# BEYOND THE MOUNTAINS

*The William Stewart Saga*

PETER CLARKE

First published in Australia by Aurora House
www.aurorahouse.com.au

This edition published 2022


Cover design: Donika Mishineva | www.artofdonika.com
Typesetting and e-book design: Amit Dey

ISBN number: 978-1-922697-50-9 (Paperback)



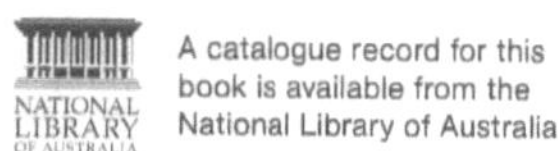


A catalogue record for this book is available from the National Library of Australia

Distributed by: Ingram Content: www.ingramcontent.com
Australia: phone +613 9765 4800 |
email lsiaustralia@ingramcontent.com
Milton Keynes UK: phone +44 (0)845 121 4567 |
email enquiries@ingramcontent.com
La Vergne, TN USA: phone +1 800 509 4156 |
email inquiry@lightningsource.com

# DEDICATION

*There's never enough time*, my father used to say. *Yet, we all squander it, as though our lives will go on forever.*

To my children—Pip, Kate and James. How much you are loved.

May these books give you an appreciation for what has gone before, and hope for what is yet to be.

# TABLE OF CONTENTS

CHAPTER 1

# MELBOURNE

"So, what are you doin' 'ere, then?"

William woke to the sound of a deep voice and a sharp pain in his leg. It took him a few moments to absorb the sight of a very big policeman, and the fact that he'd been kicked.

"Sleeping."

"Don't get smart with me. For one, you can't hang about here—sleepin' or not—and for two, any more impew-dence and I'll march you to the cells."

William didn't doubt the threat, nor that the policeman had the size to carry it out. Shocked by the sight of the policeman, the memory that he'd been dropped off at the wharves by Emma was slow to return. He'd decided to sit for a few moments before searching for a ship and a way out of Melbourne. Tired by an early start and a long day, he'd no doubt fallen asleep.

It was almost dark, but this had done nothing to diminish the activity on the docks. Men shouted orders and objections, steam engines whistled and puffed, and animals cried out in mixtures of pain and dismay. William felt sorry for the animals—they always had the worst of it. Work would have to stop soon though, as the men couldn't work in the dark.

He tried to get up.

"Not so fast," said the policeman, pushing him back. "We 'aven't finished our little chat, yet."

He studied William hard, so much so that William began to feel nervous.

"So, what're you doin' 'ere?"

"I'm looking for a ship. For work. I'm a sailor."

"I'm guessin' you're not hangin' about the wharves because you're a dressmaker or a school teacher. I figured you for a sailor. But what's a sailor doin' sleepin', I says to myself. So, I thought to wake you up and get it from the 'orses mouth, as my sainted mother used to say. Then, I find that the 'orse is a smart aleck. Too smart for a sailor, I says to myself. So, now I'm thinkin' that the 'orse is only pretendin' to be a sailor. Sailors don't have the time to be sleepin'. So, Mr 'Orse, what is it you do?"

"Like I said, I'm a sailor. I've been digging in Ballarat and now I'm going home."

"A digger. That's a good one. Where's 'ome?"

"Ireland."

"Doesn't sound like it. My sainted mother was born 'ere, but her parents came from Ireland."

"Others have said that about me. I was born in Belfast."

"Now you *are* pullin' my leg. You'd better come with me. Get to your feet, lad. We're goin' to pay a visit to Her Majesty's accommodation for sleepin' 'orses. I'm willin' to bet a month's wages we'll find some paperwork on you."

William was stunned and slow to move. Astonished at how quickly he had fallen into the hands of the police, he was sure it would end badly. He had no idea if the police were looking for him specifically, but they were certainly looking for someone involved with the event at Bacchus Marsh.

The policeman reached down to pull William to his feet. William didn't think— he reacted. As he was rising, he pushed the policeman causing him to fall over backwards with a startled cry. In that moment, William ran.

Men were leaving the docks at the end of the day's work. They were both a help and a hindrance as William weaved among them to shouts like, "Look out!" and "Take it easy, mate! There's no fire!" The men in turn helped to impede the policeman, but he followed faster than William expected. There were a few oil lamps lighting the street and William hoped that the pressing darkness, the men on the street and the lack of light would all work in his favour.

The policeman called for people to stop him, but William was mostly gone before anyone worked out that he was a fugitive. Some people thought the whole thing funny, while some called encouragement to the policeman and others to William. William's boots clattered over wood, stone and McAdam, as the road surface changed, his breath became laboured and his bag heavier by the minute. He thought to throw it away and knew there was nothing inside that would lead the police to him, but everything he owned was in the bag and he was loathe to part with it.

He saw a doorway to a pub with considerable noise coming from it. Dashing in, he hoped he might find a way out the back. Every pub he had been in had doors at the front and back and he prayed this one would be the same. Falling more than running through the door, he stood panting in front of a room packed with men, all suddenly quiet. It was as though a switch had been thrown and all the noise disappeared. The patrons could hear, "Stop him! Stop him!" carrying from outside and the switch was thrown again. The noise resumed to its previous level and a man standing near to William shouted, "Get behind the bar, lad! Quickly!"

William went behind the bar and was pushed down by the barman working there. Trying not to pant, but struggling for breath, William heard the policeman call to the patrons, "Anyone come in here?" The noise continued unabated, the patrons ignoring the question.

"Silence!" thundered the policeman. "I'll lock you all up, if that's what you want."

The room became quiet again, spreading out from the policeman as though those near to him were afraid he could do as he said.

"All right," William heard the policeman say. "Anyone come in here?"

"Yes," said a voice.

"Good. Where is he?"

"We did," said another voice. "We all came in here."

There were shouts from all around.

"I came in here."

"Me, too," said another.

"Everyone that's here, came in here," said the barman.

"No, you idiots!" shouted the policeman. "Just now!" He was gasping and wheezing for breath, and struggling to control his anger.

"No," said the barman, "no one's come in here just now."

The noise started up again, the patrons seeming to lose interest in the sideshow.

"I don't believe you!" shouted the policeman to the barman, over the rising din.

"I can't help that," retorted the barman. "You're welcome to look."

"I've a good mind to lock you all up."

The barman stood still, and William could only sense that the policeman was working out whether or not to look and, if he did so, whether he would be successful or just look foolish. The noise had returned to its previous level.

"All right," muttered the policeman. "I suppose he's run to somewhere else."

"We'll keep our eyes open for you," said the barman.

"I'm sure you will," responded the policeman.

A few minutes later, the barman nudged William with his foot and said, "You can get up. He's gone now."

William rose to his feet and looked around. No one took the slightest interest in him.

"Why did you help me?" he asked the barman.

The barman shrugged.

"Police are always chasin' people around the docks. Some're thieves, most are runaway sailors. You don't look like a thief. Anyway, you'd better go to the other side— I've work to do."

"I appreciate your help. Can I buy you a drink?"

"You can, but not right now. I'm busy at the moment. See that feller on his own in the corner? Join him. Take a drink with you. One for you and one for him. And take that coat off and put it in your bag. He might come back and if he does, he'll be lookin' for a feller wearin' a coat like yours."

"Who's he?"

"The trap."

"No. The man in the corner."

"Mate of mine. You'll be out of the way if the trap comes back. They sometimes do."

"This happened before?"

"Of course. What'll you have?"

"A whisky."

"Two whiskies comin' up."

William took the whiskies and struggled through the throng. All of the men from the docks must have come in, and all thirsty. No one paid him any mind as he pushed through. He was hot, still sweating from the run, and the heat from so many bodies in the room didn't help. The room was shrouded in smoke, mostly from pipes. He arrived at the table, unsure once he got there how he should proceed. Putting the glasses on the table, he stretched out his hand. The man looked up, contemplated William's outstretched hand for several moments, looked at the two whiskies, and shrugged.

He took William's hand and said, "Jim."

"Bill."

Jim motioned with his hand. "Sit," he said.

William sat and Jim took a sip of the whisky.

"Ed tell you to buy me a drink?" said Jim.

"Who's Ed?"

"Feller behind the bar."

William nodded.

"You in trouble with the law?" Jim asked after a few moments. "I saw you come in a few steps ahead of the constable. I suppose he was lookin' for you."

"He was, but it was a misunderstanding. I fell asleep on the docks."

"What were you doin' on the docks?"

"Looking for a ship."

"Did you tell the trap that?"

"I did."

"Most are lookin' to get off 'em. No wonder he was suspicious. What sort of ship are you lookin' for?"

"Steam or sail."

"Passenger or crew?"

"Crew."

"Do you care where it goes?"

"I want to go to Ireland."

"Why?"

"Going home."

"You Irish?"

William nodded.

Ed arrived at the table with two more whiskies.

"That'll be two shillings," he said.

"You good for it?" Jim asked William.

"I owe you a drink," said William to Ed.

"Jim can drink it," said Ed.

"Then I'm good for it," said William and counted out the money into Ed's waiting hand.

"Cheers," said Jim, raising his glass to William.

Jim looked at William intently for a few moments, as though making a decision.

"You wonderin' why Ed helped you?"

William nodded.

Before Jim could reply, the room went silent as it had earlier. William looked across the room and saw the same burly policeman, this time with two more, standing in the doorway. The policeman scanned the room, peering through the smoke.

"Who're you chasin' this time?" Ed asked.

"Same feller," said the policeman. "I know he's here and this time I'll get 'im."

He turned to the men with him.

"You stay here and watch this door," he said to one, then turned to the other. "And you, walk down there and watch the back door. I'm lookin', like I was invited to do before."

"You were welcome to do it before, and you're welcome to do it now," said Ed. "But you're wastin' your time. There's no one here that you might want."

The room was crowded, men were both sitting and standing, and the constant smoke haze made it difficult for the policeman to see clearly. Men stood, jostling each other and making a fuss when drinks were spilled or tables knocked as the policeman moved around, studying the patrons carefully, sometimes asking for papers. William was frozen in his chair, uncertain what to do. It was impossible to run with the doors being guarded. He hoped the policeman wouldn't recognise him, but didn't doubt that he likely would.

"I shouldn't have run," he whispered. "I've only made it worse."

"You should always run. He hasn't caught you yet," muttered Jim. "Here—put this on," he said, passing William his hat. "You see that table over there? The one with the two fellers, one with a hat like this? Where the policeman has already checked?"

William nodded.

"Swap seats with one of those fellers."

"How can I do that?"

"In a few moments, you'll see. None of the police will be watching."

Ed looked in Jim's direction. Jim nodded at him.

"Officer, is this the feller you're lookin' for?" called Ed, stepping out from behind the bar and pulling a man, seated near to the bar roughly to his feet.

"Watch what you're doin'!" shouted the man, trying to pull Ed's hands away. "No one's after me."

The policeman pushed back through the crowd, most of whom seemed to be badly positioned to permit him to move easily. All three policemen were focused on Ed and the man he held.

"Now," whispered Jim to William who wasted no time moving to the other table. The other man moved quickly as well, taking William's place with Jim. Most of the men who had stood to enable the policeman to get back to the bar, remained standing, making it impossible for any of the police to see what happened.

"Why do you think it's this man?" demanded the policeman when he arrived at the table where Ed and the man were still struggling.

"I don't recognise him," said Ed, puffing with his exertions.

"Christ, Ed. Are you blind?" said the man. "It's me, Alan."

"Alan? Christ, Alan. I didn't recognise you. Have you grown a beard or something?"

"No, I haven't. And I'll thank you to treat me properly, even like a customer, if that's not too much of a problem."

"Alan. I'm so sorry. I didn't recognise you. Let me buy you a drink to say sorry. Will you have another beer?" Ed hurried to the bar to get a beer.

Shaking his head, the policeman moved back through the crowd to resume his search and the other two in the doorways resumed scanning the crowd, following the other man's progress. He finished checking the room and came back to the bar, seeming not to notice that his movement around the room was so much easier this time.

"Looks like I was wrong," said the policeman to Ed.

Ed shrugged and looked at Alan. “I was wrong too, so that makes two of us. We’ll keep an eye out for you, of course. What does your man look like?”

“Young, fair haired, dressed in working clothes. Hatless.”

“Might be hard to find him. Lot of fellers look like that. Still, if anyone looks suspicious, we’ll call for you.”

The police left and the noise resumed. William and the other man swapped places again.

“Thanks,” said William as he passed the man.

“Bit of fun,” he said. “Not usually much to be ’ad around ’ere.”

William sat at the table. Jim smiled.

“I’ll have to buy everyone a drink,” said William.

“No, you won’t. Everyone has fun. It’s not always that trap. There are others, too, but it’s always fun to outwit them.”

“Alan looked like he didn’t know what was happening. Perhaps I should buy him a drink.”

“Alan’s the best. Ed usually picks him, so he knows it’s comin’. Ed bought him a drink. That’s enough.”

“So, why does Ed do it? Why do you all do it? Couldn’t there be trouble?”

“Trouble? I don’t think so. There are lots of men and lots of pubs, and not many police, so the police never recognise anyone, even if it’s been done before. If they did arrest someone, what would it be for? Stoppin’ a policeman doin’ his job? How would they prove it? Everyone here would say, ‘No, sir, I didn’t see that.’”

“So, why did Ed help me?”

“The police are always hangin’ about, lookin’ for a free drink. Chasin’ honest folk about, tryin’ to look busy. The more arrests, the better they look, so they pick on honest folk, who they then let go. Ed doesn't like it, doesn't like them. Says someone should clean them up, so he does his best to get in their way and to help people they chase."

"They don't always chase honest people, do they?"

"I suppose not. It's mostly ship's deserters. First place the deserters come is a pub, so it's the first place traps look. Sometimes, like you, they're chased here, but mostly they'll come in for a drink and get caught when the traps do their rounds."

"How do the police know they're deserters?"

"Ask for their Discharge Paper."

"What's a Discharge Paper?"

"I thought you said you were a sailor?"

"I am, but I haven't been on a ship for a few years."

"Where've you been?"

"Ballarat, looking for gold, and Heidelberg, working on a farm."

"Any luck?"

"I'm not rich, if that's what you're asking."

"Sorry—none of my business. Discharge Papers've been around for a couple of years. Have to be signed when crew leaves a ship, so police'll ask for that. Captains publish lists of deserters with the police too, so they have a description of people to look for. It's not right. Feller should be able to leave a ship if it's not to his likin', if the captain's too hard, or even if he just wants to get off."

"Are you a sailor? You talk like one."

"Yes, I am. Been doin' it most of my life. Like you, I took some time off and went lookin' for gold in Bendigo."

Jim looked at William for a few moments.

"It's thirsty work," he said finally.

"It was thirsty work at Ballarat, too."

"No. Talkin' to you."

William laughed.

"All right," said Jim. "You buy me a drink and I'll get you onto a ship."

"Where's it going?"

"Sydney first, then Liverpool."

"When?"

"Tomorrow mornin'."

"What is she?"

"Brigantine."

"Is that steam or sail?"

"Sail. Two masted. Square rig on the foremast and fore and aft on the main mast. It's a good rig. What were you on?"

"Mostly steam, but I do know how to sail a square rig."

"We're goin' under ballast to Sydney, so it won't be a hard sail and you can get used to it. Pickin' up cargo in Sydney, so she'll be harder to sail after that, but you'll probably know your way around by then. It's a good rig for coastal sailin'. We mostly do that, sailin' between Melbourne and Sydney, but we've got a good fee to take some wool to Liverpool, so that's what we're doin'."

"I thought it'd be too early for wool."

"It's last year's. Owner's been hangin' out for a good price and finally got it."

"Do you know him?"

"Yes, I do. Known him all my life."

"What's the ship called?"

"*Liza Ann.* 120 tons. She's fast, too."

"How big is 120 tons?"

"About a hundred feet long."

"How many crew?"

"Seven, including the captain. There'll be five goin' to Sydney, if you come, and we pick up two more there if you do and three if you don't. Will you join us? You won't have a lot of time to think about it. I'm going back to the ship soon, so if you want to join, you'll need to come with me."

"Can I meet the captain, first?"

"You've already met him. I'm the captain and there's a job for you if you want it. I'd take it if I were you. That trap'll be lookin' for you. He may not know you were here, but he might suspect. It doesn't matter. He and his mates will be lookin' for you, so I'd get out of Melbourne, and my ship is a good way to do it."

William looked at Jim, trying to decide if he should take the offer. Liverpool was a good destination. He could get back to Ireland from there, but he would be months at sea on Jim's *Liza Ann*. Still, he had climbed aboard the *Lady Grace* with little thought. Whatever else, Jim was right about the police, and he would be the loser in any confrontation with them.

"Thank you, Jim. I'd like to come with you."

"Good. Let me check that there's no traps waitin' for us outside, and if there's not, let's head for the *Liza Ann*."

CHAPTER 2

# SYDNEY

William stood at the ship's rail, watching Melbourne grow smaller in the distance. A warm northerly blew, which he knew would make for tricky sailing until they were out of the heads. The *Liza Ann* moved steadily against the incoming tide. The crew had been working since daylight, readying the ship for sea. The wind was perfect for their departure, and they timed their leaving such that the ship would be at the heads at high tide, or just after it, when the tide would ebb and carry them out to sea. Seagulls dipped and swooped about the ship, screaming at each other and at the ship for whatever slight raised their ire. Some took advantage of the spars where the square sails were still furled. The fore and aft sails made for more agile sailing and the square sails wouldn't be used until they passed through the heads.

None of the crew were put out that the captain had returned with another sailor, nor did anyone make William feel unwelcome. He was allocated one of the empty hammocks and had made himself comfortable and slept well, until roused by the cook for a breakfast of porridge and hot, black, sweetened tea consumed at a table in the tiny galley.

The mate whose name was John was a soft-spoken Scot with ginger hair, a big red beard and an infectious chuckle. He gave his orders quietly and firmly and seemed to take a liking to William when he saw his competence with the sails. Perhaps he had doubted the captain's assurances that William knew how to sail and was pleased to see the new man would be an asset. In any event, the men worked well together, and the sun was peeping over the horizon as the *Liza Ann* pulled away from the dock. There was a chill in the air once they were out in the bay, even though the wind was out of the north, reminding everyone that winter was at hand.

"Have you left a broken heart behind?" asked a soft voice behind William. It was Neil, one of the crew.

"No, Neil. Just thinking. I'll get back to work."

"It can wait a few moments. We've all done well and she's sailing nicely. There's not much to do except enjoy it. We'll be busy enough when we tack at the heads. I'm pleased to see you know your way around. Mate said you spent time on steamers."

"Aye. Auxiliary steamer. I was a trimmer and worked with the sails as well. The *Lady Grace*. Do you know her?"

Neil shook his head.

"I've spent most of my time on ships like the *Liza Ann*, mostly doing coastal work or doing trips to New Zealand or Van Diemen's Land. I've been with the captain a few years now."

"How did you meet?"

"Like you—in a pub. I'd been working out of Sydney, doing coastal work, trying to find a ship where I could settle. Met Jim in a pub in the Rocks and been with him ever since."

"What's the Rocks?"

"Area of Sydney, near Port Jackson. Some say it's a bit rough, but I like it. I take it you haven't been to Sydney?"

William shook his head.

“We’ll be there for a few days. You can have a look around. You won’t be needed on the ship when they load the wool. Jim’s brother and his men will do that. Sydney’s a busy place. They’re still finding gold out west and the wool trade is booming. I prefer it to Melbourne. That’s why I live there.”

“Jim’s brother?”

“Yes. He’s the one that owns the wool. Held onto it until the price was high. He’ll be a rich man when we get it to Liverpool. He has a sheep station outside Sydney and last year was the best year ever for wool.”

“And they’re still finding gold out west?”

Neil laughed.

“Not just the west—north and south too. It’s mostly mining, so we don’t lose sailors like we used to. A few years back, everyone jumped ship in Sydney and Melbourne to go looking for gold. Not so much now.”

He stopped and looked at William.

“You’re not going to jump ship are you, Bill? Mate said you were going to Liverpool.”

“I am. Going to Liverpool, I mean. I spent some time in Ballarat. Didn’t find much. Some did. Not me.”

“They say Sydney is different. Men are joining groups, mining in groups, so if the mine is successful, everyone shares in the success. Anyway, if you do have a mind to go looking for gold, don’t tell anyone. Best to keep that to yourself.”

“Jim’s been good to me. I wouldn’t think of doing that to him. Anyway, it’s time to go home.”

“Bill, it wouldn’t matter. Some of the men that work for Jim’s brother are sailors and I’ll bet they’re hoping to join the ship. They say it’s hard work on the sheep station and a change is as good as a holiday. If you're going to jump, do it as soon as you get to Sydney. That way, they'll have time to get someone else. It's not as hard to get crew as it used to be. They say most of the diggers aren't finding much, so they're happy to go back to sea. You won't get paid for a few days' work, but that won't be the end of the world."

They stood, not talking for a while, enjoying the movement of the ship and the views around the bay. William liked being back at sea but couldn't stop thinking about the gold. Perhaps he did have unfinished business in Australia.

The mate called out.

"Ready, lads! Heads're comin' up, so we're going onto a beam reach. Look lively! No mistakes now. Take it easy, helmsman. It only takes one mistake, so keep your wits about you."

The men loosened the sails, ensuring that they held their wind and the bow shifted. William wished they had a steam engine. He looked at Jim and was relieved to see no sign of nervousness, but he wouldn't feel comfortable until the heads were behind them. There was some swell coming through the heads, but not enough to interfere with the ship. Just when it seemed they'd hit the rocks, the mate ordered the ship onto a port tack and she swung easily across the wind, and they were through the heads.

William enjoyed the ship and the sailing, but the next two days were passed in total anguish. *What of the gold outside Sydney? Why would it be different to Ballarat? And what of Jim?* William had committed to go to Liverpool and, despite Neil's assurances, he was reluctant to break his word.

The wind came mostly from the north, and the northeast, so the ship was constantly tacking. Most of the crew were needed most of the time, so there was little rest. Everyone prayed for a southerly, but God appeared to have little interest in the crew of the *Liza Ann*. If the crew worked hard, Jim worked harder. William wondered if he slept on his feet. He was a good captain who was committed to his ship and his men but it only increased William's anxiety. If he was to go back to Ireland, he wouldn't find a better ship and crew. Neil assured him the job would be easier after Sydney when there would be more men in the crew. The only one that had an easy time of it was the cook. He wasn't allowed to light the stoves, so there was only biscuits and water for the crew. The ship stayed well out to sea for the whole trip to Sydney.

They'd been beating into the wind for a few hours, it was early in the morning and the crew were napping on the deck when the helmsman called that Port Jackson was in sight. The sun peeped over the water and the sky was filled with pastel blues and pinks. The wind had dropped to a breeze overnight. William heard the mate ask Jim if they should stand off the heads until the wind picked up.

"We'll check the tide," said Jim. "If it's floodin', we'll go in. There's enough wind to hold way, and I think it'll pick up soon anyway."

They did one more tack to get above the heads.

"She's doing well, Jim," said the mate. "I think you're right—we can go in. Weather looks like it'll hold, so there's no reason not to."

Jim nodded.

"All right, helmsman. Let's take her in."

The ship glided through the heads and William marvelled at how different they were to Melbourne. So high and golden yellow in the morning sun which sparkled off the water. The wind was about ten knots out of the northeast, but combined with the tide, the *Liza Ann* swept along and there was no sense of danger. William was amazed at the confidence of the crew and the fact that they didn't use a pilot.

The harbour was narrow and forked almost immediately left and right.

William saw a ship anchored about the middle of the left channel. He couldn't see anyone on board and wondered if it might be abandoned. Neil explained that it was the lightship *Rose* and its job was to mark a reef called the Sow and Pigs. William said he couldn't see the reef, or even see that water was breaking over it.

"That's the problem," said Neil. "It's hard to see except at low tide. Even the pilots had trouble with it before they put the *Rose* there."

William had not ever seen a harbour like this. The *Liza Ann* glided past the *Ros*e, east of it, the only sounds being the occasional cry of a seagull, the swish and splash of water and the flap of a sail. The air was cool, but the sun warm on their backs. Tendrils of smoke drifted lazily upwards from houses scattered in the bush that covered the low hills on both sides of the harbour and once or twice the sailors saw a hut with black people nearby. Sometimes they waved and the sailors waved back.

"You said it was busy, Neil. It doesn't look too busy."

"We've got to go a ways yet before we get to Sydney Cove and even then we go past and around two points to reach Darling Harbour. Be patient. You'll see busy soon enough, and you'll wish you were back here."

A little further and a large bay with some islands appeared at their left.

"Is this it?" asked William.

"No," said Neil. He pointed down the harbour at an unwooded rocky platform, "See that island in the distance?"

"That's an island?"

"Yes, it was once called the Rock, but its better name is Pinchgut. They used to put convicts there for punishment. Leave them for days at a time with only bread and water. Threw meat into the water to attract the sharks so that the convicts wouldn't try to swim off it. Used to hang people on it, too, and leave them hanging there. Now they're building a fort. Won't be much use if someone attacks, but no one asked me if I thought it was a good idea. On the port side of that is Sydney Cove, where the British first settled. Further on, also on the port and around the point is Darling Harbour. There'll be lots of ships there, no doubt some ready to come out and you'll get to see busy."

As they headed towards Pinchgut, William could see more buildings and farms on the shore, but mostly on the left side. Buildings were often white, in stark contrast to the grass and trees around them. The wind held and the *Liza Ann* glided on with the sailors having little to do but admire the scenery. Bright, almost white, sandy beaches came and went. Sometimes there was a fisherman, but they were mostly empty, the water lapping gently onto the sand. It was so different to Melbourne. William was enthralled. Already he loved Sydney.

"There's another fort on the point there," said Neil, pointing. "That's Fort Macquarie and those buildings behind it are Government House and the Government Stables. And near to them is the Botanic Gardens."

Without thinking, William replied, "What's a Botanic? I've not ever heard of that. Can you eat them?"

Neil looked at him and smiled. "I'll leave that between us."

William blushed, knowing that he'd said something stupid, but had no idea what it was.

A few minutes later and Neil said, "Sydney Cove."

There were big and small buildings, mostly at the end and the right side of the cove. A few small sailing ships were anchored in the cove and small vessels tied to wharves, again mostly on the right.

"Not much happens here. All the big ships go around to Darling Harbour, always have as far as I know. Any big ships that used to come in here would anchor in the stream and land their goods at the wharf by lighters, or if they moored in the cove then long, wooden stages were laid from ship to shore. That's the Rocks, there on the starboard side. We might go there if you want. I can show you a few places."

As they rounded the two points, William was startled to see how high the land was above the water. The ground was higher to his left and William could see some guns poking out above parapets.

"Is that another fort?" he asked Neil.

"No, just some gun emplacements. Better spot for a fort, if you ask me. They've got the best views, up and down the harbour. You'd see an enemy ship as soon as it came through the heads. You'd have time for tea and damper, to load the cannons, maybe even have a whisky or two before you had to worry about them being close enough to fight."

More ships were about now, even some steamers, and the helmsman took all his attention to manoeuvre among them.

"There's enough wind!" called Jim. "One sail for'ard and one aft and furl the rest."

The mate and the crew hurried to do his bidding. It didn't take long, but in those few moments, the *Liza Ann* rounded

Miller's Point and Darling Harbour was laid out in front. Some wharves made of wood jutted out into the harbour like fingers. Others, parallel with the shore, were of stone and held smaller ships. The harbour was packed with shipping, large and small, mostly moored at wharves, but some were still anchored in the channel. There were so many masts that they looked like a forest of bare wood, draped with rope. Steam tugs towed some of the larger ships, possibly headed out of the harbour. Even close by the docks, the land rose steeply from the water. There were buildings close to the wharf that were certainly related to dockside activity, but other buildings rose on the hillside above. It was hard to see if they were commercial or housing. William could see some church spires amongst the other buildings.

There was the usual shouting. William decided not much was done at the docks that didn't involve shouting.

Once they were closer to the shore, the wind was blocked by the land and the *Liza Ann* began to lose way.

"Might need some help," muttered Jim. "Hey!" he called to two men in a whale boat nearby. "Can you help us?"

"Sure can," said one of the men. "Cost you three shillings."

"It was two the last time," said Jim.

"When was that?"

"Last week."

"All right. Two it is, then. Where do you want to go?"

"Flour Company Wharf."

The man laughed.

"You should have said that earlier. Won't take long. Stern first?"

"Aye."

The men pulled alongside, took a rope, fastened it at the back of their own boat and pulled the *Liza Ann* to the wharf.

"Lower and stow all sails," said Jim.

"Lucky they were there," William said to Neil once the sails were stowed.

"Not luck at all," said Neil. "They're always there. *Liza Ann*, like most coastal ships, doesn't use the pilot, but sometimes needs help to dock. These fellers do it for lots of sailing ships."

"I didn't think a couple of fellers in a boat could pull us along," said William.

"Doesn't take much," said Neil. "If the wind is right, we can do it ourselves. If there's none, like now, we need them. If there's too much, they can't help and we'll anchor out in the stream until it drops. Been doing this a while now. It's not hard. C'mon. We're nearly there. They'll need our help."

"All right, lads," said Jim, once they were docked and securely tied. "Clean up the decks. Be quick about it too. Once you've done that, you can go ashore. They're ready to get rid of the ballast and load the wool. Come back before dark though. If they get the wool loaded today, I want to leave at first light. If they don't get it done, then we'll leave day after tomorrow."

"C'mon," said Neil to William. "Let's see to it. I want to get home and visit with family. It'll be a while before I see them."

"What about the Rocks?" asked William.

"Sorry, Bill. I thought we'd be here for a few days. Don't worry. I know you'll find something to do. All the lads are from Sydney, so they'll all be going home to see family or friends and you won't have any company. But there's plenty of hotels and lodging houses—you'll get a drink, a good meal and a bed if you need it. Look for a place called Royal Oak. It's not far."

William couldn't hide his disappointment. He'd been excited about the prospect of exploring Sydney with Neil.

"Bill, there is one other thing," said Neil, leaning in close and speaking in a whisper. "You'll have to tell Jim if you don't plan to come back. I know he'll not have trouble arranging for someone else, but he'll have to do it and will need time. If he wants to leave tomorrow, then there's not much of that."

William's heart sank. He'd been dreading the decision and now it was imminent. He turned to see what Jim was doing and was worried to see that Jim was watching him. *Perhaps Neil had already told Jim that William might not go on? Well, best to get it done.*

"Jim?" William called. "Do you have a moment?"

Contrary to what he expected, Jim burst out laughing.

"You sound more like an officer, Bill. Yes, I have a moment."

"Jim," said William and he paused, unsure how to go on.

"Bill, don't worry about it. It's good you're tellin' me and I'll have no trouble with crew. Plenty of my brother's lads want a trip to England, so I'll not be angry. You're a good lad, and a good sailor to boot."

"Thanks, Jim," said William, blushing with embarrassment.

Jim laughed again, then became suddenly serious.

"Bill, when I saw you run into the pub in Melbourne, I thought, 'This lad's in trouble' and I haven't changed my mind since. If I'm a judge, the police aren't only after you for fallin' asleep on the docks. No, lad, you've got a secret and best you keep it that way."

William stood still, unsure of what Jim knew.

"If you do have a reason to avoid the police, change your name and your appearance, lad, and get out of Sydney. Go bush, look for gold and let time run its course. Time fixes everythin'. The police'll look for you by name and description, so if you change both, chances are, they won't find you and they'll stop lookin'."

Jim stretched out his hand.

"Good luck, Bill—or whatever your name is—and be careful who you trust."

"I've heard that before."

"From a wise man, no doubt."

"Wiser than I thought at the time."

"Then probably your father."

William laughed and Jim laughed with him.

"You worked to get us here and I'd like to pay you for that. Will a pound be all right with you?"

"A pound is more than I expect, so I think that's generous."

"Good. Here," said Jim, passing the note to William. "Get your bag, say *goodbye* to the lads and go find your future. Remember me if you strike it rich."

Jim stretched out his hand and shook William's firmly, then turned and left the ship. William watched him go. *There's more good people than bad,* he thought. *Jim's a good one. I could have run into much worse in Melbourne.*

He fetched his bag, said goodbye to anyone who had the time to listen, and left the ship. The wharf was already busy with men fetching the wool to load, dragging it along on trolleys and cursing at the unevenness of the surface. Curses were also there for anything else impeding their progress, like people coming and going and other goods being loaded to and from the other ships on the wharf.

Reaching the end of the wharf, William took in his first real look at Sydney. The day was cool and mild, a few clouds scattered about, and the smell of the town was already noticeable. The breeze was at his back, so the smell would get worse when he went ashore. Even at the early hour, there was a lot of traffic, moving both ways in the street and to and from the wharves. There was the sound of metal wheels on stone roads, animals protesting at their treatment and their responsibilities, and men shouting.

*Neil was right. It's busy.*

He tried to form a plan. Mostly though, all he could think was that he was tired and dirty. Something to eat, a bath and a bed might be the first and best steps. At first glance, there was no shortage of places to go. As Neil had said, there were hotels everywhere, all were open and despite the early hour, some already had customers.

Neil had said there was one not far away called the Royal Oak, and the first person he asked pointed to it. It was easy to see. There was a man struggling with some doors, and it appeared he was trying to open them.

"Can I help?" asked William.

"Bloody things," said the man. "I keep askin' the publican to have them fixed. Mostly nothin' gets done. I suppose it's not his problem 'cause I get them open eventually. Supposed to be fixed now though. Here—hold this door."

William held the door, and the man gave it a good kick at the bottom. The doors opened easily.

"There, easy," said the man. "Thanks. What do you want?"

"A drink, a meal, a bath and a bed."

"We can do all those, but you're early. We don't usually do a meal this early. The boss said he'd had the doors fixed and I should try them and that's what I was doin'. If you want to come in, you can, but don't expect much more than a drink just yet. We're supposed to be open, so there's no harm in lettin' you in."

They went in together and William worried that he had chosen the wrong place when he noticed there were no other customers.

The man must have seen his apprehension and said, "We're always late to start. 'Late to start, late to finish', the boss always says. Take your pick of somewhere to sit. I'll get your drink. What'll you have?"

"Whisky," William murmured as he surveyed the bar. It was L shaped, with tables and chairs arranged away from the bar so that patrons could fetch their drinks at the bar and return to the tables. William took a chair nearby and waited for his drink.

An unsteady voice said, "Mornin', Tom."

It belonged to a small, bedraggled man who had just come in. He was wearing a torn shirt that was probably once white, dirty moleskins, shoes that should have been thrown out long ago and his thinning hair, no doubt a stranger to water, stuck out like an echidna's quills.

"Wally," said the barman getting William's whisky.

"Mind if I sit?" the man asked William.

"Why don't you sit in your usual place, Wally?" said Tom.

"Don't want to. Want to sit with this fellow."

"Even if you sit there, he's not buying you a drink," said Tom.

"How do you know? Anyway, I haven't sat there yet. I'm bein' polite. Mind if I sit?" asked Wally again, looking expectantly at William.

Some more, non-descript men shuffled in, taking Tom's attention.

William didn't know what to do. He didn't like the look of the fellow but could hardly deny him a seat that was available to anyone.

"If you like," said William, and he thought he noticed a brief look of triumph on Wally's face.

"What're you drinkin'?" asked Wally.

"Whisky," said William.

"I'll have one, too. Will you pay for it? I'm down on my luck. Don't have much. Can't find a job."

Tom arrived at the table with William's drink.

"You don't have much, because you spend it all here. You can't find a job because you're always here," said Tom.

"Ah, don't be too harsh, Tom. You get my money. What're you complainin' about?"

"I'm complaining about you pestering my customers for drinks, so I mostly don't get your money anyway—I get theirs. Get a job, Wally. There's plenty of work on the docks."

"It's all right," said William. "I'll buy him a drink. I'm only having the one. I'd rather a bath, meal and bed than a drink."

"Man after my own heart," said Wally.

"You wouldn't know what a bath looks like," said Tom.

"You shouldn't be so cruel to your customers," said Wally. "They'll go somewhere's else."

"There's one I'd like to go somewhere else," said Tom. "See me when you're done with your whisky," he said, looking at William. "I'll get you fixed up. That'll be a shilling for the whisky. The rest I'll get later. Next thing you know, Wally'll want something to eat, too."

"You," he said, looking pointedly at Wally. "Just the one drink, then you're to be gone."

"All right, all right. Wouldn't mind somethin' to eat though."

"Forget it," said Tom harshly, much to William's relief.

He looked about to leave but then turned back.

"What's your name?" asked Tom of William, ignoring Wally.

"Tom. Tom Smith," said William.

"Same as me."

"You Tom Smith, too?" asked William, amazed that his new name was the same as his host.

"No," laughed Tom. "Just the Tom part. Name's Thomas Stewart. I'm the publican."

*If he only knew*, thought William.

He stretched out his hand and shook William's warmly.

"It's nice to meet you. We don't often get new customers here."

"I thought you talked about a boss. How could you be the publican if you've got a boss?" said William.

"I always do that with new customers. It's better than dealing with complaints."

There were calls for more drinks and attention elsewhere in the bar, so Tom hurried off. He was back a few minutes later with Wally's drink, for which William paid another shilling. Wally stared at it for a few moments as though he couldn't believe it was there and was willing it to last forever.

"Where're you from, Tom?" he asked after taking a sip.

"Ireland," said William, hoping the response would be adequate. It was.

"I'm from England," said Wally, wistfully. "Manchester. Wish I was back there. I've got family there, but none here. Two brothers. We all worked together."

"Why did you come here?"

"Gold. Why does anyone come here? Gold diggers and convicts. That's all we have. Might be some others. I'm yet to meet 'em."

"Where were you digging for gold?" asked William, suddenly interested in what Wally might have to say. Wally appeared to notice and relaxed a little, as though expecting he might now get another drink, or perhaps a meal.

"Many places," said Wally with a smile. He looked younger when he smiled. William could imagine him getting off a ship, filled with expectation and enthusiasm. "No point in telling you about 'em, unless you want to go there. And if you want to go there, it's worth more than one whisky for me to tell you."

William laughed. He doubted Wally would tell him anything of value, but it was probably worth a whisky to find out.

"All right," he said. "We'll have another when we finish this one."

A look crossed Wally's face that William decided was a mixture of triumph and fear. Glad to be getting another whisky on one hand, and afraid that there might only be one more.

"Good-o. I was in the South, around Goulburn. There was a lot of promise. I moved around, always chasin' the latest rumour. It was very frustratin'. I'd just arrive somewhere, and the rumour would be that somewhere's else was better. I didn't get much. Others found it, but not me. Maybe I moved too often and never took enough time to learn about a place. Hot summers, and cold winters was all I got. After a couple of years, I teamed up with two fellers in the Braidwood diggin's. We all thought we'd do better together."

"I don't know any of those places."

"Wish I didn't either. Goulburn's about 120 miles south and west of Sydney. Braidwood is about 16 miles south of Goulburn. The diggin's are not far south of Braidwood, but they call them the Braidwood diggin's because you get to them through there."

William felt the old excitement stirring and remembered the first time he'd found gold.

"Not everyone had a bad experience, did they?" he asked Wally.

Wally laughed. He looked like he was enjoying himself. William decided that he didn't often get to talk to people.

"No. I don't know what gave you that impression. Feller called John Tighe made a lot of money diggin' around Bathurst. Used it to buy pubs around Sydney town. Money built on money. I think he bought the pubs for cheap grog—he certainly drinks his fair share."

"Where's Bathurst?"

"120 miles west."

"Why didn't you go there?"

"Why did you pick this pub?"

"What do you mean?"

"There's plenty of pubs. Why did you pick this one?"

William shrugged and said, "No reason." He thought it too complicated to tell Wally it had been recommended.

"That's the same reason I chose Goulburn."

"What happened in Braidwood?"

"We had a deal."

"What? A deal with the others?"

"No. You and I had a deal."

"We did?"

"Yes. You were goin' to buy another whisky."

"So I was," laughed William and he signalled for Tom, who came over.

"You ready?" asked Tom.

"We're going to have another whisky."

"That's up to you," said Tom. He walked away shaking his head.

The men sat in silence until he returned and put their drinks on the table, took William's money and left.

"We did well at first," continued Wally. His face now looked different to William. It had lost some of its weariness as he reminisced.

"We were diggin' in a wide valley near a place called Araluen. There were several hundred diggers there. The gold was in a layer of mud, sometimes five feet and sometimes twenty feet down. We'd worked out that speed was important and that's why we teamed up. You had to work out quickly if you were goin' to find gold, get it and move on. There were holes everywhere, but plenty of space to dig more. Everyone was doin' all right, so there weren't many arguments amongst the diggers. Sometimes the fellers next door would get more, and sometimes they wouldn't need to dig so deep. It was all luck, but everyone seemed to have luck in equal part."

He took a sip of his whisky and looked carefully at William, who decided Wally wasn't that old—he just looked it. Whatever memory Wally was searching for took another sip of whisky to find.

"Then, our luck ran out."

Wally sighed heavily and his hand shook as he reached for the sip. He was quiet for a few moments more and William couldn't work out if he was still trying to find the memory, or put it into words, or if it was too painful to remember.

"I've not ever talked about this," said Wally finally. "Not sure I even want to now."

"It's up to you," said William. "There are things I don't like to remember, too. Things I'm not sure I could tell anyone, least of all a stranger in a pub."

Wally laughed. The sound shocked William, as it was the last thing he had expected.

"Like a pistol duel, but with memories. My memories against yours across a table. I think mine'd beat yours at twenty paces," said Wally. "A memory duel. Doesn't that beat everythin'?"

William shrugged, unsure what Wally meant, but confident that whatever else Wally did in Manchester, he had an education.

"My partners' names were Reg O'Connell and Bruce O'Neil. They were both older than me. I don't know by how much. I never asked. They were good men. It was a Saturday afternoon in the summer. There hadn't been much rain for weeks, so it was a struggle to find water to cradle the gold. Heat, dust and flies were relentless. The gold dried up along with the rain and we decided we needed a break. We borrowed a gig and horse and headed for Braidwood to get drunk, maybe even enjoy the company of a woman. We promised we'd bring the gig back that night. It was needed for church the next day."

Wally's hand was visibly shaking as he reached for another sip.

"It wasn't too late when we got there, but it'd taken a couple of hours, so we were good and thirsty. We left the horse and gig with a blacksmith who had a yard. Said he didn't care when we got back. We could just get our horse from the yard, harness it and be on our way. Cautioned us to be careful to get the right horse.

We fell into the nearest pub and were drunk in a half hour. There were a few ladies workin' the bar who stayed with us for a while, but we got so drunk, they lost interest. Then they told us the pub was closin' and we had to go. We hadn't had enough, of course, so they sold us some bottles to take with us.

There was no moon, and we had no lantern. It was a challenge to find the yard and the right horse. Reg said he knew the horse, so he'd go in the yard and get it. I suppose being drunk didn't help and he upset the horses somethin' awful. He'd only been in the yard for a few moments and all the horses started dartin' to and fro, kickin' and stompin', pushin' against each other. We couldn't really see, of course, but we could hear."

Wally stopped again. William could see the pain of the memory in his eyes.

"Reg cried out for help several times, but what could we do? We stood by the gate until things went quiet. I suppose we'd sobered up a little by then, too. We crept into the yard, bein' very careful not to disturb the horses again and found Reg by fallin' over him. We picked him up, carried him out and tried to work out how badly he was hurt.

The pubs need to have a lamp burnin' outside at night and Bruce went back and fetched it. Reg was unconscious and in a bad way. We got some water and washed away the blood and the dirt. Reg woke up and told us he was all right. It was his friend's gig, so he said we had to get it back. We wanted to find a doctor, but Reg wouldn't hear of it. Bruce used the lamp to find the horse, we harnessed it and headed back to our camp. Even though we kept the lamp, and it was useful sometimes, we were glad the horse could find the way, because we sure couldn't.

We returned the horse and gig and slept off the whisky until late mornin' on Sunday. I checked on Reg and he looked awful. Groanin' quietly, pale, and he'd vomited at some point and it was full of blood. You know—the black blood you see from bleedin' inside."

William didn't know, but it sounded awful.

"I couldn't wake him. I woke Bruce and we tried to work out what to do. If nothin' else, we decided that Reg needed a doctor and we'd have to go back to Braidwood. I stayed with Reg and Bruce went to get the horse. Of course, he came back empty handed. The horse had gone to church.

'Find another one!' I exploded. 'Do you think there's only one horse on the diggin's?'

I waited and fretted. Reg was lookin' worse by the minute. I don't know how doctors do their job. Watchin' Reg die was too much for me.

Anyway, Bruce got back after an hour with Reg's friend's horse and gig. Said he'd looked everywhere, then he'd seen the horse and gig comin' back and went to borrow it again. Reg's friend offered to come too, but he and Bruce worked out there wasn't enough room in the gig.

We set out for Braidwood. I pushed the horse as hard as I could, but he was tired from the previous night and the trip to church in the mornin'.

It was late afternoon when we arrived and of course, bein' a Sunday, everythin' was closed. It took a half hour to find the doctor. He hurried out to the gig when I told him what had happened. Reg was slumped and Bruce was sitting in the gig.

'We'll get him down,' I said.

'No,' said the doctor. 'I'll check him first. Might need to be careful how we move him.'

He stood at the gig and looked at Reg.

'I can't do anything for this man,' he said after a bit.

'Is it too complicated?' I asked.

'No,' said the doctor. 'He's already dead—has been for a few hours. Probably dead before you started out.'

Bruce started to cry. We were crushed. We'd done our best and it wasn't good enough."

William wondered about a man crying. He knew it wasn't done, and resisted the urge to ask Wally more about it.

"'Bring him inside,' said the doctor. 'I'll need to examine him. You go and tell the police. They'll tell the coroner and he'll want to do an inquest.'

'How long will that take?' I asked.

'Weeks, at least. You can have the body after I do the autopsy.'

'What's an autopsy?' I asked.

'I check the body and determine the cause of death,' said the doctor.

'Why?' I asked. 'I already told you what happened.'

The doctor looked at me with a half-smile. I liked him. He looked like he'd seen too much sickness, sufferin' and death. He put a hand on my shoulder.

'Son. I believe you, but it's up to the coroner. Because there are no other witnesses, he's the one who'll decide if your friend died by accident.'

'When will you do the autopsy?' I asked.

'Tomorrow morning. You can collect your friend around noon. Does he have a family?'

'Only us,' said Bruce. 'Well, I think so, he never talked about a family.'

'I can arrange for your friend to be buried if you want,' said the doctor.

'How much will that cost?' asked Bruce between sobs.

'We'll do that,' I said. 'He was our friend and we owe him that much. He has a friend at the diggin's who might want to be there when he's buried too."

'Well,' said the doctor, 'I'll arrange a coffin and grave diggers. Be at the cemetery mid-afternoon tomorrow to bury your friend.'

'How much do we owe you?' I asked.

'Three pounds will cover it.'

'How much for the coffin and the grave diggers?'

"That is for the coffin and the grave diggers. You don't owe me anything for looking at your friend and the government pays for the autopsy.'

Bruce and I turned out our pockets and we had only two pounds and four shillin's between us.

'That's enough,' said the doctor. 'I'll see it's done for that. Now, let's get your friend inside. Then, see the police and go home. I'm sure it's already been a long day.'

We carried Reg inside and put him on a table. He looked so small. Death reduces a person.

As we left, I asked the doctor if we had taken Reg to him at the time of the accident, would he have lived. The doctor shrugged and said he didn't know.

'Who knows what might have happened? Maybe I can tell you once I've done the autopsy.'

'I wished we hadn't listened to him and brought him to you straight away,' said Bruce.

'You can't afford to think like that,' said the doctor. 'If wishes were horses, then beggars would ride.'

We left the doctor and went to the police station. They couldn't have been less interested. Said they'd contact us if the coroner decided to hold an inquest.

Before we left, we took the lantern back to the pub and apologised for takin' it. The publican was angry at first, then apologised when he heard what happened to Reg. Said if there was anythin' he could do, he'd be happy to help. Wanted to give us a bottle of whisky so we could have a drink to farewell Reg. We didn't take it. Bruce and I had already agreed that if we hadn't been drunk, Reg would still be alive, so we decided not to drink again.

It was already late and nearly dark as we headed back to the diggin's. We was a sad pair. The horse was tired too. He'd had a busy couple of days."

Wally had lost all interest in his drink. William continued to sip and was amazed how involved Wally had become in his story. It was as though it was the only thing in the world at that moment.

"Reg's friend, Bruce and I came back the next day for the funeral. We tried to see the doctor, but he was away. He did organise the coffin and the grave and everythin' was ready at the cemetery.

We tried to get back to normal. Diggin' each day, but our heart wasn't in it. We found gold every day, but nothin' to write home about. We didn't drink—I suppose that made it harder. We could hear everybody else havin' fun, drinkin' and singin', but we kept to ourselves. Lived in our own little world. Not talkin' much. Not livin' either, just existin'.

Then in the autumn, there was a lot of rain over a few weeks. We couldn't dig every day, everythin' was wet and mouldy. Usually, autumn was good weather, but not this time. Anyway, the rain stopped and we got back to work. Mud and water all about. We'd been workin' on a hole and were down about twenty feet. We had to keep bailin'. I was nervous that the hole would collapse, but Bruce just laughed at me. Besides, we were gettin' really good gold and Bruce wanted to work harder in case there was a collapse before we got all the gold. Anyway, I stayed at the top, bailin' out water and dirt and workin' the cradle. There was plenty of water still about, so I didn't have to go far from the hole to work the cradle.

I took a load to the cradle. When I got back to the hole, excited to tell Bruce we'd got a billy of gold from the last load, there was no Bruce. The sides had collapsed on him. I hadn't heard anythin'. I don't know if he even knew what hit him.

Some other fellers helped me dig him out, but he was dead of course. I don't know if he was crushed or suffocated to death. Neither is a good way to go, but I hope he was crushed, if that was quicker. We took him back to the tent where I cleaned him up as best I could. I sat there with him, too sad to do anythin'. I'd lost both my partners and I couldn't help feelin' that somehow, both deaths were my fault.

Some of the diggers came by, to offer any help I might need. Some of their wives brought some food, some of the diggers brought whisky. I wasn't interested in the food, but I was in the whisky and drank whatever they brought. It didn't matter how much they brought—I couldn't get enough. It didn't matter how much I drank—I didn't get drunk. For the first time in my life, I couldn't get drunk and I couldn't forget. We told some stories, sang some songs. I cried a lot and didn't care who saw me."

William thought he saw a tear in Wally's eyes. His voice certainly trembled with emotion as he told this part of his story. Perhaps in the diggin's where life is tough and dangerous, it's all right for a man to cry. Once again, he wanted to ask Wally about it but didn't.

"The next morning, I gathered up the gold that we'd found, the few things that I owned and went to see Reg's friend who owned the gig. We went back to the tent, collected Bruce and the rest of it and drove into Braidwood where we found the doctor. I told him what had happened and asked if he'd need to do an autopsy. He said that he doubted it because the reason for death was pretty clear, there were other witnesses and he'd be happy to say so.

'Son, you look like you're about to collapse. Why don't you go over to the hotel and get a meal and a bed? I'll look after your friend,' the doctor said.

I gave him four pounds.

'It's only three,' he said, lookin' bewildered.

I told him the other pound was to cover what we didn't have for Reg.

'I won't say no,' he said. 'I think I'd offend you if I did. I'll send a message to you at the pub when I arrange the burial.'

Reg's friend wanted to get back to the diggin's, so I left him and went over to the pub. I told the publican what had happened, and he said the first drink was on him. For the next few weeks, I drank my way through my money at the pub. I didn't get to Bruce's burial. I was too drunk. At first, the publican felt sorry for me, but then I was a nuisance. He wanted me to leave. Pestered me every day. Finally, he found someone that was goin' to Sydney with a wagon of produce who was willin' to take me. He dropped me and the produce at the wharf and I've been here ever since."

"Where do you live?" William asked.

"On the streets. Sometimes, the police pick me up and I spend a night in a nice warm cell."

"What do you do for money?"

"Beg. Beg for food, too. Sometimes I find scraps about the place, or find things at the wharves. Sometimes I get a job on the wharves. Dirty jobs that no one else wants to do. Fixin' broken bilge pumps. I'm still good with my hands when they're not shakin' too much."

"Is this all you'll do until you die?"

"I don't know why I'm doin' it. My parents wouldn't like it if they could see me now. I don't know, Tom. Like Bruce, I'm at the bottom of a hole."

"Wally, I'm saddened by your story. However, I'm tired, hungry and dirty. I'm going to have something to eat, a bath and a sleep. A bath wouldn't do you any harm, either. So, if you've a mind to have those things too, then I'll pay."

"I'd like another whisky."

"I won't pay for that."

"All right, Tom. I suppose if you're buyin', man'd be a fool not to accept."

"He could be something else."

"What?"

"Grateful."

"Aye. I'll be that. It's been a while since I've had a bath though."

"I can tell," said William and he signalled to Tom, who came over.

"Ready now?" he asked.

"Yes, and I'm going to do the same for Wally."

"Well, that'll be ten shillings all up. Are you sure you want to do this? Wally'll be the same drunken, dirty mess tomorrow."

"Yes, I'm sure."

"Go out the back to the dining room and get your meal. Sally'll look after you. We've only got one bathroom, so you'll have to work out who goes first. All the rooms upstairs are empty, so pick one when you've had your bath. And Wally, no bed without a bath."

"That's all right," said William. "Wally'll have first bath, so he won't be able to skip it."

"Fair enough," said Tom. "Off you go."

They walked into a hallway leading off from the bar. There was a set of stairs to the right and William guessed they went upstairs to the guest rooms. The first room they came to was the dining room. There were about a half dozen tables with four chairs at each and the room was empty. A young lady came through another doorway in the corner and introduced herself as Sally.

"Ready to eat?" she asked.

When they answered, "Yes," she nodded and went back through the doorway, coming back a few minutes later with knives, forks, a plate of bread and butter and jam, each in its own bowl. She didn't ask them what they wanted, so William presumed there was no choice.

The meal was the standard fare of black tea with sugar, chops, eggs and bread. It didn't matter though—William was hungry enough to enjoy anything.

"Off you go, Wally," William said when Wally took his last bite. "Like I said, you'll go first. Tell me when you're done."

Wally woke him some time later and he realised he'd fallen asleep while waiting. Wally showed him the washroom. They went out the door through which they had entered the dining room and continued up the hallway, past the kitchen where Sally was hard at work, cleaning pots and pans in a tub.

The bathroom was the last room. The door at the end of the hallway had a sign on it.

"What's that say?" he asked Wally.

"It doesn't matter what it says," said Wally. "It means dunny."

"Dunny? What's a dunny?"

"Where you do your business."

"Who calls it a dunny?"

"Australians."

William peered into the bathroom. There was one bathtub with black rings around the inside, and water all over the floor. The only window was open with a fresh breeze blowing in.

"What'd you do in here, Wally?" asked William. "Wash a cradle in the tub, then have a water fight?"

"Like I said, Tom, been a while since a bath. Feels good, though. Will I see you later?"

"Probably not."

"Thanks for everythin'."

William shrugged.

"Go west," said Wally. "Head for Bathurst. There's gold there and at Ophir and Sofala. Better than the south and the north. Thanks again, Tom. I won't forget."

"That's all right. Try to get home to Manchester."

"I would if I could."

"Get a job, Wally. Stay away from the drink, get cleaned up and sign on to a steamer as a greaser. If you're good with your hands, when they don't shake, it won't be long before you get a ship home. They don't ask much about what you can and can't do and a feller like you, well, he'll know how to be a greaser before they find out he isn't."

Wally turned and walked out the bathroom, shoulders slumped and feet dragging. William shook his head and set about filling the bath from the hot water over the fire at the side of the room. He guessed the fireplace was double sided—one side for the kitchen, the other for the bathroom. There was a tub of cold water too, so he could mix the water to the right temperature, and he was excited about the prospect of being clean again. He hoped the black rings left by Wally would succumb to the assault of hot water and soap.

He decided to go out back first and went through the door Wally had said was marked, 'dunny'. Apart from some rubbish scattered about, the only things of moment in the yard were two sheds—one small and one large. He decided the little shed was an outdoor privy, the same as Robert had on the farm. Pushing the door, he peered inside.

*All very modern*, he thought when he saw the seat with the hole in it. When he was done, he used some newspaper stacked beside it to clean himself. Standing, he peered in the hole and noticed it was nearly full.

*They'll have to dig another hole soon.* He wondered how the hole could be filled to above ground level. He peered again and saw that the floor was bricks and it looked like the seat might move. A little more investigation revealed that the seat was over a large bucket. *The bucket man will need to be both strong and brave. And where will they throw it?*

He headed back inside for his bath, looking forward to it more than ever. When he was finished, he went back to the bar to ask Tom which room he should use.

"Any upstairs with an open door," said Tom, and handed him two shillings.

"What's this for?" William asked.

"Wally didn't want a bed. Said he'd be wasting your money."

"Where is he?"

"You won't believe it, but he's gone looking for a job. Said he'd never look or smell better, so thought now was the best time to be looking. Said if he was lucky, he'd be off to Manchester soon. What'd you say to him?"

"Not much," said William and he put the two shillings in his pocket.

"Room's yours for the night. Sleep well."

CHAPTER 3

# LEAVING SYDNEY

William woke to the sound of rain on the tin roof. He'd not heard the sound since Robert's farm and dreamt he was back there. Robert, Alice and Emma were all arguing, but William wasn't close enough to hear what the argument was about. His feet were stuck in something, and he couldn't move to get closer. It didn't matter at first, then he saw the big policeman had seen him and the inability to move caused him to thrash about in panic. The big policeman's feet made a soft pattering sound as he ran towards William.

"I had to do it!" he called out to the empty room, the sound of his own voice causing him to wake.

It was a huge relief that there was no policeman in sight, but he resolved to get out of Sydney as soon as he could. He doubted the police would even be looking for him in Sydney, but there was no harm in being sure. He also had no desire to be hanged for murder.

The sheets were white and crisp and smelled like the ones in the surgery on the ship. There was very little furniture in the room. Just the bed, a washstand and a tall boy. The window was open, and the smell of the sea and human habitation drifted in on the breeze. There was the usual shouting from the nearby wharf and the sound of traffic in the street outside. He got up, rinsed his face and hands using the jug and bowl on the wash-stand, put on his other clothes and headed downstairs, momentarily wishing that he'd asked Tom about getting his clothes washed. He turned right at the bottom and went out back to the privy. There was no one using it and he was intrigued to see that the bucket was empty.

He went back inside and found Tom in the bar, mopping the floor. There were no customers.

"Ah, there you are," said Tom. "Sleep well?"

"Very well, thank you."

"Would you like some breakfast? Only cost you sixpence."

"Yes, I would."

"Come on, then. I'll join you. I've been waiting for you."

"Why?"

"I'll tell you over breakfast."

They went out to the dining room which was again empty. Sally must have heard them as she poked her head around the doorway and said, "Ready?"

"Yes," said Tom and Sally disappeared, again without asking what they wanted. She came back moments later with a tray full of bread, jam, butter, tea, sugar and knives, forks and spoons.

"Why were you waiting for me?"

"Police came by earlier this morning looking for a feller called Bill Smith. Said he might have arrived in the last few days on a ship from Melbourne. Said they're checking all the hotels."

"Did they have a description?"

"Young, good looking, brown hair, no distinguishing features."

Tom looked carefully at William, who blushed. Tom laughed and said, “I see a lot of fellers like that.”

“What do they want him for?”

“Homicide.”

“What’s homicide?”

“Murder, I suppose.”

William’s mind was in a turmoil. He knew he showed his emotions in his face and Tom’s scrutiny only made him more uncomfortable.

How had they followed him so quickly? *It could only be the policeman from the docks in Melbourne. Everything had gone slowly until then.*

Tom sat back, staring at William. Neither man said anything. William’s discomfort increased. Breakfast arrived—chops and eggs. William was glad of the diversion.

“Been raining most of the night,” said Tom. “I doubt it’ll let up any time soon. Looks like it’s in for a few days. We get it like that around this time of year.”

William struggled. *Perhaps I should just run? Tom hasn’t said what he told the police. They might be outside waiting for me.* His appetite had fled. His mouth was dry, his throat constricted, his breathing heavy. He picked at his food.

“You should eat up,” said Tom. “I know you’re not interested, but I told the police I didn’t know anyone by that name. I said I’d seen lots of fellers with that description. The police said they had too, that the name was the best thing to go by and I should let them know if anyone with that name came by. I said I would.”

William just nodded, afraid to show any more emotion.

“I know what I’d do if I was Bill Smith,” said Tom. “I’d get out of Sydney as soon as I could. That’s if he’s here. I’m only going on what the police said. I wouldn't use the name *Bill Smith* either, but I'll bet he's already worked that out. And I'd change my appearance, too. Grow a beard or moustache, for example. That's if he hasn't got one, of course."

"How would you recommend Bill Smith gets out of Sydney?"

"Well, if he asks around someone might tell him he could catch the train out to Parramatta. It's only two shillings in third class, but I think the police might be looking for him on the trains. They pick up quite a few ships' deserters looking for a quick way out of Sydney. No, he'd be better not to use the train. I think he should go to the docks and find someone that's collecting goods to take to the country. Docks're always busy, especially this time of day. I wouldn't look like I didn't belong, either. I'd be helping people with loading and unloading as I tried to find someone that needed me. Just little things, nothing serious. If I had a bag, I'd hide it somewhere and collect it before I left."

"Where would you recommend Bill hides his bag?"

"I'd tell him to leave it where he stayed last night. Provided it's close to the docks, that is. It might even be close enough that whoever hires Bill, can stop on the way out."

They finished their breakfast.

"I've got work to do," said Tom.

"Me, too," said William. "Do you mind if I leave my bag here? I'll come back to get it later."

"That's all right by me. I'll put it there behind the bar. If I'm not here when you get back, ask for Sally. I'll tell her we're looking after it for you."

"Thanks, Tom. For everything."

"Thanks for what you did for Wally. He was a terrible nuisance, but I did like him. Whatever you said, I hope it worked."

William stepped out of the doors and was immediately grateful for the cover that extended around the hotel. It was raining heavily and water, mixed with dirt and garbage, poured down the steep hill past the hotel towards the harbour. There were people and vehicles doing their best to move about, accompanied by cursing at the weather. He ducked out into it and was soaked in moments. Plodding through the mud, he headed to the docks. He hadn't thought that the police would be so diligent and hoped that Tom's advice was good.

Arriving at the docks, he headed for one of the large buildings, hoping that he might find someone who needed help. If he didn't, at least he'd be out of the rain. Empty carts and wagons were lined up, mostly pulled by soaked, bedraggled horses, but sometimes by bullocks, so he decided if anyone needed help, it would be these people. He stepped inside a building nearby and struggled to see in the darkness. The overcast sky did nothing to help, and it was few moments before he could make anything out. Goods were loaded from piles onto the carts and wagons. It was the same process as he had seen in Belfast.

He moved about for a while, trying to look like he belonged, occasionally stopping to help someone load a wagon. Most of his efforts evoked curses and being told to mind his own business. He decided he'd have to find another way to look like he belonged, or at the very least look busy. The wagons and carts always had two and sometimes three men, so there was never any need of assistance. It was too much to hope that someone would slip and fall and he could take their place. As time went on, he felt more and more exposed and was convinced that people were not only staring at him, but that they were talking about him too. Tom's idea wasn't paying off, but he hadn't seen any police, so it wasn't yet time to panic. It might be the rain, so if there were no police here, there might not be any on the train either. Maybe he should get his bag and catch the train. Then he realised he didn't know where to catch it. Still, he was sure Tom would help with that. He headed out of the building and into the rain.

He wasn't far from the Flour Company Wharf where he had come ashore from the *Liza Ann*. Thoroughly soaked, he thought he couldn't get wetter, so he'd take a walk down to the wharf and see if she was still there. If she was and they needed crew, he could get his bag and get back on board. He hadn't gone far when he realised that it would be a mistake. How did the police know he was in Sydney, recently arrived from Melbourne? They must know he'd come on the *Liza Ann*, so that was no place to go.

Turning back towards the hotel, he was attracted by a commotion not far away. A man was trying to drive his fully laden cart up one of the roads away from the wharf. The stone surface was slippery, and the horses couldn't get any grip. The driver had obviously decided that the horses were at fault and laid into them with his whip, lashing them mercilessly across their backs, shouting at them to make progress. All four horses were now frightened and no longer pulling together.

"Hey!" William called. "It's not their fault. Go easy with that whip."

"Why don't you try minding your own business for a change? They're my bloody horses, so I'll do as I damn well please."

"Aye, you can," said William, walking up close, taking one of the horse's heads, stroking it and whispering to it. "But you won't get anywhere and you're likely to damage a horse, and then where will you be?"

A small knot of people watched, standing under an awning attached to a shop. Others moved on, hurrying to get out of the rain. The horse he stroked became more settled and the others did likewise.

"Christ," said the driver, clearly amazed by how the horse responded to William. "Can you help me? I'll pay you if you can help me."

"Where are you going?"

"Goulburn."

"On your own?"

"What's this? Twenty questions? Can you help or not?"

"It's just that Goulburn's a long way for a man that can't deal with a team."

"Who says that I can't deal with the team?"

"Why, the horse. He said you've not done this before."

The small knot of people laughed. The driver glared at them. Other vehicles struggled to get past, accompanied by the customary shouting and curses. Rain continued to fall heavily. The man started to whip the horses again.

"Stop!" cried William. "Of course I'll help! We might need some help from the people, too."

"Will you pay us?" called one of the onlookers.

"What do you want them to do?"

"Why, get behind and push. It's not far to the top. I think if they help, we'll be able to do it."

"How many do you want?"

"As many as will help."

"All right!" shouted the man. "I'll give a penny to anyone that helps push!"

Five of the men left the crowd and stood beside the cart.

"Give us our money now," one of the men said.

"But what if it doesn't work? You'll have the money and I'll be stuck here. I'll tell you what. Half penny now, and half penny if it works."

"Don't worry. Pay us later," said the man.

The men gathered behind the cart.

"Put that whip away and get off the cart," said William. "It doesn't need your weight too. You men, wait until I tell you to push."

He went and talked to the horses, much to the amusement of the onlookers.

"You aren't the lead horse, are you?" he said to the horse he had quietened. "We'll fix that when we get to the top of the hill. Right now, I want you all to pull together. Take it slowly. Little steps will do it. And I'm going to lead you a little side to side, so we'll weave our way up."

Taking the harness, he called, "All right, men! Push!"

William led the horses and slowly weaved their way up what was left of the hill. The men behind stopped pushing, but William didn't stop the cart until they were well on flat ground and to the side of the road. The street was narrow, but the space enabled other traffic to pass by. He stroked each of the horses and complimented them on a job well done.

The men got their money and dispersed in different directions. It seemed their common bond was amusement at the driver's trouble.

"Do you want some money too?" asked the driver.

William shook his head and started to walk away.

"Will you help me get to Goulburn?" called the man to his back.

William studied the man, quickly reached his decision, and said, "Yes, I will, but I'll want some money to do that."

"I'll pay you two shillings a day and provide your meals. I can't afford any more."

"I'm happy with that."

"Get on, then."

"I've got to get my bag first."

"Where is it?"

"At the Royal Oak."

"Erskine Street? Just back where we came from?"

William nodded.

"Be quick, then."

William padded back through the rain. He was soaked but not cold. Grey clouds lay close to the ground and only a slight wind blew. There was no view of the harbour as he walked back down Erskine Street.

He stepped into the bar and saw Sally behind the counter.

"Hello, Tom," she called.

"I've come for my bag."

"Tom said you would," said Sally and took the bag from behind the bar.

"Good luck," she said, handing him the bag.

"Yes, thank you. And please thank Tom. Tell him the plan worked."

"I will."

William padded back up the hill in the rain. The man looked pleased to see him.

"I thought you'd changed your mind."

"I have to rearrange your horses before we go."

"Why?"

"The lead horse is at the back."

"How do you know that?"

"Horses told me."

"I should have guessed. All right."

William spent some time rearranging the horses, then climbed up beside the man who passed him the reins.

"I'd like you to drive," he said. "You look like you know what you're doing."

"All right," said William. "But you'll need to tell me where to go—I haven't been to Goulburn."

"You knew it's a long way," said the man, looking uncertain.

"Heard of it, but haven't been there."

"All right. We go ahead until we get to George Street, then we turn right. See that big stone building on the right? That's George Street."

"We cross this one?"

"Yes, this is York Street."

William couldn't suppress a gasp when they turned the corner into George Street. There were impressive, multi-storey buildings on both sides of the road. Some were of stone, but most were timber. There were footpaths on both sides, mostly covered by porticos and verandas. The surface of the road was more like a gravel, but he decided the cobble stones were underneath, because the wheels and hooves still made a clanging, metallic sound. Where they joined it, the street was mostly flat, and kerbed and guttered so that the water ran away, not puddling in the street as he had expected.

There was a lot more traffic, despite the rain. Horses, gigs, carts, wagons and even some bullocks all plodded along in orderly fashion. William found it was more chaotic at the cross streets, where drivers tried to push through and people darted amongst the vehicles. He struggled to take everything in and was only aware the man had been talking when he pushed William's arm to attract his attention.

"Mine's Rodney," said the man, holding out his hand. "Rodney Bagshott."

"Tom. Tom Smith."

"Where are you from, Tom? I'm glad you can help, but I'm surprised you said *yes*. Not many men can leave for Goulburn at a moment's notice."

"I just got off a ship from Ireland."

"Ireland? I didn't think they came to Sydney."

"It went to Van Diemen's Land first."

William was guessing, but it must have been a good guess. He just didn't want to say Melbourne.

"Crew or passenger?"

"Crew."

"What's she called? I might know her. I worked in a shipping office for a while."

*That's what you get for lying*, thought William. *Best to get onto another topic.*

"What are you doing here then?"

"Oh, it was my brother's idea. He saw an advertisement for a team to take goods to Goulburn."

They were going down a small hill now, but it didn't trouble the horses. They were able to get purchase on the road surface. All the vehicles moved at a snail's pace. Every now and again, a single rider would take advantage of a gap and dart through.

"Where's your brother?"

"He's sick. We came into Sydney on the coach last night and stayed at a hotel. This morning he was too sick to get out of bed. Told me to get the cart loaded and he'll meet me on the road."

"How will he do that?"

"I don't know—hire a horse, I suppose. He was too sick to say much."

"Why didn't he ride in the cart?"

"I only got the team this morning. My brother bought it off a feller in Strawberry Hills. I went and picked it up."

"So, your brother knows about horses?"

"More than me. No, that's not true. Well, it is true—it's just that I don't know anything. I was born in Sydney, been here all my life, so that makes me a currency child. Went to school here. So did my brother, but when he left school, he went with my uncle to his station in Goulburn. I stayed in Sydney, working as a clerk in offices. I've worked for the shipping line, as I said. I've also worked for the government."

"What's a currency child?"

"One that's born in Australia. A native."

"Why currency?"

"Local, I suppose."

"Now, I'm confused. You said you live in Sydney, but you came into Sydney last night?"

"Well, I work with my uncle now, too. He doesn't like me much. Says I'm too soft. So, it was my brother's idea that I'd get a team and start transporting goods. He thought it'd get me away from my uncle."

"Wouldn't you be better to get a job as a clerk in Goulburn?"

William noticed that the rain had stopped and the traffic was thinning a little.

"Where are we now?" he asked, before Rodney could answer his last question.

"Brickfield Hill," said Rodney. "You keep going straight ahead. This is Parramatta Street."

"I thought you said it was George Street?"

"It's both. I don't know when it happens, but at some point it goes from being George Street to Parramatta Street.

It doesn't matter. We'll take another road to Goulburn. Later on, I mean."

They plodded on. William was astounded how quickly the landscape changed. Both sides of the road now had rude huts and buildings. Some looked like homes, but others were clearly hotels. There was no more curbing and guttering. And while some attempt had been made to surface the road, it wasn't handling the wet and William had to be careful where he drove to avoid deep clefts of mud. Soon they crossed a bridge and not long after, the road forked to the left.

"Do we turn here?"

"No. It's about six miles before we get there. We'll turn onto Liverpool Road."

They rode on, saying nothing for a while. There was very little traffic. The road was still quite wide, so they had no need to move to one side to allow other vehicles to pass. As they drove, William encouraged the horses to move faster and was grateful they hadn't come to any hills.

He shivered when the breeze picked up.

"Are you cold?" asked Rodney. "If you are, you can use my brother's sheepskin coat. They're very good. It'll keep the rain out. I'll get mine, too. It's still a few hours before dark."

William pulled over to the side of the road. Rodney reached into the back of the cart, pulled up a bag, dragged a coat from it and passed it to William. The wool was on the inside, the skin exposed to the rain. It was like his possum skin cloak, but inside out. William pulled it on and was immediately grateful. Rodney did the same with his.

"What if your brother turns up?"

"He won't mind, but he might want it back."

"What will I do?"

"Give it to him, I suppose."

"No, I mean, you won't need me anymore."

"Might not be true. Let's see what my brother says. Anyway, I don't think he's coming."

"Why not?"

"He'd be here by now."

"What if he's up ahead?"

"I don't think he can be. I think he's still sick."

"Aren't you worried about him?"

"You asked about me being a clerk in Goulburn?"

William looked sharply at Rodney. It wasn't the question he'd asked at all.

Rodney laughed.

"I know what you're thinking," he said. "But if I answer that question, it might help to answer the other one. Don't worry. It'll take us over a week to get to Goulburn, so if I don't answer the question, ask me again."

"All right with me."

"Everybody has at least one secret, Tom," said Rodney so quietly, William almost didn't hear him. "Do you want to know what mine is?"

"If you want to tell me."

William became nervous. He didn't know this man at all, yet he'd accepted a job to take a fully laden cart with him to Goulburn. Perhaps he should have found out more about him first.

"Don't worry," said Rodney. "I can tell you're worrying, but you don't need to. You have nothing to fear from me. Besides, I don't think I can make the trip without you."

He was silent for a few moments.

"My secret is that I poisoned my brother."

William stared at him.

"Not enough to kill him, of course. I didn't want to kill him. I just wanted to do this journey without him. He says I'm weak and I'll never amount to much. We had a fight last night. He said he wished he hadn't suggested this project. Said he'll probably have to do all the work. Said my uncle was against it and told him it was better if I stayed in Sydney."

"Why did you leave Sydney?"

"I was dismissed from my last job."

"Dismissed?"

"Yes. They told me to leave."

"Why?"

"They caught me stealing."

William's mind was in a muddle and a whirl all at the same time.

Rodney smiled.

"I'm sorry, Tom. We can talk about something else, if you like."

"Something else? Why are you telling me at all?"

"You wanted to know why I didn't take a job as a clerk in Goulburn."

"I did, didn't I? Well, why couldn't you?"

"They didn't give me a reference and without a reference, I can't get a job. My brother suggested the carrier business. I think he felt sorry for me."

"I don't know about a reference."

"It's a piece of paper where they say how good you are and what a good job you did."

"If you worked for a few places, why don't you use the references from your other jobs?"

"I worked too long in the last one. I wouldn't be able to explain why I hadn't held a job for so long."

"Tell them you worked for your brother."

"They know him in Goulburn and they'd know that's not true."

"Tell them something else."

"I didn't want to lie."

*Well, he's a poisoner and a thief, but he's not a liar. He's not all bad.*

"Do you think that's odd?" Rodney asked.

"I don't know what to think anymore," William snapped. "Shouldn't we go back and check on your brother?"

"He'll be all right. I only gave him enough rat poison to make him sick."

"How did you know how much to give him?"

"I read it on the label."

"What did it say? This is how much you give a person to make him sick?"

"Now, you're making fun of me."

"No, I'm not, but I don't know how you can read it from the label."

"They told how much it takes to kill a rat. I worked out the size of my brother compared to a rat and gave him half the dose."

"Why have you got his clothes? Won't he need those in Sydney?"

"I didn't know what to do. When I picked up the horses and cart and went back to the hotel to get my bag, the feller at the hotel gave me both of them."

"Wasn't your brother still in the room?"

"He was when I left."

"Then, wouldn't his bag still be in the room with him?"

Rodney said nothing. William turned to look at him. He was smiling.

"Clever boy," he said, almost whispering.

William stopped the cart and turned to face him, half expecting to see him holding a gun. He wasn't.

"So where does the truth end and the lie begin?" he asked.

"I've only told one lie and that's about the dose. I gave my brother enough to kill him—enough to kill him ten times over. That's why I have his bag. I knew he wouldn't need it."

"Why?"

"He found out I'd been dismissed. He was going to tell my mother. She always liked me more and he couldn't wait to tell her."

"Where's she?"

"Goulburn."

"I thought that's where your uncle is."

"We called him uncle. He's actually our stepfather."

"What will they do when they find out you killed him?"

"They won't."

"Does that mean you have to kill me too?"

"No, it doesn't. I worked for the police for a while. I know what a man looks like when he's hiding from the police and you're hiding from the police. If you give me away, you give yourself away too. So, it's up to you."

"But what will you do when they find his body? They'll know it was you."

"They won't find his body."

"Why are you telling me this? You could have said nothing."

A flicker of anger crossed Rodney's face.

"It was you and your stupid questions."

"You didn't have to answer them."

"No, but I thought I was smarter than that. I thought I'd made up a good story. Anyway, the day is disappearing. Shouldn't we keep moving?"

"Rodney. You can do whatever the hell you like! But me, I'm getting off and walking back to Sydney."

Rodney burst out laughing.

"What is it now?"

"You. It's a joke, Tom. My brother'll catch up soon. He told me to take his bag, said it'd be easier to ride without it. He'll be along soon, I'll bet. I was just having fun with you, so let's get going. We need to be further along before nightfall."

William hesitated.

"C'mon, Tom. I'm sorry for my foolishness. Let's shake on it. No more tall stories."

He put out his hand. William hesitated, then took it.

They started moving again. William was still uneasy. Rodney had a funny sense of humour.

After a while, they came to a hill.

"Looks steep," said William, stopping the cart before the descent.

"It's not too bad. It's Taverner's Hill. William Taverner has a hotel here, but we won't stop unless you want to. Once we get to the bottom and cross the creek, we climb a little on the other side, then we turn on to Liverpool Road. I never feel like I'm out of Sydney until we get to here."

William took it very easy going down the hill. It was muddy, but the horses didn't slip. Another cart heading to Sydney hadn't been so lucky and was pulled to the side of the road with a broken wheel.

"You fellers need any help?" called Rodney as they went by.

"No," said one of the men. "We'll have it fixed in no time and be on our way again!"

They turned into Liverpool Road and William continued an internal debate on whether to jump off the cart and join any vehicle going in the opposite direction. Rodney was older and well dressed. He didn't look like a criminal, though William didn't think he did either. It was clear Rodney had no skill with the horses and maybe that came from a lifetime in an office. Most people had some skill with a horse. It was the only way to get around.

There was a clumping of hooves from behind and Rodney, looking back, exclaimed, "Ah, here he is!"

"I thought I'd missed you," said the rider.

William pulled the cart over to the side of the road. The rider dismounted and approached the cart.

"Who's this, then?" he asked, nodding at William.

"This is Tom and he's very pleased to see you. Tom, this is Norry, my brother."

The men shook hands.

"Why is he pleased to see me? It looks like he's wearing my coat and I'll want it back."

William started to remove the coat.

"Not yet," said Norry, holding up his hand. "Why're you pleased to see me? Has Rodney been up to his old tricks, making up stories, trying to add spice to an otherwise dull life?"

"He said he'd poisoned you," said William, still not seeing the funny side.

"Christ, Rodney! I thought we'd talked about that nonsense."

"I did get a bit carried away, but Tom's smart and saw through it all. When should we camp?"

"There's a river a few miles ahead. There'll be others there, but it'll do for the night."

Norry got back on the horse and set off, neither waiting for the cart, nor retrieving his coat from William.

"Well, you must be pleased to see Norry is alive," said Rodney.

"I am, but I still don't understand why you made up such a story. You had me worried!"

"I know. I went too far. It was fun at first, but then I realised it was upsetting you."

William shook his head briefly to show his annoyance, but Rodney didn't notice.

The country began to change, with fewer scrubs and trees and more undulating hills and grassy areas than had been the case closer to the harbour. Evening wasn't far off and a chill came in the air. There was little warmth left in the sun and it would soon disappear behind the hills to the west. William pulled the coat closer to himself and was glad he had the possum skin coat in his bag. He couldn't wear it if it rained though—it would be ruined in no time.

"We go through a few towns on the way," said Rodney. "We might be able to buy a sheepskin coat for you. It's sheep country, so perhaps there'll be some for sale. We've always made our own, so I've not ever had to buy one."

After about half an hour, they saw Norry had dismounted near a creek and William pulled the cart up nearby. The far side of the creek was bushy and rose away from the water, but the near side was an open meadow. There were several groups with a variety of vehicles already camped there, with quite a number of horses hobbled and standing about. Laughter came from a group nearby and Norry commented that they were more likely to be going into Sydney than leaving it. He said everybody loved going to Sydney.

"I'm sorry to do this, Tom, but I'll need that coat. Do you have one yourself?" Norry asked William.

"I'll wear an extra shirt for the moment but if it gets colder, I've got a possum skin coat I can wear."

William noticed that Rodney smiled, but said nothing. It wasn't until later that William realised he'd need to explain how he had a possum skin coat when he was just off the ship from Ireland.

"Can you look after the horses, Tom? Rodney and I will see to the camp."

William found a rope in the cart, took the harness off the horses and, using the rope on one of them, started for the creek. Norry's horse tried to follow, so he removed its saddle and bridle and once again set out for the creek. It was flowing briskly and muddy after the rain, but the horses didn't care. They happily drank their fill. William wondered if Norry was taking a few minutes to have a talk with Rodney. No doubt William would be part of the conversation. He led the horses back to the camp and once there, tried to find more rope in the cart, but none was obvious. Not much had been done to set up the camp. Norry and Rodney were deep in conversation.

*Nothing else for it*, thought William. *I can't stand here waiting to find out what they want to do.*

The conversation stopped as he approached.

"What do you want to do with them?" he said, indicating the horses grazing nearby.

"What do you mean?" said Rodney.

"Did you get the extra rope like I asked you?" said Norry to Rodney.

"Oh. No. I forgot."

"Christ, Rodney. Talk about sending a boy to do a man's job."

"I did bring the piece he just used as a lead!" exclaimed Rodney, anxiously.

"We'll have to let them wander," said Norry. "Can you get some wood for a fire? Rodney and I are sorting out some things."

William shrugged and set about finding some wood. It was nearly dark and obviously a popular spot, so he had to venture away from the camp before he even began to see some fallen wood, but there was none he could carry. He gave up and headed back to the creek, crossed it and found wood easily. Apparently, most people weren't prepared to pay the price of wet feet for a load of wood. He took several arm-loads back to the camp. The brothers continued in earnest conversation. He was the only one doing anything useful.

*I've drawn a poor hand here.*

By the time he had brought the last lot back and dumped it, Norry had started a fire. Rodney was sitting on a rock, arms folded, holding himself closely and looking utterly miserable.

"Make yourself useful, Rodney. Fetch the pots, meat and damper from the cart."

"What meat and damper?"

"The meat and damper I told you to buy!" yelled Norry.

Rodney looked thoroughly uncomfortable. "You said you were going to bring them!" he shouted.

"I said no such thing!" yelled Norry. "Look, Rodney, I can't even trust you to do the simplest tasks. Bugger off and see if you can beg, borrow or steal something to eat—anything—from the other camps."

"You do it!" shouted Rodney.

Norry strode over, pulled Rodney to his feet by his shirt-front, and threw him in the direction of the nearest camp. Rodney fell over, then picked himself up without a word and slunk off into the night.

*A poor hand—I haven't been dealt a hand at all.*

Norry went to the cart and brought back a sack from which he took a billy.

"Fill the billy at the creek please, Tom. I know the water's dirty, but I'll put extra tea in it. Might only be tea we're having anyway. I also know you've done most of the work so far and I appreciate it. When you get back, I'll tell you what you want to know."

William filled the billy and returned to the camp. Norry had erected a tripod of metal rods over the fire and hung the billy from a hook at the top.

"Rodney's a molly-coddled lad," said Norry, without looking at William. "He works at a grocery store in Goulburn. Uncle thinks he's simple, but I don't think so. He has no trouble in the store. The storeowner and the customers all like him—only ever say good things about him. Our father died a long time ago and our mother re-married. Feller owns a sheep station outside Goulburn. We call him Uncle. Bit silly, I know, but it works. Uncle can't stand Rodney. Most of the time, I can't either. He's such a dope. Nobody can be that stupid, I tell myself. He's making it up, just to annoy me."

Norry said nothing for a few moments as he looked in the direction of the other camps. William wondered if he was looking for Rodney coming back to change the conversation, or if he was worried about him.

"I talked him into coming on this trip. Uncle wanted me to take one of the other hands. Said this wouldn't work. Said I'd finish up doing all the work."

Then Norry smiled and looked at William. It was a wonderful, boyish smile that made him look very handsome. William was willing to bet the girls liked Norry.

"It seems he was right that someone else would do it. Rodney said you helped him with the horses?"

William nodded.

"He's hopeless. I sometimes think he'd tie the nose bag to a horse's tail."

"He was using a whip. Horses didn't like it."

"A whip? Where the hell did he get that? Maybe he bought it when he should have been buying some food.

We caught the stagecoach from Goulburn. I left Rodney at the hotel with instructions to get supplies and went out looking for some fun. Rodney's not much good as a companion. In fact, he's more likely to chase the girls away. Found more than I'd bargained for, so I didn't get back until this morning. When I got back to the hotel, he'd gone and taken everything with him. I had no idea what he might have done, so I headed to Cleveland Street in Strawberry Hills to pick up the team. Uncle had bought it through a feller there, so the idea was to use it to bring the goods back."

He looked into the night anxiously.

"Where the hell has he got to now? I'm not about to do another rescue mission, I hope."

He poked at the fire.

"I'll finish the story before I go looking—anything to delay the inevitable. So, I get to Strawberry Hills and Rodney's been there before me. I head back to the docks and you wouldn't want to know it, he's been there too. I decide he's gone to do the job on his own and prove himself to Uncle, so all I can do is go after him."

"Which is what you did," said William.

"Not quite. I had to get a horse, go back to Strawberry Hills where I pay through the nose for the horse, saddle and bridle."

In spite of himself, William couldn't help laughing. Norry was initially taken aback, but then he laughed too.

"I'd forgotten everything has a funny side," said Norry.

"I can find someone in the other camps to take me back to Sydney."

"Did Rodney offer to pay you?"

William nodded.

"I asked him. He said he didn't. Said you were happy to get a ride to Goulburn."

"It doesn't matter. If I go back with someone else, then you don't owe me anything."

"It's all right. I believe you. He's no stranger to lying. No doubt he's told you other lies already."

"It's hard to know with him. I believed the story he made up about poisoning you."

"I think he'd like to."

William shrugged.

"Let's see what's happened to him. We'll both go. There's nothing else to do here."

"All right," said William and they walked together in the darkness in the same direction taken by Rodney.

They found him at the first camp site, eating and laughing with two other men sitting cross-legged around a fire.

"Ah, here they are!" said Rodney when he saw William and Norry step out of the darkness. "We were just talking about you."

"I see you found something to eat," said Norry tersely.

"Would you like something too?" asked one of the men. "Rodney said you'd all eaten already, but we pushed some food onto him. We have plenty and we plan to be in Sydney tomorrow. If you'd like some, just ask."

"Yes, we would," said Norry.

"Good, good," said the man. "We've chops, bread and tea. Have some tea while you wait for the chops. They won't be long."

He stood up and stretched out a hand.

"I'm Matt and this is Jake."

"I'm Norry and this is Tom."

Jake stood up and shook hands too.

"I'm glad to meet you," he said.

"Not half as glad as we are to meet you," said Norry.

"How's that?"

"Well, Rodney didn't get it quite right. We haven't eaten, but we'd sure like to."

Rodney kept his head down while Matt grabbed a bag from the cart, took half a dozen chops from it, put them in a pan and then onto the fire.

"They won't be long," he said, pouring some tea into two pannikins. He gave them a spoon and a bag of sugar. "There's plenty of sugar. Water's a bit dirty, so we've been putting lots of sugar in the tea. Sorry about the wet ground—we tried to find a log or some stones to sit on, but we didn't have any luck."

"Don't worry about it. We're just glad to have something to eat, and very glad for your generosity."

As they waited for the chops, Jake said, "Well, Tom, I expect you're glad that Rodney came along."

"How's that?" asked Norry.

"Oh, Rodney was tellin' us that Tom got the horses jammed in the street in Sydney and no traffic could get past. He made it sound pretty funny. We was just laughin' about it. Sorry, Tom—it must have been very embarrassin'."

Norry started to move towards Rodney, but sat down again, his face grim.

"Rodney said you was sick from drinkin' too much, Norry, so he and Tom had to start the journey. Said he thought Tom needed a chance to prove himself. He's right you know, Tom. You have to put the bad experience behind you. Keep practisin', mate. That's the best thing to do."

It was all William could do not to laugh. He'd never met anyone like Rodney who had no problem with lying. His da had told him not to trust anyone, but he'd be willing to bet his da had never met anyone like Rodney, even though he was living proof that his da was right.

"It was very embarrassing," said William. "We had to pay some men to help as well. They pushed the cart from behind."

"Rodney told us. Said he had to belt one of them on the nose when they laughed at you."

William couldn't help it. He burst out laughing. He'd just seen Norry throw Rodney out of the camp and Rodney did nothing.

"Let us in on the joke," said Matt, smiling and clearly eager for more of William's misadventures.

"Oh. The feller looked pretty funny, flat on his back in the gutter, covered in water and mud and begging Rodney to stop."

"I'll bet that was funny," said Matt. "Hey, the chops look ready. Jake, grab some bread for the boys."

After the meal was done, they all chatted for a while, though Rodney offered very little comment—Norry and Matt did most of the talking. Several times, William was about to ask for a ride to Sydney the next day, but then hesitated. He wasn't sure he could maintain the lie of Rodney's skill and valour for the time of the journey. As it turned out, he was glad he'd said nothing.

Matt had taken another half a dozen chops from the bag for himself and Jake and pressed the rest on Norry. "They'll only go off anyway, so you might as well use 'em. No point in 'em goin' to waste." Norry accepted them graciously when they left and the three men walked back to the camp.

"I'm tired," said Rodney when they arrived. "Looking forward to sleep."

"Tom and I are sleeping under the cart. You can sleep in a tree for all I care."

"What if it rains?"

"You'll get wet, Rodney. But you deserve a lot worse for the rubbish you told those fellers. Get your blankets and bugger off."

Rodney got his blankets and stole off into the night.

"He'll go back to Matt and Jake with some story," said Norry. "Well, all they'll get is another helping of the same fairy tale. Tom, stay with us tonight, then take my horse and leave in the morning. You can go back to Sydney, or on to Goulburn, whichever you like."

"How will I return your horse?"

"You can keep him by way of payment for helping Rodney. You can have the saddle, too. How about the horse, the saddle and a shilling? You didn't need to support Rodney's silly story back at the camp, and I admired you for it."

William didn't know what to say. There'd been plenty of twists and turns since leaving Sydney that morning.

"Don't worry," said Norry, misunderstanding William's lack of a response. "I'll sign the bill of sale over to you, so you won't be accused of stealing. If you're agreed, let's shake on it and get to bed. I'm tired too, but for better reasons than Rodney. I didn't get much sleep last night and it wasn't the grog, either."

They shook hands and Norry fetched the rest of the blankets from the cart.

"I always carry spare, in case it rains," he said.

They curled up under the cart, wrapped in the blankets, and William knew nothing until he was woken by Rodney whistling at the fire. Norry was still asleep, so William crawled out, pissed on a tree and went to join Rodney. He'd done a good job and the billy was already boiling.

"Where'd you sleep?" asked William.

"Oh, over there," said Rodney, waving his arm in the direction of Matt and Jake's camp. William looked up in time to see them driving their cart away.

"Early start for them," he said.

"Yes," said Rodney. "They wanted to get their produce to market as early as possible."

"Where are the horses?"

"Dunno."

"Should we look?"

"I suppose. Norry'll be mad if I don't."

"That'd be reason enough for me to look."

"All right," said Rodney, irritably. "Let's go. Where do you think we should look?"

"Well, you go down the creek that way, and I'll go the other way. One of us will find them."

"How far should I go?"

"I don't know what's down there. If you haven't found them in a while, come back."

"What's a while?"

"You'll have to work that out for yourself."

"All right."

William told Rodney to take a nose bag. The horses would think he had food and would follow him back. They took one each and set off.

The morning was clear and fresh with only a light breeze blowing. He loved the smell of the creek. The air was always sweet, and the bubble of the water over rocks was so soothing.

William hadn't gone far when he wished he'd had some tea first. He walked past a couple of other camps with men seated around fires, drinking tea and having some breakfast.

Then he saw the horses. It looked like they had joined some others that were hobbled.

He approached the horses carefully and showed them the nose bag. They came over to him and he turned and started walking back to camp. A couple of the other hobbled horses tried to follow, but soon abandoned the task. Their hobbles prevented them from moving fast enough, and they stood looking mournfully as William led his back to camp. A few times he had to encourage them by showing them the bag.

When they got back, Rodney was nowhere to be seen and Norry was snoring loudly under the cart, so he set about noisily harnessing the horses. Sure enough, he woke Norry who took a piss nearby then asked if he'd seen Rodney.

"Yes," said William. "Last I saw of him he went that way looking for the horses."

"But they're here."

"They weren't at the time. I went the other way and found them further up the creek."

"He's probably found someone to have breakfast with and I'll have to go fetch him. Let's you and I finish this, we'll have breakfast, and then decide what to do."

Norry cooked the chops while William finished the harness.

"Should have got their bread, too," said Norry. "A few chops isn't much. Still, Liverpool isn't far and we can get some there. What are you going to do?"

"Go to Goulburn."

"Why? I thought you'd go back to Sydney. What do you do, anyway?"

"I was crew on a ship. I had no plan on what to do next when I stopped to help Rodney. I could go back to Sydney and sign onto another ship, or go south and maybe look for gold."

"Gold? There's not much alluvial gold left anymore. They're mining for it now."

"Mining's all right."

"Have you done mining?"

"One of the crew was talking about it." William was already afraid he'd said too much.

"There's some fields around Goulburn, but west is best."

He stopped for a moment, laughed and said, "Sounds like something you'd read on a bottle of beer from the west. You haven't come too far. You could go back and go out on the Bathurst Road through the Blue Mountains."

"Is there gold around Goulburn?"

"Yes, there is," said Norry. "In fact, some recent finds on the road between Goulburn and Bathurst. You can go that way too, although it'll take you longer to get to Bathurst, if that's where you want to go."

"Doesn't matter where I go, or how long it takes me to get there."

"Then go through Goulburn—it's pretty country. Well, not so much this time of year because winter's coming on, but if you stay until spring, you'll like what you see. Would you like another tea?"

"Yes, I would," said William, holding out his pannikin.

"Rodney said he thinks you're running from the police."

"The police?"

"Yes. He said he told you some story about him being a criminal and you agreeing not to tell the police because you were both criminals."

William laughed.

"All right, all right," said Norry. "I should have known better. I was going to say that you have nothing to fear from me. You seem like an all right type and if you are avoiding the police, I'm sure it's not because you're a criminal. Anyway, I'll go find Rodney and you go find Goulburn. Liverpool is about twelve miles further along. There's several inns and shops there, so you can stock up with whatever you need. You'll be there around the middle of the day, and it's not a hard ride. Just cross Cook's River here and follow your nose."

"Looks more like a creek," said William.

"I know. It gets bigger further downstream. They come through this way because it's easier to cross here."

He walked over to the cart and fetched one of the blankets.

"Here, take this. You might need it and I have some spares."

He stretched out his hand.

"See you later, Tom. Look for us in Goulburn, if you've a mind. Thanks for being kind to Rodney. I think I would have given him a black eye if I was you."

William took Norry's hand and shook it firmly.

"Aye, a few times I thought I might do that. See you. Good luck! By the way, what's his name?"

"Who?"

"The horse."

"The feller called him Kelly."

On hearing his name, the horse snorted.

Norry headed off to find Rodney. William mounted his new horse and headed off across the river. It was neither deep nor wide and in no time at all, William had left the river behind. The country was a strange mix of scrub and open fields. The sun poked weakly through any trees that he went under and did little to warm him when he was in the open. A breeze blew, from what William judged to be the south, that had a cold edge and he was glad he wore the possum skin coat. He glanced nervously at the sky. It looked like it might rain, and he urged his horse along.

The horse's head bobbed up and down as he plodded along. William thought his might be doing the same. He was happy—happier than he'd been since leaving Robert's. He'd never owned an animal, much less a horse, and he was delighted to be riding one of his own. There was no concern he could look after him, as Rocky had shown him all he needed to know. He felt a sense of freedom as well—beholden to no one, not working for anyone, and his future in his own hands. He could go forward or back, and the decision would affect no one but himself.

He thought about his family and wondered how they were. The sense of freedom and his ability to be in charge of his future were due to his father and his decision to send William into the world. His father had been right to send him away of course, but quickly following the sense of freedom was a sense of loneliness. He had the means and the opportunity to decide what he wanted to do next, but he had no one to share the moment with. Once again, like when he left home and when he joined the ship to journey to Australia, he was alone in the world.

It didn't take long to decide what to do. He would go to Bathurst where he'd been told he'd find gold, and it appealed to him to go through Goulburn, even though it was a longer route. There was other traffic on the road and most people either ignored him or muttered, "Mornin'", "'Day", or just poked a finger to their hat and said nothing. He supposed this was a busy road and no one had time to stop and greet any passers-by.

At one point, he came to a magnificent bridge over a river and was annoyed to have to pay a toll of a few pennies to cross it. He asked if there was another crossing where he wouldn't have to pay, and the man just laughed at him.

He rode into Liverpool around the middle of the day, as Norry had said he would. There was no trouble finding a shop and he bought matches, flour, sugar, tea, a billy and pan, some oats and two tarpaulins. The store owner looked quizzically at the purchases and suggested that William must have lost his supplies on the road, since he was buying all the essentials. William ignored the question and asked if he could buy chops and a sheep skin coat, but was told he couldn't.

"Why don't you just buy a sheep?" asked the owner with a smile that faded when William showed no expression.

He was a big fellow with a ruddy complexion, white hair and a huge white beard. His hands were big and strong, and everything he did was quick and competent.

"Chops next door at the butcher. As far as the coat goes, most people make their own," said the storeowner. He suggested William would be better off with an oilskin coat—it would take up less space and could be used in summer and winter. It was expensive at fifteen shillings. William had seen the officers wearing them on the ship, and the occasional one around the gold fields, and he and Tom had kept one in the store in Ballarat. He decided to buy it as he'd need something to keep the rain off, and by the look of the sky as he came into the shop, there'd be no shortage of that. The bill came to twenty-two shillings. Sure, he had it, but he now regretted the coat. He'd either need to conserve his money, or find some work.

"Where are you goin'?" asked the owner.

"Goulburn."

"Been there before?"

William shook his head.

"Well, head southwest out of town and you'll come to a crossroad—'bout three miles out. Head down the right fork. It's the busiest anyway, so if you're on a road that doesn't look busy, you've taken the wrong one. After that, just keep goin' until you get to Goulburn."

"How long will it take?"

"You ridin' I suppose? You didn't buy much in the way of oats, so there's only one horse."

William nodded.

"Well, two or three days dependin' on how hard you push it. I think we're in for a few days of rain, so you might want to stay at an inn. Be cold, lonesome, wet and miserable outside."

William thanked the man and left. He wasn't sure he had enough money to stay anywhere but out in the bush. If it took two or three days to get to Goulburn, then he had supplies enough, so he wasted little time and set off.

*Looking after myself,* he thought ruefully. He hadn't ever had to do that and was daunted at the prospect. The rain was misting, so he stopped and pulled on his new jacket. It wasn't long before he wished he'd bought a hat, too. His old one was well worn, and the rain came off his head and shoulders, running under the coat and making him damp and uncomfortable.

The crossroad was easy enough to find and like the man had said, the right fork showed more sign of use. There was an inn right on the corner too, but he didn't bother going in to check he was making the right choice. It was still early afternoon with plenty of day left, although he knew that darkness would fall early due to the rain. He'd put a couple of the biscuits in his pocket and was glad he had done so as he nibbled at them as he went along. The horse was sloshing through sizeable puddles now, and mist and rain reduced visibility to no more than a few hundred yards.

CHAPTER 4

# GOULBURN

It was evening as he rode into Goulburn, four days after leaving Liverpool. William couldn't remember four more miserable days in his life. Even on the ship he'd been able to get warm again in his bunk after being on deck in the wind and the rain. Now, there'd been no respite from the rain and he'd been soaked both day and night. Each night, he'd tried to keep the rain out by using one tarpaulin as a ground sheet and the other as a tent, but every effort was to no avail. He'd not bothered to buy a nose bag in Liverpool and hoped to feed his horse with oats by hand as best he could. The plan had been to use a small area of grass where he could put a ration of oats, but that hadn't been possible due to the downpour. There'd be no other choice but to buy a nose bag in Goulburn.

The oilskin coat did little to keep the water out, but it did keep him warm. "Be grateful for small mercies," his mother used to say. Notwithstanding the cost, he was glad he'd bought it.

There'd been several bridges with water lapping on the deck, and swollen rivers and creeks to navigate. The part of the journey he decided was most dangerous was an area he later found out was called the Razorback Road. It was everything the name implied, and perhaps the only saving grace was that it was hard to see in the mist, so it might have been more dangerous than he realised. He saw very few other travellers and decided that everyone else had more sense. Whatever the cost, he'd long since decided he'd seek accommodation in Goulburn.

As far as challenges went, the biggest hurdle was starting a fire to boil a billy, cook his chops and make a damper. He never bothered to try at night, stopping somewhere suitable once or twice a day. Most times it was under the trunk of a large, partly fallen tree where he could sometimes also find some dry wood. One time, he came upon a hut. It was a sad affair of timber poles and bark slabs and looked ready to fall down. There was evidence of some use, but it didn't look like a permanent home. He decided that if the owner came and threw him out, it wouldn't matter as he'd at least have a chance to cook a meal and get warm.

There was no room for his horse, so he fed him some oats in the doorway and left him free to graze. He didn't bother with hobbles and doubted the horse would go far. It was so warm and dry in the hut, he took a chance to dry his clothes and the blanket and while doing so, he fell asleep. When he woke, it was nearly dark, so he decided to stay at the hut overnight. It was tempting to stay until the rain stopped, but he would run out of food quickly, so one night would have to be enough.

*Which would kill me first—starvation or cold?*

Next morning, he cooked breakfast in the hut while the rain pattered on the roof. There was no shortage of leaks and holes, but he'd contrived a platform using stones, poles and bushes that enabled him to keep away from the water. It was easy to get water—he had only to put the billy under one of the many leaks.

Once breakfast was done he called his horse, fully expecting him to be nearby. When Kelly didn't come, he poked his head out the door, but couldn't see him anywhere. He sighed as he pulled the oilskin coat tightly about his shoulders. It wouldn't be long before he'd be wet again, and the warmth of the hut would be a distant memory.

He spent the next hour walking all about, trying to find his horse. Finally, he found him close to the hut, where he'd been sheltering in a dense clump of trees. It was obvious the horse wasn't ready to move on either. At least if they stayed there would have been plenty of grass for him to eat, but there was nothing for William so he told Kelly there was no other choice. He put the lead on and led him back to the hut to saddle and load him. The rain continued to fall, and he was thoroughly wet before they set off.

The lights of Goulburn were visible before they got there. The bush and terrain hadn't changed for miles, the road was muddy and rutted and never difficult to follow. He prayed it was Goulburn and, from what he'd heard from others, the size was about right. Descending from a ridge, he saw lights in the gloom of the early evening. They were still well in the distance, so William knew the town must be in a valley.

As he came closer, he crossed a long bridge with the sound of rushing water echoing beneath it. Approaching the buildings, he saw that not only were some better lit than others, but the lights themselves were brighter. He sighed. In different circumstances he might be more interested, but right now all he wanted to do was get out of the rain and get warm.

One particularly well-lit and imposing building caught his attention. He stopped his horse out the front, tied him to one of the posts supporting the floor above, and walked out of the rain onto the veranda and through its doors. Warmth and the sound of music and laughter struck him like a blow.

"You look tired," said a young woman, standing behind a desk.

"That's because I am," William responded, smiling despite his discomfort. He looked down. Water was dripping onto the floor. "Oh, I'm sorry!" he said, embarrassed. The establishment looked too good for him anyway. He turned to leave.

"Please don't worry," said the woman. "There's no carpet here and water will do no harm. Besides, I'll have only to mop it now, so I'm most grateful, sir." She made a little curtsy.

"There's nothing good to say about this weather," said William.

"Did you see any flies or mosquitoes?" she asked.

"No," he replied.

"Then, that's good, isn't it?"

William laughed. What a wonder to find someone like her at a time like this.

"Would you like a room?" she asked. "Not making any comment on your appearance, but we have one left on the ground floor at the back that we can let you have for five shillings for the night."

"What's the cost of one upstairs?"

"Why, they're fifteen shillings."

"Then, Miss, I'd like the one at the back. Or is it Mrs?"

"It's Miss. Please sign the book here."

She saw William hesitate and said, "I'll do that for you. You're all wet, of course. What's your name?"

"Tom Smith."

"Then Mr Tom Smith, if you'll get your wife, I'll show you the room."

"Wife?" asked William. "There's only me—and my horse, of course."

"You can't bring your horse, only a wife. And if you don't have one of those, all the better," she said, and laughed. William loved the laugh. It reminded him of Mary.

"Why all the better?"

"It's only a small room."

"What will I do with my horse?"

"You can stable him for sixpence."

"I'd like to do that. Can I do that first?"

"Of course! But let me show you your room first. Then you can take him around back and come through the back door to your room."

"I'd like a bath and something to eat, too."

"A bath? You look wet enough already. We don't charge you to use the bathroom, and the dining room is through that door there. You pay for whatever you order. I'll tell the cook that you are here, so you can have your bath first, if you'd like."

"Where's the bathroom?"

"It's at the back. You'll come past it when you come through the door. Come on— I'll show you that, too. I doubt anyone will be using it. Not many of you fellers ask to use it, and upstairs have one of their own."

William hesitated.

"What's wrong?" she asked.

"Well, I'm still dripping water."

"All right. See to your horse first then. See the door down the end of this hall? That's the back door. Come through that when you've seen to your horse and then call for me. I'll still be here, and I'll show you everything then."

"How will I know which door to use?"

"There's only one. You won't have trouble."

William went out front, back into the rain, collected his horse and walked around the back of the hotel. The side street was a sea of water and mud. The horse sloshed through, and William did the same. He found the stables easily enough and took the saddle off his horse before putting him in a stall. There was a bag of oats nearby and some stacked hay. He put some oats and hay into a trough in the stall and made sure there was some water in the other trough. Kelly wasted no time attacking the food with enthusiasm. It made William realise how hungry he was, but he hadn't finished with his horse yet. He found some rags and a brush and rubbed Kelly down.

When he was done, he gave Kelly a final pat and headed for the only door he could see at the back of the hotel. He pushed through before he realised, he hadn't found the girl's name.

*Call me*, she had said.

*All right*, he thought. *I can do that.*

He stepped through the door and called, loudly, "Me!"

The girl appeared in the hallway almost immediately, laughing.

"I was wondering how you might do that," she said. "I'm Ruth, by the way. You're all wet again, but your room is right here, and the bathroom is right there."

"Thanks Ruth Bytheway. I'll use the bathroom first. I've got some other clothes I can use in my bag."

She laughed again.

"Ruth Jones is my name. They'll be wet, no doubt, but I suppose there's not much anyone can do about that," she said.

*She's really nice. She's at least the happiest person I've ever met.*

"Come on then," she said and pushed through a door into a room without a bath. It was hot in the room. It had a fireplace in the corner, built of bricks with a large tub built into it. There wasn't much of a fire under the tub, but the water was steaming. There was a long table with several tubs stacked on it. The floor was slats of wood, all crossing each other.

"This is actually the laundry, but you can use it. We're not doing any washing at the moment, as you can see. We thought the rain might stop today, so we got the fire going. The water will be nice and hot. Use one of the tubs. There'll be cold water in the pump. Have you used one?"

"I've seen them used."

She turned up a lamp on the wall so William could see a little better.

"Here's your towel," she said, passing him some cloth.

William studied it in the half light. He'd not seen anything like it before.

"It's a Huckaback towel," she said. "All the best places are using them. Soap's on the table there. Don't take too long—you don't want to get the cook angry with you."

"What will I do with the water when I'm finished?"

"Do you think someone might want it?"

William blushed and struggled for a response.

"Don't mind me. Throw it out into the yard. Your room is straight across the hall. You can put your things in there when you're finished. How long are you staying?"

"Why?"

"Well, if it's more than a day, you can leave your clothes in here to be washed."

"They might get stolen."

Ruth looked at him and smiled. "I doubt it," she said. "Hurry up. Like I said, you don't want to get the cook angry. Come to the dining room when you're ready."

"Where's the dining room?"

"Down the hall. If you can't find it, ask someone."

She turned on her heel and left, closing the door behind her.

William took little time to wash. He stood in one of the tubs and rubbed himself down. It wasn't as good as a bath, but he was happy enough with it for the moment. Besides, he wanted to get to the dining room. He was hungry enough to chew his own leg off.

He put on his extra clothes. They were a wet, sorry lot of rags and needed to be replaced. He decided to do that once he had earned some more money. Thinking about Ruth, he was tempted to put his old clothes back on, but they were in an even worse state being soaking wet, mud streaked and stinking of horse. He left his clothes on the table, threw the tub of water into the back yard, dropped his bag into his room and went to find the dining room. It wasn't hard. He found it beside the kitchen.

The door was open and he stepped into the room. There was no one there. He looked outside again, but Ruth wasn't at the front, so he turned back and studied the room. To his left, there was a large opening into the bar where it looked like a person in the dining room could order drinks. In the corner to his right was a door that he decided must lead to the kitchen. He headed for that to check with the cook.

As he reached the door, Ruth came out of the kitchen.

"Ah, here you are. That's an improvement," she said, studying him.

"I'm ready."

"What would you like?"

"What can I have?"

"Steak or chops, eggs, bread, jam and tea."

"I'll have steak, eggs, bread, jam and tea."

"It won't be long. Cook thought you'd have that, so it's nearly ready. Sit there," she said, pointing at a table in the corner.

"Can I have a whisky?"

"If you like. Put your head through that hole there and Angus will get one for you."

Ruth went back into the kitchen and William walked over to the bar opening and poked his head through. The only man William could see behind the bar was standing down the other end, talking with some customers. It was a long room, like every bar he'd seen in Australia. Some people were sitting at tables and chairs, and others were standing. There weren't too many people, perhaps the rain had kept them away. He tried to signal, to get the attention of the men talking to Angus who were at least looking in his direction. One of them saw him and tapped Angus on the shoulder. Angus detached himself from the group and strolled over.

"I'd like a whisky," said William.

Angus nodded, poured one and returned.

"That's a shilling," he said.

William counted out the money and went to his table, where he pulled his money from his pocket again and counted what was left. It took some time and concentration, but he decided there were four pounds, three shillings and sixpence remaining. He'd need to be very careful with his money. Sipping his whisky, he tried to work out what to do next. It didn't matter that he'd left his clothes to be washed. That didn't commit him to another night at the hotel, and the hotel was too expensive anyway. He'd crossed a bridge coming into the town, so there'd be a river where he could camp for a few days if he could find some work. On the other hand, there might be a hut or a room he could use. It'd be miserable camping in the rain, so the camping would work only if it stopped.

Ruth arrived with his meal. He'd taken only one sip from his whisky but gave it no further attention and set into the meal without delay. Ruth stood for a few moments watching him, looking pleased that he was clearly enjoying his meal, then left and went back to the kitchen. He could hear scrubbing and rattling of pots, so he guessed she was cleaning up and wondered why the cook didn't do it. Then he realised, Ruth was the cook. He burst out laughing.

"Is everything all right?" asked Ruth from the doorway. "Not many of our customers laugh at our meals."

"It's all right. I'm laughing because I just realised that you're the cook."

"Why is that funny?"

"It's not."

"Sounds like it is," Ruth said tersely before turning and heading back into the kitchen.

William thought about Ruth. She looked about his age with dark hair pulled back into a bun, bright and lively eyes, a beautiful figure, and certainly a sense of fun. She was not as tall as him, though he was tall compared to most, so it would be surprising for her to be that tall anyway. Her dress was bright and colourful and added to the air of happiness that surrounded her. He wondered how someone could be that happy in Goulburn.

*Nothing wrong with Goulburn—it's just a long way from anywhere.*

He had no idea of how to approach Ruth, or even what to say. *What would I do with a wife, anyway? I'm not sure I even earn enough money to look after my horse. It would be nice to talk to her though, and be in the company of a woman for a change. I liked it at Robert's place where the women were around and there was always something to talk about.*

Ruth came back and silently cleared away everything but the whisky and the tea. Once again, he could hear things being washed in the kitchen. *Perhaps I could ask Ruth to sit with me? Have a cup of tea? Is that what people do?*

He finished his tea and his whisky, but Ruth didn't come back. He could buy another whisky, and stall for time, but wasn't sure he could afford it. On impulse, he got up from the table, went to the kitchen and poked his head through the door. The room was empty, so he presumed Ruth had gone out and was back out front. He went out to look, but she wasn't there either. He wished they'd finished on a better note. She thought he'd laughed at the meal, and he'd given her no reason to think he did otherwise. He couldn't sit waiting in the dining room, so he had no choice but to either go to bed or buy another whisky in the bar and hope he could see her again to reassure her that he wasn't laughing about her cooking.

Deciding on the latter, he went out and around to the bar. He stood in the doorway, uncertain about his decision. Most of the customers were gone, but the group with Angus still stood at the bar. One of them saw him, waved and called out, "C'mon, stranger! Come and join us. I'll stand any man a drink that's brave enough to be out on a night like this."

"He's not out," said Angus. "He's stayin' at the hotel."

"All the more reason he should join us!" said the man. "He'll have nothin' better to do than enjoy a drink at the bar. And it won't do us any harm to meet someone new."

The man moved away from the bar, approaching William to shake his hand.

"I'm Joseph," he said. "But everyone calls me Joe."

"I'm Tom."

They walked back to the group together. None of them moved. William wished he'd gone to bed.

"This is Hugh," said Joe, indicating one of the men. The man slowly put out his hand. "Tom," said William, taking it.

"And this is Mac. He's Andrew McArthur, but everyone calls him Mac." Mac, too, was slow to extend his hand. William took it and said, "Tom."

"And you already know Angus." Angus made no move to extend his hand, but waved and smiled.

*What's with these men? It's not as though I've done anything to them.*

"The boys were just tryin' to convince me to go into a business with them. They—"

"That's enough, Joe," said Hugh, cutting Joe off. "We don't know who Tom is. Might be that he takes our idea and uses it for himself."

"I doubt it," said Joe. "Angus, get Tom here whatever he wants to drink. I'd like to buy him a drink and I'd like you to tell him your idea, Hugh."

"Like I said, Joe, I don't like the idea of tellin' anyone else about our idea."

"Joe," said William. "I've been on the road for a few days and I'm tired out. I didn't really come in for a drink. I was looking for Ruth to thank her for a wonderful dinner. I think you men have matters to discuss, so I'll thank you for the offer of a drink, but I'll be on my way."

"Well, now, Tom. That's a very fine speech and spoken like a true gentleman," said Joe. "But these fellers have been talkin' for a couple of hours now and me, I think it's all nonsense. Besides, if it's Ruthie you want to see, then you'll need to see me first—I have a rule that says that no one sees Ruthie before I buy them a drink."

William stared at Joe in astonishment.

"What's the matter?" asked Joe, smiling.

"It's just that… I mean… Ruth said she's a miss," blurted William, red with embarrassment.

"Joe, enough of this nonsense!" said Hugh. "I came here to talk serious business and if you've not a mind to do so, then I'll take my leave."

"Me too," said Mac.

"All right with me, boys," said Joe, smiling. "I'll think on your idea, and don't worry—Tom here won't find out about it. From me, that is. I'm not sure it would matter if he did because I'm not too sure it's such a great idea."

"Told you," said Mac.

"Shut up!" said Hugh to him. "No need to insult us, Joe."

"I didn't think I was, but if you want a serious business discussion, then you have to expect a serious response. Come and talk to me in a week's time. I'll have an answer for you then. 'Night."

Joe dismissed them with a wave of his hand. They left, Hugh thumping his feet on the floor and clearly angry.

"I don't envy them going out on a night like this," said William.

"They haven't got far to go. Do them good, anyway. Might dampen their enthusiasm a little," said Joe. He looked up. "Angus, what're you doin' here?"

"I don't know what he wants."

"Are you daft? A whisky—and one for me. I want to wash a bad taste out of my mouth."

"No, I meant I didn't know if he wanted anythin'. He said he was goin'."

"You're still daft! He's not goin' anywhere. Are you, Tom?"

"No," said William.

Nothing more was said until Angus brought the whiskies back. They clinked their glasses.

"So, young man, what brings you to Goulburn?" asked Joe, sipping the whisky and pursing his lips. "This is my best. Angus wouldn't dare serve us anythin' else. Would you, Angus?"

"No, Mr Jones," said Angus, laughing.

William was trying to piece it all together. Angus had looked angry, but just laughed. He decided nothing made sense and hoped that it all would, sooner rather than later.

"I'm heading for Bathurst."

"Where'd you come from?"

"Sydney."

"There's shorter ways than goin' through Goulburn."

"I know. It's a long story, but I'd started out this way and thought I'd keep coming."

"What's in Bathurst?"

"Gold."

"I thought so. You're right to go there. There's not much left around here. You could try Tuena on your way to Bathurst—they say there's steady, payable gold there. All the diggers say they won't find enough to get rich, but every now and again there's a find that proves them wrong. If anyone's goin' to be lucky, might as well be you."

Joe studied William for few moments, sipping his whisky while he did so. Then, he laughed. On hearing the laugh, William understood.

"Ruth's your daughter, isn't she?" He instantly regretted the statement. "I'm sorry," he stammered. "It's none of my business."

Joe just stood there smiling.

"C'mon, lad. Let's find somewhere to sit. My legs are about finished. Bring your drink and I'll get you another when that's done."

He walked over to a table and sat heavily. William followed.

"Yes, she is, and a finer girl never graced the earth. She's a wonderful comfort to her mother who is scarce able to rise from her bed these days. She'll be with her now, readin' her to sleep. You see, this is my hotel and Ruthie works here, so she can take time when she needs to see to her mother."

Joe reflected for a few moments.

"C'mon lad, if I'm to share a drink I'd like it to be with a man that enjoys one. There's more where that came from."

"I don't have the money, Joe. I'm grateful for this one, but I'm afraid it'll have to be enough."

"Nonsense. It's not often I get to share the company of an educated man, especially one that rides a horse and dresses like he doesn't have a penny to his name."

William flushed.

"I'm sorry, Tom. Now it's my turn to apologise. I didn't mean it like that. Well, I suppose I did. I saw you come in, then when I heard you speak, I couldn't put it together. Your appearance belies your education."

"I'm not educated, Joe. Why, I hardly went to school."

"You speak like you've been educated."

"People say that, but I don't know why."

"It's no matter, Tom. Let's forget about it. How long are you plannin' on stayin' here?"

"I'm not planning on staying at all."

"It won't do you any harm to stay a while. I've some jobs that need doin', if you'd like to earn some money. Most of the fellers have gone to the gold fields, so it's hard to find help these days. It'd be a good idea to earn some, then head to Bathurst. At least, you'd arrive there better dressed."

Joe smiled, then laughed and William laughed with him.

"I'll pay you three shillin's a day for any day you work, a room and rations. How does that sound?"

"Sounds good."

"And, any drink you have with me will be to my account."

"Sounds even better."

The men laughed together.

CHAPTER 5

# TROUBLE IN GOULBURN

William settled into an easy life with Joe. He didn't work every day but when he did, Joe worked him hard. It was mostly work around the hotel—helping Angus, fixing things that were broken, running errands and sometimes, working behind the bar. Best of all, he got to spend time with Ruth. He found it to be a blessing and a curse.

Ruth intrigued him. She was the same laughing, courteous, almost flirtatious person with everyone. On the days William worked around her, he couldn't suppress his pangs of jealousy when she would greet young men with, "Hello, handsome!" or "Good morning, handsome!" He wrestled with his feelings every day, struggling to control his need to be around her all the time. Many a time he longed for his mother or father, who could advise him on how to approach Ruth, or what to say to her. He'd listen carefully to conversations around the bar in case someone would discuss a similar problem and expose a likely solution to it.

Joe treated him very well and they would have a whisky most evenings together before supper. He'd often dine with Joe but never with Ruth, who mostly dined with her mother after cooking a meal for any guests. Several times he nearly blurted out to Joe that he'd like to call on Ruth. That was an expression he'd heard when he'd been fixing a floorboard in the ladies' parlour. They thought he was listening to them, which he was, but he'd heard the expression before they asked him to leave, and not to come back until they were finished. He told Joe they'd asked him to leave, just in case they complained, but he just laughed.

The days he didn't work, he'd go for a ride on Kelly. He enjoyed exploring the countryside, though he did find it became terribly monotonous after a time. His riding improved all the time and he no longer hurt like he did after he'd arrived from Sydney. He'd forgotten how much it would hurt to get back in the saddle.

One time when Joe said he wouldn't be needed on either the Saturday or Sunday, he took a ride over to the Braidwood diggin's. There wasn't much to see, and he decided it only confirmed what he'd been told. He camped beside a creek overnight. It was summer and hot, so he had to endure a night where the mosquitoes found him a tasty morsel. Nonetheless, he had the best sleep he'd had in a long time, his dreams untroubled by images of Ruth. He'd hardly had a night in the last few months where he didn't wake hot and troubled, so the night by the creek was a wonderful respite. He wondered if it was time to leave and head for Bathurst, but he knew he couldn't. He'd fallen in love with Ruth, or at least, he imagined that's what it was. There was no one to ask, but he wanted to be with her, and to marry her, so he presumed it was love.

Then, close to Christmas, Joe said they were having some friends over for a Christmas lunch and asked if William would join them. It was a welcome invitation, but not without obligation. Joe wanted him to help arrange the dining room, make sure the kitchen fire was good and hot from early morning. There would be about twenty people and, while some of the guests' wives would help with the meal, there would be no time for them to tend to the fire. William had to help with the stabling too, as many of the guests would come from outlying wheat, sheep and cattle stations. He didn't mind, as he knew many of the men already and he enjoyed being part of the family. It was times like this when he missed and wondered about his own family the most.

The biggest shock was that Ruth had a married older sister—no one had ever mentioned her. She, her husband and her husband's brother all came down from Camden, where they had a cattle station. The men were tall and, in William's view, incredibly handsome. They were very well dressed and everything about them said that their business was going well. When they pulled up outside the hotel in their gig late on Christmas Eve, William wondered about the excitement. He was told their decision to come was as unexpected as it was welcome.

When the excitement died down, Joe introduced William to Eve, her husband Brian and Brian's brother, Ned. William knew that Joe was only being courteous since the family were still talking excitedly and not much interested in him. Brian smiled broadly and shook hands firmly, Eve smiled sweetly, but Ned could not have been less interested. He shook hands absently, all his attention focused on Ruth.

On Christmas morning, William was up early but decided not to yet dress in his good clothes. He'd bought some better clothes with the money he'd earned from Joe, but thought he'd make a mess of them stabling, tending to the fires and doing odd jobs. Helping Ruth in the dining room and kitchen was first prize. He enjoyed resolving the many problems that Ruth confronted. At one point, she kissed him on the cheek and said, "You're wonderful, Tom." He had to make a quick retreat in case she saw his embarrassment and misunderstood it.

*No*, he thought, ruefully. *Understood it.*

Gigs, carts and buggies arrived from early morning. William saw to it that the horses were unharnessed, fed, watered and turned out into a paddock at the back. Some of the men helped, and others just nodded their thanks and went to find Joe.

Ned was about Ruth's age, and it took William no time to decide that Ned was competition. William had been jealous when Ruth had been nice to young men who came by the hotel, but Ned was entirely different. He and Ruth flirted openly with each other, although Ned did nothing to help with the preparations. William did all the work and, apart from the kiss on the cheek, Ned received all the credit. William wondered if Ned had been Ruth's intended all along, as everyone seemed to think he was the ant's pants. At one point he admired how well the dining room had been decorated and Ruth said, "Just for you." The wives helping Ruth tittered their appreciation. Ned put his hand lightly on Ruth's cheek, smiled and whispered, "Thanks." William muttered that he needed to get more wood and went out back, his face red, and his heart racing and aching at the same time.

William knew his emotions were out of control. He'd imagined the Christmas lunch would be good food and laughter, some drink, some toasts, him possibly sitting beside Ruth, chatting about things, and her finding him interesting, hopefully, very interesting. Now he hated everything about it. He wished he'd not been invited. The thought crossed his mind that he could quietly saddle Kelly and go for a ride and come back in a day or so. They'd miss him, might even come looking for him, but at least he wouldn't have to endure watching Ned and Ruth.

Joe called, "Tom!"

William looked up and saw him standing in the doorway.

"You're workin' too hard, Tom. You're all red in the face. C'mon in. We're havin' a whisky in the bar, and we'd like you to join us. I've checked and the girls don't need you for a while. Everyone's here, so there's no more horses to look after. C'mon, lad. I'd be pleased if you'd join us."

William knew he didn't have much choice, but it was all he could do not to turn and run. He and Joe walked up the hall together, heading towards the bar.

"I'm so pleased you're with us," said Joe, putting a hand on William's shoulder. "You're like family now and I'd like you to think of yourself as one of us."

Tears were close to the surface, but William forced himself to walk into the room. There were half a dozen men standing around, including Brian and Ned. He recognised the others as Paul, Andrew, George and Phillip—all regulars and good friends of Joe. They all knew each other well enough that only a nod to say *hello* was needed.

"Here he is," said Joe. "Found him, workin' as hard as ever!"

"C'mon, Tom," Andrew said. "Here, take this," and passed William a glass of whisky. "Joe's best, and we all know there's none better. Joe?"

Joe raised his glass. "To Christmas, to present friends, and to absent ones, and thank you all for comin'. Brian and Ned, it's so good you could make it, comin' so far and all."

William wished Brian and Ned weren't there as the sight of Ned strained his emotions and threatened tears again.

"Bottoms up!" said Andrew, and they all drained their glasses. The whisky burned all the way down. The glasses were all refilled. William knew it was dangerous to drink so early, but decided not to care. With luck, the whisky would drown his disappointment, smother the hurt, or at least give him something else to think about.

"Have you got family, Tom?" asked Brian, sympathy in his voice.

The last thing William wanted was to be the centre of attention, but he forced a smile.

"Yes."

Andrew refilled all their glasses.

"Where are they?" asked Brian.

"Ireland."

"You're a man of few words," said Ned, laughing. It wasn't a pleasant sound and William knew it wasn't meant to be. He imagined Ned with a glass smashed in his face and whisky all over his nice clothes.

"Well, bottoms up!" said Andrew again.

William did so, before Joe said, "Whoa! Let's take it easy. I've got beer and wine to have with the meal and whisky and brandy for after, so we've got a long day ahead of us and best not disappoint the girls by being too drunk to appreciate the food."

"Too late now," said Andrew. "Tom's got the right idea. It won't do us too much harm and that's for sure."

"Ned, go check on the girls. See how long before lunch."

"Sure, Joe. Happy to," said Ned, and winked at Joe.

Now William's image was Ned lying in a ditch, clothes all dirty and muddy and too drunk to move. The room started to sway.

"Tom, are you all right?" asked Brian.

"Yes," said William, but didn't feel all right at all. He'd not bothered with breakfast, being too busy attending to his chores, and whisky on an empty stomach had been a mistake. Still, even though the whisky had gone to his head, if he didn't have another before he ate, he'd probably be all right.

Ned came back.

"Ruthie said they'll be a while yet. Time for another whisky, she said."

"All right," said Joe. "But let's make this the last one before we eat. And let's drink slowly—Tom here has been workin' like ten men and is probably the only one with a real thirst."

"All right," said Andrew. "I'll pour him a double."

"That's not what I meant," said Joe, tersely.

"Too late," said Andrew, shrugging his shoulders.

"Well, let's all take it easy then. I'm sorry, Tom, don't drink that if you don't want to."

"It's all right," said William. He already felt better. In fact, he felt more than better.

The sun blazed on the building and the room became hotter.

"Shall I open the doors?" William asked Joe. "It's getting hot."

"No," said Joe. "Best we don't get noticed. I can serve drink on Christmas Day, but I can't sell it, so best the police don't think to check. We have nothin' to hide, but a visit from the police might spoil the day."

The men discussed local matters, including some proposed changes to the town. It was idle chatter that held no interest for William. He was trying to work out how he could compete with Ned, or at least make his intentions known.

William was only halfway through his whisky when Ruth called from the doorway, "C'mon, everyone! Lunch's ready!"

"Bring that with you," said Joe.

"I was planning to," said William. He was feeling light-headed and had a little trouble walking, but thankfully there wasn't far to go.

When they got to the dining room, William marvelled at the food on the table. There were slices of every kind of meat imaginable, vegetables, pickles, paste and sauces. The table was composed of all the smaller tables pulled together. There were bumps where they joined on the uneven floor.

Joe organised everyone to their seats.

"I don't want any husband and wife together," said Joe. "I want to mix you all up, so you can all have a chat to someone else for a change."

"Oh, Pa!" said Eve and Ruth at the same time.

"No exceptions. Ruth—you and Ned sit together, and Eve—you and I sit together. Tom, I'd like you on the other side of Eve. You can get to know each other. The rest of you can fit as best you can."

William did as he was bid and sat in the chair. He'd been sitting for a few moments when he realised Eve was standing beside her chair.

"Am in in the wrong chair?" he asked her.

"No," she said sharply. "That's all right—I'll do it myself."

She pulled her chair out and sat.

William knew he'd done something wrong, but didn't know what it was.

"C'mon, Evie. You're embarrassin' the lad," said Joe. "It's all right, Tom. Don't mind Evie."

The day was falling apart by the minute. He was off to a bad start with Eve, he was sitting opposite Ruth and Ned—but far enough way that he couldn't engage Ruth in any conversation—and he knew he'd already had too much whisky.

Joe stood and rapped a spoon against a glass.

"Now, everyone, welcome to our home. We thank the Lord for his bounty, for all this wonderful food, and for the special friends with whom we get to spend this day. My Beth can't be here with us, but she's here in spirit. I know she would bid you all welcome. I know she would love to see you if you have a few moments to visit with her. There's bottles of claret, ale and whisky on the table, so please help yourselves. Now let's enjoy this wonderful lunch, thanks to the marvellous and talented cooks."

The lady on William's left passed him a plate and said, "Here you are, dear. You help yourself now."

William leaned forward, pulled some food off the plates where it was closest and began to eat. He could feel Eve looking at him, so he cast her a guilty look. Once again, he knew something was wrong. He looked at her and she was staring at him. Wondering what was wrong, he looked to Joe, but Joe was deep in conversation with a lady on his right.

"What's wrong?" he asked Eve. He knew his face was burning and thought it had been most of the morning.

"A gentleman would assist a lady before beginning to eat himself."

William tried to speak, but it came out, "Shorry."

He took Eve's plate to put some food on it, but she pulled it back.

"I'll do it," she said. "I do believe you've had too much to drink to be useful anyway."

As she pulled the plate, his arm came with it, and he knocked over a bottle of claret on the table. It fell towards Eve and spilled on her dress.

"Oh, you clumsy oaf!" she said. "You've ruined my dress! Pa, where on earth did you find this imbecile?"

"Evie, don't speak to Tom like that. It was an accident. Besides, he's family."

"I don't know where you got that foolish notion," said Eve. "He's not now, and he never will be. You're always doing this—trying to find the son Mother couldn't give you. This one's trouble. Look at him, everyone. He's drunk already! What have you had? A glass? Is that all it takes? He's probably stealing your alcohol when you're not watching."

William looked at Ruth. She was still, deathly white, with her hands clasped to the sides of her face. Ned had a smile on his face. Joe looked enraged.

"Eve!" said Joe, harshly. "You—"

"Well, Tom? Do you have anything to say for yourself? Are you still *shorry*?"

William just stared at her. *What is going on? What did I do to Eve?*

"I see the way you look at Ruth," Eve continued. "You should crawl back into whatever swamp you came from. As if you'd ever be good enough for my sister."

Eve looked at Ruth.

"There's only one man for you," she said. "And he's sitting beside you."

"I will not permit this to continue, Evie!" thundered Joe. "This is my home and Tom is my guest. He's always welcome here. I was so pleased to see you at first, but you can't help yourself, can you?"

"Can't help myself? What does that mean, Pa?"

"You pretend to be so high and mighty. Let me remind you that we aren't so far removed from the swamp ourselves. We're ordinary people, we're all ordinary people," he said, looking around the table. "And with one exception, proud to be. Your mother would be distressed to hear you talk like this."

"Mother would only be distressed if she thought Ruth was the least bit interested in this drunken excuse for a man."

The room was so quiet, they could all hear the sounds of insects buzzing and the breeze moving the trees outside.

Eve and Joe stared at each other. Joe looked angry enough to burst, but Eve wore an angelic half smile.

After a few moments, Eve looked at Ruth who had remained motionless, her hands still clasped to her face.

"Well, you're not interested in this fool, are you? Please tell me you're not."

Ruth looked at William who remained motionless. He'd never been shamed like this, by someone he hardly knew. The sailors on the ship had their fun, in the end Hall had even tried to kill him, but he knew them all and he could at least decide on a reason for their behaviour. Ruth took her hands from her face.

"Oh, Tom," she said. "I'm sorry. I didn't know."

William tried to get up, but in his haste, he fell backwards, crushing and splintering the chair as he fell. Eve laughed loudly—a combination of triumph and derision.

"My dress, your chair, Pa. What next? Look out, everyone—it might be you!"

William struggled to his feet, humiliated beyond anything he had ever known, and headed for the door. Joe stood up and tried to stop him.

"Don't go, Tom. We can resolve this. It's only Eve that wants to hurt you."

William looked around the room. Eve and Ned looked triumphant, the others looked either sympathetic or confused.

"There's no place for me here," said William.

"Yes, there is Tom," said Joe, putting his hand on William's arm. "Please stay."

"No, Joe. Eve has taught me a lesson I'll not soon forget. I'll be going now. I'm very grateful to you for all you have done. Merry Christmas, everyone."

He stopped in the doorway and looked back.

"Good luck to you, Brian. I have a feeling you're going to need it."

He was nearly at his room when Joe stopped him.

"I know you have to go, Tom. I would too, but there's someone I'd like you to meet first. It won't take long."

"I'm not up to meeting anyone, Joe."

"You said you're grateful for what I've done. Then, please, for me. Just a few minutes."

"All right, Joe. Who is it?"

"This way."

They turned, went up the stairs and stopped outside a room where Joe knocked softly.

"Beth? Are you awake?" he called.

"Yes," said a voice from inside the room.

Joe pushed the door open, turned and said, "C'mon, Tom. I know you won't regret this."

The room was dark—the curtains were drawn and there were no lamps lit. It took a few moments for William's eyes to become accustomed to the gloom. He saw a woman sitting up in bed, leaning back against some cushions. She was pale and thin, her head crowned with thick, grey hair.

"Oh, Joe, why aren't you with your guests? Is something wrong?"

"I've brought someone to meet you."

"Who is it?"

"It's Tom."

"Oh, Tom—I've heard all about you. Come closer. Don't be afraid. What I have is not catching."

She reached out, both arms extended, fingers probing the air.

"Where is he, Joe? I know you're there, Tom. Please come closer."

"Don't be afraid, Tom. Beth is blind, so she needs to touch you. It's all right. She's been wanting to meet you and I wasn't sure, but now I have no choice."

"What do you mean, Joe? Why do you have no choice? Tom, please come closer."

William went up to her, standing close enough for her to touch him. Her touch was gentle, lightly moving over his hands, arms and clothes. He noticed she wore the same perfume as Ruth.

"Ah, a working man. That's good," said Beth. "Let me feel your face."

Beth touched William's face and cried out.

"Oh, what's happened? Oh, Joe, this is awful. What's happened to this poor boy?"

Beth moved a little sideways in the bed and said, "C'mon, Tom. Sit here beside me. Let me hold your hand. Joe, I know there's a chair by the window, so you sit in that. Joe usually sits on the bed beside me, but I want you to do that now."

William looked at Joe who nodded, even though it was hard to see him in the darkness, before sitting on the bed while Joe sat in the chair.

"I can't get up, Tom," said Beth. "I can't see, and I can't walk, but apart from that, I'm all right, so it's not all bad. Other people do the seeing and the walking for me. Your heart has stopped racing, so I think you are comfortable. Are you comfortable?"

"Yes, I'm comfortable," said William, thinking it was an odd question.

Beth was looking at him so intently that William wondered if she really was blind.

"Do you mind it being dark?" she said.

"No."

"It's strange. I can't see anything, but I prefer it to be dark. Might be woman's vanity. If it's dark, you can't see how badly I look. It might not be fair either. You see, I can see you, but you can't see me. I can't see with my eyes of course, but nature replaces eyes with other senses. Do you understand?"

"No."

Beth laughed and despite himself, William laughed with her.

"That's better. Now, tell me what's happened?"

Both men remained silent for a few moments.

"Evie's up to her old tricks," said Joe.

"Ah, the princess," said Beth. "Worst thing we ever did was send her to finishing school. Finished her all right. You'll understand one day, Tom. Parents see their children as people too, and they don't always like what they see. You'll always love them, of course, but it doesn't mean you have to admire their actions. 'Love the sinner, despise the sin', my mother used to say."

The room was quiet for a few moments. There was a clock ticking somewhere.

"Do you like the clock, Tom? Every tick puts us closer to the end of our time here. Best not to squander it. Wouldn't it be awful if when your time is up, there were still some things undone? Joe, you go back to your guests now. They must be wondering where you are. I think Tom and I are going to be friends, even if we shall have only a few minutes together. Say your goodbyes now, both of you. I think I'm right that Tom is leaving us, and I think with good reason too."

Joe stood and came over to William, who stood and shook his hand. William was glad it was dark. Once again, tears were close to the surface.

"Good luck, lad. You know you are always welcome here. No one will think the less of you for what happened today. None of it was your fault. You are probably the only one in this family that needs to shoulder none of the blame."

Once Joe was gone and William was seated, Beth said, "Give me your hand again, Tom. There, that's good."

Her hand was soft and feathery, so light, so feminine.

"You have a nice hand, Tom. You've come from far away, haven't you? You've done a lot in your few years, but nothing you should regret. That man on the ship, your friend was right. No one will miss him, and the world is better without people like that."

William was startled. *How did she know about that?*

"I know what you're wondering. Like I said, lose one gift and gain another. The other men, too. They were very bad men, Tom, and no one knew about all the bad things they had done. The police won't find you, so you can stop worrying about that, but you can't go back to Victoria. Keep going, Tom. You'll find what you're meant to find around Bathurst, but you won't get there for some years yet. Tuena will be good for you, too."

"How do you know all this?"

"Ruthie's not for you, Tom. I can feel your broken heart, and it's not the first time it's been broken. You left one behind, and the other one thought she was too old. More fool her. Take your time, Tom. You'll die an old man, but you must use the time you have here wisely. Don't waste it on the wrong ones, like my Ruthie. Perhaps she'll make a mistake, but there's no way I can stop it. Still, she'll find, as will you, that your heart will mend in time and once it's mended, it opens again to other opportunities. And they'll be there, so you have nothing to worry about."

The ticking of the clock and the insects flicking at the window were the only sounds in the room.

"You're wondering if things would not have gone so badly if you'd put on your good clothes."

William didn't reply and Beth laughed.

"No, Tom, it wouldn't have made any difference, although you would have looked and smelled a little better. Evie's had her heart set on Ned since she met him, but she didn't have the courage to tell Brian. She's decided if she can't have Ned, then Ruthie will. So, Tom, it's nothing to do with you. You found your way into the middle of a war and got hurt in the crossfire."

"Does Joe know?"

"No, Tom. And what would he do if he did? No, it's my secret. I wouldn't have told you except you're going away. You need to know that the things Evie said about you aren't true, and you should know why she said them."

"Shouldn't you tell Ruth? Stop her making a mistake?"

"It's only a mistake, Tom. We all have to make mistakes. That's how we learn."

"Learn? What do you mean?"

Beth laughed. William loved her laugh. It reminded him of Mary—she laughed like that. And Ruth, too, he thought sorrowfully.

"It doesn't matter that you didn't go to school. You don't have to go to school to learn. You'll learn something every day in the school of life, even if you don't always like learning it. Remember though, that the lessons are not to stop you experiencing life, they are there to help you enjoy it. Promise me, Tom, that you'll forgive Evie for what she has done today. I know she's not nice, but it's too late to do anything about it. Don't let bitterness make you angry, too. There's enough anger in the world."

Beth was silent for a while and William thought she'd gone to sleep. He liked sitting there, holding her hand. It was comforting, and he was in need of comfort after his world had turned upside down.

"I'm still here, Tom, and you haven't said anything. Will you forgive her?"

William thought for a while. He was not of a mind to forgive her—the things she did and said, the complete humiliation in front of everyone. And Ruth? What of Ruth? He'd had his heart set on Ruth and that future was gone now too, thanks to Eve. And for what? To serve Eve's own ends. It wasn't fair.

"No. Well, not yet anyway."

Beth laughed again, and William laughed with her. He enjoyed her company and wished he could have met her earlier.

"Does God have a plan, Beth?"

"I hope so," she said and laughed. "What a waste, otherwise."

William thought about Beth's answer. He hoped she would say more. He wasn't disappointed.

"But I often wonder about it, sitting here in bed, each day, all day, and every day. Before my accident when life was so simple, I didn't wonder about anything. I had a husband and two beautiful girls. Now, when I wonder what good purpose I serve, I realise it's not my job to wonder, but to make best use of what I have. It's not my plan, it's His."

William stood, not sure he could control his emotions any longer. "It's time for me to go," he said.

"I know. I enjoyed meeting you. You're a good man, Tom. You've got a strong heart and body, and a good mind. Ruthie would have been happy with you, but you're on different paths. So tread carefully, young man, and beware the likes of Evie."

"I will."

He stooped and kissed her carefully on the forehead, turned and started to leave the room.

"I will forgive her," he said. "Just not this afternoon."

He left the room to the sound of Beth's laughter, went down the stairs and to his room, where he packed his few belongings into his bag. As he went out into the sunshine, he could hear laughter coming from the dining room. He was glad the day had not been completely spoiled for Joe and his guests.

Kelly was in the paddock but came quickly when William called him. He sometimes brought him some oats or apples if they were in season, so he would always come quickly. It didn't take long to saddle and make ready for the road. The whisky had mostly worn off and his head was clear enough to think that he wouldn't get far in what was left of the day. He had no food or provisions and would need to remedy that before leaving.

"Tom," a soft voice said. He turned and saw Ruth, standing partly in the stall, a sugar bag in her hands. "Here," she said, handing him the bag. "Pa said you're leaving, and you'll need some provisions. It's not sugar—I just used the bag. It was all I could find."

William was at a loss for words. He stood silently, studying her.

"I'm sorry, Tom. I didn't agree with Evie, but I didn't have the courage to stand up to her. She's always bossed me around."

They stood, she only a few feet from him, neither one saying anything, but the morning's events widening a chasm between them.

"I must go back," she said finally. "Pa saw you leaving and asked me to give this to you. It's only he that knows I'm here. The fight would start again if Evie knew, and we've already had enough fighting for Christmas."

She started to walk away, then turned. "Good luck, Tom. I didn't know you felt like that about me. Evie has always wanted me to marry Ned, but I don't know. I don't always like him that much. Still, I suppose it's what I'll do—Evie usually gets her way. If you ever come back, please see Pa. I know he'd like that. He really likes you, and Evie wasn't too far wrong. He did think and talk about you as though you were his son."

William watched her turn away again and walk into the building. He would later think there was a moment when he could have called out and stopped her going, but he didn't. *The rest of your life starts with the next moment*, he thought, but the moment was gone, and it was too late to change it.

He mounted Kelly and after a while, he was on the Bathurst Road. It wasn't far to the Wollondilly River, and it would be as good a place as any to camp overnight. The events of the day had already caught up with him, and he dozed as his horse plodded along. It took no time to find a good camping spot by the river. Somewhere slightly raised, but flat. He spread one of the tarpaulins on the ground and rigged the other as a tent using some nearby trees. It didn't take much effort as it didn't look like rain, so it didn't have to be too flash. Supper took no time and he then rolled into his blanket under the tarpaulin, using the spare blanket as a pillow. He could no longer sleep without a pillow.

He tried to sleep. *Sleep might not have the power to cure all my ills, but it sure does help to forget them, at least for a while.*

It was not to be—the incessant heat, the mosquitoes and the lack of practice at sleeping on the ground gave him ample opportunity to review his treatment at Evie's hands. His face burned with the heartbreak and the humiliation. He promised himself that he would never allow that to happen again. Yet he didn't know how to make good such a promise. He didn't even know that Evie existed before he met her on Christmas Eve, so how would he avoid it? Then he found himself laughing loud and hard. *Of course! Christmas Eve. What else? And what a present she turned out to be. But it was Eve I had to avoid, not Christmas. If Beth could be grateful for the good things in life, well, so can I.*

He promised himself that he would enjoy the next Christmas, wherever he was. As he lay in the dark with the nightlife chirping and rustling, and the river bubbling and gurgling nearby, he thought that everything wasn't so bad. Once again, he was on his own—the future in front and the past behind. Within moments, he was sound asleep and didn't wake until the sun was well up.

CHAPTER 6

# THE ROAD TO TUENA

It took him two days to get to Tuena and it wasn't an easy ride. He took the shorter way, avoiding Taralga, but it wasn't much more than a bush track until he got to Kiamma Village. A few times he thought he might be lost, but relied on his instinct and the sun. There was no shortage of sun to guide him, the days being blazing hot and windless. He saw a few small farms along the way, but he didn't stop for either directions or company. For the moment, he was glad to be alone and thought more about Joe and Beth, helping to make him feel better about himself and his role in the events of the day. There was no shortage of creeks along the way for water for both himself and Kelly.

The country didn't change from hour to hour—undulating hills, creeks, ponds and scrubby clumps of trees. Sometimes the road skirted the hills, at other times it went more or less over them. He saw no other travellers and even though he didn't think he was lost, it would still be a relief to arrive at Kiamma Village. Towards the end of the first day, the country changed a little and he saw more huts and cultivated fields. He was just thinking it was time to find somewhere to camp when he saw some buildings, not long after he'd crossed a river. It wasn't much of a river but it was bigger than a creek, so he elevated its status to river. He thought about camping beside it but pressed on in the hope he would reach the village. It was only two or three buildings and, whether it was Kiamma Village or not, he decided he'd prefer to stay somewhere if he could and conserve the provisions Ruth gave him.

He pulled up outside an inn and let the reins drop. Kelly had been trained well. Every now and again he had to repeat the training by tying the reins to something heavy on the ground, so Kelly would think the reins were always anchored.

The inn was only a small building, low to the ground. He had to stoop to go through the door. It was too dark to see the construction, but he guessed it to be timber with bark slabs or wooden slats for a roof. He came into a small bar room where there was a man behind the bar chatting with two others. No one smiled. They stopped talking and viewed him with suspicion. William asked if he could stay and the man behind the bar said he could have supper and a room for three shillings, and it wouldn't cost anything to stable the horse. He asked about the stable and the man advised him to turn the horse loose in the paddock beside the inn. William couldn't help smiling.

"Grass is free," William said.

"Yes," said the man. "But it's still our grass."

"Then I'm grateful for it, as will my horse be eating it. Where can I put the saddle?"

"There's a shed out back—put it in there with the others."

"Can I get some oats?"

"I don't have any. You might get some at the store. I'm sure you saw it as you came in. Probably not open now, but you could try in the morning. Do you want breakfast?"

"What time does the store open?"

"After breakfast."

"Then I'll have breakfast."

"That'll be sixpence."

William counted out the money.

"I'd like a whisky, too, before supper."

"That'll be another one shilling and four pence. You'll have time before supper. You've got to wait for the cook. She's gone visiting, but she'll be back before dark."

"It's dark now."

"All right, then she'll be along directly."

"I'll see to my horse and come back for the whisky."

The man nodded and William saw to his horse and saddle. He came back into the bar carrying his bag.

"Can I put my things in the room?"

"Yes. It's just down the hall. The first room on your right. There's a jug of water and a bowl if you want to wash before supper. Privy's out back."

"You'll have no trouble findin' it," said one of the customers. "Just follow your nose."

His mate laughed with a hee-haw noise that sounded like a donkey.

"All right, you two. That's enough. Here—take this lamp. Leave it in your room when you come back."

"Better not to take it," said the same customer. "Better you don't know what the room's like."

*Hee-haw, hee-haw,* laughed his mate.

William picked up his bag and the lamp and headed down the hall. The whole place was hot. If it stayed like this, he would have been better camping. He pushed the door of his room open and was pleased to discover that, despite being small, the room was comfortably furnished. He put his bag on the floor, poured some water in the basin and washed his face and hands. He thought back to the lady in the farmhouse outside Belfast where he had first learnt the process. *I hope she's well.*

He threw the water into the yard and used the privy. The customer had been right—it didn't smell too good. It was a small shed that had a door but it was open, so he could see there was no one inside. There was a seat with a hole in it where he sat and did his business. There was the customary newspaper hanging on a nail on the wall and he tore some sheets to clean himself. He made something of a mess of it and resolved to have a bath in the first creek he came to the next day.

Walking past his room on the way to the bar, he thought he'd wash his hands again. *Might as well,* he thought, regretting the mess he'd made with the paper. He smiled ruefully, wishing he could make better use of a newspaper.

When he entered the bar, there was a short, stout woman standing with the barman. The other men had left.

"This him, Fred?" she asked. Fred nodded.

"Mine's Betty," she said and stuck out her hand. William had never shaken a woman's hand before and hesitated before taking it. He wondered if she might be playing tricks on him. Betty laughed.

"I won't bite you, I promise, but it is nice to meet a gentleman."

William shook hands. "This is Fred," said Betty.

"Fred," said William, shaking hands with him too. Fred and Betty looked at William expectantly.

"All right, mister," said Betty, less friendly than before. "You don't have to tell us your name if you don't want to, but there's bushrangers about and you don't want me thinkin' you're one of them."

William blushed. "Sorry," he said. "Tom."

"That's better, Tom. You'll be dinin' with us. It'll be ready in a jiffy. Fred says you're havin' a whisky, so when you're done, your supper'll be done. Bring the lad through, Fred, when he's had his whisky."

Fred poured a whisky for William and one for himself.

"Where're you headin'?" he asked.

"Bathurst."

"Gold?"

"Yes."

"There's gold at other places, too. Tuena is not far from here."

"So I hear. Where's best?"

Fred shook his head. "There's no best—every place is as good and as bad as the rest."

"What's at Tuena?"

"Couple of pubs, some stores and a few hundred diggers. People seem to like it. Quiet place, not too much shootin' and most men have their families with them."

"Which way you plannin' to take?" Fred asked after a few moments.

"Is there more than one way?"

Fred shrugged. "Depends," he said.

"On what?"

"Fastest way is through Laggan. High road is through Binda, and there's more water."

"How much faster?"

"You ridin', I suppose? I mean, you've got an 'orse."

William nodded.

"An hour or so. Go through Binda—road's better marked and like I say, there's more water, so it don't matter so much if you get lost."

"How do I take that road?"

"Stay on the road you're on. You have to go back to go to Laggan. When I think about it, that's as good a reason as any to go through Binda. You'll go through Tuena. You might like it, too."

"Where are all your customers?" asked William.

"A few locals come each night, but tomorrow's the big night."

"What's tomorrow?"

"Saturday. They'll start comin' around the middle of the day and be here 'till I throw 'em out at nine o'clock. It's no way to make a livin' though. Betty wants to go to Sydney. Says we should get a pub there. She's sick of the bush—heat, dust, flies, mosquitoes and bugger all women to talk to."

"That's what I like about it. The bugger all women to talk to, I mean."

"You're not one of those fellers, are you?" asked Fred, peering suspiciously.

"No, I'm not. I just don't like women."

"I agree," said Fred, sounding relieved. "I don't like 'em much either. Always causin' trouble around 'ere. The men want me to 'ave a special room for 'em. 'Ladies' Parlour', they call it. Have you ever 'eard of such a thing?"

"Yes, I have. I think it's a good idea. Men can drink on their own. Play cards, do what they want. Same for the women. They can enjoy each other's company, too."

Fred looked disappointed, as though William's answer had not been the right one.

They finished their whiskies and went out to supper. Betty had cooked a beautiful stew and William could have kissed her—he'd been dreading the inevitable steak and eggs. She also produced a damper that she said was her specialty. When William admired that, too, she insisted he take what was left.

William went to his room and spent a restless night. It was hot, so he needed no bed coverings, and that meant the mosquitoes had an endless feast. Their whining and frequent stops when they landed to feed meant he was slapping at himself and the air most of the night. When dawn appeared through the only window, he got up and dressed and let himself out of the inn. He didn't see either Betty or Fred. He saddled Kelly and set out. He didn't wait for the store to open for oats, or for Betty to cook breakfast. As he put the saddle on, he again marvelled that it was still useable despite its poor condition. Sooner or later, he'd need to spend money on repair or buying a new one.

He set out, the rising sun to his right. The morning was cool but there was no breeze to speak of. Already the cicadas made an almighty racket and the grasshoppers flicked against his legs. Birds called to each other, possibly warning of his approach, and the kookaburras laughed at him incessantly.

The narrow, dusty road climbed up a hill away from the village. He hoped to find a creek or a river soon so he could have the promised wash. It may have been more sensible to backtrack and use the river he had seen on his approach to the village, but he didn't want to see Fred or Betty and have to explain his early departure. Betty may already feel justified in her assessment of him as a bushranger. He smiled to himself. *Tom the Bushranger doesn't sound too threatening.*

After an hour or so, and continual climbing through the same monotonous scrubby country, he reached the top of the hill he'd been on since starting out. He could see into the valley in front, although the trees beside the road largely blocked his view. It didn't matter but it was now very hot, and he looked forward to washing himself more than ever.

About an hour later, after moving through a succession of rolling hills, a creek appeared beside the road but there wasn't enough water in it to even make a cup of tea. He let Kelly have a sip, but he wasn't too interested.

Finally, he rode down to a river. It was neither wide nor deep, and the water wasn't running fast but it was plentiful and welcome. He was always amused by the difference in the rivers he was accustomed to back home. *Still, who am I to argue whether it's a river or a creek?* It didn't matter. There was more water in it than the creek he'd passed earlier.

He let Kelly graze nearby, stripped off his clothes and waded in. The bottom was all rocks and very hard on his feet. He decided to go no further, sat on a rock and washed himself as best he could. The water wasn't all that cold, and it felt so good against his skin. He rubbed some sand he gathered from between the rocks onto his mosquito bites and they started to bleed. *It's no better than scratching them*, he thought, and stopped doing it.

Stumbling over the uneven bottom and back to his clothes, he wished he'd found a better spot. He hadn't bothered to look. For a few moments, he contemplated washing his clothes and staying by the river until they dried but decided against it. He didn't have enough supplies to waste time hanging about, so he thought it best if he pressed on. He put on his clean clothes from his bag and stowed the others in their place.

He filled his bottle with water and corked it. It would fit in his saddle bags later. Joe had explained the trick. "Saves you dying of thirst if you get lost," he'd said. Well, he always found plenty of water on his rides but it was good to sip from time to time when he was thirsty. Besides, he didn't know the country and he'd already ridden several hours before finding good water. He looked around before setting out. It was a pretty spot with trees growing close by. The ground was uneven and there was debris scattered about, so he supposed the river could swell and be violent when in flood. It was in the bottom of a valley, so it was likely the valley would gather a lot of water when it rained. Clouds dotted the sky and some of the heat was gone from the sun.

Kelly looked at William expectantly and sniffed the bottle when he approached. "Not for you," William said, putting the water in his saddle bags and tying the bag across the back. The bag wasn't looking too good either. A few things needed fixing, as well as his heart—he wasn't sure if it could take another beating. His pride, too, needed to be restored.

He rode up the bank and set out again, first looking up and down the road. Already he was a little worried that he hadn't seen anyone. Perhaps he should have asked for directions back in Kiamma Village before setting out on the same road he had used yesterday. If he saw anyone, he'd ask for sure. The road wasn't much more than a track through the trees, but he did see the odd wheel mark. He hadn't seen those before Kiamma Village, so this road was more used. "I'll go wherever it leads," he announced to the trees. Kelly plodded along, nodding agreement with every step.

About an hour later, he rode into a town. *This is it*, he thought. *Tuena*. There was a man driving a cart, heading in the same direction. The first person he'd seen all day. It didn't take long to ride up beside him.

"Is this Tuena?" William asked.

"No," said the man, smiling. "Where did you come from?"

"I stayed at Kiamma Village last night."

"How long did it take to get here?"

William was puzzled and must have looked so.

"Well," said the man, "this is Binda. You're about a third of the way there."

"Took me about three hours," said William, proud of knowing the number. He was good with anything up to ten.

"Then you've got six to go. It'll be a long day. This is a nice town, and you could stay here if you wanted."

"Why should I stay here?"

"All the men have gone looking for gold, so there's work that needs doing and girls that need meeting."

"You've just talked me out of it."

The man laughed. "Good luck then. Ride carefully—there's bushrangers about."

William went on his way. The countryside was the same undulating hills, but there were signs of cultivation and it looked like good country. Creeks crossed or ran beside the road from time to time, and there was no shortage of water to replenish his horse and bottle. The sun blazed down again, the little black flies continued with the same monotonous personal intrusion, and the wind picked up a little. Hour after hour he continued, with a sense that he was now climbing. If he looked back, he could see wooded hills in the distance. It seemed desolate, lonely country—just hills, trees and a track that he hoped would lead somewhere.

Hills were all around him now and gave him a sense that if it wasn't for the track, it would be easy to get lost. Everything looked the same, and he began to fret that he had bitten off more than he could chew. He should have either stayed at Binda or waited for someone that knew the way.

He was going through more mountains than hills, and the trees grew thickly on both sides of the track. Almost anywhere would be a suitable place for a bushranger to attack, so he made sure there was no threat ahead as he moved along, eyeing the trees and nearby scrub nervously. He hoped Kelly would be alert to any other horse and would snicker if he sensed anything. It would have been better if the man hadn't alerted him to bushrangers as the threat probably wasn't real, but it made him worry and he knew that to be pointless.

The country reminded him of Ballarat, and he supposed he was once again in gold country, though there was no evidence of any digging until he saw some tents and huts off to the side of the road. He couldn't see anyone and decided since it wasn't Tuena, he'd press on.

It was coming on dusk, and he knew he was close to Tuena. He could smell it and was reminded of Ballarat again, although the stench was not quite as strong. Gold fields had a smell all of their own, and it was far from pleasant. There were creeks to his left and right, but the one on the right was closer and showed signs of digging. The noise of the town came to him, and he could see lamps and fires from huts and tents, and see and smell smoke drifting into the air.

He rode into the town as rain began to fall, stopped outside the bigger of the two pubs, and stepped wearily from his horse. People were packed under the roof on the veranda, the noise of chatter and laughter deafening. Dropping the reins to the ground, he headed towards the door.

CHAPTER 7

# TUENA

He stayed in Tuena for about two years. He would later say he grew up on the ship, found out about life in Ballarat, and became a man in Tuena. There was always work with the diggers, for which he received twenty-five or thirty shillings a week. If it was at the diggin's far enough from town, he'd also get food and lodging. Food was always good and plentiful. It was not only grown in the town—it also came from both Bathurst and Goulburn, and the competition meant it was never expensive.

The work was hard, the nights harder. Fred had been right that most men who had a family had brought them. It meant there were more wattle and daub huts scattered among the tents, as those families wanted more comfort than a tent could provide. William always thought that the huts provided little more, but kept those thoughts to himself. The men that didn't have a family gathered at the bigger tents each night to play cards, smoke their pipes and drink whisky, and William embraced the lifestyle as though he'd been born to it. William made few friends and moved among the groups, sometimes winning, sometimes losing, but always enjoying himself. He loved the company of the men—the laughter, the thrill of winning, the whisky, the stories and poems—but most of all, he enjoyed being away from the women.

His reception at the pub endeared him to the town straight away. There'd been no suspicion when he entered the noisy room, and no antagonism as he pushed his way to the bar. The barman gave him a friendly smile when he asked what he'd like, nodded when he asked for a whisky and said, "First one's on us," when he returned with it.

Some of the men standing beside William asked where he'd come from. Not in a way that was intrusive, but by way of starting a conversation. When William answered, "Goulburn," one of the men laughed and said, "Before then."

"Well, Ireland," said William, which started chatter and questions about Ireland. The men asked if he'd like to join them and the laughing man said, "You'll have some friends, being from there. This is a good place. People from everywhere. Publican's a limey, but not even you Tipperary boys care. He's all right and looks after his customers. We've got Americans and Germans too, and some say the Chinese are on their way."

It was hot in the room with the press of people, but William didn't mind. He liked these men, liked being made welcome. He was near to the end of his first whisky when a man appeared in the doorway and called for everyone to listen.

"There's a 'orse out 'ere," he called. "Says it's sick of standin' in the rain. Wants 'is owner to come see to 'im."

"Mine," said William to his new friends, feeling embarrassed and guilty for not taking better care of his loyal companion.

"Owner's over here!" called the laughing man.

"I'll see to 'im," said the barman.

"No, you won't," said the laughing man. "You'll see to us. We'll see to him."

The laughing man took William by the elbow.

"C'mon, I'll show you where. The boys'll set up another while we see to yer horse."

"I haven't got much money," said William.

"Then you're one of us. No one's got much money. We'll take yer horse out back. It'll be all right until morning. You staying here tonight?"

"I'd like to, but I haven't asked as yet."

"I know he's got room, so you'll be all right if you want to stay. You get yer horse and I'll show you where to put him."

Once they settled Kelly, the man told William that he'd arrange a room and that William should rejoin the others in the bar. He said there'd be a meal on later if William needed one and he'd arrange that too, if William wanted.

William was overwhelmed by the man's hospitality and said so.

"Think nothing off it," said the man. "Be good if you stayed in Tuena for a while, if you've got nowhere else to go."

William put out his hand and shook.

"Tom's mine."

"And James is mine. Yer welcome, Tom. Go and join the others. I'll be back directly. If you decide to stay in Tuena and don't have enough money to take a shout, just tell the barman. He'll keep an account for you. They do that here."

"I've not heard of that."

"You live long enough Tom, you'll've heard of everything. They do it for the diggers 'cause they aren't always lucky, and they all deserve a drink when they feel like one."

William went and joined the others. They introduced themselves, but William forgot all their names moments after he heard them. The noise in the room, the heat, the humidity and the whisky all played tricks with his mind. He tried to follow the conversation, which was all about the rain and how hard it was to dig when there was so much water. Some of the men had claims along the creek and there was talk of getting pumps to help.

"I don't know," said one of the men. "Maybe we're better to wait."

"Might be waitin' a while," said another one of the men. "Rain doesn't look like stoppin'."

"I suppose it's happenin' everywhere, but I've never known a place to get as much water as 'ere," replied another. "What about you, Tom? You a digger?"

"I've done a bit. Always working for someone though. Mostly I do help-about. I've worked in a store, in a pub—things like that."

"You'll like it 'ere," said one of the men. "There's always someone that needs 'elp."

The chatter and the laughter continued all around William but, as much as he enjoyed it, he was grateful when James came and announced supper was ready as he was hungry enough for two suppers.

"Will you all be here when I'm done?" he asked the men. "I haven't had my shout yet."

"Might be," said one of the men. "No harm done if we're not. Buy us a drink next time we're all here, or next time you come to town if you don't stay in Tuena. You look like you need supper and a bed right now, so off you go. Hope to see you soon."

These were William's kind of people and he'd already decided to stay in Tuena for a while.

He went to supper and was a little embarrassed when he discovered James was the publican, but settled into an easy conversation over supper when he realised James thought nothing of it. James didn't join him for supper but was kept busy bringing food from the kitchen and generally helping where needed in the dining room and at the bar. The other guests lived nearby and had decided to treat themselves to supper at the pub. They ran the store over the road.

William learned that Tuena was there because of the gold, and that anyone associated with the town was proud of it. He heard again that there were two pubs, five stores and several hundred diggers scattered up and down the valley. Most were alluvial diggers, but a few had started mines where it looked promising. Like the others, his dinner companions encouraged him to stay.

"James would like you to stay," said one of his companions. "I think he's not too well and would be glad of some help. He's about run off his feet with one thing and another."

"How do you know that? That he'd like me to stay, I mean," asked William.

"Well, I heard him talkin' to his wife. Told her there was a new young feller had just ridden into town, said he'd worked in a pub and might help if he stayed. Would that be you?"

"I suppose so."

"Well, are you stayin'?"

"I suppose so."

James gave William a room at the back of the hotel. It wasn't much as rooms go but, despite being small, it was comfortable and adequate. William was free to come and go as he pleased, and James told him on the evening before if there was any work for him the next day—for which he received ten shillings. It was mostly a full day's work, but William also found itinerant work with other diggers and miners about the valley. He would sometimes be gone for a week at a time but James never seemed to mind, or to fault him for not being available.

Tuena Creek was fast flowing and prone to flooding. It was sourced in the mountains about fifteen miles to the southwest, meandering its way between the heavily-timbered and closely-packed hills to the Abercrombie River, three or four miles to the north of Tuena. Payable gold could be found all along the creek, but the water made digging difficult and dangerous. Consequently, some diggers used pumps but others sought gold elsewhere, and mines were scattered amongst the hills all along the creek and nearby valleys, and the miners working them were glad of whatever help they could get. Sometimes William was paid for his labour and at others, he shared in what they found.

The digging was mostly shallow, through alluvial soil, never going down more than thirty feet or so.

Occasionally a new field would be opened, causing excitement among the diggers that perhaps Tuena would fulfil a promise for all of them and they would become rich men, as had others in gold fields to the north. About six months after William arrived, a new ground adjacent to the Commissioner's Camp was opened, and miners queued from midnight to be the first to stake claims. Unfortunately, only a few claims paid and then often not more than wages, so disappointment was again the diggers' troublesome companion.

There was controversy in the valley about the permanency of the town. The two innkeepers strove hard to create a town with an identity, encouraging settlers as well as gold diggers to buy supplies from the stores, as well as patronise the inns. This wasn't all to do with the town. The innkeepers owned stores as well. Despite their efforts, there was a sense of failure amongst the diggers, many not digging or pursuing gold enthusiastically. This contrasted with the huts that the miners had built, and the families they had with them, seeking permanency in the hope that Tuena would fulfil its promise.

These things didn't matter to William. He loved the lifestyle, the drinking, the cards and the companionship. The want of energy and commitment to the task in hand, the rain and the flooding meant there was never a shortage of men to gather for a drink, a smoke and a few hands of cards.

It astonished William that there was no gold escort from the town to either Bathurst or Goulburn. The task fell to the two innkeepers, James and Alexander, who worked it out between themselves as to who took the gold, mostly to Goulburn.

James told William over a whisky one night that he'd been robbed at the Shepherd's Inn in Bathurst in the year before William got to Tuena. He'd been carrying over one hundred and fifty ounces of gold in two bags, but had arrived at the Inn too late to find buyers. Stashing the gold in his room, he'd gone to the bar for a whisky.

"It had taken a lot of men a lot of time to find that gold, so perhaps leaving it in the room was stupid. I'd been doing it for a number of years and there'd been no trouble before, so much so the police hadn't bothered to establish an escort—they just left it to the diggers to organise, and the diggers left it to us. I tried to take trips to Bathurst that didn't involve transporting gold, so that bushrangers wouldn't know if I had gold or not. Once Alexander became an innkeeper, he carried gold too, and mostly to Goulburn.

Strange thing, you know. He never hesitated to tell the papers about what he carried. Said he wanted to put Tuena on the map and the best way to do it was to tell the world about how much gold came out of Tuena."

"Was he ever robbed?"

"Never. I was held up on the road one time. 'Bail up!' was the cry. 'Hand over yer gold!' Of course, I had none and even when I turned out my pockets, there was only a pound or two and some shillings. The bushranger was disappointed, but it was a good thing for me. I suppose the word got around then that there was no point in holding me up. They left me alone after that—well, until last year.

Getting back to my room after a whisky and supper, I found the bags were gone.

You can imagine my distress. I should've kept the bags with me, but I thought they'd only attract notice.

I wasn't sure what to do. If I told the police, they'd go looking for the robbers and everyone would know that I sometimes did carry gold. If I didn't, I'd have to explain to the diggers, without evidence, that their gold had been stolen. After a long night of uncertainty, I went to the police next morning. I decided the diggers' trust was the most important thing."

"Did the police find the robber?"

"No, they didn't. I even posted a reward in the hope that someone might turn them in."

"Do you carry a gun?"

James hesitated a few moments before responding, "Why do you ask that?"

"I thought you might carry one to protect yourself and the gold. The police carry them."

James sighed, a sound of resignation.

"Yes, they carry a lot of them. But not me. No—I decided that gold is not worth dying for."

He shook his head before adding, "I know many diggers that disagree with me."

"I don't. I agree with you," said William. "So much so that I'm not sure if there's anything worth dying for. I've seen men killed in a fight. Good men."

"Not much good ever comes from a fight," said James.

William, thinking he'd said too much, did not reply, hoping he could talk about something else.

James took a sip of his whisky.

"Last year, I was at a pub in Bathurst and a fight broke out. I didn't know the reason until later, but one man pulled out a knife and stabbed the other. I tried to intervene and got stabbed for my trouble. It wasn't a bad wound, but my wife was very angry that I became involved."

"What happened?"

"Both of us who were stabbed lived, and the feller with the knife got five years hard labour."

"What were they fighting about?"

"The feller that got stabbed refused to buy the other a drink. Said he'd had enough."

They were silent for a few moments, both sipping their whisky.

"Who found the gold here?" asked William, relieved that James had stopped talking about fighting.

"Story goes that a feller called Butler was up by the point that now has his name, sat down to comfort himself with a smoke after fossicking the area for months and finding nothing. He absently scratched at the ground and found a nugget. There's as many sizes to the nugget as stories about the event, but whatever else, Butler and others went on to make a fortune."

"It's all luck, isn't it?' said William.

"I think so. It's why I run the store and the Inn. Takes the luck out of it. I know though, that when the gold is finished, I will be, too."

"Some people don't think so."

"They keep peddling the story that there's more gold to be found, and they're always right. There's always more gold to be found, but there's no doubt there's less of it and it's harder to find as time goes on. No, Tom—the settlers go to Bathurst or Goulburn. Oh sure, they come here for a drink sometimes, and maybe to buy some things from the store, but there's nothing like the adventure of a trip to Bathurst or Goulburn. It's the diggers that keep this town alive and when they're gone, that'll be it."

"You sound like you don't care."

"Oh, I care all right. But there's caring, and then there's being sensible."

* * *

Life rolled on, the days becoming weeks and the weeks becoming months.

There was fun, but sadness and melancholy too. Those that wanted the town to prosper kept pushing for a church and a school, but their letters to the authorities and the papers went unanswered.

Then, a miracle happened. A minister was appointed to Goulburn whose ministerial duties would include Tuena. It was of little interest to William, but he was glad for his friends who rejoiced that their prayers had been answered. William on the other hand had more experience in the futility of prayers, but kept this opinion to himself.

The Reverend Betts was only a young man and had made friends and an impression in the first few months of his appointment to Goulburn, and after his first visits to Tuena. It was returning to Goulburn after one such visit that he met his untimely end in the waters of the Wollondilly River at Marsden's crossing place, about a mile and a half outside Goulburn. He'd joined another traveller who lived in Cook's Vale—about three miles further out—and, both being on horseback, they agreed to ride together for the remainder of the journey. His travelling companion was able to report the circumstances of his death to a group gathered at James's one evening. William marvelled that a person not much older than himself would take such a risk, and that it would cost him his life.

"We don't need to hear this," said one of the listeners. "It was all in the paper."

"It's all right for you," said another. "You can read, but not many of the rest of us can. So if it's still all right with John, we'd like to hear the story."

William thought John looked like he was more than ready to tell the story and in fact, would welcome to do so.

"I asked the Reverend, 'What shall we do if the river is up?'" John said, starting his story.

"He replied that it would be of no consequence, as he would swim the river. When we reached the river, he went down to the crossing immediately, but I held back. I didn't like the look of the river and told him so. The sky was overcast and there was a distant rumbling of thunder—storms could be adding to the flow further upriver. I called out that the Wollondilly was not a river to be taken lightly, but the Reverend ignored me. I suppose being born in Australia, he was as familiar with the rivers as I was, but he seemed to me to be incautious. I decided that, having God on his side, he could afford to take more chances.

He was some distance from the bank when his horse went underwater and upon rising to the surface, tried to return to the bank. The Reverend didn't let him, maintained control and forced the horse to continue swimming to the other side.

I called to the Reverend to preserve his life and that of his horse and return immediately. He ignored me and continued his course for the other bank. The current was flowing swiftly, and I knew the bottom to be uneven. It seemed then that the causeway had been washed away by the flow, and the Reverend was forced to swim his horse for some spot on the other bank further down. The horse then fell on his side and the Reverend was thrown from his seat. He tried then to swim, and I saw him and his horse striking out for the bank.

The horse found some obstruction and remained motionless, no doubt tired from his efforts. The Reverend reached the bank, took some foothold, and I was relieved to think him safe. When he stood, he turned and as he did, he pitched forward into the water. Perhaps the cold of the water and his exhaustion made it impossible for him to gain more than a foothold on the bank. Maybe he even turned to tell me that he was safe but lost his footing.

I was shocked to see him fall, and once he fell into the water, I saw him no more."

"What about his horse?" asked William.

"He eventually gained the bank and headed off in the direction of the town."

"The Reverend should have stayed with his horse," said someone.

"He shouldn't have gone into the river," said another.

"For God's sake, everyone, let John finish his story," said James, ever the peacemaker.

"Well, there's not much more," said John. "There was another witness. He was on a hill, on the other side of the river. Seeing the whole affair, he apprehended the horse, came to the river to check with me as to who had been drowned, and then rode to Goulburn to give the alarm. Hundreds of people came out. They even found a boat to assist with dragging the river for the body, but it was several days before it was found."

"I don't suppose they'll find another reverend," one of the men said, unable to hide the sarcasm in his voice. Everyone ignored him.

"It's a sad thing to happen," said James. "No one expects when he wakes any day, that it will be his last on earth."

"I met a few bushrangers who did," called a voice.

"And good thing, too," said James. "The world's better off without those fellers."

"John speaks very well," said William to James later, who laughed. "I suspect he's memorised the story from the paper. He usually speaks no better than anyone else around here."

Christmas came and James invited William to lunch. He was having a few friends around. William was wary but thought it might not be showing proper appreciation for all James had done if he said 'no'. He hoped there'd be nothing to worry about, but was still consumed by his humiliation the year before. He'd promised himself that such a thing would never happen again but, being very grateful to James for all he had done, felt compelled to say 'yes'.

James had six children, the eldest of whom was about ten, all of whom thought well of William and he of them. Given the ages of James, his wife, the children and their respective friends, it was unlikely an affair of the heart would occur. Still, to be sure, he took time with his grooming, made sure he had nothing to drink until invited to do so—then only in moderation—and so spent a very easy and pleasant time. He'd taken time to buy presents for all the children and although his taste was not equal to the task, because the little children all but ignored the presents, the older ones and the adults were both gracious and grateful. William emerged from Christmas unscathed.

There was some excitement around the middle of the following year, when a rush occurred at Paine's Point and some thirty to forty shafts were put down. One or two were very good, many produced payable gold, and William was once again unfortunate to join a group that had a shicer. Then, within a day or so, a group on Douglas' Flat bottomed and produced over a pound of gold. The hole was about twenty-two feet deep with about eight feet of water, so it was nothing but determination and perseverance that produced a result. Still, gold was all the talk and William became caught up in the excitement.

For the next few months, he moved from group to group, opportunity to opportunity, and found nothing but disappointment. It was time to move on.

CHAPTER 8

# THE ROAD TO BATHURST

William woke one Sunday morning and decided that today was the day to leave. He'd been hinting to James for weeks that he was thinking about it, but he hadn't yet made up his mind.

"I'm expecting it," said James once, with a soft smile.

It was late in the year, summer was coming on, and the news from travellers was that the roads were passable.

William found James cleaning the bar after a busy Saturday night.

"Are you 'ere to help?" James asked him.

"No," said William.

"I thought not," said James, placing his broom against a table. He sat down in a chair beside it and signalled with his hand that William should sit in a chair close by.

"Will you join us in prayer before you go?" he asked, and laughed. "Come on, Tom. A first time for everything."

"You know I'm not much for prayer, James."

"I know. But I also know that if I didn't ask, you wouldn't volunteer. Where will you go?"

"Bathurst."

"Why don't you wait and go with me the next time I go? Bathurst is a wild sort of place. I've told you about my troubles there."

"I'll be all right."

"I know you will, but I'd enjoy yer company—it's a long ride."

"I'm eager to go now. Travellers are saying they're still finding good gold around there, and I'm keen now to take a serious look."

"Don't get too serious, Tom. I've watched yer disappointment these past months."

"I came to Australia to find gold and it's time I found some—before it's all gone."

"Every time we think it's all gone, they find some more."

"Not so much around here."

"I'll grant you that," said James with a sad smile. "We'll miss you. The children, too. Everyone will miss you. You're popular, Tom. You would be with the girls, too, if you give them notice."

"Now, it's definitely time I was going."

"You're sure about the prayers?"

William nodded by way of reply.

"Is that 'yes, you're sure', or 'yes, you'll come'?"

"Yes, I'm sure. I'll go while you're at prayer. It will be easier that way—no goodbyes. I'm not much at goodbyes."

"Will you not say goodbye to the children?"

"It's hard enough going as it is, James. I don't think I can do that."

"I understand. You get yer things and I'll organise some food for yer journey. Don't try to do it in a day. Best if you arrive in Bathurst in the afternoon, so you can find somewhere to stay. You can go to the Shepherd's Inn, of course. I've told you about it."

He laughed and William looked at him quizzically.

"Be careful of yer money," James continued. "Speaking of money, I still owe you a few pounds—I'll get them together, too."

James stood and William put out his hand. James shook his head.

"Yer're not getting out of here that easily. You get yer things. I'll get yer food and yer money, and I'll see you in the bar shortly."

William went and packed his bag. Then he went out the back to get Kelly, saddled him, and walked around to the front of the Inn. Spring was well advanced, and there were some hardy plants still flowering in some of the houses nearby. He dropped the reins and walked into the bar. There was no trading, but there was no such thing as a locked door in Tuena. There was also the possibility of a traveller, and they were not excluded from accommodation on a Sunday.

James sat at a table, two whiskies in front of him. There was a bag on the floor beside him and a roll of pound notes beside the glasses.

"I'd like us to have a drink together, Tom."

William sat down beside him, nervous about what was coming.

"You don't have to be nervous, Tom. You look nervous, but you don't need to be. I've enjoyed you being here. I always knew you'd move on. Tuena is more about families and it's no place for a single man. What I want to say is, if you do get married and yer're looking for somewhere to live, you could do worse than Tuena. I'd really like you to come back one day, if you've a mind to do so."

William was overcome by James's thoughtfulness and struggled to hold his emotions. James raised his glass and said, "To the good times."

"To the good times," said William, raising his glass and choking back tears.

"You don't know yet, Tom," said James, after savouring his whisky, "life is not all about gold, cards and whisky."

"You could have fooled me," said William and the men laughed together heartily, the tension broken.

They finished their whiskies, chatting easily about the summer, gold and Tuena. Then it was time to go. They both stood and shook hands.

"May God always be with you," said James.

"I'm sure He has better things to do," said William.

"I doubt it."

The men shook hands again, William picked up the money and the bag and turned for the door. He didn't look back, went straight to his horse, pushed the money into his pocket, tied the bag behind the saddle, mounted Kelly and set off towards Bathurst.

He'd been on this road before, but not as far as the Abercrombie River, which he knew was about four miles away. The road climbed for a while, bending about, working its way up the hill between the trees and rocks. It was rough, dusty, and scrubby country. The noise of the insects was constant, chirping and buzzing, the heat came off the road and there was an occasional call from birds. Once, the kookaburras laughed at him and he knew why—he'd have to be crazy to be out in this heat. Then he laughed at himself. He was used to the heat now and knew that summer heat was a part of living in Australia.

Once again, he was on his own. It was easier this time, although leaving James and his family had been hard. He didn't doubt he'd find more men to play cards, whisky to drink and chances to dig for gold. Gold had been on his mind in the last week or so. If he was going to find some and become rich, as others had done, he'd need to get on with it.

He was used to the false tops now, too. As you climbed a hill, it didn't matter if you were walking or on a horse, it always looked like you were near to the top, but when you reached that point, there was always another top. Climbing. Climbing. Kelly plodded on with endless patience and loyalty. The road was more like a track. Stones and rocks littered his path and there were obvious signs of ruts cut by a combination of rain-water and wheels. He reached a point where there was a good view, both behind and in front. There was a welcome breeze up there too. The view was nothing new— mostly hills, trees, and sometimes grass. He supposed the grass was where there was a natural meadow beside Tuena Creek, or an area cleared by settlers.

Kelly sometimes stumbled when the ground was uneven, and where it was steep. William was glad he wasn't driving a team with a cart or wagon.

He was a long way past where he'd been before when he crossed a creek he thought might have been the Tuena, but there was no way to know. After a while he crossed a river that might have been the Abercrombie, but there was no way to know that either. He didn't see any diggers, or any settlers' huts, so there was no one to ask. The river was easy to cross, and he was glad of it. The sides looked steep, and it looked as though it would carry a lot of water in flood.

Leaving Tuena, there'd been no real plan other than to take James's advice that he should do the trip in two days. He guessed there must be a place to camp about halfway to Bathurst, or perhaps he was best to go on until he found somewhere to camp around mid-afternoon, then push on the next day. Not being sure how long it would be before he found water again, he stopped for a little time to allow Kelly to drink, himself to do the same, and to top up his bottle.

Starting out again, he was apprehensive at how steeply the road rose not far from the river. It would be an easy place to have an accident, or to be robbed for that matter. The gullies fell away steeply first on one side and then the other as he climbed. There wasn't much cover for bushrangers, but there weren't many ways to get away from them either. He kept a sharp eye out for anything that didn't look like it belonged and hoped that Kelly would alert him to any horses that might be in the area. James's stories had spooked him, and he thought it better to be over than under cautious.

Finally, after so many false tops he'd decided there was no such thing as a top to this hill, he came to a flat section and thought he saw a creek through the trees to his left. He was tired and decided that even if the place wasn't a good camping spot, he'd still spend the night there. There was an obvious track from the road, so he took it and pushed on through the scrub. He was relieved to see there were already two groups there. It wasn't likely the two groups would both consist of bushrangers, so he approached the first group—three men sitting around a fire, drinking tea. There was a loaded cart and five hobbled horses nearby.

"Afternoon," he said, staying on his horse, ready for a quick escape if needed.

The men just nodded.

"Where are you off to?" he asked them.

"Bathurst," one of them replied.

"Where are you from?" William asked, comforted by the lack of friendliness. They weren't certain about each other yet, so the men probably weren't bushrangers.

"Abercrombie," said the same man.

"We've been diggin' there," said another.

William knew better than to ask if they'd found anything.

"'Bout ye?" asked the man who hadn't yet spoken.

"Tuena," said William. He waited a few moments before asking, "Mind if I join you?"

"Suit yerself," said the first man.

William stepped down but held the reins as he approached. He dropped them when he came near, and sat on a log. It seemed there'd been bigger groups in the area before and there were enough logs scattered about for them all.

They obviously decided William was all right, as the tension had gone from the group and they offered him a pannikin of tea.

"What's this place?" asked William.

"Camp Creek," said one of the men.

"I suppose yer'll want to know why it's called that?" asked the first man.

"I think I can guess," said William, smiling. They all smiled back.

It wasn't long before they were all chatting about gold and comparing Abercrombie and Tuena. William decided that he'd had the best of it. They told William he would easily get to Bathurst by midday if he left at dawn, and that he'd be better to go on without them as they'd be slower with the cart. They told him that he'd been through the worst part of the road since he left the river and that it wasn't a hard ride from here on to Bathurst. Sharing their food, they ate a good supper and drank a lot of tea, and all turned in as darkness fell.

William was up and gone the next morning before the men had even stirred. He was keen to get to Bathurst and work out what to do next, and was sure they wouldn't care if he left before them.

CHAPTER 9

# BATHURST

William approached Bathurst around the middle of the day. He'd passed some inns and cottages earlier but decided not to stop and ask for any directions. He'd already made a plan to find the Shepherd's Inn and, since this was in Bathurst, there was no point in asking for directions until he got there. The road was wide enough to cater for the many vehicles, for there were horses and vehicles of all kinds moving both ways, but it was in very poor condition. No one had time for anyone else. No one waved, nor did anyone even pass the time of day. Ruts and potholes abounded. Kelly plodded on. They were both hungry and thirsty now, but William decided to solve both those problems in Bathurst.

Bathurst was a revelation. One moment, William and Kelly were plodding along, with no town in sight. Then all of a sudden, Bathurst was there. It was as though he'd fallen asleep, then woken up to find the town at hand. There were substantial buildings, and that was wonderful to see, but more impressive was the layout of the streets. It was clear that Bathurst didn't just happen—it was planned. The streets were both wide and long. He came upon it from the south on what he later learned was Vale Road, through a wide valley, with long sloping hills on both sides.

There were two men standing chatting amiably beside the road, holding their horses' reins and allowing them to graze on the plentiful grass.

"Can you help me?" William asked the men, stopping nearby.

"Depends on what help you want," one responded, smiling and looking friendly.

"I think he wants a bed," said the other.

"Why's that?" asked William.

"Well, you look tired."

"I think he might need two beds," said the other man.

William laughed.

"And why two?" he asked.

"Your horse looks tired too."

"You're right—I am tired and so's my horse. But I'm wanting to go to the Shepherd's Inn. Can you tell me how to get there from here?"

"Aye, we can do that, but you be careful when you get there. It's run by an ex-sergeant of the police."

"And why do I need to be careful?" asked William, bristling.

"Why, young feller out here all alone, you could be a bushranger."

"Sorry to disappoint you."

The friendly man laughed.

"No, I'm not disappointed. That street there is Rocket Street. Stay on that until you get to William Street. It's the fourth street. Turn right into that and continue until you see the Shepherd's Inn."

"Thank you. I hope to return the favour one day."

"You stayin' for long?"

"Don't know. Depends."

"Depends on what?"

"Whether or not I get arrested."

They all laughed and William set off, counting on his fingers to know when to turn. Then he wasn't sure whether he'd heard the number correctly, or counted his fingers properly. He'd just have to keep asking. One day he'd learn about numbers and letters.

He kept asking as he went, and no one seemed to mind. There were plenty of people to ask and in little time he found William Street and set off down it. There were lots of vehicles and people about and the street wasn't in such poor condition that he needed to avoid potholes and ruts. Everyone seemed friendly and if he smiled at anyone, he always received a smile back.

It wasn't long before he saw inns, with horses and vehicles out front. He'd hoped there might only be one inn but there were several, and he had no way of knowing which of them was the Shepherd's Inn.

"Is this the Shepherd's Inn?" he asked a man standing on the street outside an inn, wiping his brow with the back of his hand.

"No, this is the Oxford—Shepherd's further down. Why don't you come in here? This is the best in town. Well, as far as I'm concerned."

"And why is that?"

"I'm the publican."

"Then I'm not surprised, but I need to meet someone at the Shepherd's."

"Come back here if you don't find him."

"I might," said William, touching Kelly on the sides with his boots to get him moving. "Nearly there, Kelly. You can have a rest soon."

He had to ask several more times before he found the Shepherd's Inn. It was on the same side as the Oxford, and he had to cross a few more streets before he reached it.

Pulling up outside the Shepherd's, he dismounted and let the reins drop to the ground.

The Shepherd's was a big, two storey building, with a number of horses and vehicles out front. It, like the Oxford and the others that he had passed, was popular. He went through the doors and found the inside gloomy until his eyes became accustomed to it. There was a fair noise from the patrons, and he had to push through people to get to the bar.

"Name your poison," said the man behind the bar.

"I'd like to speak to John."

"Publican?"

"Yes."

"I'll get 'im for you," said the man and nodded. "Wait over there."

He turned to another man behind the bar. "Bill, back soon." The other man nodded.

It wasn't long before he returned with another man. He wasn't old, though he was older than William. He was solidly built with dark hair and a big dark beard. His face looked friendly and he had a twinkle in his eye, as though he'd enjoy a laugh if the opportunity presented itself.

"This is 'im," the barman said, indicating William.

"What can I do for you?" John said in a distinctly Irish accent.

"My name's Tom. James who has an inn in Tuena said you might help me."

"Ah, James. How is James?"

"He's well."

"Good. That's good."

John thought for a moment, as though deciding whether to ask more questions about James.

"Tom, what help do you need?"

"A drink, something to eat, a bed and some advice on where's best to dig for gold."

"Well, the first ones are easy—that's what we do. As for the last, everyone is wanting an answer to that but I'll see what I can do. Take your horse 'round back. There's a man there that'll see to him. Then come back and we'll talk."

"How did you know I've a horse?"

John just looked at William, laughed and walked off shaking his head.

William took Kelly down the side of the building and sure enough, there was a man at the stables, mucking out one of the stalls.

"How much?" asked William, handing him the reins.

"You'll have to ask the boss," said the man. "It's nothing to do with me."

William took his bag, walked back to the bar and found John talking with a group of men. He saw William and called him over.

"Fellers, this is Tom. He's from Tuena. Tom, these fellers are from Sofala. They're in town for a few days to wash away the dust, sell their gold, get some supplies and then they're going back. I'll leave you fellers to talk. Tom, first drink's on me. What'll you have?"

"A whisky."

John signalled to the bar. "Bill, whisky for Tom here. Tom, supper's out back later and rooms are upstairs. Bath's down the end of that hall if you are so inclined."

"Thanks, John. How much do I owe you?"

"No need if it's one night. You're a friend of James and a friend of James is a friend of mine. Anyway, we'll talk later over supper. Enjoy yourselves, gentlemen. Here, Tom, give me your bag—I'll put it in a room for you. Make sure there's nothing of real value in it."

"If someone wants some dirty clothes, they might find it valuable."

John laughed, took the bag and walked off.

Standing alone after John left, the group introduced themselves. The three men from Sofala were Reginald, Harvey and Maurice—all came from England and were married. Their wives and children lived with them in huts at the diggin's.

"It's all right," said Maurice, "there aren't many of us left now. Most of the gold and the diggers are already gone."

"There's enough for those of us left," said Harvey. "We make a living, but that's about all. What's Tuena like?"

"Like Sofala by the sound of it. Most of the diggers are married and their wives and children live in huts along the creek. Not much gold there, either. Oh, they make a new find every now and again, but it never amounts to much."

"Why're you here, Tom?" asked Maurice.

"Well, I'm looking for somewhere to dig. I didn't make much at Tuena, so I'm hoping to find somewhere else—feller said Bathurst is a good place to start."

"It all started here, of course. Feller called Hargreaves got it started over at Ophir. Now, there's about a dozen places around here and they're all as good and as bad as each other. Doesn't mean there aren't other places, of course, but most of the ones we know about are down to the last of it."

"I wouldn't know how to go looking for it. I've only ever gone where others have already found it."

"They say there's such a thing as gold country. They say that's how Hargreaves found it over at Ophir. He'd seen gold country in America, so he knew what to look for."

"Look for a whole lot of people diggin'," said Reginald. "They can't all be wrong."

"I went through places on the way here that looked like Tuena, but I didn't stop and look for gold," said William.

"Well, maybe you should," said Reginald. "That's how others found it. It's called prospectin'. Maybe we should do it."

"There's a lot of country to look in," said Harvey. "I'm happy with our lot and we get enough. People that get lots just waste it anyway, on whisky and women."

"That's not wasting it," said Maurice. "Besides, shall we have another drink? Would you like another, Tom?"

"Let me buy," said William. "You're teaching me about gold, so let me buy."

"I don't think we're saying anything you don't already know. But why don't we all have a shout and then go for supper?"

Bill was watching all his customers from the bar and saw William signal with his hand. He was there in moments with four whiskies.

They were all focused on their whisky in companionable silence, then William asked, "What would you do if you were me, Maurice?"

"I'm not sure why you're asking me, Tom. If I knew what to do, I'd do it myself."

"You've got a wife and children to look after, so there's only some things you can do. I don't have anybody, so I can do as I like."

"I'd leave the wife and little ones in a heartbeat if I thought that was all it would take to make my fortune. I'd go back to them of course, but if I only had to be single, then that's easy. No, Tom—there's nothing you can do that I can't."

"You've only got two choices, Tom," said Harvey. "Join the diggers on a field or go prospecting."

"He can't go prospecting on his own," said Maurice.

"Some do," said Reginald.

"That's right," said Maurice. "And often we never hear from them again."

"You don't know that," said Reginald, hotly and signalling for another round, "why, I've a good mind to go prospectin' myself."

"You can do what you like, Reg. No one's stopping you. You're part of this team only while you want to be. Harvey and I will be fine, so you can go prospecting if that's what you want."

"You'd like that, wouldn't you? You two would have my share then. And don't call me Reg."

"Now take it easy, Reginald—you get a share because we all work hard for what we get. We'd get less if we didn't have you working with us, but it's not about that. I'm saying you're not stuck to us—you can go whenever you want but if you'd like to stay, then of course, you're welcome. I'm thinking it might be time for supper."

"I'm havin' another drink. It's my shout anyway, so you all have to join me. Supper can wait." He signalled Bill for another round of drinks, which arrived quickly.

William was wary of what might happen next. There was clearly tension in the group.

"Harvey hasn't had a shout yet," said Reginald.

"I'll get whiskies to take to supper," said Harvey.

"Aren't we goin' to 'ave wine with supper? We usually 'ave wine with supper," said Reginald. "I'm 'ere to 'ave a good time. We usually 'ave a good time. Dunno what's got into you two."

"I'm having supper with John," said William. "He asked me before."

"John has supper with everyone that's in the room," said Reginald. "He goes from table to table. Spends a little time with everyone."

"Reginald's right," said Maurice. "He says he'll see you at supper, but he sees everyone at supper."

Reginald, Maurice and Harvey all laughed. The tension was broken. William was glad—he hated tension.

They finished their whiskies, had another, and chatted amiably about Sofala and people they knew. There were many funny tales about what people got up to on the gold fields. William thought they might be making it up, but Maurice reassured him. "You can't make this up," he said. There were sad stories, too—diggers being trapped, crushed and drowned, women dying in childbirth, children dying of disease, and people being bitten by snakes. William was amazed at the diggers' ability to endure hardship and to laugh at trouble, and said so to Maurice.

"No, they don't always laugh," said Maurice. "Not everybody laughs. There's those that put a bullet in their own head. It's a hard life. Sometimes, for some, too hard."

Supper was enjoyable. John came and went from their table several times. There were about twenty other people in the room, many of them known to each other, and John passed messages back and forth as he went from table to table.

One time, he whispered to William, asking if he'd found the information that he sought. William said he didn't know and acknowledged there was a lot to think about. William tried some wine at supper, but found he preferred whisky.

When supper was finished, they went to the bar for a final whisky. William was so tired he could hardly keep his eyes open, but thought it might be rude not to join the others.

"What ye doin' tomorrer?" asked Reginald. "We've got supplies to get, but thought we'd have 'nother drink around midday. Want to join us?"

"Tom'll probably be too busy," said Maurice, firmly.

"He can answer fer himmsel," said Reginald, equally firmly.

"I'll see how I go. I have no plans at the moment, and I'm worried I'll run out of money before I run out of thirst. Right now, I'm so tired I think I could sleep right here."

He stood and shook hands with each of them.

"Make sure you're there tomorrer," muttered Reginald.

"Goodnight," William said, too tired to show interest. He walked unsteadily to the bar and enquired which room was his.

"Take the first one with an open door and with your bag on the floor inside."

William climbed the stairs, unsettled to discover them something of a challenge. He found his room, lay on the bed and went to sleep immediately.

## CHAPTER 10

# A CHANGE OF APPROACH

William woke to a quiet room, with just a splash of sun from the window. He was fully clothed and desperate for a piss. His head throbbed and it took him a few moments to remember he was in Bathurst. He remembered the men from last night and he hoped he would also remember most of what they talked about. However, if he was going to find gold enough to make him wealthy, he doubted drinking away the evening hours with a group of strangers was going to help.

It was a few moments before he realised the bed was more comfortable than any he'd used before. He got up and peered at the bed, trying to work out what was different. The needs of nature were too pressing for a proper investigation. He picked up the towel from the washstand, and his bag from the floor, and headed for the washroom that he remembered was on the ground floor at the back. Then again, they were always on the ground floor at the back.

There was some noise from the bar as he passed it, but he had no time to investigate. He found the washroom empty, so he dropped his bag and towel there and headed out back for the privy. It was also empty, so he hastened inside and tended to his needs.

Returning to the washroom, he found it was still empty. He ladled some water into the bath from the steaming tub over a fire that he guessed backed onto the kitchen. Then he added some cold from another tub nearby and, when the temperature was right, he selected the cleanest of his clothes, threw the rest into the bath and climbed in with them. There was a bar of soap on a stool beside the bath that he used it to wash himself and the clothes. By the time he was done, the water looked like he'd washed a bag of potatoes in it. He lay in the water for a while, thinking about the night before.

*Digging or prospecting—they're my choices. I've made more money working for other people, but that won't make me rich...* He sighed. A long, sad sigh. *I've probably wasted all my opportunities, though I really don't know anyone who has become rich digging for gold... I've heard about them, of course. Nevertheless, I'm still young and everyone says there is more gold to be found.*

He got out of the bath and dried himself on the towel. After he put on his clothes, he pulled the rest out of the bath and draped them over a line in the backyard he hoped was there for that purpose. It took several trips and there was water everywhere by the time he was done. Finally, going back to the washroom, he picked up the bath and threw its water in the yard. He hoped that's what they did.

Feeling a lot better, he went in search of John. He found him eating breakfast in the dining room. His companions from the previous evening were nowhere to be seen.

"Tom! Tom!" called John. "Join me. I'm having a late breakfast. We let you sleep— you looked like you needed it."

"I did," said William, seating himself opposite John.

"What'll you have?"

"Steak, eggs, bread, tea."

"That's good. That's what I'm having. I won't be long. Wait here."

John was gone only a few moments and came back followed by the same woman who attended tables at supper. She put down a plate of bread, some knives, forks and spoons, some jam and butter, salt, pepper and sugar. Everything was a trifle more elegant than was customary for William, but still obviously of the Australian bush.

"Now, Tom, I'm glad of this moment for a talk," said John. "I asked you last night if you'd solved your problem. Let me ask you again. Have you?"

William shook his head.

"They said my only options were to dig or prospect. What do you think?"

"I think that's about it."

William studied John.

"What do you think I should do, John?"

"It's not for me to say, Tom."

"Then why did you want to talk?"

"Ah. Good question. I think if you decide to prospect, Reginald might ask to come along. I thought you should know that."

"Isn't he working with Maurice and Harvey?"

"Indeed he is, but I think he'd like to change. I think he, like you, would like to make more money. I think he thinks Sofala is nearly done, so they're not even working for wages."

"He seemed upset last night."

"It's been going on for a while. They always talk him out of prospecting. I think he's looking at you as an opportunity."

"Is he a good man?"

"Of course he's a good man."

Their meal was delivered and both men ate contentedly for a few minutes.

"Do you think you'll go prospecting?" asked John.

"I might."

"Will you take Reginald?"

"I might."

"You can't go on your own, and Reginald is a good man."

"Why can't I go on my own?"

"Too dangerous out there. A lot can go wrong and when you're on your own, you can't always fix it. Some men go on their own, but they're more foolish than brave."

"I might think on it. If I do, where would you go?"

"Well, that's the question, isn't it? I think I'd go where no one else goes. Plenty of men already prospected the easy places, but not so much where it's difficult and dangerous."

"Where are those places?"

"Follow the rivers. The Macquarie, the Cudgegong, the Abecrombie, the Meroo, and the Turon for example. Reginald will know. He's heard about all the places, and he'll be able to help. He's a good man."

"You said that."

"I did, didn't I? Tom, I'm not trying to persuade you either way, just suggesting that if you have a mind to do it, then do it properly. I owe James that much. Like I said…"

"Reginald is a good man."

"That's right," said John, laughing—his beard, belly and shoulders shaking.

They agreed to catch up later in the day when Maurice and the others would be back. William went to check on Kelly and take a look around town. Kelly was happy, with his own stall and a small paddock that he could share with three other horses.

There was no point in taking him out as William didn't plan to go far.

He went back up the lane and decided to continue on down William Street. He liked that he shared a name with it. It had been a long time since he had such a thought, and James would say *the gentle hand of God was guiding his footsteps*. Many of the diggers he had met saw God in everything. William not so much, but he did sense that there must be something that made everything happen. He saw little point in going to a church when he was told God was everywhere, but others did seem to gain comfort from community singing and praying.

The day was already hot, insects whizzed and buzzed, and flies gathered around his head, signalling the imminent arrival of summer. William Street was very wide and composed of a type of white gravel. Houses and commercial buildings were interspersed, and both were at times magnificent. Whatever else the town had, it had money. There was a lot of traffic about, mostly courteous, but there was some shouting about unexpected moves from carts and drays. Mostly the pedestrians stuck to the sides, but when they needed to cross, they would carefully manoeuvre between the traffic. It was obvious there were no rules.

William admired some of the goods in the shops and was equally awed by the number of pubs. Some people were already drinking, although that wasn't unusual. When the miners came to any town it was usually with only one purpose in mind.

He reached a river where it was marshy and boggy, so he decided to go back. Besides, he thought the others might be back by then and he was excited to discuss prospecting with Reginald—if it wasn't all a dream. He realised Reginald might have changed his mind, or Maurice might have changed it for him.

When William returned, the others weren't back yet, so he got a whisky and sat at a corner table. There were a few people in the bar—drunks, locals, business people and diggers. A game of cards was underway at another table. William presumed it to be a group of regulars, as the game was conducted wordlessly.

He took his time with the whisky—he would need his wits about him if Reginald wanted to discuss prospecting together. Conversation around him was quiet, so it wasn't possible to amuse himself by listening to others.

Eventually, a commotion at the door announced the arrival of Maurice, Harvey and Reginald. The commotion was to the effect that Reginald wanted to see if Tom was there, but Harvey and Maurice said they still had work to do. When Reginald saw William, he told the others to attend to their work while he spoke to Tom.

"I thought we were in this together," said Maurice, loud enough for William to hear and to draw vexed looks from others in the bar, "but I might have to rethink that, I suppose."

Maurice and Harvey left, and Reginald got himself a whisky and joined William at the table.

"Glad you're here," he said.

William nodded, trying to wear his poker face.

"Have you thought about prospectin'?" asked Reginald.

"I have."

"And what have you thought?" asked Reginald, a slight tone of exasperation in his voice.

"Where do you think we'd go?"

"Depends on how long we go for."

"How long are you thinking?"

"Six months to a year."

"What about your family?"

"They'd rather me gone and rich, than around and poor. Besides, they'll be all right. Maurice and Harvey will see to them."

"I thought Maurice doesn't want you to go."

"He doesn't, but he'll get used to the idea."

"What'll we take?"

"You got a horse?"

William nodded.

"We'll need to get another horse. Picks, shovels, pans, supplies for us 'n' the horses. And I don't have much money, so you pay for it and take it out of what we find."

"Why don't we share?"

"Like I said, I don't have much money. If you don't pay for it, we can't do it."

"I don't have much money either, and what I do have may not be enough."

"Tom, it works like this. We decide to do it, then we work out how. Maybe we can't afford an extra horse, so we make do. Maybe we get less supplies at first, then get more if we find gold. When we can't afford to do it anymore, we stop."

William nodded, deep in thought.

"Have you got a gun?" asked Reginald.

William nodded again. He still had the pistol Tom had given him, but he hadn't used it in a long time.

"Why?" he asked.

"Protection and huntin'."

"Hunting?"

"Yes—we can kill the odd 'roo or bird or wombat. They make good eatin'."

William continued to think. Reginald had just made the decision much harder by not offering to contribute any money.

Every instinct told William this was madness. The cost was all to him and failure would wipe out all the money he had. Of course, he still had money with Scott and Robert, and it was only a matter of writing for it. Robert's letter was long gone, but he was confident he could find someone to write another. He was sure they wouldn't have forgotten, and it would be a shame to waste it.

"I'll get us another whisky," said Reginald.

"I thought you didn't have much money."

"A man who can't afford a whisky shouldn't go into a pub. Anyway, bein' in a pub and prospectin' are two different things."

While he was getting the whisky, Maurice and Harvey arrived. Reginald got a whisky for them, too.

"So, what've you fellers been talking about?" Maurice asked William.

"Christ, Maurice," said Reginald arriving back with the whiskies, "you know damn well."

"When are you going?" asked Maurice, crestfallen.

"Tomorrow," said William.

"Suits me," said Reginald.

CHAPTER 11

# THE DECISION

All the men stood around outside the Shepherd's Inn except for Harvey, who sat on the cart laden with supplies. Everyone was awkward. No one liked goodbyes.

"Will you see to my family sometimes?" asked Reginald of Maurice.

"Of course. They'll be all right."

William wished they'd taken more time over the preparation. It had been a spur of the moment decision to leave so soon, but he'd thought that if they sat around in the pub drinking, he'd only be spending money they'd need, so they were better to go sooner than later.

The picks, shovels and pans had been easy. John had some that had been left in lieu of payment and he was glad to part with them.

"Always been in the way," he said, "I'm glad to be rid of them."

Another horse had been easy too—there were plenty for sale.

Planning the supplies had been a little harder. They settled on dried beef, plenty of tea, sugar and flour, and some fruit and vegetables.

"How long before we can buy more?" he'd asked Reginald.

"Well, we'll see towns and farms along the way, but the less we see the better. We want to look where no one's looked."

William's heart sank. He was already regretting his decision and they hadn't even left Bathurst.

"Where will you go?" asked Maurice. "Do you have a plan?"

"I think we'll go towards the Abercrombie, then sweep back around. I think it's all gold country, so there's no reason we won't be lucky."

"I can think of a few," said Harvey.

"Well, keep 'em to yerself," said Reginald, tersely. "Let's go, Tom. Let's find it before someone else does, or these fellers talk us out of it."

They mounted and rode back the way William had come. William looked back after a few minutes to see Maurice still standing beside his horse, as though expecting the riders would return. William was hopeful, despite all the signs to the contrary, that they would be successful. He knew other successful ventures had started equally foolishly.

There was almost nothing to distinguish these two riders from others in the street. They wore the same cabbage tree hats, checked shirts, moleskin pants and boots. Their faces were sunburned, despite the hats, and sparsely covered in badly shaven hair, their mouths set in firm lines.

The sun was already warm, the flies attentive, and there was little breeze as they threaded their way through the morning traffic. Pans, picks and shovels clicked against each other gently, and the horses snorted from time to time to clear their nostrils of dust. There was no conversation. William was off to find his fortune. His emotions were mixed. He was nervous about the unknown, nervous about the country, and nervous about

Reginald. Why, he hardly knew him! And despite John's reassurances, he was nervous Reginald hadn't the faintest idea of prospecting. Yet, he was excited to take such a bold step. What would his ma and da think if they could see him now? He hoped they'd be proud.

CHAPTER 12

# THE LIFE OF A PROSPECTOR

What followed next were the most difficult, disappointing and exhilarating months of William's young life.

After a bad start, he became quite the marksman with the pistol. By the time they were done, he could bring down a running kangaroo at fifty paces.

They called in at farms to add to their supplies, and most settlers were pleased to see them. They were usually a little wary at first, expecting William and Reginald to be bushrangers, but when they found it was two prospectors down on their luck, they made them welcome. Once or twice, William and Reginald stayed a few days and helped around the house when the man was away or too sick to attend to his duties. Those were the best days—good food and warm beds. The beds were mostly bark stretched across wooden poles, but they were always better than the cold, hard ground.

Storms came too frequently and many times the rivers were too swollen to cross. Even though Reginald had a compass, William was impressed that he could navigate through the bush. He always seemed to know where they were. William asked him about it once and he said, "We find gold, we better know where it is."

William wished he'd known more about Reginald before they started but did have to admit to himself that even if he had, it may not have changed anything.

They used William's tarpaulins, a tent and a groundsheet, which meant they shared the tent. Reginald could make more noise at night with his body than twenty horses in a yard. He blurted, farted, belched, snored, shouted in his dreams, scratched endlessly, and thrashed about as though he was trying to release himself from being bound. From time to time, William couldn't stand it and slept with the horses on the pretext that Kelly needed attention.

There was nothing nice about Reginald's eating habits. He slurped and chomped his food, smacked his lips, licked his fingers, took more than his share at any meal and showed little interest in cleaning up afterwards. Not that there was much to clean up. Living was primitive.

On several occasions, they thought they'd struck payable gold. William remembered the excitement when Tom had first shown him how to pan. When it came to panning, William and Reginald were on an equal footing. They never argued about where to look, nor held each other accountable for failure—and there were many failures. But in the moments when the gold would sparkle in a pan, they were the best of friends. They'd grip each other by the arms, holler for joy, and hide their disappointment when the pocket would falter.

"It must be here somewhere," they would encourage each other, but it never was.

One night, smoking their pipes, sitting on a log by the fire after supper, Reginald said that one of them must be unlucky.

"We can't both be unlucky," he said. "One of us must be holdin' the other back."

"I've never heard such rubbish," said William. "We'll either find it, or we won't. It has nothing to do with luck."

"Then, why do some people find gold and others don't?"

"I think that's just how it is."

"Sounds like luck to me."

Another night, Reginald said they should stop at the next town they came to and sell the gold they'd found. "It's not much, but if we sell it, you can get some of your money back."

"Why don't we sell it and drink it?"

"No, Tom. We had a deal, and a deal's a deal."

William decided that even if he lived two lifetimes, he would never understand Reginald.

Then one night, after a week of disappointments, Reginald told William about himself. He wasn't drunk. They agreed there was no space to bring whisky, so it was to be a dry exercise. However, Reginald spoke about himself without being prompted and William decided he must have been lonely.

"I was a convict, you know. Not many know it. It's a shameful thing, so I keep it to meself."

He paused, and William wondered if he was already thinking he'd said too much. Then he went on, and William realised he was most likely searching for the words.

"I was only young, and I stole some food. My little brother was dyin' of the hunger. My ma was sick and my da dead, so it fell to me to look after the family. I tried to find work, but there was little work and too many lookin', so I tried to steal from the market. Went there with the idea of stealin'. Must've been like I was holdin' up a sign, 'cos they grabbed me straight away and handed me to the traps. They wasted no time sendin' me 'ere."

William asked, "What happened to your mother and brother?"

Reginald shook his head. "I dunno. Dead, I suppose. I wrote some letters, but I never heard back. It was bad, there, Tom. People said it was bad in Ireland, but it's always been bad in England, if you're poor."

"You can read and write though?" asked William, wonder in his voice.

"Enough."

Again, Reginald paused before continuing.

"I was indentured to a feller at Hawkesbury. He was a good man with a good family. I didn't mind workin' there. Good meals, fresh air and hard work. Some of the other convicts kept talkin' about clearin' out, but I was happy to see out my time. One day, the master asked if I wanted a wife. He thought if I had a wife, I might stay on when my time was up. I'd not ever thought about a wife and told him so. Said I didn't know anyone anyway. He said I didn't need to—we could get one at the Female Factory. I said I'd never heard of them makin' women and if they could, how come some of them turned out so bad?"

"I've not ever heard of them making women either. How do they do that? I suppose if they can make women, they can make men. Was there a Male Factory too?"

Reginald laughed. He didn't do that too often.

"Turns out they're convict women. You could get one as a wife or a servant. There were so many the government didn't know what to do with 'em, so they came up with the idea to make wives of 'em."

"What if you didn't like the one you got?"

"Oddly enough, if it didn't work out, you could take 'em back and get another one."

"Did it work out for you?"

"Yes, it did. Turns out the master had been workin' on it for some time and had already picked one out for me. He was a good picker and he picked well. We're still together."

"But you're not with the master?"

"No—that's another story."

"I've the time."

Reginald laughed.

"We do, don't we? Master gave us a cottage. It was awkward at first. We found it wasn't easy just to do what married people do. We had to get to know each other. We were very shy. We got there in the end. She was a tough girl at first, all hard language and full of bitterness. She'd stolen a blanket to keep her sister warm, been caught and sentenced to seven years. She thought it unfair and was angry at the whole world. I agreed with her, of course."

"Why'd you leave the master?"

"One of the other fellers thought she could be a wife for him, too. One day he left the work early sayin' he felt sick. I came back later. I didn't make too much noise as I came to the cottage. When I opened the door, I found he'd torn off my wife's clothes and he was trying to get her on the bed. Her face was all bloody where he'd punched her, tryin' to control her. She'd obviously fought him all the way. His back and arms were all scratched, the room was a mess with furniture smashed. He didn't hear me come in, but I was angry enough for ten men—and had the strength of them too.

I pulled him off and threw him against the wall. He slid to the ground and tried to get up, but couldn't, his trousers around his ankles. My wife was sobbin', a mixture of relief that I'd arrived and from the pain she'd suffered. It only increased my anger.

He was trying to pull up his trousers and get up at the same time.

'Christ, mate!' he shouted. 'What's wrong with you? It's not as though she means anythin' to you.'

Well, he'd got that wrong. She was my wife. She meant everythin' to me and it wasn't until that moment that I realised it. I strode over and pulled him to his feet. I dragged him over and tried to throw him out the door. It's not right to say I didn't mean him any harm—I wanted him to suffer all the harm there was. I wanted him to suffer like my wife had suffered, and I wanted him to hurt like I was hurtin'."

Reginald stopped talking and William said nothing, overwhelmed by what he'd just heard.

"But I didn't mean to kill him."

It was a while before Reginald continued, as though he had needed time to gather his thoughts or control his emotions.

"He hit his head as he went through the doorway. There was a pulpy, kind of bang and he spun about in my hands and fell like a log to the floor. I thought I'd knocked him out, so I went to help my wife dress. She was sobbin', holdin' me fiercely, less interested in getting dressed than in holdin' me.

'Thank you, oh, Reg. Thank you. I thought you'd never come,' she sobbed, 'I couldn't bear him touchin' me.'

'It wouldn't have mattered. He could have killed you. I'd rather you alive than dead,' I said.

'Of course it would matter. I'm your wife and you're the only man I'll ever lie with. I'd rather be dead than with anyone else.'

In that moment, I didn't think I could love someone so much. I started to cry. I know men aren't supposed to do that, but the idea that she was prepared to die was too much for me.

We got her dressed and cleaned the place up a little. He was still lyin' in the doorway and hadn't moved or made a sound. I checked him and he was dead."

"Your wife called you Reg," said William.

"Oh? Yes. I used to be Reg. I'm Reginald, now. Master said I should change my name, so I did."

William thought about when he joined the workers on the docks in Belfast. A man asked his name and he replied 'William'. "You can't be William here," the man had said, "call yourself Bill." He thought most people used a short name, and also thought it odd that a man would go to the longer form of his name. Surely people, even the police, would notice.

"Didn't you think that people would notice someone using their full name? Why didn't you choose another name? Anyway, there's not much difference between Reg and Reginald, so perhaps the police could still find you."

"Oh. I thought there was," said Reginald, dismissing all the questions with a single answer.

"What did you do then?"

"I went to the master. Explained everythin'. He was angry and upset. At first he said we should go to the police, but then decided that since my wife and I were still indentured, it may not go well for us. My wife's face was all puffed and bloody. She looked like she'd been in a boxing match. The master's wife tried to clean her up, but it didn't do much good. The master said we'd sleep on it and he'd work out what to do overnight. My wife and I went back to the cottage. I'd forgotten the body was still lyin' in the doorway. I wondered when I saw it why the master hadn't wanted to see it."

"I suppose he believed you."

Reginald nodded. He looked sad and lonely, the light from the fire flickering across his face, highlighting the curves, valleys and sadness.

"I dragged the body into a shed nearby and covered it with some hay."

"Did he have any family?"

"No. He was just another indentured convict."

"Why didn't he get his own wife?"

"Master wouldn't hear of it. Master had to approve, but there was no way he'd arrange for that feller to have a wife. He was bad, through and through."

"Perhaps he got what he deserved."

"Perhaps, but I'd rather someone else'd done it. Like I said, I wanted to hurt 'im, not kill 'im."

"What'd the master do?"

"Next mornin', we rearranged the body in the shed to make it look like he'd fallen from a cart and 'it 'is head on the way down. He told my wife and me to go work in the fields, and not to come back until he came to fetch us. He went to the police and told them one of his workers had fallen and killed himself. Police weren't very interested. Didn't even come to the farm. Just accepted the master's word."

"So, why'd you leave?"

"How do you know I left?"

"You're here, aren't you?"

"I could have served out my time."

"I suppose."

"But, I did have to leave. Master struggled with what we'd done. Said he'd need to tell the reverend and ask the Lord's forgiveness. I tried to tell 'im that the Lord would be on 'is side, but it didn't do any good. A couple of months later, when there was enough time gone after the accident, he told me to change my name and to leave. I was really sad—my wife, too—but the master'd been good, and so I went along with it. I changed my name to Reginald and finished up in Sofala."

"Have the police ever come looking for you?"

"Not that I know of."

"How did the master explain that you'd gone?"

"Don't know that either."

William fussed getting some more tea and when they finished their pannikins, they went off to bed. Reginald must have still been thinking on the past, because he made no noise at all that night.

Over time, William had become a bushman. He could find food, shelter, and cope with the snakes, flies and mosquitoes. Setting up camp became easy—find a flat spot near to water, but high enough not to be affected by flash flooding, put some brush and leaves down to soften the effect of any rocks underneath, put the ground sheet down, tie a rope between two trees and stretch the tent sheet over it, collect some wood and get a fire going. If it looked like rain, they'd keep some food from the previous meal and use that in the tent while they listened to the rain patter on the tent above them.

He even learned to cope with cattle duffers.

They'd saddled up one morning, deciding to push on. They'd spent the last two days working the sides of a creek and had nothing to show for it.

"Perhaps we'll stop in Carcoar," said Reginald. "Might take a day or so to get there. We need some oats and we can sell the gold to pay for it."

It wasn't long before they were on a track.

"I don't like this," said William. "What's a track doing here? I thought you said we're miles from anywhere."

"We are, but it could be animals. I think there's a creek up ahead, so it could be how they get to it."

"Do you think the animals would light a fire? I smell smoke."

"Might be other prospectors."

"They don't make tracks through the bush."

"Might be some diggin's we don't know about."

The track suddenly broke into a clearing. There was a hut to one side. It was a rude affair—mostly bark and poles and looked like an Aboriginal gunyah, but there were no Aborigines to be seen. There were three men, seated on logs around a small fire. A billy bubbled and steamed on a tripod over the fire. Utensils and plates were lying beside them, so the men must have just finished breakfast.

"Ah, well," said Reginald quietly, such that only William heard him.

Then, he called to the men, "Can you spare us a cuppa?"

"No," one of them responded, "bugger off."

"As you wish," said Reginald, and he began to turn his horse to ride back the way they had come.

"Just a minute," said another man. "What's your business?"

Reginald stopped, putting himself between the men and William. It gave William a chance to see the men clearly, even though they couldn't see him. There were two young men, not much older than himself, and one older man, certainly older than Reginald.

"Make yourself ready," whispered Reginald. "If anything happens, ride like your life depends on it."

"I'm not leaving you alone with this lot," whispered William in reply.

"What did he say?" called the older man.

"Who?" said Reginald.

"Don't play games with me!" said the man angrily. "The man behind you."

"Said he doesn't want a cuppa," said Reginald.

The older man stood and pulled a gun from his belt.

"Aw, Pa," said the young man standing beside him. "Let them go. We don't have the cattle anymore."

"You young fool!" barked the older man, and he belted the young one on the side of the head with his gun. "I've always said your mouth is bigger than your brain!"

The young man fell and lay unmoving on the ground.

William took the moment to fetch his pistol from his saddle bags. It wasn't much use anyway—it wasn't loaded—but it might be handy to hit someone if he got the chance.

"You. The one behind. Come out where I can see you," called the older man.

"He doesn't want to," said Reginald. "It'll spoil his aim."

"What do you mean? Spoil his aim?"

"Well, like you, he's got a gun and it's pointed right at you."

"You don't know that—he's behind you."

"I do know that. He told me. You asked what he said, and that's what he said. So, here's an idea—why don't you both lower your guns and we'll back off out of here, and no one will get hurt."

"How can I be sure he's got a gun?"

"You can't."

"I can. Boy, go over there and see if he's got a gun."

"Don't want to, Pa."

"You'll do what I tell you!"

"He might shoot me!"

"He might too, lad," said Reginald. "He's a pretty good shot. Then you'd be dead and your pa there, why he'd shoot one of us, but there'd still be one left to put an end to him. And by the looks of him, there'd be few to mourn him."

"You watch your mouth!" called the older man, but there was uncertainty in his voice.

"Do as he says, Pa. We don't want trouble for trouble's sake, do we?"

"You've a smart lad there, Pa. Must take after his mother."

"I told you to watch your mouth!" This time, there was anger in his voice.

He stood still, staring at Reginald as though deciding his next move.

"Well, we can't wait all day," said Reginald. "I might just get my friend to shoot you anyway."

"I'll shoot you too!" shouted the older man.

"How will you do that? You'll be dead."

Reginald started walking his horse forward, but keeping William hidden from the older man's sight.

"Stand still, damn you! I will shoot!"

William held his hand in front, the pistol now obvious.

"He has got a gun, Pa!" shouted the lad, his voice trembling with fear.

"All right, all right," said the older man. "I was just funnin'. Didn't mean you no harm."

"Of course you didn't," said Reginald, moving his horse up beside him. When he reached the man, he stopped his horse and swung down from the saddle.

"No hard feelings," he said, stretching out his hand as though to shake the other man's.

The older man's face broke into an uncertain smile, he transferred the gun to his left hand and put out his right to shake. In a single movement, Reginald reached down swiftly with his left hand, grasped the gun and swung it up to smack the other man on the side of the head. He fell to the ground instantly.

"What'd you do that for?" shouted the lad.

"Dunno," said Reginald, "but give me time and I'll come up with a reason. All right, Tom, you can come over now. I believe the threat has passed."

"No, it hasn't," said the lad, pulling a gun from his own belt and pointing it at Reginald.

"Now, be sensible," said Reginald. "Put that gun down. It can all end here."

"You had no call to hit Pa."

"I think I did."

"He was about to shake your hand."

"Tom," called Reginald, "you got this lad covered?"

"Aye," said William.

The lad turned to look at William and as he did, Reginald reached down, picked up his father's gun and pointed it at the lad.

"So, now it's two against one," said Reginald. "C'mon, lad. Let's be done with this."

"You hit my pa," said the lad again.

"Your pa hit your brother."

"He's allowed to. He's our pa."

William got down from his horse and started walking towards the lad, who swung his gun back and forth between William and Reginald, uncertain as to who was the greater threat. His hand was shaking so much, it was a toss-up as to whether he'd pull the trigger, or the gun would go off by accident. The gun was pointed in Reginald's direction when William reached the lad and went to take the gun from him.

"All right, mister," said the lad, and tried to pass the gun to William. It went off before William took it, the bullet thudding harmlessly into the ground. The lad fell to the ground, crying.

"I'm sorry, mister! I didn't mean it!"

"That's all right, lad," said Reginald, walking over and pulling him to his feet. "C'mon—we don't want your pa to see you cryin'. There's no need for it now and there's your pa and your brother to see to. They need your help, so there's no time for cryin'. We're all alive and that's the main thing, but I'd find another line of work, if I was you. Somehow, I don't think you're suited to this one."

Reginald helped the lad pull his father and brother into a sitting position, their backs against a log.

"The brother's in a bad way, Tom. I think his pa hit him a mite too hard. He's still unconscious, there's a lot of blood and he's hardly breathin'."

"He'll be all right," said his brother, "it's happened before."

"Tom, collect all their guns."

"You can't take our guns, mister," wailed the lad.

"We'll dump 'em down the track. You'll have no trouble finding 'em. I just don't fancy you havin' 'em when we leave 'ere."

"My pa'll get you for this."

Reginald glanced at the still unconscious Pa lying against the log, and his seriously hurt and pale son lying beside him.

"I doubt it. I think your pa will have his hands full when he wakes up. He's got a severely injured son, he'll have a headache and a bad temper too, so you might want to stay away from him for a while. I don't know who you are, or I'd tell the police about your cattle duffin'. You'll get caught anyway, before long. You always do. If you want my advice, I'd be tellin' my pa to lie low somewhere else for a while."

"I don't want your advice."

"That's the most sensible thing you've said all mornin'. However, for once, I think it might be good advice. C'mon, Tom, we've wasted enough time on this foolishness. Here, I'll help you carry those guns. There's enough weapons here to equip a small army."

They'd walked only a few steps when the lad called after them, "Can you help my brother, please, mister? I think he's dying."

"I think he is too," said Reginald, "but he's got a father. And if you believe in Him, there's a God, too. It's not my job, and it was your fool of a father that hit him. Men like that don't deserve to have sons."

"Can't we help?" whispered William.

"No, Tom—the poor boy is past help. There's no help anywhere near enough to take him and he'll be gone before long. It's sad, but that's how it is. Like I say, men like that shouldn't breed. C'mon, let's put the mornin' behind us."

They took turns holding the weapons as they mounted, before continuing on through the camp.

"We'll go some ways before we dump the weapons," said Reginald. "I don't fancy not findin' a way out of here, havin' to come back and runnin' into an ambush. We'll make sure we can get out before we dump 'em. I don't think the lad's father will be thinkin' kind thoughts about us."

It was around noon before they came to a meadow and Reginald was comfortable to drop the weapons.

"What if they don't find them?" asked William.

"It doesn't matter. Someone will find them."

"Should I keep my pistol loaded?" asked William.

"I wouldn't. Might shoot your foot off. It sure did come in handy though, and you backed it up with a mean face. Didn't know you had that one. I hadn't seen it so far. Seen pretty much all the others."

They continued on, speaking very little, until they got to Carcoar the next day. They'd both had a narrow escape and had come to appreciate each other's resourcefulness. William would now be able to reassure John that Reginald was, indeed, a good man.

CHAPTER 13

# BACK TO BATHURST

They sat in a pub in Carcoar, a whisky each, and said little to each other for some minutes.

Riding into town around the middle of the day, they'd hardly excited any interest. William guessed there were many travellers like themselves, merging like chameleons into the background of the gold fields. Carcoar was a pretty town with plenty of buildings, some impressive, but lacked the planning of Bathurst. William guessed that the hills surrounding the town prevented the planning, and their steep sides and the narrow valley dictated how the town could be laid out and develop. They went into the first pub they saw, although they had a choice of several. This one had the advantage that the publican's name was James, or so Reginald said.

The town was busy enough, with carts, drays, pedestrians and horses making enough noise for twice the number. Winter was already upon them, and it didn't pay to spend too much time in the open, so everyone was in a hurry.

William looked at Reginald. He looked and smelled like something from a swamp. William had taken time to clean himself up every now and again, but Reginald never bothered.

Their gold had fetched quite a few pounds, and Reginald insisted William take most of it. William wondered why, but was soon to find out.

"I've had about enough," said Reginald. "We had a good try and don't have much to show for it. I would probably have earned more if I'd stayed with the others, but I'd always be wonderin' if prospectin' was for me. Now I know it isn't, so I'm ready to go back to Sofala. What about you?"

"Well, I won't go on alone. I'd have been lost plenty of times without you to find our way. John was right—it's a dangerous job."

"Like all jobs out here. Anyway, I'm headin' back in the mornin'. I'll go back through Bathurst and give John what's left of his gear."

William laughed. "He was glad enough to get rid of it. I doubt he wants it back."

"He doesn't have a choice. I only borrowed it."

"As you wish. I'll come with you. I might as well—there's nothing for me here."

They had a few more whiskies and camped by the river overnight, upstream from the town, conserving their money. William offered to pay for rooms for the night, but Reginald wouldn't hear of it.

"Besides," he said, "we can use the rest of our provisions for supper and breakfast. No point in wastin' 'em."

Leaving at daybreak the next day, they arrived in Bathurst by late afternoon. The early morning was crisp and the day warm enough, with little breeze and only passing clouds. The road was awful—full of pot holes and ruts—but the country was beautiful, though there were hills from time to time that made hard-going for the horses. By any measure their expedition was a failure, but they were both in a happy mood.

"What will you do next?" asked Reginald.

"Not sure. What do you think of the find at Snowy River?"

"I think it's all talk."

"Have you talked to anyone that's been there?"

"How could I? I've been with you."

"Why do you think it's all talk?"

"What I read in the paper. You should try it sometime."

"Feller told me you can't always believe it."

"That's my point."

"So you're telling me the paper says it's an exciting find, but I shouldn't believe it?"

"Yes, that's what I'm sayin'."

They stopped briefly in Blayney where they got some bread and jam, and then stopped outside of town by the river to boil the billy. It wasn't long before they were back in the saddle.

William thought he'd never been so pleased to see anywhere as he was to see Bathurst. They pulled up outside the Shepherd's Inn and dismounted wearily.

"Let's take the horses to the stables, then we'll have a whisky," said William.

"No. I'm goin' to give the gear to John, then I'm pushin' on to Sofala."

"That's foolishness, Reginald. It'll be dark soon and I'm guessing there'll be no moon. Stay here tonight and go on tomorrow. I'll pay for a room, so you don't need to worry about that."

"No, Tom. I'll push on. If it gets too dark, I'll pull up for the night."

"You haven't got any supplies. What's one more night? You can push on early tomorrow."

"I've got what's left of the bread and jam. There's plenty of tea and sugar. There'll be others on the road too, so I won't be alone. My mind's made up. I can't wait to see my wife and the little ones. It's an ache now and only gettin' worse since I decided to go home. Wait 'ere—I'll take this to John and be back soon."

He came back a few minutes later, still carrying the shovel, pick and pan.

William couldn't help smiling.

"Get that grin off your face and don't say a thing. He can be rude when he puts his mind to it. Anyway, said you should see him first thing."

Reginald stretched out his hand and William gripped it warmly.

"I hope to see you again, Tom. I know I'm not always the best company, but I think we worked well together. I'm sorry we didn't find much, but that's how it goes. Good luck with whatever you do next."

He swung up onto his horse and headed off down the hill, casting a long shadow by the setting sun. There was already a chill on the night air and William wished he'd convinced him to stay. As Reginald had said, he wasn't always the best company, but William was still sad to see him go.

William walked Kelly down to the stables. The same man was there, attending to two other horses.

"Here, give me those," he said, taking the reins. "You look all in."

"A whisky, supper and bed will see me right."

"Then get to it. I'll see to your horse."

"Thanks," said William, taking his bag and wondering if he should give the man a penny for taking the extra trouble. He put his hand in his pocket and pulled one out. "Here," he said, holding out the penny.

"What's that for?"

"Why, for taking the extra trouble with my horse."

"It's your money—you keep it. It's no extra trouble and I'm paid to do a job."

William felt a little embarrassed, muttered a quick 'thanks', and walked back up the lane. He went inside and found John.

"Well, well, the traveller returns. A bit worse for wear, I think, although you look and smell a little better than Reginald." He stretched out his hand and shook William's warmly.

"Now, my boy, let me buy you a whisky. I understand from Reginald that you aren't exactly rich from your prospecting, but no harm. 'Nothing ventured, nothing gained' I've heard them say. After the whisky, you'd better go and have a bath. Leave all your clothes that you're not wearing out there—I'll have them washed for you. Then we can have supper and you can tell me a little of your adventures."

"I'd rather a bath first."

"Good idea—I think I'd rather that for you, too." He laughed and William thought how good it was to be back.

William went out back and used the privy. He thought that good things keep happening, and how nice it was to use a proper privy for a change. When he was done he went back inside, had a bath in which he fell asleep, and was woken by the water going cold. He picked the best of his clothes to wear and decided most of them were now rags and should be replaced. Going back inside, he found John talking with a group of men, who told him they were about to send out a search party.

"We thought you might have either drowned, or got stuck in the mud," said John.

"What mud?" asked William.

"Why, the mud in the bath," said John.

William blushed.

"Don't worry," said John, "we're just having fun. Here's your whisky—this one's on me."

He had a good time chatting with the men, none of whom he knew. They were all locals and knew John well. John introduced them all to William, but he soon forgot all their names. It didn't matter. They laughed loudly when William told them about Reginald's nightly antics. Most clamoured for more tales from the adventure, but John said that William needed supper and bed and took him away to the dining room when their whiskies were finished.

John sat with William for supper, not joining other groups as was his custom. William wondered at that, but said nothing. John was thirsty for information and quizzed William endlessly about the journey. They had another whisky and some wine over the meal, then John announced that he had things to do and William could either go back to the bar, or go to his room. William chose the room and fell into a deep sleep where he dreamed that Reginald was attacked and killed by bushrangers.

William woke to a great sense of unease, regretting that he didn't argue more forcefully with Reginald. He got up and dressed hastily before heading downstairs to discover that it was already late morning. John was nowhere to be found, but he did find one of the men from the night before in the bar, enjoying a whisky and reading the paper. He was the only customer there.

“Do you mind if I join you?” asked William.

“I’d be delighted,” said the man, folding the paper and putting it on the table. “I’m sure you don’t remember my name from last night. It’s William, but everyone calls me Will.” He put out his hand and William shook.

“Mine’s Tom.”

“I know.”

“Of course you do. I’m sorry.”

“You don’t need to be. I enjoyed your stories last night. I hope you’ll be here later to tell some more.”

The man was well dressed in a suit that looked expensive. Nonetheless, he didn’t behave as though his money elevated him to a position above William, who hoped to learn more about him. He enjoyed talking to a man who was clearly educated and well-to-do.

“No reason why not,” said William after a few moments of thought. “Although, there aren’t many more that are funny. It was mostly hard work and better looking back at it than at the time.”

“I’ve heard that from others who went prospecting.”

“Can I buy you a whisky?”

“No, thanks. I’m only having the one. I’ve some business matters to attend to, but I’ll be back later, and you can buy me one then.”

Bill arrived with a whisky.

“That’s for you,” said Will. “I took the liberty of ordering it for you when I saw you walk in.”

William smiled in gratitude and the man smiled back.

“I didn’t see you order it, but now we’ll have to catch up later,” said William.

“That was my plan.”

"What do you do for a living, Will? If you don't mind me asking."

"I don't mind at all. I sell shoes and boots. I've been looking to set up in Bathurst. I've already got a store in Sydney, but I like it out here too."

"At the rate that I've gone through boots, I could probably keep a store going on my own."

"I've heard that prospecting is hard on boots."

"Aye, you've said that right."

"I sell only the best."

"Then I should come to you."

"I have to set up here first."

"Well, when you do."

"Do you fancy some lunch? My shout."

"I can pay for myself."

"I know you can, but you could accept my offer with a little more grace. After all, it's only lunch."

William blushed, affronted.

Will looked embarrassed.

"I'm sorry, Tom. I didn't mean to offend you", he said hastily. "I meant nothing by that comment."

William was confused as to why Will would make such a comment, and yet assert it meant nothing.

"Are you wondering why I said that?" asked Will.

William nodded in response.

"I was offended that you didn't want to accept my offer. It's not often I make such an offer and it's refused."

"I like to pay my own way."

"Well, I can understand that you might, but if the price of your company is a lunch, I'm happy to pay it."

"You can have my company without any price."

"Ah, I see. I often have lunch when I want to discuss a matter. If it's my idea, I pay."

"What do you want to discuss?"

"Well, nothing really. I just wanted to get to know you a little. I suppose I'm just accustomed to asking and people accepting. Let's have lunch and we'll just pay our own way. It's not worth an argument."

"Thank you, kind sir."

"That's better," said Will, laughing.

They had some lunch and Will departed about his business. William went out to buy some clothes. There were several stores and he took his time, going back and forth until he found one he liked. Most of the people were offhand and not very interested, but in the one he chose, a pretty young girl said, "You're really tall. You'll be hard to fit, so let's take our time and make sure we do the best we can."

She was friendly and chatty.

"I'm helpin' my pa. He's a bit crook at the moment, so he asked me to help. I said I didn't mind. It's what I should do, I told him. He's always been a good pa, so it's my turn now."

She tried hard to find pants that would fit. The shirt was all right, but she couldn't find any pants the right size.

"That's the trouble with store bought stuff," she said, exasperation in her voice. "Fellers like you are hard to fit. I'll tell you what—I'll get my ma. She makes dresses, so she'll take the best of these and change it to make it fit. You wait here. I'll be right back. Look after the store for me, will you? If anyone comes in, tell 'em I won't be long."

"Before you go, how long will it take to change it? And how much will it cost?"

"Dunno. You'll have to ask Ma. She'll know," she said, before disappearing out a door at the back.

She was gone before William could say anything else and back before he'd worked out what to say.

"This is him, Ma," she said as she came back through the door, followed closely by a buxom woman with a scarf tied around her head, a floral apron and a ruddy complexion.

"Mine's Shirley," said the woman, hands on hips and eyeing William up and down.

"Mine's Tom."

"Well, Tom, you're a tall feller, so it won't be easy. But I'm happy to give it a go. What've you done before?"

"Before what?"

"Before now."

"About what?"

Shirley made an exasperated sound.

"About the pants. What else do you think I'd be interested in?"

"I usually get ones that are too long and fold them up."

"Haven't you got a wife? Can't she do this?"

"No, I haven't got a wife."

"Ah," said Shirley, looking at her daughter, who coloured immediately.

She pulled a pair of pants from a shelf.

"Here, young man. Try these. Go out the back there, through that door and put them on. Come back once you have them on and I'll see what needs to be done."

The bell rang to indicate another customer had arrived.

"Do I still go out back?" said William, thinking Shirley might not have time to attend to him.

"Of course," said Shirley, "and be quick about it—I don't have all day."

William left and as he put on the new pants, he could hear everything said in the room next door.

"There you go, young lady," said Shirley, "off you go and see to the new customer. You're not needed here. And keep your eyes off Tom—you can't go falling in love with anything in pants that walks through the door."

"Ah, Ma. You hadn't oughta talk to me like that. I'm sure I've done nothin' to deserve it."

"If you haven't yet, you're about to, if I'm any judge."

William opened the door and was about to come back when he saw John, who was apparently the new customer. He was embarrassed to be found by John trying new clothes, so he stayed in the room with the door slightly open.

"Shirley, Annie. I heard you talking back here. How are you both?" said John.

"You heard us back here? Oh, dear," said Shirley, glancing quickly at the door. "Well as can be expected with winter comin' on and all. What can we do for you, John?"

"I'm looking for Tom. I thought he might be here."

"Why, of course he is! He's out back, tryin' on some new pants. He's a devil to fit. Annie here has said I'll adjust his pants, since we can't find any to fit him."

William walked into the room, struggling in pants that were too long.

"John," he said. "Are you buying some clothes too?"

"No, I came to find you. I've someone for you to meet."

Annie looked crestfallen.

"Is he at the Inn?" asked William.

"He?" said Annie, looking slightly happier.

"No, he's up the road at the Rankin and Piper. It's not far. We can walk there together."

"A *he* then?" asked Shirley.

"Yes, it's a *he*," said John, laughing and smiling at Annie, who reddened again.

"We won't be a moment and you can have him," said Shirley, stuffing some pins between her lips, bending down and folding the legs of William's pants.

"I think these ones were made for a giraffe!" she exclaimed.

"What's a giraffe?" asked William.

"They're taller than you," said Shirley, as if that was enough to answer the question.

"Do you need any help, Ma?" asked Annie.

"Now I just bet you'd like to help," said Shirley, taking the pins from her mouth and handing them to Annie. "Here—hold these."

She fussed about the legs and then the waist.

"There—that's done. Won't you be the one when they're all fixed? Be turnin' heads all about the place, I'll warrant. Out back you go and take 'em off. Come back tomorrow mornin'—they'll be done then."

"How much do I owe you? The shirt, the pants and the fixing?"

"We'll sort that out in the mornin'. Off you go and meet John's gentlemen friend."

"My gentleman friend?" said John.

"The mystery man," said Shirley.

"Oh, it's no mystery—it's Daniel."

"Which Daniel? I think a few people are called Daniel."

"Daniel of the Rankin and Piper."

"Ah. He's a right good man, is Daniel. Best you don't keep him waitin'. Come back in the mornin', Tom. It'll all be done."

"I'll be here, Tom, if you need any help," said Annie, smiling openly again.

John and William walked out of the shop and up the street. Darkness was falling and little light was thrown from the lamps burning outside the hotels and inns. There were still a few people about and they had to thread their way through the pedestrian traffic. They walked past several inns before John said, "This is Piper Street. We go along here."

"Should I be better dressed before we meet your friend?"

"It won't matter. I'm sure how you're dressed will not be important."

"Why are we meeting your friend?"

"He's the publican and he's looking for some help. I think you might be the right man. I know I haven't discussed it with you, but I thought you could at least meet him and if you like the sound of it, you can work for him before he finds someone else."

"What's the work?"

"Helping around the Inn—the usual stuff. The man he had has gone to the Snowy River, so there's work to be done and you might be the right man to do it. See what you think."

"I was thinking to go to Sofala and maybe work with Reginald and the others."

"There's no money in that, Tom. You'll at least get wages here, so you can build up your money a little, then decide what you want to do next."

They walked on silently, each man lost in his own thoughts. After crossing another street and reaching the next corner, John said, "Here we are."

Stepping into the bar, William thought it was the same as any he had seen. But after a few moments, he realised there was an air of order, and a certain gentility. Most people were well-dressed and conversation was low, not intrusive on those nearby. Drinks were ordered by signals to the bar.

It must have showed on his face, as John said, quietly, "I thought you'd like it."

A well-dressed and well-groomed man walked over to them.

"John. I'm so pleased to see you."

They shook hands.

"Let me introduce Tom. Tom, this is Daniel. Daniel, this is Tom."

William held out his hand. It was gripped firmly and held a few moments, while Daniel studied him. Daniel had a well-formed beard, cut neatly and close, and the bluest, brightest eyes William had ever seen. He always thought his father had blue eyes, but they weren't blue at all compared to Daniel's. Daniel wasn't tall, William supposed medium height, though he clearly prized personal grooming. His clothes were immaculate, well cut and beautifully presented. William decided John should have told him to dress as well as he could, but on a moment's reflection realised that perhaps John was right—it was only a job, so maybe rough was best.

"John tells me you might be looking for work. Is that correct?"

"Well…"

"He and another feller are just back from prospecting," said John.

"Did you do any good?" asked Daniel.

"Oh, we got some, but it didn't make us rich."

"Please sit down—both of you. Would you like a whisky?"

Both men nodded and Daniel signalled the bar. Two whiskies arrived promptly.

William was about to ask Daniel was he having a whisky, but he remained quiet when he saw John shake his head a little.

"The work I have is a do-all around the Inn. Not serving, but cleaning up, moving the kegs, stacking the shelves, and keeping the fires going. I'm sure you've seen those jobs being done."

"I've done the job, Daniel. I worked for Joseph in Goulburn."

"For how long?"

William blushed. He couldn't answer the question.

"It's not important, Tom. A silly question, really—my fault for asking."

Daniel appeared to gather his thoughts for a moment, then asked, "Who did you go prospecting with? How many of you?" He stopped. "There I go again. The numbers don't matter, Tom. Sorry."

"Just Reginald from Sofala."

"He's a good man," said Daniel.

"Yes, I found that out. To be fair, John did tell me."

"I did, didn't I?" laughed John.

"Tom, if you've a mind to take the job, it's yours, but I won't apply pressure. I know you're just back from prospecting, so you might be thinking of trying again. The job pays two pounds a week with board. There's a room out back you can use, it's small but it's comfortable. You mustn't drink alcohol while you're working and if you have a drink on your own time, you can't drink here. You get most Sundays off for yourself. Sometimes there are jobs that can only be done on a Sunday, so those days you'll work. For the rest, you're here first thing in the morning until the morning chores are finished, then from when we start lunch until supper is finished. I think that's all. Do you have any questions?"

"Just one. I have a horse. I can't leave him at John's."

"Of course not. I have some land not far from here. You can put him in the stables, or if there's no space, you can put him in that paddock. Anything else?"

William shook his head.

"Well then, you think about it and come back and tell me your answer day after tomorrow."

Daniel was watching William carefully. William put on his best poker face and nodded.

"Thank you, Daniel. That's fair and I'll give you an answer then."

"Good, good. Now, you two finish your whiskies and there's more where that came from, if you've a mind to stay. You'll be my guests, so just ask for whatever you want. I've work to do, things I must attend to immediately. Good evening to you both."

He stood up, nodded and disappeared out back.

"What do you think?" asked John.

"He's a good man," said William, his face still impassive.

John laughed heartily. A few heads turned to look.

"Ah," said John. "Let's finish these and go. It doesn't pay to prey upon another man's hospitality when he's not with you. Besides, I know there's a group back at the Shepherd's looking forward to enjoying a whisky with you and hearing more of your stories. By the way, since you won't be able to drink here if you take the job, you are most welcome to have your drink at the Shepherd's Inn. I'll even give you a special rate."

They laughed, finished their whiskies and stepped out the doors into darkness and drizzling rain.

"I hadn't expected this," said John. "The rain I mean. It will make for an unpleasant walk home, so let's not dilly dally."

He set a brisk pace, but the ground was wet and muddy underfoot and they had to walk carefully to avoid the deeper puddles and the bigger areas of mud.

"I should have worn a pair of Will's boots—better suited to the conditions than what I'm wearing."

"Will told me he's thinking of setting up a store out here."

"I hope he does. His boots are the best you can get. He brings them out from Sydney."

"Why hasn't he set up yet?"

"You'll have to ask him. It's none of my business, but the sooner he does it, the better."

They arrived back at the Shepherd's Inn thoroughly wet and with mud-clad feet. William tried to clean his boots before he went in, but John told him it was a waste of time.

"No one else will do that," he said. "You might as well just come in and we'll sort the mess out later."

Will and the others were sitting just inside the door.

"Ah, here they are!" cried Will. "It's about time. We've all been wondering what's happened."

"We got stuck in the mud," said William. "Well, almost, but this time there really was some mud."

"There you go, Tom," said John. "You join the others. I've got some things to do, but let's see each other sometime tomorrow. I'm sure you've got some questions. Perhaps we'll have lunch together?"

"Yes, John. I'd like that."

William sat and Bill brought him a whisky. The men clamoured for more stories, but none that William told had the same effect as what he told the night before. It wasn't long before they all took turns, and the stories became more outlandish and less believable. It didn't matter though—they all had a wonderful time and there was much slapping of knees and many shouts of encouragement. It wasn't long before the whole bar became involved, and the stories had an international flavour.

John came back and William thought it might have been to ask them to quieten down, but John did the opposite and encouraged others to join. Then William realised that the drink was flowing freely, as patrons bought drinks for themselves and sometimes for the best storytellers.

The Irish mostly told stories about the English and vice versa. No one seemed to mind. William was glad the problems from home hadn't followed them there. On the other hand, perhaps there were only Protestants or Catholics in the room.

"Did you hear the one about the Irish digger?" shouted Will, standing up. "No? Well, he was having an affair with another digger's wife. He thought he saw her husband go out, so he crept up to her tent and whispered, 'Is the coast clear?'"

He looked around at his audience, pausing for theatrical effect, a smile spreading from ear to ear.

"'I don't know,' she whispered back. 'I can't see that far!'"

The room roared its appreciation as Will sat again, his face beaming with pleasure.

"What about the English Lord who was having trouble with his eyes?" asked a man with a heavy Northern Irish accent once the noise had died down. He also stood.

"No? Well, he went to see a feller who he was told was very good at fixin' eyes. 'My eyes are bad,' he said. 'Are they?' said the man. 'Come with me.' And took him outside the store. 'What's that?' he asked pointin' at the sun. 'Why, it's the sun,' replied the Lord, unsure of what was happenin'. 'Well, how far do you want to see?' asked the feller."

Again, the room roared and the man sat, also looking very pleased with himself.

The stories went on and on until finally John called a halt, telling them supper couldn't wait any longer.

William joined the others for supper and stumbled more than walked to his room afterwards. The next morning, he remembered laughing at the stories but couldn't remember what they were. He had breakfast and wandered around the town for an hour or so until he thought it might be time to get his shirt and pants. When he arrived at the store, Annie looked pleased to see him.

"Good morning!" she called. "I'll just finish with this customer and I'll be right with you." She looked more attractive than she had the day before, but William couldn't work out what was different.

Finally, she finished what she was doing and joined him.

"I thought you may not be coming back," she said, holding her skirt at the sides and dipping down slightly, making a pretty curtsy.

"Oh, I've just been looking around," said William, hoping he sounded vague.

"Your clothes are ready. I think you should try them on. I can help you if you like."

"It'll be all right. How much do I owe you?"

"Ma said nothing for the sewing. Said she was happy to do it. I think she likes you," said Annie, smiling shyly. "She was waiting for you to come back, but she had to go out, so maybe you can come back another time. Maybe you could come for supper? I'm sure she wouldn't mind."

William started to feel very uncomfortable—he was unaccustomed to the attention and not sure what to do.

"Perhaps," he said, again as vaguely as he could. "What do I owe you for the clothes then?"

"Ma said four shillings. I hope that's not too much."

"No, that's not too much," he said and counted out the money.

"Ma said she stitched some extra pockets inside for you, where you can keep your money. She said you can't be too careful. Do you want me to show you how she's done it?"

"No, that'll be all right. I'm sure it won't be hard to work out. Thank you very much, Annie, and please thank your mother for me."

"Of course I will, and don't forget to come back for supper. You're welcome anytime. I'll tell Ma to expect you."

"Oh, no—I might be going away, so don't expect me. Perhaps if I come around and tell you when I'm able to come."

"All right, but don't make it too long," said Annie, sounding disappointed. "Perhaps you could come before you go? You're not going today, are you?"

"Oh, I might be. I don't know yet, so perhaps it's best to wait."

He hurried out of the store and left the welcome sound of the exit bell in his wake. He didn't know why he was so nervous. Annie was pleasant to chat to, was certainly attractive and seemed to like him. Perhaps it was because she was the first girl that had ever shown obvious interest at their first meeting, that he had noticed anyway, and he didn't know what to do.

*Should I go back and arrange to have supper with them tonight? I'm not going anywhere, so I'd just look like a fool... and I don't need any practice at that. No, best to keep going. Perhaps John might be able to help me.*

Back at the Inn, he found John but he was still busy and asked him to wait. There was no one he knew in the bar, so he got a whisky and waited in the dining room. He didn't mind being on his own. It gave him a chance to think, and he hadn't thought about Daniel's offer yet. It was more important to think about that and what to do, than to think about Annie just at the moment. Daniel was expecting an answer the next day, so there was little time to think about such an important decision.

John sank into the chair opposite him.

"I'm sorry to keep you waiting, Tom. It's been a busy morning with one thing after another. Perhaps I should give you a job, rather than letting you go to Daniel."

"Do you think I should take the job?"

"That's up to you. It's none of my business. I introduced you, so my job is done."

"I thought we'd have lunch together and talk about it."

John laughed and shook his head.

"No, Tom. I know I said we might have lunch, but I don't have time. You do what you want about Daniel. I want to talk to you about Annie."

"Annie? Annie at the clothing store?"

"That's the one."

William burned bright red. He hated blushing. He'd forgotten about it, and now it was back.

"I'm sorry, Tom. Please don't be embarrassed or take offence. It seems she's quite taken with you."

"How did you find out?"

"I've got eyes, Tom."

"Well, what about Annie?"

William was acutely, severely, deeply embarrassed. More than he'd ever been. He'd never discussed his emotions with anyone, and it was all he could do to sit in the chair. His heart pounded, his pulse raced, and he couldn't stop his hands shaking. He folded them in his lap, out of John's sight.

John looked at him with real concern. "Are you all right? If you're not well, we can talk of it another time."

William shook his head. *Better to do it now. Get it over and done with. I'd rather face a death sentence than wait for such a conversation.*

"All right. I just want to tell you a little about her. Is it all right if I do that?"

William nodded again. He still didn't trust his voice, wasn't even sure he had one.

"How old do you think she is?"

William blushed again. He thought he didn't have enough blood to keep blushing like that and decided that all his blood must be in his face.

John shook his head.

"Stupid me—I should have realised. I'm sorry, Tom. Please forgive me. It's just that you speak so well, I assumed… well, you know what I mean."

William nodded.

"She's older than you. Well, I don't really know how old you are, but she left school early and got married. Her husband was killed in an accident right outside the store. It was very sad. He was run down by a drunken rider. Her ma and pa thought that Annie and her husband would run the store, and they did for a few years. But the good Lord decided it wasn't to be, long term. Unfortunately, her father is not a well man, and he does his best to run the store, but can't do it all the time. She's gone back to school and hopes to finish it before her father passes on, but she struggles because she has to help in the store."

*Where's this heading?*

"I suppose you're wondering why I'm telling you this? Well, if you're the least bit interested, I'm sure you'd make a fine pair. She's a fine girl with fine parents. The store is good, but could be better with someone smart like you running it."

John became a little embarrassed then, and William didn't mind the shoe being on the other foot for a change.

"You might need a little schooling, and I mean no offence by that. I'm sure you've thought of it from time to time. It's strange—you speak so well, I thought you were an educated man. Oh, you know I'm sorry, Tom. Like I said, I mean no offence."

John stopped talking and William still struggled with the urge to get up and run.

"I think I'm making something of a mess of this," said John, finally. "I was going to ask my wife to help. I think I should have. It might be more appealing from a woman—they understand these things."

"John, I appreciate your words and your thoughts, but I'm still finding my way in this world."

"You'll find your way easier with a good woman at your side."

"That might be right, John. But right now, I can go anywhere, do anything, and I have no one to consider. I like it like that."

"Don't you get the urge?"

"Urge?"

"You know what I mean."

If John was embarrassed before, it was nothing compared to the embarrassment showing on his face now. William couldn't help smiling.

"All right," said John and sighed heavily. "I deserved that. I don't have any children of my own, you know. I've never had this conversation with anyone. I didn't realise it would be so hard."

"Of course I get the urge, but I'm not ready to be married."

That wasn't strictly true. He thought of Mary, Bridie, Emma and Ruthie and smiled to himself.

"That was a lie, wasn't it?" said John, smiling warmly.

William was glad John smiled. The tension was past. He liked John a lot and admired him for wanting to help his friends, even if it meant wandering into unknown and difficult territory.

"Yes," said William, smiling again. "But the older I get, the more afraid I become. I see people that marry young and live a life of regret."

"You can always run away," said John, chuckling. "Plenty do."

"I'd rather not have to run away."

"That's a very good answer and a very good philosophy. Anyway, think about Annie and if you change your mind, I can introduce you to her father."

"All right, I will."

"You should play poker, Tom," said John. "You lie so easily. And I mean that as a compliment, before you challenge me to a duel."

"I do."

"What? Challenge me to a duel," said John, looking suddenly very serious.

"No—play poker."

"Why didn't you say so? Let's go out to the bar and get you into a game if there's one going, or get one started if there's not."

"What about the police?"

"They don't worry about friendly games. Some do, but I know the fellers here, and it'll be all right."

William went and saw Daniel the next day and accepted the job on the condition that if there was a gold strike that sounded promising, William was free to go.

Daniel shook his head.

"I'm not saying no, if that's what you think," he said. "Just marvelling at the human condition. I'm not disappointed you ask me for that. It gets in your blood, doesn't it? The fever, I mean. Anyway, that's all right with me. I'm gambling the big strikes have all been made."

They laughed together and shook hands.

"There's something you should know, Daniel," said William.

"Oh, what's that?" asked Daniel, looking a little uncertain.

"I can't read or write."

"Oh, dear me. Is that all? You don't have to worry, Tom. I'd worked that out already. You just have to be strong, fit and well to do the job and I think you'll fill the bill admirably."

As it turned out, it would only be a few months before William was on the move again.

CHAPTER 14

# LAMBING FLAT

William was helping serve lunch at the Inn and heard some men talking about Lambing Flat. Diggers had found surface gold there, and the men at the table were talking that they might go and try their hand. It was all the talk around the Inn over the next few days and William fretted he might be missing out. He took a chance to talk to Daniel, knowing in advance that Daniel wouldn't be excited for him to try.

"It's a lot of talk, Tom. There's always a lot of talk first, then the reality sets in. These things often don't hold their promise for long."

Daniel studied William for a few moments and sighed.

"It's still in your blood, isn't it? You're doing a very good job here and I'd hate to lose you, but I won't stand in your way."

"Where's Lambing Flat?"

"It's about one hundred and twenty miles south and west of here. Being winter, it's two or three days' unpleasant ride."

"Will they bring any of the gold here?"

"More likely go to Goulburn. Why?"

"Well, if they bring it here, we'll hear how good it is and how much there is."

William was struggling to contain his excitement and Daniel looked like he could see it. Daniel shook his head, a look of resignation on his face. Then he startled William by putting his head back and laughing.

"I suppose you've still got your gear stashed away somewhere?"

William nodded.

"You'd better go then. You don't want to be late to the party. I can't promise your job will be here if it doesn't work out, but I expect that's of no concern to you."

"That's not true, Daniel. I like it here, but I'd still like to find gold if I can. I came to make a fortune and I don't think I've tried hard enough yet."

"I understand, my boy. Leave first thing in the morning and may God go with you. I'll get you the money that I owe you—I'm sure you'll need it. I can keep a few pounds if you like, then there'll be money to come back to, even if there's no job. I'll get you some supplies, too—perhaps enough for a week. I'll keep your job for two weeks as well, so if it doesn't work out you can come back quickly."

"Thank you, Daniel."

He stretched out his hand and Daniel took it warmly.

"I hope it works out, Tom. But don't be ashamed to come back if it doesn't. We'll miss you—I'm sure you know that. I'll arrange the supplies and you can collect them from the kitchen when you get breakfast before you go. I'll get your money now, so wait here for me."

"How do I get there?"

"You go through Blayney and Cowra. I'm sure you'll have only to follow the crowd."

William waited and Daniel came back in a few moments and pressed a roll of money into his hand.

"Be careful, Tom. There's many that would think nothing of murdering you for that."

William went and fetched Kelly. Being dark, he thought it wouldn't be easy, but Kelly came as soon as he arrived at the gate. He put him in an empty stall behind the Inn and headed off to bed.

He was up before dawn and cast a last look at his small, but comfortable room. He fetched his supplies from the kitchen, made sure his money was pushed deep into his false pocket and went out the back of the Inn to saddle Kelly. Pulling the shovel, pick and pan down from their storage place, he was glad they still had some life in them. It hadn't been long since he last used them, and seeing them only increased his enthusiasm. The tarps were there too, and he either put things in his saddle bags or secured them to the outside.

Setting off in a strong, cold wind from the west, the misty rain clung close to the ground and visibility was limited. The rain crept in everywhere and in no time at all he was soaked and frozen. At least he knew the Blayney Road, so the first stage of his journey would be unpleasant as Daniel had said, but not unknown. No, it was more than unpleasant—it was downright uncomfortable, close to unbearable, and he almost turned back. Daniel had said that he shouldn't be ashamed of failure, but he was sure that even by Daniel's measure, it was far too early to give up.

Stopping after several miles to adjust the load on Kelly, he saw some other figures emerge from the mist. There were three men also on horseback, but they moved on by without a word.

It was too early for the comradeship of the gold fields. Everyone at this point was competition, and experienced diggers knew there was only so much gold. No point in making friends now when you might have to clash later.

It took William two hard days to reach Lambing Flat. The ride—wet and monotonous, the country not visible due to the mist and rain, and the night—cold. The wind was incessant and always either strong or very strong. He camped not far from some other men overnight. They didn't come near him, or he near them. There was a surprising number of travellers, and it took a while for William to realise he'd not ever been this early to a new gold field. As Daniel had said, it was the first time he was on time for the party.

In the end, he was glad there were others heading to the diggin's, as he doubted that he would have found them on his own. There were about ten diggers all slogging through the mud and rain. The diggin's were in a broad valley, spread out along a creek. It turned out they were on private land, so part of his licence fee went to the owner and the rest to the government. He'd taken care earlier to separate his money, such that it appeared all he had was the licence fee when he paid it.

A few stores and sly grog shops had already been set up. Enterprising vendors were always quickly behind any gold find.

It wasn't hard to find a spot to claim. There were only a few hundred diggers, though the number of Chinese was unexpected. Most diggers were pegging close to the creek, and the diggers around him seemed to go down only two or three feet before they either found gold or abandoned their claim. William was well pleased with his first claim. He found gold and was grateful that he made the effort to join the rush. It wasn't long before he regretted being on his own though. He couldn't leave his claim for fear of it being jumped, so he'd have to work any claim fully before taking his gold for sale or going for supplies.

The misty rain was perfect. It meant he could catch water to drink and that there was enough in the creek to wash dirt, but not so much that he had to fight with water as he dug.

There were other problems that arose, but they were solved for him. It was good fortune that the gold field was on private land, as the owner had discovered other ways to make money. A man came by offering to take care of Kelly for sixpence a week, said he'd put him in the paddock with the other horses. There'd be no oats though, and if William wanted to give his horse better treatment, then he'd need to see to that himself.

Another man came by offering to sell wood at two pennies a load. A load turned out not to be very much but, by being careful, William was able to make do. Using some of his sailing skills, he lashed some pieces together and used them with his tarpaulin to make a tent.

His first claim played out and he fetched Kelly, took his gold to Boorowa to sell, and to get more supplies. It wasn't far but took a day and already when he returned, there were more diggers. He mused on the problem of finding a partner. With a partner he would not only have freedom to move, he would also be able to reserve a bigger claim. It wasn't going to be easy, as it wasn't like any gold field where he'd been before. There were no gatherings for singing or poker, the grog shops saw little patronage and diggers only used the local stores when there was no other choice. Worse still, he had to keep a sharp eye on his possessions. Thieving was rife and, as he heard another digger say, "If it's not tied or nailed down, it'll be stolen."

Fights over possessions broke out regularly. Sometimes it was a welcome distraction, but mostly it made him aware that his could be the next fight.

Then summer came early, the rain stopped, and the flies came out. The heat meant that human waste attracted the flies, and the fields took on that awful smell associated with digging. Worse, water became scarce, and the diggers fought over it in the creek. William was making good money, but he wasn't getting rich—the costs were higher than he'd experienced before, and the inconvenience of digging was almost beyond bearable. Several times, he nearly gave it away, then he'd find more payable gold and be content, although reluctant to stay.

The water scarcity became so severe that the wood man sold him drinking water as well. It was harder to find places to wash the dirt now too, which meant that any claim he now staked had to be close to water.

The number of diggers continued to grow, some moving away from the creek, collecting dirt, then bringing it in for cradling. The new chums blundered around the diggin's, sometimes trying to wash their dirt on other diggers' claims. It was sometimes funny, but mostly caused trouble.

There were more Chinese about than William had seen before, although he'd heard back at the Inn that they were flocking to the diggin's, hoping like all the diggers to make their fortune he supposed. He heard from the wood man that a lot of diggers were angry with the Chinese—they were using more water in the creeks, making a bigger mess because they worked in groups. Some said they were thieves, attributing most of the missing goods to their actions and claiming their dirty habits led to disease.

William was amused that they were accused of dirty habits. He did his best to stay clean, but it was an uphill battle. As far as he knew, none of the other diggers bothered, and you could smell most of them a mile off.

The Chinese were content to try a claim once it had been abandoned and often found gold missed by the original digger. That got the other diggers angry too. They'd do all the hard work, loosening the soil, and the Chinese would capitalise on it. It didn't seem to occur to them that they'd abandoned the claim.

William left a little present for them. He solved the problem of where to do his business by using the first hole he dug in the claim once the hole was played out. He used it at night or early morning in the interests of privacy, though he'd learned to ignore issues of privacy on the ship. He'd just shovel a little dirt over his business when he was done, and the hole was reserved for the purpose while the claim lasted. It bothered him that the flies had undoubtedly visited places like that before settling into his eyes, ears, face and mouth.

He found out later that it didn't matter to the Chinese. They used human waste as fertiliser, so it was of no consequence to them, and they probably thought he had tried to grow something. The use of human waste was one of the dirty habits attributed to them.

It was dangerous for the Chinese to be caught alone, as two or three diggers would beat them up. Word filtered through the diggin's that if more diggers made them unwelcome, they might go away.

William worked on through the summer and into the autumn—working hard, making reasonable money, but given the privations and cost, he worried he was hardly working for wages.

The sly grog shops presented a chance to meet someone to take on as a partner, or at least to meet a group to play cards and enjoy a drink. It never worked out that way though. The cards were mean and competitive, and it seemed to him that he would take his life in his hands to join a game. Everyone was angry all the time, and rumour suggested it was mostly caused by the Chinese, but anger needed an outlet and any outlet would do.

Sundays were the most difficult. It was generally agreed that it was a day of rest, the Lord's Day, and there would be no work. The Chinese didn't care that it was Sunday, and they worked on, incurring the ire of others in the gold fields. William usually pottered about his claim, fixing things or cleaning up. He sometimes took Kelly for a ride but never wanted to be away from his claim for too long. If there was a visiting minister, the diggers would go to the service, sometimes regardless of their denomination, so it meant there was a lot of movement around the camp.

It didn't seem to matter if it was a Sunday or a working day, if you left your claim, it was likely to be jumped.

William spent the autumn of the next year trying to decide whether to stay or go. He missed Ballarat and Tuena, and all that had been good there. He did think of getting a job at one of the stores but couldn't suppress the feeling that it would be a mistake. He was here to make his fortune and that wouldn't happen in a store—unless he owned it, of course.

Eventually, his mind was made up for him.

The days became shorter and colder. He found there was more interest around the diggin's in getting together now, but the topic was always the Chinese. The diggers brought drink, plenty of drink, and took out their frustrations with their lot on the Chinese. It reminded William of Ballarat and the diggers' disputes with the Government, but there was more bloody-mindedness and irrationality. It didn't matter which way William looked at it, he couldn't find a way to blame the Chinese for everything. As far as he could tell, he was alone with this opinion.

One night—a particularly cold, but moonlit night—there was a large gathering nearby with fiery anti-Chinese speeches accompanied by shouting, drinking and cursing. William could hear some of what was said, and thought he'd go along out of interest and, perhaps, boredom. A few fires were going, which seemed to William more for effect than anything, as they provided little warmth against the cold for the several hundred gathered.

"What about their bloody clothes and those bloody pig tails they wear?" cried a voice.

"They're different!" shouted another, deeper voice.

"They're thieves and they're dirty!" shouted a woman.

"What about their bloody writing?" shouted someone near to William. "Who can make sense of that?"

There were murmurings of assent.

"Makes as much sense to me as our own," said William.

A few people laughed.

A big man arrived, pushing through the crowd to stand beside William.

"You? You! You on their side?"

"I'm on no one's side but my own."

The man took a swing at William, who dodged it easily, but the man was so drunk he fell off balance and thudded to the ground, cursing that someone had tripped him.

More people laughed and William moved away—he had no interest in fighting.

"There's more of 'em comin'!" someone shouted now. "I hear there's more of the bastards on the road to here! Thousands of 'em!"

"It's bad enough already!" shouted others, almost in unison.

"Somebody should do somethin' about it. The Government won't."

"We should do something about it! After all, it's our bloody country and they're our bloody diggin's!"

The shouting and yelling continued, but the mood of the crowd changed. It suddenly went from talking about the Chinese menace to deciding to do something about it.

"Let's go and sort 'em out! Give 'em what for! Crack a few 'eads!"

The crowd started moving off in the direction of the Chinese camp, swelling as it went. People picked up pieces of wood, rocks, and digging equipment. Some were so drunk they couldn't get out of their own way, others who were drinking but not drunk were ready to fight the world and everyone in it.

William stood undecided. Curiosity alone made going seem a good idea, but William had no stomach for violence—he'd seen enough in his short life. He also had no issue with the Chinese.

"C'mon, mate!" shouted a man passing by, "you don't want to miss the fun!"

Watching the mob swell, William decided that whoever was making humans had to go back and redesign them. The combination of mob excitement and a common enemy made for unpredictable and often deadly behaviour.

On the spur of the moment, William went back to his tent, crawled in and tried to sleep. There was a lot of noise from the Chinese camp and the noise grew louder by the minute.

Whatever was happening, it appeared the mob's desire to teach the Chinese a lesson was being put into effect.

"Let's check this one," whispered a voice outside the tent. "I've seen this feller—I think he's doin' all right."

"He might be inside."

"Nah. Everyone's gone to see the fun."

*There's always someone who'll take advantage of any absence.*

William reached for his pistol. It was always loaded these days and never far from reach, although it had been some time since he last loaded it. The thought that it may not work briefly crossed his mind. William's tent was a tarpaulin stretched across a pole, so it was easy for someone to access it from either end. The thieves must have thought William's body was a stack of his possessions, bundled up on the ground to keep them out of the weather. Lucky for William, the intruders came into the tent from the same end and headfirst. William lay quietly, not moving, waiting for his moment. He could see the men clearly framed against the moonlight.

When he judged the moment right, William sat up and pointed the pistol at the two men.

"Evening, fellers. I don't remember asking you to drop by. Is there something I can do to help?"

William couldn't see the men's faces, but he could see their shapes against the moonlight and smell the unwelcome stench of their bodies.

The men froze, clearly uncertain what to do next.

"We just came to make sure everythin' was all right," said one of the men, hopefully. "You can't be too careful, you know. There's some bad'uns about,"

"Yes, that's right," said the other, both men still on their hands and knees, faces only inches from William's pistol. "Now that we know you're all right, we'll be on our way and check some other tents."

"Check some other tents?"

"Yes, just to make sure everythin' is all right."

"And, how will you know if everything is all right?"

The men didn't respond.

"How will you know if everything is all right?" asked William again.

William's back ached from his sitting posture, but he was sure that whatever discomfort he was enduring, the men's was greater. There's something very uncomfortable about a loaded pistol pointing at you in the darkness.

"Now that we've found everythin' is all right, can we go, mister? I thought a feller'd be grateful, us goin' out of our way and everythin'."

"Why, I'd be grateful if I was confident you'd come by out of a sense of concern on my behalf, but I can't help thinking you might be lying, which is why I'm wondering how you'd know if everything was all right."

"We know everythin's all right because you're here."

"And if I hadn't been here?"

The thief on William's left moved quickly. He probably had a good view of William's pistol in the dark, helped by the moonlight behind him. The men were only shapes to William. One minute the shape was stationary in front of him, the next it had a vice-like grip on his pistol hand, forcing it upwards. It was a bold move and caught William off guard. He'd enjoyed humiliating the men too much and realised he might be about to pay for his arrogance with his life.

William tried to free his arm using his other hand to claw at his attacker's arms and face. The pressure on his arm caused the pistol to fire and the noise was shocking in the confined space of the tent. No one would notice though, as there was plenty of shooting and shouting coming from the direction of the Chinese camp. The second thief must have decided that his mate had been shot and took the chance to roll from the tent and could be heard running away. At least there was only one of them now, but the situation wasn't really any less dangerous for William.

The man took one of his hands off William's arm to protect his arms and face. Neither of them could get the upper hand, the thief lying across William and both using their hands and arms. William was using one hand to protect his pistol and the other to attack the man, the man using one hand to maintain a tight hold on William's pistol hand and the other to protect his body. William knew the pistol could only fire once, and the man might have guessed it, but both fought for it nonetheless. It was a valuable weapon, even if it wasn't loaded.

Whisky and body odour offended William as they struggled in the dark, neither one giving an inch. There was no sound in the tent other than grunting and the occasional exclamation of pain, all smothered by the noise coming from the Chinese camp.

Once again, William was in a fight for his life and was sure he'd get no quarter from his opponent.

He didn't know how long they'd been scrambling around in the darkness—it must have only been minutes, but it felt like hours. Sometimes, he thought he was about to lose his pistol, then he'd land a solid blow on his attacker's face. The man tried to hit William with his other hand but was more focused on making sure William couldn't use the pistol, so most of the time he kept two hands on William's pistol arm and that allowed William to batter his face.

Then, without thinking, William used his elbow. The man had put one of his hands down on the ground, trying to get leverage to push himself further up William's body, perhaps to smother him. Rather than punch the man's face, William threw his elbow across and must have caught the man on the side of the head. The man slumped across William's body, motionless.

Pushing the man off, William reversed the positions. The man now lay on the ground and William knelt over him. Just for good measure, William belted the man on the head with his pistol.

A voice whispered from outside the tent, "Did you get 'im, Louis? I knew you would, I knew you wouldn't need me."

"No, Louis didn't, and you'd better clear out if you don't want the same."

"Christ," said the voice, "I'm sorry, mister. We didn't mean you any 'arm. I'll be goin'. Please don't shoot me too."

"I won't, but you'd better clear out, if you know what's good for you."

William dragged the unconscious man from the tent and wondered what to do next. The police, such as they were, would be busy trying to restore order at the Chinese camp, or might have even left to ensure their own safety. Whatever they were doing, William and his problem would not be top of their priorities.

He could tie the man up, but the last time William left a man tied up, his mate had come and freed him in the night. This fellow's mate thought he was dead, so chances were he wouldn't come back to free him, but the fellow had fought like the devil. If he got free, he may well come seeking revenge.

While he contemplated his limited options, the man stirred. William hit him over the head again with the pistol to give himself time to think.

The noise from the Chinese camp continued unabated, so whatever had started over there was still going on.

William was exhausted, overwhelmed by what had just happened and by the noise from the Chinese camp. He was surrounded by violence and the thought made him sick to his stomach. Getting some water from his barrel, he sat and sipped it, looking at his adversary.

The man didn't look old, although William had no idea how you judged years. He really only judged people as older or younger than himself, and this man was older. Despite what he had just endured, he had a vague sympathy for the man. The man looked like he had little money, though he must have spent what he did have on whisky. No doubt, the belting over the head would not be the only source of his headache the next day.

Still, William couldn't sit there all night, sipping water and belting the man over the head every time he woke. He needed a plan and, exhausted or not, he had to come up with one.

There was no one around, so he could reload the pistol and put a bullet in the man and dump him. No one would be the wiser, and it would doubtless be associated with the drama unfolding around him. He thought he should reload the pistol anyway, as a precaution, but wasn't sure he could do it in the dark and hesitated to light a lamp.

He could tie the man up and turn him over to the police in the morning. Hopefully his mate wouldn't bother to return during the night to free a dead man so, provided William did a decent job of the knots, the man would still be tied in the morning.

Or he could pack up and leave. There would be a sense of failure, a sense that he couldn't make it alone, a sense that he couldn't or wouldn't ever be able to find gold. As to the last, he had come to believe that a person didn't find gold, gold found the person. Some people just had the good fortune, the way that others didn't.

The noise at the Chinese camp diminished and as he turned to look in that direction, the man struck. William hadn't seen him stir, much less get to his feet. He must have lain awake a while, waiting for the right opportunity, and William would always say that it was his own exhaustion that gave the man the opportunity. He would also say that because he spared the man, the man spared him, but he didn't know for sure. It might have been that a shot would have been heard now and someone would investigate, or that the diggers were returning from the affray and there would be a witness to murder. Perhaps the man had wanted to shoot him, found the pistol to be unloaded and so couldn't because he didn't have the means to reload it. There was no doubt William was lucky to be alive, lucky that he'd put Kelly elsewhere, so he couldn't have been stolen, but that was as far as his luck went. When he woke later, all he had left was a tent and Kelly. All his money, his kit and his gold were gone.

## CHAPTER 15

# CAROLINE

He'd been penniless before and he was certain he'd be penniless again, but the theft of everything enraged him like nothing before in his life. All his work, the privations, the loneliness, the heat, the dust and the flies—all for nothing. He'd spent nearly a year of his life digging gold to enrich a thief.

When he woke from the blow on the head, he knew immediately that it was a waste of time to look for his possessions but did so anyway. A vague, short-lived idea was that the man wanted only to escape, but that notion failed to recognise what the man was doing there in the first place.

Around him the camp was in an uproar, with police trying to work out what had happened the night before at the Chinese camp and trying to determine the ringleaders. Despite a concerted effort on the part of the police, it was a pointless exercise. There were no witnesses, and the Chinese who also spoke English were beaten senseless when they tried to persuade the diggers to leave them alone. William's problem was of no interest to anyone.

He still had a few supplies that the thieves hadn't bothered with, or hadn't seen, more likely. If he left that morning, he could be back in Bathurst the next day—his supplies would last, and he could see Daniel to get from him the money that he'd sensibly kept. Thank God for Daniel.

He felt like he did when he left Ballarat. Overwhelmed by the violence, and in this case by the theft as well, he only wanted to run. Run away from there and leave the memory of all the pain, the hurt and the humiliation as far behind him as possible.

When dawn came, taking his few remaining supplies, he quit his claim and went to get Kelly. He could stay a day or two and try to get a little gold to pay his way out but without his kit, it was a waste of time. Perhaps, he could try to find some work, maybe work for the wood man, but the idea of staying in the valley was not appealing on any level. His head hurt terribly, and he was sure he had an open wound, but couldn't find any blood when he searched for damage with his fingers. Perhaps the man had used a rock as a weapon—as there were plenty about—so there was only a bruise. Whatever he used, it was effective.

It wasn't until he arrived at the paddock that he realised he had no money to settle his account for Kelly. It was only sixpence, but without any money he was afraid the man would want to keep Kelly in exchange for the debt. But he needn't have worried.

"Don't worry, mate," said the man that managed the paddock. "Happens a lot. I'm sorry you've been robbed, but others just give up looking when they run out of money, so they don't pay me either. I don't want to kick a man when he's down, so you take your horse and saddle and good luck. Maybe you should see a doctor—you look really bad."

"Thanks," said William, moved and grateful for the man's kindness. He knew Kelly was worth a few pounds to the man and he could easily justify keeping him. Getting his saddle from the shed where it was stored proved a task beyond him. As he reached to pull it from the rack, he passed out and woke to the paddock man, and a few others, bending over him and looking concerned.

"I'm gettin' a doctor for you," the paddock man said, turning to walk out of the shed.

"No, you're not," said William. "I couldn't pay you for looking after my horse and saddle, and I can't pay a doctor for looking after me either."

"I'll pay him," said the man. "You've paid well and on time for the last year, so I'll do it."

"No, you won't. I've got nothing and I won't be beholden to any man just because I've got nothing. Just help me saddle my horse and I'll be on my way."

"I can do that, but I don't think you're bein' sensible, mister."

"Sensible or not, there's a lot happened here since yesterday and I want to be on my way."

"Did you get involved in the fight with the Chinese fellers?" the man asked suspiciously. "Police are lookin' for some fellers. Is you one of 'em?"

"If I am, then I'm not sure what trouble I was to the Chinese, as the bump's on the back of my head, so I must have got it running away."

Some of the men standing around laughed.

"I suppose that's right," said the man. "From what I've heard, the Chinese got the worst of it, so I suppose you're tellin' the truth."

They'd not long finished saddling Kelly and the drizzle started. William thought it a fitting conclusion to his time in Lambing Flat.

William didn't remember much of the two-day journey back to Bathurst. His head hurt constantly and he didn't have any bedding apart from his blanket and tarpaulins, so the night was miserable. He was up early and on the road with daybreak, munching on his supplies and finding water plentiful due to the rain.

It was almost dark when he reached Bathurst and he'd already decided to see Daniel, as he thought he could use the money he'd left with him to cover any immediate costs.

He heard later that he arrived more dead than alive, soaked to the skin despite his oil skins, and looking like he'd be better in a graveyard than a pub.

Putting out his hand, he said, "Hello, Daniel," before collapsing.

William also learned later that Daniel and his wife had cleaned him as best as possible, put him in a bed and fetched a doctor. The doctor, advising that William had a concussion, shocked Daniel by saying he may not live. When William finally woke, he'd been unconscious for two days and Daniel and his wife had kept a constant vigil by the bedside.

William woke, wondering at the unaccustomed soft bed.

"Where am I?" he asked.

"In good hands, I hope," said Daniel.

"Ah, Daniel. I suppose that means I'm back in Bathurst?"

"It does, and right pleased we are to see you. Especially alive, as the doctor said you may not be. The doctor said you'd been hit hard with a rock or something on the back of the head. He thought you might have fallen from your horse, as the roads are flooded and slippery. May I ask what happened?"

"Where are my clothes?"

"They've been washed, though they might be ready for the scrap heap. They're over there, but you shouldn't be thinking of getting up yet."

"I'm not thinking of getting up. Was there anything in my pockets?"

The lamp beside the bed exaggerated the movement of the shadows on the wall behind Daniel, making him look like a giant.

"Have I got my old room back?"

"Whoa! One question at a time, or I won't know which to answer. No, there was nothing in the pockets which we all thought strange, although the doctor said things might have fallen out. But there was nothing in the hidden pockets either, so I thought you might have been robbed."

"Nothing? I was hoping it was a bad dream."

"And yes, you've got your old room back. Now my turn, what happened?"

William recited the whole sorry tale, and he felt the rage, humiliation and shame course through him again, undiminished by the lapse of a few days since it happened.

"I'd like my time over again," he said. "I would have shot him."

"No, you wouldn't," said Daniel. "You're not that kind of man."

*You don't know the half of it.*

"I had a lot, Daniel. I don't know the number, because I don't know numbers, but it was a big bundle of notes. Maybe it wasn't a fortune and maybe it was no better than wages, but I worked hard for it."

"Too hard for it to be stolen is my guess."

"That's what makes it so hard to take. I suppose he didn't just steal it, it came at a cost to him too, as he nearly lost his life. But then, I nearly lost mine trying to protect it. But in the end, he won."

"We'll tell the police here—they may be able to do something. Can you describe the men? Do you know their names?"

William shook his head. "One was called Louis. It was night, and they were only shadows in the dark of my tent. I didn't even get a good look at the one I knocked out. I could see he was older than me, but he looked like every other digger on every other gold field—unshaven, ragged and dirty clothes and smelled like he thought water was only for making tea and cradling. No, Daniel, it's a waste of time."

"That's a shame, but concentrate on getting better."

"I'm done with digging, Daniel. It's a lot of hard work for nothing," William said, bitterly.

"Then why don't you get well, take your old job back, and think about what to do next? You could do worse than work here for a while."

"I thought you'd have found someone else by now."

"We tried, but put simply, no one else was as good as you and they didn't last. It's good to see you, Tom. Rest here and go back to work when you are ready, but not a minute before."

William couldn't wait to get back to work. Lying in bed gave him too much time to think, so concussed or not, and despite Daniel's protests, he was back at work the next day. He was strong, young and fit, so it took him no time at all to get back into the old routine.

As Daniel had said, his clothes were too far gone to be retrieved, so he went back to see Annie. She was annoyed at him for leaving without so much as a *goodbye*, but soon her chatter turned to other things. A man had come into her life, and it was all she could talk about. William was mildly jealous of his exalted position and was glad when Shirley came in from the back to say *hello*. She did the fitting again, saying she couldn't remember the details, but William was suspicious she only wanted to get him in the back room for a chat.

"I don't like him that much," Shirley said, "but Annie, well, she's over the moon. I worry she might get her heart broke again. Poor lass—once is enough. Life can be cruel, Tom, but as my ma used to say, *There's a reason for everythin'*. I wonders at the reason in this though. You come for supper some time, Tom. It'd be nice if you did."

"Shall I come back tomorrow and collect everything?"

"Yes, tomorrow will be fine. You speak so nicely, Tom. I wish others were as well educated as you."

William decided there was no point in correcting her knowledge. He hurried back to the Inn and made sure he hadn't missed any chores while he'd been away. It was only afterwards that the doctor had told him about Daniel and his wife's nightly vigil, and he was overwhelmed with gratitude. As a result, he couldn't do enough for Daniel and his business.

It was around this time that William's teeth began to hurt. He didn't think much of it at first. It started as just a general soreness but, after a week or so, it became a constant pain. One morning, he thought he'd ask Daniel, who said it happened to everyone at one time or another. Some people were lucky and kept their teeth all their lives. However, most people lost all their teeth over time. He thought it was something to do with the amount of sugar people put in their tea.

"Here, sit in this chair and let me have a look," said Daniel.

William did as he was told and sat.

"You'll have to open your mouth," said Daniel.

Once again, William did as he was told.

"You've got problems," Daniel stated, after a brief inspection. "Looks like quite a few of them are rotting."

"Is there anything I can do?"

"People say you can do all sorts of things, but I've never heard of anything that worked. Feller told me once you can stop the holes, and the pain goes away for a while."

"Stop them hurting?"

"No. They fill the hole with something."

"Something? What do you fill them with? And how do you do it if you can't see them yourself?"

"Oh, they've got fellers now called dentists. They do it. I believe there's one or two in Sydney. They'll stop them for you."

"I don't want to go to Sydney." He didn't need to tell Daniel why.

"I can understand that. I go there sometimes myself, and I'm always glad to get home."

"What would you do?"

"I'd go to a surgeon. There are a few storekeepers who'll remove a tooth. They'll charge you a shilling, but I think the surgeons are better because they've been trained."

"Do they cost more?"

"They do."

"Is there one that you go to?"

"Yes, here in Bathurst. I can take you there, if you want. He travels a lot, so I'll find out if he's there, and if he is, I'll take you there in the morning. It isn't far."

Daniel told William the next morning that the surgeon was there and would be happy to see him. They walked there together. As Daniel had said, it wasn't far. Spring was nearly on them, making for a pretty walk.

They entered the surgeon's shop and a bell attached to the door announced their arrival. The surgeon was busy with another patient, but it wasn't long before he shook the patient's hand and ushered him out the door.

He nodded at Daniel, then turned to William.

"I'm Patrick O'Connell. Now, what can I do for you young man?" he asked.

"My teeth are aching."

"It happens. Sit in the chair. Let me have a look."

William sat, and Patrick started pulling his head and jaw about.

"There's two should come out now. And some more later."

William had heard of people having their teeth pulled out and dreaded it.

"Do you have to pull them out?"

"No. You can leave them and they'll fall out eventually, but they'll hurt until they do. If I pull them out, then your jaw will hurt for just a few days and the toothache will be gone. It's up to you. Costs two shillings a tooth. Think about it for a moment if you like. How are you, Daniel? Family good?"

The men chatted briefly while William considered his options.

"How do you do it?" William asked suddenly, interrupting.

"Pull the teeth?" asked Patrick.

William nodded.

"I've got some forceps. Let me show you."

"Tom, don't fool around," said Daniel. "If you want it done, just agree to it. Delaying will only prolong the apprehension. I've had it done—it only hurts for a while."

"All right," said William, "I want it done."

Patrick nodded, went to a drawer and brought out a tool that looked like tongs William had seen used by blacksmiths, although much smaller.

"Help me, will you, Daniel?" asked Patrick.

"I'd rather not," said Daniel. "I'll wait outside on the street."

"As you wish," said Patrick. "What's your name, young man?"

"Tom."

"Well, Tom, I want you to hold the sides of the chair. Press your back firmly into it and try not to struggle. It works best if I take a few moments to get a firm grip with the forceps, I'll say *now*, you brace yourself and I pull the tooth."

"All right," said William, "are you going to do both teeth?"

"Yes—one after the other. No rest between. Just hope the teeth don't break. If they break, I have to cut the gum with a scalpel to get a grip on what's left. In future, you're better to have them pulled when they first begin to hurt. That way, there's plenty of tooth to hold onto."

Patrick was quick. In less than a minute, both teeth were out. William had hardly recovered from the first tooth being pulled when Patrick pulled the second. He thought Patrick was going to pull his head off, so hard did he have to pull to dislodge his teeth. William decided that in the future, he'd rather a toothache than to have his teeth pulled.

His gums hurt and bled for several days, and he never again had a tooth pulled— he let them rot and endured the pain.

As spring rolled into summer, the Inn was doing very well, and Daniel was pleased and told everyone so. After nearly a year had gone by, Daniel told William his Inn's popularity had increased severalfold and he thought he might get some help for William.

"You don't have to do that," said William. "I'm happy with the job and I think I'm getting everything done. Some days I work hard, but I'm happy to do that. You looked after me, I'm happy to look after you."

"Oh, it's not just that, Tom. I'd like to get someone to help clean the rooms, to serve on the tables, and to welcome people when they arrive to stay. I'm thinking of a girl I know. She's only young, but she's keen. I think you might work well together."

"Well, it's up to you, Daniel. But if it was me, I'd leave things as they are."

"I think people like to see a woman when they arrive, so if it's only for that, I think it's a good idea. See if you change your mind when you meet her."

William felt miffed, but didn't know how to say it. He thought he'd been doing a good job, and if the Inn's popularity had increased, then he must have been.

"Her father is bringing her in tomorrow. I'll certainly value your opinion, so let's have a chat once you have a chance to meet her. I'm not a gambling man, but I'm willing to bet you'll change your mind."

William spent that night and most of the next morning planning how to stop the new appointment. He liked how Daniel valued him and how his contribution mattered. Not that he had a lot of time to think. Winter was on them again, and there were many tasks that needed doing to prepare for cold weather. Odd jobs around the building, fixing broken glass, holes and cracks, gathering and storing wood for the fires, mucking out the fireplaces and making sure the stables would keep out the weather. They needed to store plenty of spirits, whisky and wine as the roads weren't always passable, and the customers would brook no excuse when it came to drink being available.

Daniel stuck his head out the back door and called, "Tom? Do you have a moment? There's some people I'd like you to meet."

Reluctantly, William dropped the shovel he was using to muck the stables and followed Daniel into the parlour.

There was a tall, solid man with a big beard and a shock of white hair. Most noticeable of all was the size of his two hands, and the way he was holding his hat and moving it ceaselessly between them, dwarfing it. William could imagine one hand alone would be enough to pick up an axe and split a sizeable log in two. He wore boots, drab cords, a checked shirt, and a vest and coat.

Then, his eyes moved to the girl seated beside him. She wasn't tall, and she had the prettiest face he'd ever seen—and the most radiant smile. Her hair was dark, almost black, pulled away sharply from her face and caught up in a bun at the back. William was instantly red in the face, because he thought everyone could hear his sharp intake of breath. He knew he stank of horses from mucking the stables, and wished he'd taken more notice of Daniel's warning that he might change his mind. If only he had made himself more presentable.

He smiled back and thought it not possible that her smile could become more radiant, but it did.

"Tom, this is James, and Caroline—his daughter. This is Tom. I told you about him. We're very lucky to have him here."

William was red again at the compliment.

"Yes, Tom, another James, but this one doesn't own an inn," said Daniel.

"And not likely to," said big James, laughing. "But my Caroline, well, she wants a job. She's young and keen to start work somewhere that's not at home."

"Now, Pa—you know I'm happy at home. I'd just like to get a job," said Caroline, putting her hand on her father's arm. He patted it.

"Now, now, lassie. Don't you take on so. It's the truth, so there's no harm in saying it. Perhaps Daniel can tell you what he wants you to do."

"Mostly cleaning, tidying, greeting guests, and making people feel at home."

"She's only young," said big James. "What if people are causing trouble?"

"Tom'll take care of that, won't you, Tom?" said Daniel. "He's no stranger to trouble and knows how to take care of the rowdy elements."

William didn't trust himself to do any more than nod. He was enchanted with this lass and wondered how he might make sure Daniel would give her the job.

"She won't need accommodation," said big James. "She can live with a widow and her son nearby. They're not too far from here and I know he'll walk her to and fro each day."

"I can walk her home, if it's late," said William, blushing furiously when he saw Daniel smile, clearly noting that William had changed his mind about help around the Inn.

"Well, that's all, Tom. I wanted you two to meet. You'll be working together, if Caroline joins us here."

William, still red and uncertain what to do, mumbled more than spoke, "Thank you. I am pleased to meet you both."

Turning to walk out, he turned back and said, "I hope you get the job."

Caroline turned her most radiant smile on him and said, "I hope so too."

William left the room, smitten like he'd never been before—his emotions out of control, his pulse racing, and head over heels in love.

## CHAPTER 16

# LOVE

Caroline started the job and William's life became a blur. She occupied his every waking moment, and he used every contrivance he could to be with her. Several times he caught Daniel looking at him and shaking his head. It was hard to keep his feelings a secret. If he was near Caroline, he mumbled and stumbled his way about.

After about a week, he resolved to walk her home. He heard the wretched son had been coming to pick her up, so there'd been no chance so far. For the first time he could remember, he prayed to God, so that the widow's son would meet with an accident and William would be able to take over the role. Perhaps if she had to help with something late in the day, she wouldn't be ready and he would leave and William could walk her home later.

The days were cold, short and wet—not appropriate for walking—but William couldn't wait for the spring. Somehow he had to find a solution, but no amount of thought or scheming paid off. Plans were formed, reformed, and then discarded.

William was often around Caroline—fetching, storing or carrying—but there was never any opportunity to talk.

Exchanges were mostly single words of permission, gratitude, or regret. Perhaps she went to church on a Sunday? If he could find out where, he could go there too. He tried to quiz Daniel about her, but Daniel hardly knew anything, or at least pretended that was the case.

Caroline was an instant hit with the patrons. She called them all by name and gave of her wonderful smile freely. The men wanted her to work in the bar, but Daniel told them to abandon those notions as her father wouldn't hear of it. One of the conditions of her being able to work was that she would only be in the bar to clean, and never when it was open.

John sometimes invited William to the Shepherd's for a drink and a game of cards when he'd finished work. He quizzed John, but he didn't know anything either.

It had been the same with Bridie and Ruth—hopelessly in love and no way to express it. At least Caroline was younger than Bridie, so it wasn't doomed from the beginning.

Then, out of the blue, Daniel said that he'd invited Caroline and the widow's son for lunch on the next Sunday, and would Tom like to join them? He said that the widow would be away for much of the day, and it wasn't right they'd be on their own. William couldn't keep the elation out of his voice when he said he'd really like that.

"I thought you might," said Daniel, again shaking his head.

The Sunday came and William spent extra time on his appearance. He tried to shave but found he was no expert with the razor. When he was done, he looked like he'd been in a bare-knuckle fight, and wished he'd just left his face alone—his beard had been coming along, though it was still scraggly and nothing to be proud of. He took extra time with his clothes, made sure they and his boots were clean, and slicked his hair down with water.

All morning, William kept creeping up to the dining room to see if anyone was there. He'd already seen to the fires, but couldn't maintain a pretence of looking after them as often as he would have liked. Daniel and his family had gone to church and with luck, Caroline and the widow's son would arrive before they got back. It wasn't until late in the morning that Daniel and his family arrived back from church, but still no Caroline.

Not long after, their guests arrived, and the widow's son turned out to be younger than Caroline. William was relieved. He had supposed the widow's son was older and certainly competition. The widow's son was so young, William doubted he'd be of any assistance if there was trouble. Then, there was no reaction when he was introduced to William, so William fretted that Caroline hadn't even mentioned him. Still, it paid to be courteous, so he shook hands warmly and heard the lad mutter the name, "John".

There was a gnawing fear that even though he was head over heels in love, Caroline had no interest. Already he regretted accepting the invitation, dreading another humiliation. When it came time for lunch, Daniel's wife casually suggested that William sit next to Caroline.

"I'm sure you don't get much time to chat when you're working, so now is as good a time as any to get to know each other. Besides, I think John wants to find out about managing an inn, and I need to get on with the cooking. C'mon, girls," she said, rallying her two young daughters to their tasks, "we'll see if we can impress our guests."

"I can help too," said Caroline, hurrying to the kitchen with the others.

"She'll be back," said Daniel, smiling, "don't fret—we have all afternoon."

William sat quietly, watching the fire, while John and Daniel talked about running an inn. It wasn't long before all the women were back, carrying plates laden with chicken and vegetables. The young girls were excited to see what the others thought and watched every plate arrive, anticipating a reaction.

Daniel called them to order and said grace. William knew to cast his eyes down and be quiet.

There were *oohs!* and *aahs!*, and other expressions of delight over the meal, some friendly banter and laughter. William thought that Daniel had a lovely family, and was delighted to be there. He even forgot about Caroline briefly when he looked at the girls and remembered Missy and Polly—so long ago and so many memories, not all of them good.

"Where are you from, Tom? I can't work out your accent at all," asked Caroline. She'd turned her chair a little, so she was angled towards William. It made him feel special and he relished the moment.

"Ireland."

"That's funny—you don't sound Irish. I can hear the accent now that you've told me, but you don't use the words like they do."

"Some say that."

"How long have you been here?"

"A few years." William blushed. It was too early for her to find out he could neither read nor write. He'd been through this before. Even though he was older now, he was no more able to handle it. He resolved to do something about the reading, writing and numbers. Without an education, he'd never be able to marry someone like Caroline.

"Do you like working here?"

William nodded. "Yes, I do."

"So do I. But most of all, I like working with you."

William was stunned. He hardly got to work with her at all and they'd never exchanged more than a few words. Looking quickly at the others, he saw no one taking any notice of them and was pleased.

"I like working with you too," he said stiffly, trying to hide his pleasure.

A look of concern crossed Caroline's face.

"Have I upset you? I hope not," she said. "I wasn't meaning to be forward, but I did want you to know that I like how hard, and how well, you work."

"Where are you from?"

"Guyong. I was born there. Pa came from England to work as a sawyer in the mines. Ma and my two older sisters all came with him. Do you know that word, *sawyer*? It's hard to say. I always tell my father I wish he was something else."

William thought she had said *lawyer*, but thought it better to check.

"No," said William. "I don't know that word. What does it mean?"

"Pa says timber cutter is the closest thing, but he's not really a timber cutter. He's a *sawyer*."

Caroline laughed and her laughter made William's heart swell. He felt the laughter surround him, embrace him, and bring new life to his spirit. His losses, difficulties and humiliations belonged to another time, another man. A brand-new William was sitting beside Caroline, he hoped forever. Already he loved this girl and was aching to tell her. He wanted to fold her in his arms, protect her, and care for her. Thoughts of regret flooded his mind when he thought of the stolen money. Her father and family might think better of a man who had successfully dug for gold. He had little more to offer her than the shirt on his back, the sweat on his brow, and the love in his heart.

William wanted the lunch to go on forever, but it was finished all too soon.

"Perhaps we should all go to the parlour now?" interrupted Daniel. "I have two lovely daughters and, if we're lucky, we may persuade them to sing."

William stood, took Caroline's chair and held it for her as she rose. His misadventure with Evie had taught him a valuable lesson. Daniel's wife smiled approvingly. He then took Caroline's arm, and she smiled at him in such a way that he thought he might faint. They all went into the parlour and William sat Caroline on a lounge and quickly sat beside her. Daniel caught his eye and winked. William blushed, but Daniel only smiled.

The girls sang. They had beautiful voices and mostly sang English songs, none of which William had heard before. However, they did sing some Irish ballads, some of which William had heard on the gold fields and one or two he thought his ma might have sung.

Finally, with dusk approaching, John and Caroline took their leave. William was sad to see Caroline go and was already planning chores for the next day that would involve them working together.

They stood in the doorway, thanking everyone for a wonderful day. Then Caroline focused on William, only briefly, but definitely purposefully, and they were gone.

"Would you like a whisky, Tom? I know I said you'd need to do your drinking elsewhere, but I thought you and I might have a whisky in the parlour, if you'd like."

"Yes, Daniel. I would like that."

"I don't drink much myself, but I think this is a special occasion, so today is an exception."

"Why is today a special occasion?"

"Why, I was proved right and it's not often that happens."

"What were you right about?"

"Why, come into the parlour and I'll tell you. I'll get the glasses and you bring that bottle. That's it—the one near to the back."

They were seated in the parlour, sipping their whisky, and William was desperate for his pipe. He knew Daniel would disapprove as he didn't like smoking around his family, so he didn't bother and enjoyed his whisky.

"What were you right about?" William asked again.

"That you would change your mind," said Daniel, chuckling. "I thought you'd like her."

William blushed.

"I thought so," said Daniel, nodding. "Well, if you want to know, I think she likes you too—wanted to know all about you, right from day one. I told her what I could, but it wasn't much."

They sipped their whiskies, comfortable in each other's company.

"Don't rush this, my boy," Daniel said at last. "A long time will seem longer if you make the wrong decision and marry the wrong person."

"Marry," said William, blushing again.

"Don't worry, lad. Your intentions are writ large, as they say."

"There's intentions and there's reality, Daniel. I doubt her parents would find me a suitable husband. After all, her father's a lawyer."

"A lawyer? Where did you get that notion?"

"Caroline told me."

"She said he's a lawyer?"

"Yes. She said he came out from England to work in the mines."

"Oh! You mean *sawyer*. A man that cuts wood."

"She said that, but I thought she was joking."

"No, James is a good man, a working man, just like you." Daniel paused before continuing. "Talking about that, you can't work here and live in the room at the back if you are married."

"Why not?" said William, startled.

"Well, think about it—have you ever seen anyone bring up a family in one room?"

"We did back in Ireland."

"Perhaps that's why you came here—a bigger and better place to live, land that's your own."

William nodded. There was more to getting married than he realised.

"I'm thinking of buying a place out near to James. I've had my eye on it for a while. I bought some land in Guyong last year. I think the whole area is go ahead, so I'd like to buy a farm out that way, too. If I bought it, you could live on it, work it, and you'd be near to James and his wife, Philis. I'm sure Caroline would like that, especially when the little ones start to arrive."

"Little ones?" All the colour drained from William's face.

"Ah, Tom. There's a lot to think about, I see."

"How would I pay you?" asked William, desperate to move to any other topic.

"Pay rent. That would do. You could sell what you grow, make some money, perhaps enough to buy the place from me one day, if that's what you wanted."

"What would you do then?"

"Oh, it's an investment, so it doesn't matter if you buy it or not. If you don't, someone else will. I've a lot of confidence in the area."

"Daniel, how would I manage a farm? You know I can't read or write, and I'm only able to use small numbers."

"I know, Tom, but James can't read or write either and he manages a farm. None of his family can read or write. I suppose James is out of the old school that says your wits and your hands are all you need. I've not ever asked him, but I suppose it to be so. Although, I'm sure that if Caroline wanted to learn, he would have permitted it. She's bright and determined enough. No, Tom, your only concern should be to be sure she's the right one. So, work together here for a while, see if the feelings stay. There may be small, annoying things that will become much bigger later."

William already knew—Caroline was the girl for him.

CHAPTER 17

# MARRIAGE

William made a terrible mess of asking Caroline's father for her hand. Caroline and Philis planned that Caroline would be home visiting one Sunday and William would ride across on Kelly. It wouldn't be a long ride, and he could do it easily. If he set out early, he would be there in time for lunch. Philis sent a message to Caroline through a neighbour that James had to bring some equipment into Bathurst for repair, so he'd bring it in one Friday, take Caroline back to the farm when he left, and bring her back to work again the following week. William had been dreading it since Caroline first talked about it, and now the time was at hand.

Daniel and his wife fussed on the previous evening, trying to be sure William would wear his best clothes and take a gift for Caroline's mother. Daniel's wife helped him to buy some scented soap—she was sure it would be acceptable and welcome.

William set out early, in pouring rain that didn't stop for the whole journey. His oilskins had stood the test of time, not getting much use recently, and still useable, although useless in the volume of rain that fell. Kelly plodded on, taking

William to his destiny. William was terribly afraid that James would say *no.* He had no plan if that happened, just prayed that it wouldn't. Caroline had assured him that her father was expecting William and was ready to say *yes.* It seemed a long journey, made longer by anxiety and the weather.

It wasn't easy for William to find his way around when he wasn't going to a town. There were no road signs, rarely anyone to ask, and William couldn't read written instructions, or count well enough to confidently take the third road on the left, for example. He sometimes got away with the task by using his fingers, but it didn't always work. Caroline had given him instructions that he had memorised, involving landmarks. Thankfully, through the mist and rain, he could see a few properties scattered about, so if all else failed, he could ask. But he really didn't want to delay—he just wanted to get there and get the task out of the way.

Eventually, he turned off the road at a place that Caroline told him was called Vittoria, he hoped at the right point. In the near distance, he could see cattle and sheep huddled in groups under still-standing gum trees. It looked like James was a progressive farmer, as there were both wire and pole fences. There was a hut in the middle distance and a rutted, pot-holed track wound its way towards it. Kelly sloshed through an already swollen creek and then climbed up the gentle incline towards the hut. There was an outbuilding too, which William presumed was for the animals, and what looked like fruit trees.

The buildings looked a lot like the huts at Tuena, although the house was bigger and had a sense of permanence about it. The roof, like the walls, was wood and bark. Great sheets of bark from huge trees that he supposed had been felled in the surrounding fields.

No prisoner facing the severest punishment would have a heart that beat faster, and have more fear of the future, than William at that moment. He'd been schooled by Daniel on what to say, but try hard as he might, the schooling wouldn't come to mind and all he could think was that James would say *no*.

Caroline came running out from the hut, mindless of the mud and rain.

"Oh, Tom, I was afraid you had changed your mind!"

He stepped down from his horse and Caroline hugged him fiercely.

"Come on, you two!" called a woman from the doorway. She was a bigger version of Caroline, with the same hair and features, wearing a crisp white apron over what had to be her best dress. "You'll both catch your death. There you go, young James—you help that boy with that horse. Put him in the barn and see to it that he's rubbed down and fed. Then wash up and come back for lunch. We'll all be waitin' for you."

Young James, who looked to be not much older than Caroline, hurried out and took Kelly. As he led Kelly to the barn, Kelly nearly broke into a run, clearly keen on the idea of being out of the weather.

Caroline and William stepped up onto the veranda that ran along the front of the hut. It had a board floor, and the roof was the same bark that wasn't completely effective at stopping the rain.

"You must be Tom," said the woman. "No one else would be so foolish to be out on a day like this."

"This is my ma, Philis," said Caroline.

"You may call me Ma, or you may call me Philis. Plenty do both, and I'll answer to both. Hang those wet things on the wall there—it's wet enough inside already."

She disappeared inside.

"She likes you," whispered Caroline.

"I hope so," said William.

They stepped inside, still on a wooden floor, straight into a combined kitchen and eating room. It wasn't a big room, and perhaps had been originally designed for a smaller family because everything was jammed into it. A fire glowed at the end of the room, away from the doorway. Pots hung from hooks above it and wood was stacked on both sides of the chimney that disappeared into the roof. *Whatever is cooking,* thought William, *it smells delicious.*

He reached into his pocket to get the present for Caroline's mother, and pulled out a sweet-smelling, sodden mass of pulp. It was impossible to hide the present now that he'd taken it out. He'd been looking forward to the moment. It was always a pleasure to give someone a present, but there was no way it could be turned back into soap now.

"It's a gift for your ma," said William, shuffling his feet, embarrassed that he hadn't thought to take better care of it.

"For me?" declared Philis. "Why, that's wonderful! And don't you mind that the rain's got to it—I can fix that in no time. Thank you, Tom. That's a very thoughtful thing to do. It's not often these days a girl gets a present."

During the lull in conversation that followed, water that dripped through the roof in several places could be heard falling into various bowls.

"It's better than going to the creek for it," said James, noticing William looking at the bowls and standing from the kitchen table where he'd been working on a harness. The table almost filled the room and there were eight chairs, four on each side, fashioned from bush wood.

"Get those things out of here," said Philis. "Lunch will be on soon. You young ones, you can set the table, and Caroline—you can help too. Don't just stand there like a lovesick puppy. There'll be time for that later."

The room sprang into life, James removing the harness and dumping it in a corner near to where a small child lay sleeping on some blankets. The rest of the family busied themselves with their allotted tasks. William wished he had something to do and tried to adopt the same uninterested look and stance as James. He knew it didn't work and that he just looked clumsy and out of place.

Young James came back from seeing to Kelly and lunch was served in no time. The family bowed their heads and James said grace. William knew to sit still until it was done.

"We usually go to church on a Sunday, but it's too wet today. I know the Lord might take issue with our cowardice in the face of the weather, but we thought with you comin' and all, He might forgive us," said James from his place at the head of the table.

"Perhaps the next time you come, you'll join us at church," said Philis from her place at the other end near to the fire, where she could see to the cooking pots and to the littlest, who sat in a high chair beside her. William wished that James had made the invitation. It was clear that Philis was onside, but it looked like James was still to be convinced.

*Maybe I can ask Philis for Caroline's hand in marriage... Whose idea was it that it had to be the father?*

The meal was delicious but William struggled with every mouthful. *The next time I do this, I'll ask first. Then at least I'll be able to enjoy the meal.*

Conversation was about small matters—the animals on the farm, the rain and the leaks and floods it caused. At one point, young James asked William about Kelly, but his father shushed him and said, "Now, James, that's Tom's business and not for us to pry." William was disappointed. He would have liked to talk about Kelly. It must have shown on his face as he received a look of concern from Caroline across the table.

They finished the meal with apple pie and cream.

When they were done, the whole family helped with cleaning up, washing the dishes in a tub Philis put on the table, and stacking everything away. James didn't help and William was told to just sit. They both sat wordlessly at the end of the table. William would have given anything to help, to take his mind off the moment that crept inevitably closer.

Then, like a sudden sunset, Philis announced that the family needed to go to the barn to check on the livestock.

James started to get up, but Philis put her hand on his arm.

"No, my dear, I believe you have other things to do. And Tom, we won't need you either, so you stay here with James—I'm sure you'll find something to talk about."

"Aw, Ma, it's wet out there!" cried the youngest boy. "Can't we stay here?"

"No, Georgie," said Philis, scooping up the baby, who had fallen asleep. "Not this time. Come on and hurry up, too. Time's passing by and Tom has to get home before dark."

"Can't Tom leave now that we've had lunch? What's Tom going home got to do with us going to the barn?"

"What indeed, young Georgie? What indeed?" said Philis, laughing, and she led her brood out the door into the rain.

The moment had arrived. He sat with James in a room on a property in country Australia, a long way from where he was born, about to ask the most important question of his life and with no one to help. He'd felt alone before, but nothing like this. Of all the situations he had faced, of all the decisions he had made, and all the questions he was ever to ask, this was the most important and his mind and mouth refused to work.

He tried to clear his throat, but all he did was squeak. He tried to open his mouth, to form a word, any word, but it still refused to work.

"Out with it, lad," said James, not unkindly and smiling.

"I have something to ask," stuttered William, finally.

"I know, lad, so you'd best get on with it—the others'll catch their death in the barn."

"I'd like… If it would be all right… If there are no objections…"

James kept smiling.

*What did Daniel tell me to say? I can't remember!*

"I want to marry your daughter," he said eventually.

"Which one?" said James, after appearing to give the question serious consideration.

"Which one?"

"Yes, I've got three."

"Caroline," blurted William, crimson with embarrassment.

"Oh," said James, "why didn't you say so in the beginnin'?" He appeared to give the question further consideration.

William sat still, terrified and embarrassed all at once. He wished himself anywhere but there.

James chuckled.

"It's all right, Tom. Of course the answer is *yes*. Settle down, my boy—I was just havin' some fun. I'd give you a whisky, but I don't keep it in the house."

"Thank you, sir," stammered William, afraid he might pass out.

"Where will you live?"

"Daniel says he has a farm, not far from here. He said he'd rent that to me and I could be a farmer."

"Daniel?"

"From the Inn."

"Ah—too many people called Daniel. I didn't know he had a farm here."

"He doesn't yet, but he says he's thinking about it."

William blanched, hoping he hadn't broken a confidence.

James must have noticed as he said, "Don't worry, Tom—I'll not tell anyone. I think it's a good plan. It would be good if it happened. It's up to you, of course. Farmin' has been good for us, but I'm sure it's not good for everyone. If it's not too far away, we can all help. Let's get the others back. I'm sure you want to be on your way shortly."

"What happens now?"

"About what?"

"About us getting married?"

"Well, now that I've given permission, we'll work out when. No point in rushin' it and we'd like to know where you'll be livin'. Nearby would be good, so when Daniel is ready, tell us about his farm. It's a good community here, I'm sure you'd like it. I know Caroline does. So, my boy, have a talk to Daniel and let us know what he says."

He went to the door and waved. The others were back in a moment, so William judged they must have been watching the house.

"I must go soon," said William, exhausted by the day and its stress. "I'd like to get back before dark."

"That's a good idea," said Philis. "This will be no night for ridin'."

William already knew that Caroline wouldn't be coming back with him, as she wasn't expected back for a few days. He would have loved to ride with her, no matter how bad the weather.

"I'll get your horse," said young James, hurrying out the door.

"He's a good boy," said his mother.

"Thank you for the lunch, Philis. It's been very nice to meet you. And you, too, sir," said William, nodding to Philis and James in turn.

"What about us?" asked George.

"Yes, it's been nice to meet you, too," said William, putting out his hand. George took it and shook, as though he'd seen the adults do it but wasn't quite sure how to do it himself.

Caroline took his arm and they walked out the door together. The rain had stopped, but the wind whipped the low flying clouds across the valley. William shivered, even colder once he put on the oil skins. He wished he'd brought his possum coat, then was glad he didn't, as the rain might have ruined it.

"Thank you for coming," said Caroline, holding him close. "Did it go all right with Pa?"

William nodded. "He did say *yes*, but I was very embarrassed and glad when it was over."

"You silly boy—you had nothing to worry about."

"Didn't stop me worrying."

"I know. Please come to see them again soon. It'll be easier the next time. I know they all like you."

Young James brought Kelly over, all rubbed down and looking ready for anything.

William nodded and thanked him. He put his foot in the stirrup and swung up into the saddle. At least his backside was dry for the moment.

Leaning down, he pecked Caroline on the cheek, not wanting to make an exhibition in front of her parents, who he was sure were watching, and rode off down the track. He'd be glad to reach home. It'd been a long day and it wasn't finished yet. On the way back, he thought he saw where Daniel's farm was, but didn't bother to look any closer. If he was wrong, or there was someone there, it would be a waste of time and he had little of it, so he pressed on. Daniel said they'd come to look at it in a gig one day, if he bought it, so that would be soon enough.

They did come back about a month later, on a Sunday in a gig that Daniel borrowed. Daniel was driving and, without hesitation, pulled into a farm that was on the other side of the road from James's. *Perhaps it's too close*, thought William, but kept the thought to himself. His heart sank when he saw the buildings. They were rough—the hut with a dirt floor, and if there'd ever been any farming, there was no evidence of it anymore. The buildings and the land looked rundown and neglected. It looked like bush animals had taken possession and it would need a pitched battle to get them out. The privy looked like it was about to fall over. All he could see was a lot of hard work.

Daniel suggested they call in to see William's future family after they inspected the farm. He thought that William would do best to think about what lay ahead—what would be involved in being a farmer and if the property was suitable, and how much work was involved in fixing it. Armed with more knowledge, he'd be better able to discuss his future with Caroline. Seeing the farm and not knowing a thing about farming, William wondered if he wanted to be a farmer at all.

"How much will it cost?" asked William, as they climbed back into the gig.

"The farm?"

William nodded.

"I don't think you can bring a wife to live here yet. You've some work to do first. How about I don't charge anything for three months while you fix it up, then three pounds and ten shillings a year after that?"

William had no idea about that as a deal. He supposed it was all right, as he'd been earning two pounds a week working at the Inn.

"And," Daniel continued, "if you're making fences, or buying things for the buildings, I'll pay the cost of materials and you do the work."

"All right," said William. "Thank you, Daniel. When do I pay you?"

"You can pay me when you come to Bathurst, or even once a year when you sell goods from the farm, and you have the money. You'll find when you start farming, you'll pay for most things once a year when the money comes in."

"I've always paid for things as I go along."

"Works all right when you're on wages, but not so well when money doesn't come in all that often."

"But if you can't pay when it comes time, what do you do?"

"That happens. Most people are patient provided you pay them something."

They crossed the road and, once again, William approached Caroline's father with trepidation. It was good news that he now had somewhere for Caroline to live, but bad news that it wasn't ready yet. In fact, it was a long way from it. He was sure James would ask him about being a farmer, too, and he had no idea how to answer. They drove up to James's place, knowing they weren't expected, and William was more than ready to leave quickly if everyone was too busy to see them.

"Hello!" called a voice from the barn as they pulled close. "And what brings you two out here on such a fine morning?" It was young James, acting all grown up.

"We came to see your father," said Daniel.

"He's not here. They've all gone to church."

"Why're you not with them?" asked William.

Young James squared his shoulders and told them he might have to help a cow to calve. "It's due, real soon, I think. Pa said to wait with it. If it got into trouble, I'm to fetch him quickly."

"I see. Can we have a look?" asked Daniel.

"Of course," replied young James. William thought he heard a tone of relief.

He led them into the barn. The cow was lying on its side, moaning. It was obvious the birthing process had already started.

"Your pa was right to worry," said Daniel. "Is it her first time?"

Young James just nodded, looking concerned.

"Shall I fetch Pa?"

"Too late. Here, Tom, give me a hand."

"What do you want me to do?"

After checking the cow, Daniel glanced up with an anxious look on his face.

"The calf is not positioned properly. We'll have to help her. C'mon—it's not hard, just messy."

He reached in and started pushing the calf.

"C'mon, Tom, I can't do this on my own. Here—push that foot."

Liquid started flowing.

"What have we done?" exclaimed William.

"Nothing," said Daniel. "It's normal—we're just helping. Nature mostly knows what it's doing, but sometimes needs some help. You hold mother's head, young James. There's the lad."

The next thing, the calf came with a rush, liquid and some membranes splashing about. Daniel held its nose up and got it to breathe.

"It's a fine calf. Well done, mother," said Daniel. "Do you have a pen for mother and calf?"

Young James pointed and said, "Over there."

"Good. Help me to clean up the calf and then we'll put them both in the pen."

Once that was done, William and Daniel stood looking at each other, smiling, their arms and legs soaked.

"We'll need a wash," said Daniel. "We can't go home like this."

"I'll set up a tub," said young James. "I don't know about washing your clothes though."

"We might be lucky," said Daniel, laughing. "It might rain."

They cleaned themselves up as best they could, but there was little they could do about their clothes.

"My wife will be upset," said Daniel. "I'll have to explain that it was for a good cause. She'll probably say it's the Lord punishing us for coming out here and not going to Church."

They stood around for a few moments.

"Let's see to the calf and, if all's well, we'll be on our way."

"I can make some tea and damper," said young James, hopefully.

"That's all right. Next time."

They saw to the calf. It was happily feeding and the cow fussing over it. Climbing into the gig, they waved *goodbye* and set off for Bathurst.

William looked at his clothes dejectedly and Daniel said, "It's a farmer's lot. Nature doesn't always get it right, and you'll have to help when it doesn't. There's still time to change your mind."

"About being a farmer?"

"Why, about everything."

Caroline had been nervously waiting for him when he got back, wrinkling her nose but then laughing when she heard about the adventure with the cow. William didn't mention his apprehension about being a farmer and the fact that the adventure with the cow had done nothing to make his mind easier.

CHAPTER 18

# BECOMING A FARMER

A week later, after supper one evening, William and Caroline talked with Daniel and his wife about the next step. They suggested William couldn't take Caroline to the farm until it was ready, so fixing it was the most important thing. As a result, William and Caroline agreed that Caroline would continue to work at the Inn, but William would stop working there the next week and devote himself to fixing the farm. Over the week, he bought an axe, a hammer, some nails and a saw.

On the day he set out for the farm, Daniel gave him some supplies.

"They'll last you a week or so. But I think you'll need more tools," said Daniel, when he saw what William had bought.

"What else?" asked William, apprehensive again that he hadn't a clue what he was doing.

"It doesn't matter—you'll work it out in time. I know your future in-laws are just across the road, but you don't want to be bothering them all the time. Settle in for a few days first. And don't try to get it all done at once. There's a lot of work there. And come back here if you need a break, or just to say *hello*. You're always welcome. There'll always be a bed for you, Tom," said Daniel, out of the hearing of Caroline.

Kelly was laden down as they headed out of Bathurst. The supplies, axe, saw, hammer, nails, tarpaulins and his gold-digging kit were all strapped on and packed in the saddle bags. Daniel, looking sad, shook his hand and wished him well. Caroline, the girls and Daniel's wife all came out and stood in a group, waving. William was overcome with emotion as he realised one chapter of his life was now closed and another was starting.

Nearing the turnoff from the main road, he looked at the valley, appreciating the clearness of the air and the blueness of the sky. There was no doubt early autumn was a good time of year, perhaps the best time, for him to be taking up residence at his new home. Autumn and winter would give him a chance to clean up, repair and build, and hopefully be ready for the spring. There were other huts about, smoke curling from their chimneys, animals grazing, sometimes calling to each other. If anyone noticed him, they didn't wave. He supposed there was enough passing traffic in the area not to excite interest.

There were rolling green hills all about, some steep, others passing subtly from one to the next, and the road wound its way along in typical country fashion, taking the easy way when possible.

Arriving at the turnoff to the farm, he rode up to the hut that was to be his home. It was about lunch time, but there was no time to waste if he was to make the hut habitable for the night. If he didn't succeed, he could always use the tarpaulins, but decided that if he could, he'd spend the first night under his new roof. He unsaddled Kelly, hobbled him so he wouldn't stray too far, stacked his gear and took a long look at what lay ahead.

The first job was to clean out the hut and to let the bush animals know they no longer had free rein. He brushed away the spider webs, pulled out the weeds and creepers, and resolved to put down a wooden floor as soon as he could. The floor was damp and smelled.

Standing back to admire his handiwork, his heart sank. Nothing looked better. It was a single roomed hut—fireplace at one end, table and chairs in the middle, and a bed at the other. There was a door and a window at the front, and again at the back. The windows and doors were pieces of wood nailed together and to a frame that hung from leather straps. If the windows and doors were closed, it was almost completely dark in the room. He'd need to get some candle lamps, or he wouldn't be able to see a thing.

The land had only been partially cleared, so there were plenty of trees about. William found some fallen branches and cut some wood for the fire, stacking it up inside the hut alongside the chimney where he hoped it would dry out.

Unfortunately, the creek was at the bottom of the land, so he fretted how to get water. The barrel that stood outside the hut was empty and rotting, so it would be useless, even if he could work out how to get water to it. He got his billy, slipped the hobbles off Kelly, and the bridle on, and rode him bareback to the creek. The idea of camping beside the creek was once again attractive, but he decided to stay with his plan to sleep in the hut. Night was falling as he rode back, so again he hobbled Kelly and went inside.

He got the fire going—perhaps brighter than it needed to be for him to see—and prepared a meal of bread and cheese. Sitting beside the fire in the best of the chairs, he wondered about taking Kelly and going over the road, then decided that was surrendering too early. The billy bubbled and he made some tea, putting more sugar than usual in the pannikin. He sipped at it and fell asleep in the chair. When he woke, the fire was only embers, and he had no idea where he was at first. He shivered and put some more wood on the fire. He grabbed his blanket from the table, wrapped himself in it, and went to lie on the bed. The bed collapsed as soon as he put his weight on it. He went back and spent a miserable night in the chair, grateful when it became easier to see in the room and he knew dawn was imminent.

Leaving the hut, he went to use the privy, which met his expectations and fell over when he tried the door. He decided to use the bushes instead. He spent the morning after breakfast re-erecting the building and making sure there were no spiders under the seat. Removing the seat, he saw that the hole was still deep enough for plenty of use—one small mercy. Standing back to admire his handiwork, he realised that it might still fall over again at any time. It was a dispiriting end to a hard morning's work.

The next two days were a succession of triumphs and disappointments. The bed frame was useless and needed to be completely rebuilt. Fortunately, there were plenty of saplings and branches about, and enough bark to use for covering. He decided there'd be a bed for him for right now, and another one when Caroline joined him, so he'd do his best for now and redo it later.

It hadn't rained yet, so he had no idea how good the roof would be. He tried to see if there were any holes, but knew it was a waste of time until it rained.

The barrel was a different matter. He tried to repair it but it was way past that, and he'd need to get another.

He was delighted to find some tools in the barn, to add to his meagre supply. It looked as though larger animals had made their home in there and he was nervous about snakes as he cleared away some rubbish. He stacked all the rubbish, and the old bed, outside and set the pile on fire. There was a lot of satisfaction watching it burn, although more smoke than he had expected billowed skyward.

*I'll get to meet the neighbours*, he thought. *Someone will come to investigate.*

No one did.

Then on the third day, the neighbours began to drop by.

"Saw some smoke—thought someone might be here. Name's John. I'm just down there, not far. You need anythin', you come by. Missus sent these. They're only potatoes, but she thought you might be able to use 'em. Said she'll be by to meet your missus, later."

John expressed concern to discover that William didn't have a missus. "Why, you'll be here on your own!" he said, and made no further comment.

"Name's Tom," said another. You probably rode past my place gettin' 'ere. Missus sent a pie. Made it fer ye this mornin', so it's good'n fresh. Your missus and little ones about?"

Tom, too, was disconcerted that William was on his own, but did no more than raise an eyebrow.

In between visitors, William finished the barn and the chicken shed. The shed looked like it hadn't been used in some time but was still in reasonable condition. He just made sure the chickens would be safe from marauding dingoes and snakes, although he wasn't too confident about the snakes. It looked like there were plenty of places for them to sneak in, so he just made the structure as sturdy as he could. *Might be a waste of time without any chickens yet, but it's another job out of the way.*

Then, late that afternoon, Philis and young James arrived in a cart. Philis scolded William for not stopping by.

"Here you are, soon to be family, and you've not even stopped by to say *hello*? Young James said he saw you here the other day and thought this might be the farm. What are you doin' here, anyway? Why, it's been ages since anyone lived here! I'll bet nothing could live in there."

"I'm sorry to disappoint you, Philis, but I think there's been snakes, spiders, wombats and kangaroos here from time to time. I'm trying to fix it all up."

"I admire your courage, young man, but you fetch your horse, come back with us now for supper, stay tonight and come back here in the mornin'. You can do that until more'n a blind snake down on its luck can live here."

William laughed.

"I appreciate the offer, Philis, but I'm all right and I can make do."

"Hmm. I hope you don't turn out to be hard to get on with."

"It's a job, Philis, and the more I do it, the sooner it'll be done. Besides, I've slept in worse."

"Do you need anythin'?"

"A lamp and a barrel might help."

"I'm sure we can do that. I'll have young James fetch them right back for you. Now, the invitation stands, so you come by when you run out of supplies or feel like someone to talk to."

She clicked the reins and went back the way she had come. It wasn't long before young James was back with two lamps and a barrel.

"You sure got Ma all stirred up," said young James. "She told Pa she had a good mind to come back and give you another scolding."

"What'd he say?"

"Just smiled and shrugged."

They dragged the barrel down and put it beside the hut.

"Don't you want it down by the water?" asked young James.

"No—I'll bring water to it."

"How?"

"Still thinking on it."

Young James laughed as he got back on the cart. He passed the two lamps to William.

"Ma says you've got to come to church Sunday and she won't take no for an answer."

"When's Sunday?"

"Dunno. Maybe in a day or so. Do you want me to come back and tell you?"

"No. Just thank your ma and tell her I'll do my best."

"She won't like that. She'll think that's *no.*"

"Then you tell her it's not *no*, it's *I'll do my best.*"

Young James laughed again as he drove off into the gathering darkness.

William was glad Kelly didn't wander far, but knew he'd have to build a holding yard for him sooner rather than later. He slipped the hobbles off and the reins on, and took him for a drink in the creek while he filled the billy. It was dark when he got back to the hut. He got the fire going easily, had some supper and slept well on the new bed.

*Good job,* he thought as he drifted off.

He had breakfast at dawn. His supplies were holding well, and he didn't yet need to go begging to Philis, or to go into town.

He built a structure he could hook up to Kelly to drag the barrel to the creek, fill it and bring it back to the hut. It took a little ingenuity, and he was well pleased with it, though Kelly didn't share his enthusiasm. To make up for it, he built a holding yard not far from the hut, incorporating one of the big trees so that Kelly could use it for shade. The fence wasn't very strong, but it didn't need to be as it only had to be good enough to stop Kelly wandering at night. He could strengthen it over time, if it became necessary.

Working hard all day, he didn't notice the time pass and it was nearly dark when he finished. He took Kelly for a drink at the creek and sat on a rock, enjoying a few moments in the cool of the evening. He shivered. Winter would be on them soon enough and he hadn't even begun to clear the fields yet. Then he realised with a shock that, apart from some chickens and Kelly, he had no idea what he'd produce on the farm. It was time to find James and ask him what to do, although he supposed, like James, he'd have cattle, sheep, wheat and maybe rye.

*Good in theory*, he thought, but he'd never get the fields cleared and ploughed in time for planting. He couldn't keep cattle, because he couldn't make enough strong fences in time either. He might be able to keep sheep, if he got a dog and brought them back each evening.

*Well, at least I can talk it over with James. He might even like that.* He resolved to go to see him the next evening. As he drifted off to sleep later, he thought that many of the small jobs were done and the ones remaining might be too big to do on his own.

He was up early, had a simple breakfast, and took Kelly to the creek to water him and to have a wash. The water wasn't fast flowing, but there were some reasonable sized pools where he could stand and wash himself down. He just finished dressing when he heard his name called, and *coo-ee* from the direction of the hut. Hopping back onto Kelly, he went back at a canter, wondering who was there. It was all of James's family, sitting on the cart and all dressed for anything but work.

*Uh-oh, it's Sunday.*

He stopped Kelly and slid down from his back in a single movement.

Philis looked young, pert and gracious in a floral cotton dress and bonnet with a shawl draped around her shoulders.

"You gettin' ready for church?" asked Philis. "I hope so."

"Why, yes," said William.

"A lie's a bad way to start the Sabbath," said James, smiling. "C'mon, lad—be quick about it. Join us and meet some of your neighbours. I understand you might have already met some, but there's still plenty left."

"This is the best I can look," said William, hoping it wouldn't do and he wouldn't be able to go.

"You look as good as new," said Philis. "So put your horse away and climb up here with us. I've been wantin' to show you off, and now's as good a time as any."

William did as he was told. Kelly looked forlorn as he was put into the new yard. Returning to the cart, William went to climb into the tray with the children.

"Steady on," said James. "Up here in front. There's room for three, and four at a squeeze."

It was as beautiful an autumn morning as he had ever seen. There wasn't a breath of wind, only a few wisps of cloud masked the brilliant blue in the sky, and the morning air had a sharpness to it.

"The Lord has given us a pretty day to celebrate His goodness," said James. He was dressed in the same clothes he wore on the day William first met him. It would appear he was a man of habit, or perhaps one with a limited wardrobe.

He flicked the reins and the cart moved off. Kelly snorted his disapproval and set about exploring his new yard.

*I'll have to build a trough for him to water. Just one more thing to do.*

It wasn't far to the church and Philis talked up a storm on the way, chatting about the neighbours. It seemed they were a topic of great interest.

When they reached the church, William was shocked by how small it was. Philis had given the impression there'd be a lot of churchgoers. Nonetheless, he'd not ever taken much interest in churches and hoped he wouldn't have to take too much interest in this one either.

There were gigs, carts and even some saddled horses scattered about. It wasn't yet time for the service so, true to her word, Philis took William around and introduced him as her 'soon-to-be son-in-law'. A few eyebrows were raised, and William wasn't sure why. Then they stopped by an elderly suited gentlemen with a long, flowing, white beard.

"This is Pastor Tom," said Philis. "And this is Tom—our soon-to-be son-in-law."

"Ah," said Pastor Tom, "are you of the faith?"

William had no idea what to answer. *What did the question mean?*

As he was trying to come up with an answer, becoming more embarrassed by the second, both Pastor Tom and Philis were called away to other matters. Pastor Tom to see to the imminent service, and Philis on a community errand. William decided not to go back to the cart to join James and the children, but to study what he was about to join.

There were about fifty people there—men and women and children of all ages. He supposed most of them were his neighbours and, with certainty, he would become like them over time. Most of the women were dressed like Philis, although some did look like they had more money. Some of the men wore suits, most had beards, all looked serious and gathered in small groups, talking quietly. The children did what children always do—engaged in noisy games, rushing about, talking and shouting excitedly.

He noticed James and the children had left the cart, doubtless to join more desirable pursuits. A young woman came up to him. She looked like she might be around his own age. Her dark hair was pulled back tightly and she had a full face, a hint of humour in her eyes and an easy smile.

"Hello," she said, "I'm Annie. Who do you belong to?"

"I came with Philis and James."

"Good people. Are you a friend of theirs?"

"I'm going to marry Caroline."

"Ah, I've heard she is engaged to be married. Congratulations. We haven't met before, so I suppose you're not from here?"

"No, I'm not. I've been working in Bathurst."

"Will you live in Bathurst?"

Annie had such an air of seriousness that William couldn't repress a smile as he answered, "No. We'll live on a farm near James and Philis."

"Wonderful. I'm sure they will like that."

She paused a moment and went on, "Are you of the faith?"

"I've been asked that before, and I don't know what it means, so I don't know what to say." William was comfortable to be honest with her, being similar in age.

She laughed. "Ah," she said, "I'll suppose that Philis made you come here today."

"She wouldn't take *no* for an answer."

She laughed again. "That's Philis."

"So, what's it mean?"

"It means are you a Wesleyan Methodist?"

"What's that?"

"I don't suppose Philis had time to explain. It's a faith—a belief in God and His goodness."

"I think I'm a Protestant."

Annie laughed again. "That's good. You're part of the way there."

Once again, she studied him carefully, looking at him as if to judge his worth, as if he was to be sold.

"What's your name?" she asked finally. "I don't believe you told me."

"I'm Tom."

"That's a nice name. I used to be called Tom."

"But it's a boy's name!" exclaimed William.

"Not always. Now, you'd best go and find James or Philis. We'll all be going in soon. I hope you enjoy the service—my father will be conducting it."

"Pastor Tom?"

"Yes, that's the one. Off you go now—I'm sure you'll want to be close to the front."

"But if your name used to be Tom, then you'd have been Tom Tom."

Annie chuckled. "No, I'm married—I used to be Annie Tom."

William laughed too. He liked this girl, a lot.

She hurried away, stopped and searched the crowd. She spotted a young man, took his arm and they walked into the chapel together.

William scanned the crowd and saw both Philis and James in separate groups. He didn't know which to join, so he stood waiting until James called him over. When he got near to James, James disengaged from the men and rounded up his children, put his arm around William's shoulders, and led them all over to extricate Philis from the ladies to whom she was chatting.

They went into the chapel, found a space to accommodate them all, and took their seats. What followed was an extraordinary hour for William. There was some singing, and William was astonished at all the good voices. Some people were reading books to follow the hymns. He didn't know any of the words, nor could he have read a book if one had been offered to him—although none was.

But the singing was only part of it. Mostly, Pastor Tom thundered at them from the front of the chapel. William was enthralled. Pastor Tom spoke as though he had a direct commission from God, as though he'd worked out in advance the type of human frailties and failures with which he was confronted, and the words he'd need to turn people back to the right path. At times, William was convinced the Pastor could read his mind, that his thoughts were on public display and all in the chapel could hear them. He seemed to be aware that William liked whisky, tobacco and cards, but that these things were evil and a source of trouble for William. It was disconcerting. William had always liked those things, and apart for some losses at cards, a burnt mouth from smoking and a headache from drinking, he'd had none of the trouble that Pastor Tom assured him was in his future.

*No wonder James doesn't keep whisky in the house. He'd be in a lot of trouble with Pastor Tom—and God too, for that matter.*

When the service was over and they'd said their goodbyes, the trip home in the cart was a quiet one. William didn't want to discuss the sermon with either Philis or James. He thought it best to discuss it with Caroline first. He had no idea his future might be one without whisky, tobacco and cards, and wasn't sure that such a future was the right one for him.

William struggled for a conversation on safe ground and finally asked, "Did we meet all our neighbours at the church? Were they all there?"

"No," said James. "There are quite a few nearby that don't go. I'm sure you'll meet them in due course."

Philis asked William if he wanted to come to supper but William said no, he'd need to make up for lost time. He asked Philis and James when Caroline might be back, but neither of them knew.

As he was getting out of the cart, young James leant over and whispered, "Don't worry about it. I know it'll be all right."

William got down, thanked them for taking him to the service, waved goodbye and went to get Kelly to take him to the creek for a drink. It would be nice just to sit under the tree and think for a while.

Settling into a comfortable place by the creek, William looked around. It was a beautiful place—a clear blue sky and still not a breath of wind. Birds flitted about the tree, doing whatever birds do, insects buzzed and, while wondering if there were fish in the creek, William drifted off to sleep. He awoke with a start, and after looking about for a few minutes, he realised that Kelly wasn't to be seen. He had probably wandered off and now William would have to waste time finding him. It was nearly supper time when he finally located him further up the creek, and not down as he had first thought.

When he got back to the hut, he turned Kelly loose in the yard and went inside to prepare supper. The meat was nearly off, so he cooked all that was left. There wasn't much anyway, and he'd need to get more supplies soon. He could go to Bathurst and see Caroline while he was there, or to Guyong, which was closer. After a terrible night's sleep, he resolved to go to Bathurst—he missed Caroline terribly and was desperate to talk to her. Fixing the hut and the yards had been a great experience, but he was no longer sure of what he was doing, and he could only resolve it by seeing her.

Dawn was only breaking when he had a hasty breakfast of damper and black tea, saddled Kelly and headed for Bathurst.

## CHAPTER 19

# COPING WITH CHANGE

Arriving in Bathurst, he startled Caroline when he appeared at the Inn.

"What are you doing here?" she asked, scanning his face anxiously. "Why, what's wrong?"

"I'd like to talk to you. Can we walk together?"

"I'll check with Daniel. I'll be back in a moment."

She came back a few moments later with Daniel.

"Hello, Tom," said Daniel, concern on his face. "What's wrong?"

"I'd like to talk to Caroline. Can you spare her for us to walk together?"

"Of course, of course. Is there anything I can do?"

"No, thank you, Daniel. Just spare us a few minutes."

"Well, once you've talked, if there's anything I can do, you know where I am."

"Thanks," said William, taking Caroline by the arm and steering her out onto the street, still holding Kelly by the reins.

Daniel called out after him.

"You can leave Kelly with me if you like. I'll put him in the stables, so he'll be there when you need him."

"I'm sorry, I wasn't thinking. Thank you," said William as he passed the reins to Daniel.

He and Caroline walked up the street towards some vacant land, thought to one day be a park, the day's traffic moving around them. A young couple, walking arm in arm, both looking anxious and doubtless dealing with a problem, receiving sympathetic looks from passers-by.

"Oh, please, Tom—talk to me. Tell me what's wrong. I'm so frightened! What's happened?"

"I went to church with your ma and pa."

"Oh. What happened?"

"Well, nothing. But tell me about being a Wesleyan Methodist."

"Why do you want to know that?"

"Aren't I supposed to become one?"

"I don't think so. Who told you that?"

"No one."

"Then why do you think it?"

"I went to church with your ma and pa. I think they think it."

"So, what's wrong with going to church? What's wrong with them thinking it? You're not making sense, Tom. I thought you were a Protestant. That's good enough for me. If you want to become a Wesleyan Methodist, you can. But you don't have to, if you don't want to."

"Pastor Tom said people shouldn't drink or smoke or play cards, but I like doing those things. I grew up in the gold fields, and it's what we did. I don't want to give up those things, nor do I want people to think less of you because you married a man that drinks and smokes and plays cards."

"Let's sit here, Tom, under this tree."

Caroline folded herself gently and modestly to the ground, pulling William by his hand to sit beside her.

"I thought perhaps that you didn't want to get married anymore. You might have even met someone else?"

"Who would I meet? There's only snakes, spiders and wombats at East Guyong. Although I must admit some of the wombats look pretty good."

Caroline laughed and he couldn't help smiling.

"Tom, I want us to get married. I know you smoke and drink in moderation and don't play cards all that much. We can get married in Orange. There's a young minister there. He's not like Pastor Tom who wants us all to follow his way and do what he does, although his own sons go their own way often enough. You'll like the young reverend. We'll go to him. You'll see. It'll be all right."

"That's what young James said."

"What?"

"That it'll be all right."

"When did he say that?"

"When I was getting out of the cart, after church."

Caroline laughed again. William delighted in the sound.

"Good boy. He's right, you know. There's many paths to heaven, Tom, and as far as I know, any or all can be right."

"I don't think much about heaven."

"That's all right, Tom. That'll be my job."

They were both quiet for a while, then Caroline said, "What did Ma and Pa say?"

"About what?"

"About what Pastor Tom said."

"I didn't discuss it with them. I wanted to discuss it with you."

"They'd say the same thing. I know Pa has a whisky sometimes."

"What does your ma say?"

"Oh, she loves him, so there's not much to say. People talk, Tom—about each other, about their neighbours—and it's not always complimentary. But it doesn't matter. Talk's cheap. It's what people do that matters—how they treat each other, their children, and people that are sick or dying. That's all that matters. It'll be different when we're married. You'll see. We'll have each other, and that will be enough for me."

"I'm sorry. I should have talked to Philis, shouldn't have taken you away from work. Shouldn't have worried you."

"That's all right. I'm glad you did. I've been desperate to see you. I'm thinking of coming home, Tom. Live at home and help you fix the farm. We can't get married until it's ready, so the sooner it's ready, the sooner we can get married."

They stood. William was overwhelmed with love for this girl. She was so reassuring, and so sensible. He was very lucky to have found her.

Kissing briefly, not wanting to make a scene, they went back to the Inn—the future clear, William's doubts dispelled and his heart bursting with love.

"How do we set a date to get married?" asked William when they neared the Inn.

"Why, when the farm is ready."

"It's almost ready now."

"Then let's talk to Daniel and set a date for me to finish work. You can tell Pa to come and get me and we'll be married as soon as can be."

They talked to Daniel, who shook William's hand furiously. He asked that Caroline stay on for another week while he found someone else, and invited William to have lunch in the dining room. William was grateful, thinking he might spend more time with Caroline or Daniel, but both were too busy. So he had a quick meal on his own, for which Daniel refused to take any money, and set off for East Guyong.

"Tell Pa to come for me next Sunday!" Caroline called to William as he rode away. He was so glad that he'd come, he resolved that he'd always discuss any problems with Caroline as soon as he could. She was certainly very wise and understood many things better than he did.

He stopped and bought supplies at the first store he came to. It was silly not to have brought a cart, then it made little sense as Guyong was closer and it would be quicker to take a cart there. He also resolved to spend more time with James and Philis, hoping to get to know them a little better, although Caroline would be home soon and he could discuss any problem with her. The future looked good and even some scudding rain on the way home failed to affect his high spirits.

True to his resolution, he went to James and Philis's for supper. They had a lovely evening, and didn't discuss their visit to the church, for which William was grateful. He did talk about what he and Caroline had decided, and James said he would go and collect Caroline on Sunday and bring her by on the return trip, so she could see his progress with repairs.

It was mid-afternoon before they arrived. James had borrowed a gig from his neighbour John to speed up the journey. He didn't need supplies, so taking the cart would have been too slow and a waste of time.

Caroline got down from the gig before either James or William could help her. She strode confidently to the hut, showing no visible signs of either elation or disappointment as she approached, and stepped through the doorway. She came out after a few moments, put her hands on her hips and said, "Who lived here before, Pa? I don't remember."

"It was Michael."

"Yes, of course. It's a pity he didn't leave it in better condition. But no matter—I'll get it sorted out soon enough. It'll be easier done if I'm Tom's wife. I can live here as it is, so the sooner we get married, the sooner I can get on with the job."

"Perhaps Philis should see it?" said James.

"She doesn't need to, although she might help if she has time. We'd like to get married by the young minister in Orange. Can you arrange that, Pa?"

"We'll ask him next time he does the service in Guyong. That's how most people arrange their wedding—choose a minister, and ask them the next time they do the service."

"Well, if that's what worked for others, that's what we'll do."

She looked around at the work that William had done, put her hand on his arm and said, "Oh, Tom. You've worked so hard and it's looking really good. I know we'll be happy here. And Pa will help of course. We'll need to plant some wheat and buy some animals. There's a lot to do and I can't wait to get started! Will you come for supper?"

"I'll come over later—there's still some work to finish first."

"You shouldn't be working on the Sabbath," admonished James.

"I'm hoping the Lord doesn't mind," William responded absently.

"I know, I know," said James, "sometimes we need more than seven days in the week."

He and Caroline rode off in the gig and William went back to building some fences in the house yard, using wood he had collected from the hills.

Caroline became more and more impatient as Sundays went by and the young reverend didn't appear for service at Guyong. Then Annie told them he was attending to more services in Orange, and they'd be better to see him there. She had a service schedule from which she reassured them he would be doing the service in Orange the next Sunday.

They were all up early and collected Tom from his farm just as the sun appeared on the horizon. James had explained that Annie had told him the service was earlier in Orange and it wouldn't make a good impression if they were late. As it turned out, they were late anyway and made a disturbance when they tried to find seats at the rear of the chapel.

The minister stood at the front of the chapel after the service. James approached, along with the other parishioners and in turn, explained his daughter wanted to be married.

"I won't be long here," said the Reverend. "Please just wait and I'll be with you shortly. I'll have a talk with your daughter and her intended."

"What does he want to talk about?" asked William, nervous about his hopefully secret habits.

"Oh, he just has a talk to you about the seriousness of marriage. Don't be nervous, Tom. It's nothing to worry about."

It wasn't long before the Reverend was free and came over to join them. He looked like he wasn't much older than William, had dark hair, a nice, round, open face and a twinkle in his eyes. After being introduced to William and Caroline by James he asked, "How old is your daughter?"

"She's underage," said James. "I don't know how old she is exactly."

"That's all right. Do you give your permission?"

"Yes, I do."

"All right. Let me talk to Tom and Caroline." He ushered them to one side and said, "Well, you two, have you thought about this?"

"Thought about what?" asked William.

"Why, about the very serious step of getting married!"

"I've thought about little else," said William.

"Me too," said Caroline.

"You know once you get married, you are together for the rest of your lives?"

"I hope so," said Caroline.

"Me too," said William, nodding.

The Reverend laughed.

"Your mother and father know what to do. Your father will need to be here to give his permission, and you'll need two witnesses. Come back next Friday, around this time, and I'll have you married quicker than you can say 'Jack Robinson'."

They did as they were told, returning on the following Friday with James and his son's wife Bridget as a witness. All were dressed as best as they could be, proudly displaying their finest clothes. Philis had taken special care with Caroline.

"It's a special day," she had said, "you need to look your best." She hugged her daughter. "I'm glad you'll be living close. I'm glad too, that you went to work in Bathurst. I have already become used to you not being around all the time."

They apologised to the Reverend.

"We only have one witness," said James. "My son had to stay behind and see to a sick bull."

"All right," said the Reverend, "I'll be back in a few minutes."

He left the room and came back a few minutes later with a man he called Samuel.

"Samuel's done this before," he said. "People always have trouble finding witnesses. It's a good thing you brought one, though—Samuel's father could only spare Samuel."

As the Reverend had promised, Caroline and William were married in no time at all. There was a little confusion when it was found that William's name was William Thomas, but the Reverend resolved that by agreeing that many people used their second names, or even a nickname, so William being called *Tom*, wasn't unusual. Both Caroline and William made their mark, and William was grateful that he understood the process of making a mark—he was nervous enough already. Bridget made her mark too; only Samuel knew how to sign his name, and he confided to William that his ability to read and write was almost confined to his name.

They didn't stay after the ceremony, and the trip back to Guyong was a sombre affair. Bridget was anxious to get back to her husband Warren in case he needed help, worrying that young James may not be enough. James fretted that they'd be gone the whole day when there was so much to do. Caroline and William just wanted to get back and to be alone, to talk about their future.

James dropped them off at the farm and gave Caroline two bags.

"These are from your ma," he said. "One bag's yours—just some special things your ma made. The other is some supplies. She said you may not want to be fussed with cooking tonight."

As was normal at the time for people of little means, there was no talk of any celebration. Getting married was simply another step in the daily process of living.

Once the others had gone, William and Caroline stood, holding hands in front of their home.

"It's not much, is it?" said William, looking at the slabs, the bark, the weeds and the vines. Darkness was already falling and they were about to spend their first night together as husband and wife. The hut looked anything but welcoming.

"It's all we need," said Caroline. "C'mon. Let's take our first step into the rest of our lives."

CHAPTER 20

# MAKING A HOME TOGETHER

It took William a long time to get used to sharing a bed with someone. He was used to noise from the ship and from his time with Reginald—it was reaching out and finding someone there that was strange at first.

Lovemaking was awkward and difficult, and it took them some time to grow accustomed to the process. It wasn't something they ever found easy to discuss. If one felt the need and the other didn't, the sense of rejection would last for days, and any conversation about it was uncomfortable.

Caroline threw herself into the business of making a home with an enthusiasm that astonished William. He admonished her sometimes, saying the hut wasn't theirs, but Caroline said she didn't care. She wanted it to be as much their home as possible. She convinced her pa and young James to come over and lay a wooden floor for them. William helped, working harder than the others. It took two days, and he was thrilled with the result. He was already sick of the dirt floor, the ants, the bugs and the damp.

Every passing day found William and Caroline working more as a team. Almost by default, they worked out a program of tasks that involved cooking, cleaning, washing and the myriad jobs around the farm. They sometimes went to have supper with Philis and James but never stayed long, hurrying back to tend to the animals.

They got some chickens, some pigs and a cow. Some they bought and others were given to them. They tried to put the cow in with Kelly, but they would have nothing to do with each other. William spent several days building a new enclosure for the cow. It had to stay in the barn until he finished the job, and they had to feed it by hand. Caroline did that job, as well as the milking, without a moment's complaint. They lost a chicken from time to time, mostly when they forgot to close the door to the coop. It might have been dingoes or feral cats—there were enough of both around. It didn't matter what took them, the loss was always keenly felt.

One time William woke in the night to the sound of the chickens squawking. He hurried out to the coop and was just in time to see the blur of a white chicken being carried into the scrub. He was always amazed at how quickly the other chickens settled down. It was as though they were satisfied to lose one of their number to protect the rest.

It was too late to plant wheat that year, so they had to content themselves with vegetables. Caroline reassured William that it wouldn't pay to hurry with the wheat. It would be a lot of work to clear, plough, tend and harvest, and they were busy enough getting the farm ready.

"Next year," she said, "we'll get Pa and young James to help. Maybe if we save some of our money, we can hire some help, too."

William knew that hiring someone was a faint hope. They had little enough money left and would need to be very careful with it. Not a day went by that he didn't regret losing his money at Lambing Flat. Caroline tried to tell him that it could have happened to anyone, but he was always ashamed at having been so stupid. Of course, there was still the money with Scott and Robert, but getting the money would involve telling Caroline where he had been, and he'd never quite worked out how he would do that. He didn't know how either she or her family would take the news of what had happened on the ship, or on the road near Bacchus Marsh.

He enjoyed being married, enjoyed working with Caroline and facing their day together. They would often skip lunch, having only breakfast and supper and then being so tired in the evening, they would crawl into bed, and be asleep before they even said *goodnight* to each other.

The days went on with monotonous regularity. They sometimes went to church on Sunday, but William didn't enjoy the Sundays when Pastor Tom railed at him from the front of the church. He always knew that Pastor Tom was speaking to him personally. Mostly, he liked the days when the young reverend conducted the service, and regretted that he couldn't read, so he could tell the days to go to church when the young reverend would be there. James and Philis never put pressure on them to come, but always called by to see if they wanted to go.

It was a simple life. Close to nature, driven by it, controlled by it, and regulated by it. If there was too much or too little rain, they lost their crops. They fretted when the creek was low or swollen, when the animals looked sick, when the heat burned, or the cold froze. William remembered some of his mother's tricks for growing things and regretted that he'd not taken more notice of the ones he couldn't. Nonetheless, he and Caroline spent hours in the garden, nurturing vegetables, hoping to grow more than was needed and sell some to neighbours, or in Guyong and Orange.

Then, one morning, Caroline announced that she was pregnant.

William was stunned. He just hadn't thought of children. Of course, he'd learned over time that children would be a natural consequence of their coupling, but he hadn't thought such a thing would happen. Caroline was so excited, and clearly expected him to be excited too. Unfortunately, he struggled to show it and could see the disappointment in Caroline's face. They agreed they should see Philis as soon as possible as, being Caroline's first, she would need to do everything properly to ensure a safe and successful birth.

When they saw Philis and James, William was more embarrassed than anything. Caroline's pregnancy meant that her parents would be aware that she and William were intimate. He supposed that everyone who had children were intimate, but it wasn't something anyone acknowledged or talked about. Oh, some of the men on the ship and in the diggin's had made fun of it, but it didn't last long and mostly others' embarrassment was enough to move the topic on quickly to other matters.

That was when William was introduced to Euphemia, the local midwife. She was proud of the number of babies she had brought into the world, and proud that most women preferred her to be in attendance, rather than any local doctor. William was told she lived not too far away in another man's hut, had a large family—not all hers—and an absent husband. Nobody knew quite where he was, although he'd been seen on a visit two or so years ago. She looked tired and old, and only brightened up when the discussion turned to babies.

Caroline said that Euphemia had gone bankrupt the previous year and since then had lived mostly on charity and the little work she could find, other than being a midwife, and what she could grow.

It took Caroline some time to explain the concept of bankruptcy to William.

Euphemia's sister and her sister's husband had both died within a few months of each other. She had taken in all their children, in addition to her own, leaving her with ten little ones to look after. She'd been buying goods on credit from different shops, and finally a storekeeper in Orange had demanded she pay her bill or sell all her goods to cover it. He took her to Court and forced her into bankruptcy. It didn't seem fair, as she got so little by selling all her things and then she had nothing. Her debt to that storekeeper alone exceeded what they got by selling everything, so in the end, all the storekeepers only got a small part of their money.

Caroline said Euphemia's son helped where he could, but life was in no way easy for Euphemia.

*Then, it's not for anyone,* thought William.

Not long after, the unthinkable happened. Caroline lost the baby. William was devastated. He thought they'd done everything correctly, doing all the things Euphemia had recommended. William had gone from being unsure, to being excited. Now it wasn't going to happen, and he couldn't contain his sadness. Caroline was no different, and also struggled to manage her emotions.

"I think Caroline is too young," said Euphemia. "Her body just isn't ready. Care for each other and wait a little while before you try again."

*Try again? We weren't trying in the first place.*

"It's for the best," said Philis, one night after supper. "Everythin' happens for a reason."

William couldn't imagine what reason there might be, but was glad it was autumn again and he could concentrate on his wheat. He borrowed James's plough and horses, rejected his offer of help, and ploughed every day while there was sunlight. Caroline would sometimes come to help, but there wasn't much she could do. She would sometimes bring lunch, which William would eat quickly, explaining that he was wasting daylight.

At night, after supper, Caroline would want to talk but William struggled to find things to talk about. There seemed little point to him talking about the child they had lost or those they had yet to make. Nor did he want to talk about some of the things in his past. Those things were better left there. They often sat like strangers, lost for words, gazing into the dying embers of the fire, the winter winds howling outside, and the bark and timber clattering as it was pushed about in every which direction.

Caroline sometimes went to James's and Philis's for supper, but William always said he was too tired. He'd tried to buy a cart so Caroline could drive rather than ride to her parent's home, but they could never afford it. Kelly was happy for Caroline to ride him, as though he knew she was now part of the team.

Once the memory of the lost child began to fade, they were intimate again, but it was more physical than caring. It didn't happen too often either, as they were both afraid that Caroline would become pregnant again. William was at a loss to know how to bridge the widening gap between them. It seemed to William that Caroline didn't know either, and they lived and worked as two people with separate lives under one roof.

They had some good years with their wheat, but William was overwhelmed by how hard he had to work to cut and thresh it. Hour after hour in the heat of the day, with no respite from the burning sun, he was cutting, stacking and later threshing the wheat. James suggested he engage help, but William wouldn't hear of it, preferring to maximise his own profits. He was able to get forty or fifty bushels per acre, which he added to James's yield for transport to Sydney where they would get ten or eleven shillings per bushel.

Of his land, he had about a quarter under wheat, so he could sometimes get a hundred pounds after costs. William didn't know what a hundred was, just that it looked like a lot of money when he received it. He and James let the other farmers in the district do all the negotiating, as the numbers were a mystery to them. But the back-breaking work for the hundred pounds made digging for gold look like child's play. The money certainly seemed like a lot but was really very little when he had to make it last a whole year.

William realised that the successful families in the district were made so by large, extended families that could share the work at the critical times of the season. He, James and James's son Warren all had separate farms so, while they could pool their resources, their operations were nowhere near as successful as those where eight or ten grown children were available to share the work. Thoughts of returning to digging for gold, or even moving to mining, were never far from William's mind.

Then Caroline announced she was pregnant again. William had tried to avoid intimate contact since their loss, fearing that he might somehow be at fault, but it hadn't always been possible. Once again, he was wracked by guilt.

One day in Guyong, he met Euphemia at the store, and she told him that she'd heard congratulations were in order. His look must have said otherwise as she inquired how it was going for Caroline.

"I don't know," said William. "I try to do as much as I can. I'm worried, though. I know she is too, but we don't talk about it."

"You shouldn't worry, Tom. Everythin' will be all right."

"I suppose you're going to tell me to pray more often."

"I'd be the last person to tell you to do that. He wasn't much use when I tried to do the right thing and found little in the way of help. Caroline's older now, is what I mean."

"Will you be able to help us?"

"I'm afraid not this time. I have to go away for a while. I'm tryin' to find somewhere to live, tryin' to find someone to look after my sister's children. I've heard that my husband died in Bourke not so long ago, and as useless as he was, it still hurts, and I still miss him."

William thought he'd never seen someone so hurt and broken by life and hoped that such a thing would never happen to him. He couldn't imagine going bankrupt and not be able to pay people for anything. Everything had been so much easier when he was single. Now that he was married, he took his responsibilities very seriously and not a day went by that he didn't worry that he wouldn't be able to take care of Caroline and the baby.

Finally, Caroline was due, and once more she moved over to Philis's. Her mother would know when to call for help, and the plan was to ask Caroline's older, married sister Charlotte. Winter was around the corner and William could occupy himself with the ploughing. He tried to do his best, but his mind was constantly distracted by the imminent birth and how their lives would be different once caring for a baby.

Then, early one morning, young James came galloping into the yard, shouting that William was now a father and he had a baby girl.

William jumped on Kelly, without saddle and bridle, and rode him frantically—more excited than he had ever been. He'd been over the road to see Caroline most evenings but hadn't gone over the previous evening as it had been too dark when he finished ploughing.

He rushed into Philis's yard and all the children were gathered on the veranda, shouting excitedly, "Here he is! Here he is!" Chickens darted about, scared by the commotion. Sliding off Kelly, he strode into the hut and saw James by a doorway to their room.

"In here," was all he said.

Entering the room, he saw Charlotte holding a bundle, which she passed to William with the words, "I believe this is yours."

William started crying, tears rolling down his face, unable to speak and overwhelmed by the miracle of birth. He and Caroline had made another person.

Caroline, lying on the bed, looked tired and drawn but was smiling like she had when they first met. That wonderful, dazzling smile that said all was well in their world. He couldn't stop crying, making him feel like such a fool, especially in front of James.

"Out of here, you two!" snapped Philis at James and Charlotte. "These young ones have a lot to talk about."

James moved away from the doorway and Philis and Charlotte followed him out.

"Come sit beside me," said Caroline, and she moved a little to give William space, grimacing as she did.

William sat, still holding the baby. He marvelled at her exquisite little fingers but was frightened by her redness.

"Why is she so red?" he asked, trying to keep the fear out of his voice.

Caroline laughed.

"That's normal," she said. "The first is always the hardest—they get a little squeezed coming into the world."

"Did it hurt?" he whispered.

"Not so much now, but I'll be sore for a while. I'm glad Charlotte was here. I was nervous, but she kept reassuring us that it would be all right. Ma said not to worry, too."

William continued to marvel at his new daughter.

"She's so small. We'll have to be careful, I suppose."

"For a while, perhaps."

"When will you come home?"

"I might stay for another day. I'm very tired, and Ma can look after me. Are you still ploughing?"

"Yes. It gave me something to do while I waited. I suppose while waiting wasn't easy, it was nowhere near as hard as producing one of these."

Caroline chuckled. "It had its moments."

After a while, she said, "Would you like to be here the next time?"

William was stunned. He's never heard of a man, other than a doctor, being present at a birth. He'd always thought it was a very private thing, a 'women only' domain.

It must have shown on his face. Caroline smiled.

"Don't worry—you don't have to be if you don't want to. Will you stay for lunch?"

"Do you want me to?"

"I'm going to sleep, but I know Ma would like you to stay. Da might even find a whisky."

Caroline had no idea how much the thought of a whisky was welcome news to William.

"I'd like that," he said.

"Give her to me. We're both going to sleep now. It's been a hard time for both of us."

William passed their baby to Caroline, in some ways glad to do so. He was afraid he might drop her—or do something else stupid.

"I'll come back each evening, and you can come home when you're ready."

He leant forward, kissed her on the forehead and left the room.

Charlotte was no longer there, but James and the children were gathered around.

"Congratulations," said James, shaking William's hand.

"Me, too," said Philis, leaning in to kiss William on the cheek.

"Will you stay for lunch?" asked James.

"Caroline said we might have a whisky?"

"Oh, Tom—I don't have any."

"Then I might ride to the Commercial in Guyong and have one."

"I'd rather you stayed for lunch," said Philis. "You look tired out. You can stay the rest of the day and sleep here, too, if you wish. There's a spare bed, even with Caroline here."

"I am tired, but I'd like a whisky more, so I'm not troubled by the ride. It's not far. I'd like to celebrate. It's hard to believe that I've just had a child! Philis, James, I know you're used to it, but I'm confused and overwhelmed all at once."

"All the more reason you should stay for lunch," said James.

Philis studied William carefully, so much so he became embarrassed. Then she chuckled.

"Let the lad go. You've forgotten what it's like, James. My da used to say that you're not fully grown up until you've had a child. Everythin's different now, and Tom won't be able to ride off for a whisky whenever he wants, so let the lad enjoy his last few moments of freedom."

"All right," said James, looking slightly cross.

"Can I go too, Ma?" asked young James.

"No, lad, you can't," said James.

Young James looked crestfallen. William put a hand on his shoulder.

"Next time, young James. We'll go together."

"No," said James, "not this time, and not next time either."

William looked at James in confusion.

"I'm sorry, James—I didn't mean to offend."

"I'm not offended. James is my son and I thought I'd just make sure he knows the rules. He's of the faith and knows what's expected of him."

"I'll be going, then," said William. "I'll be back tomorrow evening to see if Caroline wants to come home. I told her I'd come back each evening and she can come when she's able."

"Good boy," said Philis. "Now, give me a hug and you go and enjoy yourself. Lord knows, you've earned it."

He hugged Philis, shook both the James's hands, patted the children on the head, and left.

CHAPTER 21

# BEING A FATHER

He'd gone back home to saddle Kelly, get a warm jacket and some money. However, he was irritated after his discussion with James and took his time over preparations to go into town. There was a nagging feeling that, somehow, he would offend his father-in-law by going into town to celebrate. Besides, there were a few jobs to finish and at least now he could give them his full attention. In the end, he'd spent most of the day working and then decided it wouldn't hurt to have one drink, so he took a couple of pounds, thinking he might get some supplies, too, and possibly pay the bill at the store Caroline used. Like most farmers and their wives, she bought supplies and the storekeeper kept an account.

As he rode into town, he couldn't shake the feeling that he'd had a disagreement with James, though didn't understand it. James told him once that the reason they couldn't enjoy a whisky was that he didn't have whisky in the house, which implied he would drink it if he had some. Also, Caroline had said James might have a whisky with him. He didn't understand why James was suddenly against whisky, and would really have liked to share one with him to celebrate the moment. It's only once that a man has his first child.

It was close on dark when he arrived in Guyong and there was very little street traffic. Walking into the bar for the first time was no matter. He'd been in plenty of other bars, but he did wonder who he might meet and if there'd be someone he knew to have a whisky with him. If he was to celebrate, he'd rather do it with somebody. Besides, he thought the Commercial might be acceptable to James and Philis because it was run by a man he had seen at the church.

The Inn was two storeys, so it was substantial, but it looked run down, as though the owner didn't care, or couldn't afford to care. It had the temporary look of all country inns—built to satisfy an immediate need. Slipping off Kelly, he let the reins fall and walked through the door.

Pushing the door open and standing in the doorway for a few moments, he was still undecided, unable to eliminate the feeling he was doing something wrong. The room was L-shaped, with a fire glowing at the end of the long part of the L and a bar all along the side. There were several patrons sitting at a table near the fire, playing cards, and another group nearby chatting. A bored-looking barman was reading a paper spread on the bar, squinting hard due to the poor light from a lamp nearby. Despite the fire, the room had no heat and William shivered.

There was a distinct look of apprehension from the card players when William stepped into the room, but they quickly relaxed when they saw he was just another farmer.

"Welcome," said the barman, looking up. "It's Tom, isn't it?"

William looked again and realised it was the man from the church. He nodded and walked to the bar.

"What brings you here? I don't think I've seen you here before?" said the man, pushing his paper away.

"I'm celebrating the arrival of a baby daughter."

"This is as good a place as any to do that," said the man behind the bar. "Let me shake your hand. We've not been introduced, although I've seen you at the church. I'm William, but people call me Bill. I think it's your first, isn't it?"

William nodded.

"What'll you have?"

"Whisky."

Bill put a glass on the bar and filled it. William took a sip and turned to watch the card players. He didn't recognise any of the men, but the group nearby looked like some of the men from around the town—storekeepers and the like. There was obvious tension in the game and nothing friendly about the calls and responses. He decided his best chance was to talk to Bill, but he'd already gone back to the paper, squinting again in the half light.

Not knowing anyone in the other group, he thought he'd wasted his time coming for a drink, as the prospect was anything but a celebration.

Then one of the card players stood up quickly, threw his hand on the table and said, loudly in the quiet of the room, "That's it! I'm out." The group at the table nearby stopped talking, Bill looked up from his paper and said softly to William, "Good. He always loses and he's a poor loser."

The man reached into his pocket, pulled out a pound, threw it on the table and stomped out of the bar, slamming the door closed behind him.

"Would you like to join them?" Bill asked William. "As you can see, there's a spare chair."

"What's the stakes?"

"Threepence, but they play for matches and settle up at the end. That way, it doesn't look like they're gambling, just playing cards. It's against the law for me to allow card games, but most police ignore them when they're only playing cards."

"I'd like to. I haven't played for a while."

"They won't mind. Hey, fellers—a player here if you'd like one."

"C'mon over!" called one of the men, standing and stretching. "Good chance to top up our drinks, anyhow."

William went over and the men introduced themselves as Frank, Nicholas and Joseph.

"Pleased to meet you all. I'm Tom."

The men looked like farmers and their friendly smiles made William welcome. All the tension had gone with the departed player.

"You from around here?" asked Nicholas.

"Yes," said William, "I've a farm on the Pretty Plains Road."

The game started and William found he was well out of practice. Even though he lost, he loved the whisky, the cards, and the company. The men knew each other well, there was banter among them, and they brought William into the fun. Whisky flowed freely, and due to his losing, William was relieved when they called a halt to the cards.

"Time to stop," said Nicholas. "We'd been playing for a while before you got here and we all have to be home for supper soon. You too, I suppose, Tom."

"No, my wife is with my in-laws. I'm celebrating the birth of a daughter."

"Well, congratulations!" said the men all at once, and Nicholas shook William's hand.

"We'll be off now," said Nicholas. "We normally play on a Saturday night. There's seven of us, so you'd be more than welcome to join us, if you've a mind. Stephen can be difficult, but he's not always here."

"Why are you playing tonight then?"

"Why, Stephen couldn't get here last Saturday, so we agreed to come tonight. I'm glad we did, since we met you—there aren't many regular players around here."

"C'mon, Nicholas," said William, "you like the fact that I lost."

"There is that," said Nicholas, laughing, "but I think that might just have been tonight. By the way you played, I think you might be out of practice."

The men left and William joined Bill at the bar.

"Will you have a drink with me?" he asked Bill.

"Of course—Wednesdays are quiet, so I'm unlikely to have anything else to do."

Sipping his whisky, William asked about Stephen and why he was a bad loser.

"He's a carrier here in Guyong," said Bill. "He earns good money and is never without it, but he hates to lose. He's too confident in his ability and always thinks his hand is better than it unfortunately turns out to be. I'm sure you've seen the type."

"No, not really. Most of the men I've played with set a limit on their losses."

"He never does that. He always chases his losses."

"You said he's a carrier. What does he carry?"

"Lots of things, but mostly produce to market. He sometimes goes to Sydney, but mostly to Bathurst and Orange. He was popular at first and he found it easy to get work, being a young man with a gentle manner and an easy smile."

"What happened?"

"Some say he fell and hit his head. Others say his marriage is not good. No one seems to know. All I know is that he acts angry all the time. I think if there was another carrier, they'd get all his business."

They had two whiskies, but when William suggested a third, Bill said, "No—I always stop at two. You have more if you want."

William was the worse for what he had drunk, but was sure he hadn't had enough. He'd not forgotten Kelly either, who by now would be sick of standing outside the pub. So he decided to buy a bottle of whisky and continue the celebration back at the farm. Counting out five shillings for a bottle, he realised that he'd spent most of a pound on the celebration—a pound he could ill afford. Still, it wasn't every day that a man celebrated the birth of his first child.

Saying goodnight to Bill, he promised to come back another day. It was dark outside now, and Kelly looked like he might have been dozing. He was in the slumped position horses adopt when they sleep on their feet. William felt a momentary pang of guilt. He could have at least put Kelly in the stable, though he hadn't realised he'd be so long. The saddle bags proved a challenge to open in the dark and after the whisky he'd drunk, but he finally succeeded and put the bottle away.

All the way home, he thought about his pipe and how much he'd enjoy filling and lighting it. It had been a long time since he'd last used it. He supposed that would complete his degeneration. Whisky, gambling and smoking. Despite the chill in the air, and his befuddled head, he laughed out loud. He had really enjoyed himself and had forgotten how much he loved the three things most frowned upon by society.

When he got home, he put Kelly in the barn with some oats and some water.

"Good boy," he said, "I wish you could have enjoyed yourself too."

Then he went into the hut, and it took a while to get a lamp and the fire going. It was hard to think straight, and he decided perhaps a whisky and pipe would help. He found the pipe and tobacco, but the tobacco was dry. And although it was easy to light, it burned his mouth. A few sips of whisky helped. He was hungry, but couldn't be fussed cooking, so he found some apples Philis had given him. They didn't do much to ease his hunger, and didn't taste all that good with the tobacco and whisky, but it was the best he could do. He fell asleep in front of the fire, missing Caroline and wondering what his baby daughter thought of the world so far. At some point, he was driven into the night by a need to piss, and when he came back inside, he fell into the bed and pulled the covers around himself. The fire had long gone out, and winter's chill gripped the room, so it seemed to take forever for the bed to become warm.

CHAPTER 22

# BECOMING A CARRIER

When he woke, he knew straight away that the day was well advanced. His head was sore, and his mouth terribly burned. As he struggled to get up, he realised there was mud on the bedding where he tracked it in during the night. He supposed Caroline would understand but thought perhaps he'd better wash the bedding before she came back, just in case. No point in trying to explain what had happened, when he could easily remove the evidence.

He got the fire going and went outside for a piss. It looked like it was already around the middle of the day. He breakfasted on several pannikins of scalding hot tea and golden syrup on damper. Going outside again, he set about making sure the animals were fed and watered, enduring a few pangs of guilt when he set the chickens loose and they almost ran out looking for something to eat. Kelly, too, looked agitated in the stall and wasted no time going to his paddock when he was let out. William decided that his excess was probably forgivable in that a man only celebrated once the arrival of his first child.

Looking at the fields, he knew there was the ploughing to finish, but he didn't want to do it now. He could finish and sow the wheat anytime in the next week or so. Then the realisation hit him like a physical blow—he'd enjoyed himself so much the night before, but he couldn't do those things anymore. It wasn't just the animals. He now had a wife and child, and he was responsible for all their welfare—a roof over their heads, clothes on their backs and food in their mouths. There'd be schooling, too, and doctors' bills. All sorts of things he didn't yet know about. Whisky, cards and a pipe were things of the past. No wonder James had frowned when he talked of celebrating in the town. James took his responsibilities seriously and William would have to do the same.

Perhaps adherence to a faith would help him to avoid things like whisky, gambling and tobacco, things that consumed money with little benefit to a family. But maybe all he needed was a little more discipline. He didn't have to be of the faith to deny himself, he just needed to be stronger. Being stronger wouldn't be all that hard. He'd done hard things before.

For a part of the day, he thought about Stephen the Carrier and the suggestion that people might be looking for an alternative. He could spend part of his money on two horses and a cart. He might even be able to get a cart cheaper if it was broken and he could fix it, then he could be a farmer and a carrier. The idea grew on him over the day. There was a problem in that he didn't understand money, but if he did only local work, he'd only be dealing in small sums. Towards the end of the day, he was so excited, he couldn't wait to tell Caroline.

William suffered a self-flagellating dip in the creek to help with his appearance, enduring the cold. He was sure he looked and smelled badly after the whisky and tobacco. The handle-bar moustache was coming along well, but no doubt it would smell from last night. He'd need to steer clear of Philis and James. Of course, they'd think the smell of the whisky would by now be long gone, so they'd be disappointed to smell both whisky and tobacco. Yes, he'd better steer clear of them.

It was nearly dark when he saddled Kelly to ride over to see if Caroline wanted to come home yet. He'd already decided the bedding had no hope of drying outdoors and had draped it around the hut, hoping it would dry in the heat of the fire. So if Caroline came back tonight, then he'd have to either tell her the truth, or manufacture a credible reason. Seeing the bedding draped across the rude furniture only emphasised his sense of irresponsibility.

"He's here!" young James called out as William rode up to the house.

Philis stepped outside.

"We almost sent young James to fetch you. Caroline was worried, but I told her you'd probably just got caught up in your chores."

William didn't say anything, just slipped off Kelly. As he walked towards Philis, she reached out to hug him.

*Can't steer clear of this,* he thought, and gave Philis a hug. She wrinkled her nose as she stepped back and looked at him. She shook her head, but said nothing further.

*Ah, well,* he thought. *Just as well I didn't say anything. She knows.*

"Is Caroline ready to come home?" he asked.

"No, not yet. I want her to stay one more day. Young James will bring her over in the cart tomorrow afternoon."

She stepped further back and studied William, a smile on her face.

"Will you be all right until then?" she asked.

"I think so."

"Will you stay for supper?"

"If I may."

"Of course you may. Caroline has been asking for you all afternoon. She feels like she's neglectin' her husband. So off you go—have a talk to her and then we'll have supper."

She turned to young James, who had been watching with interest.

"See to Tom's horse, would you? Then come in for supper."

Young James led Kelly away and William went inside to see Caroline.

Caroline was still in bed, the baby sleeping in a cradle nearby.

"Oh, Tom, I've been wanting to talk to you all day!"

"Oh?"

"Yes. Pa said he didn't have a whisky with you and you went into town. I'm sorry I misled you—I thought he'd have a whisky."

"It doesn't matter. I had a whisky in town."

"But you don't know anybody! It must have been awful celebrating on your own."

William smiled at her. "I met some people. It was all right. I had some whisky and came home." *No need to trouble Caroline with the details.*

"Pa used to have a whisky sometimes, but when I asked him after you left, he told me not anymore. I was wrong to tell you otherwise. I'm sorry."

"It's not important. How's our baby? Can I pick her up?"

"She's sleeping. Best to leave her be. Are you staying for supper?"

"Yes."

"Good. Have it in here with me. I want to talk to you about something."

William stiffened, slightly nervous.

"About what?"

"What do you think of Elizabeth?"

"Who's Elizabeth?"

"Your daughter."

"Oh. Are you going to call her Elizabeth?"

"If you agree. Do you have any other thoughts?"

"No, I'm happy with Elizabeth, if I can name the next one."

"The next one?"

"Are we going to have more than one?"

Caroline laughed. He loved that laugh. He started laughing too. All was good in his world, and he forgot to tell Caroline about his idea to be a carrier.

William was up with the sun the next day, feeling much better after a good supper and a good night's sleep. He had a quick breakfast, saw to the animals, saddled Kelly and rode into Guyong to see about some horses and a cart. It was the most exciting thing he'd done in a long time. As he rode, he thought that he only became a farmer because it was easy. He hadn't thought too much about doing it, it was just an obvious choice at the time. But this was different—he was making a conscious choice to change his job.

The idea of being a carrier appealed to him, not the least because he'd be working with horses and travelling around. It wouldn't be the same monotonous tasks, day after day. He'd still have to care for the animals and do some work around the farm, but it was as though someone had lifted a weight off his shoulders. There was no doubt in his mind he'd be a better provider for Caroline and his daughter, because money would be paid for each job instead of once a year at harvest. The simplicity of it all was wonderful, and he marvelled he hadn't thought of it before.

Caroline would be back some time in the afternoon, so he wanted to get into town, find out about the horses and a cart, and be back before she arrived. He wasn't worried that it was so early nothing might be open. It didn't matter—he'd knock on doors if need be.

The plan was to see Bill at the Commercial—he'd know who might have what he was after. If that didn't work, he'd see the blacksmith. Many farmers did their own smithing, but most horses and carts would pass through his hands at some point. Perhaps he should have discussed the matter with James the previous evening, but instinct told him James wouldn't like the idea and would make it seem foolish. No, this was the right way, and he wouldn't make the final decision before he talked to Caroline. He'd brought all his money—just in case of, he didn't know what. But bringing the money wasn't spending it. Besides, he was struggling with the idea that it was no longer his money—it belonged to both him and Caroline because they'd earned it together, working the farm.

He pulled up outside the Commercial and was grateful to see it was open. Dismounting, he walked into the bar. Bill was stacking wood beside the fireplace.

"Hello, Tom," he said, standing and turning when he heard the footsteps. "If you've come for cards, you're a day early."

"I came to ask for your help."

"If I can help, I will."

"You talked about there being an opportunity for another carrier."

Bill looked relieved.

"That's right. I think there is. Do you know someone?"

"I was thinking I might do it."

"You? I thought you're a farmer."

"I thought I'd do both."

"Why?"

"Make some more money—farming doesn't pay a lot."

"I agree, but you'd be kept busy doing both."

"I'm not frightened by that."

"I suppose not. Do you have horses and a cart?"

"That's why I came to see you."

"It's not what I sell," said Bill, laughing.

"I know, but I thought you might know someone who wants to sell their cart, and someone who wants to sell some horses."

Bill stopped laughing and looked hard at William.

"You're serious, aren't you? I thought you were having some fun at my expense." He thought for a moment, while William waited. "If you don't mind a broken cart that you can fix, you can get one at the mines. They treat them pretty badly, so there's always the odd one for sale. The horses are another matter."

"What would the cart cost?"

"Four or five pounds," said Bill, holding up five fingers.

"And the horses?"

"You might get them around here. You could try the mines, of course. They prefer them young and fresh, so you might get a bargain. Otherwise, you'd need to go to Bathurst or Orange. Keep an eye on the paper—Bathurst in particular—I often see advertisements for horses."

"That won't work, Bill—I can't read."

"I'll keep my ears and eyes open for you. If I find something, I'll tell you about it on Saturday night here, or Sunday at the church. In the meantime, take a ride to the mines and ask around."

"What mines?"

"There's a few, most of them private and maybe not what you're after. The best would be Cadia. It's a big operation involving big machines and hundreds of people. The machines do most of the work, but they still use a lot of carts and horses."

"Where's Cadia?"

"Through Millthorpe. It's about as far from here as Bathurst."

William was bitterly disappointed and must have shown it on his face.

"What's wrong?" asked Bill, concern in his voice.

"I was hoping that I could go today, but I'd not get there and back in time."

"In time for what?"

"My wife is coming home today."

"Ah. You'd better be there to meet her. It's an important day for you both. What time will she be home?"

"This afternoon."

"Good, you've got time enough to continue our chat. Tom, it's cold in here. Set the fire for me and get it going. I'll shout you a whisky and we'll sit by the fire and talk some more. There might be another way to solve your problem."

William got the fire going and Bill brought him a whisky, as promised.

"Aren't you having one?" asked William, perplexed.

"I've a whole day to get through, Tom. It's too early for me. But you have this one and let's talk."

They sat by the fire and William took it easy with the whisky. He was sure it would have been better not to have one at all, but he didn't want to reject Bill's hospitality, especially when he was helping him.

"Tom, I've a cart out back that I once used for fetching supplies from Bathurst, but Stephen does that now, so it's not used anymore. You can buy that at a good price, on the condition that you fetch my supplies at a better price than him."

"How much do you pay him?"

"We'll discuss that in a few moments. Joseph who you played cards with, amongst other things, raises cart horses—best in the district, some say. He might lend you some horses if you fetch his supplies. If he made a saving, and the deal looked good to him, he might be interested."

William's hopes rose. He might have a surprise for Caroline yet.

"I'm not much good with numbers either, Bill, so I'm worried if I work for you for a good price and Joseph for nothing, I won't be able to do both farming and be a carrier and make any money at all."

"It's a good point. How about you borrow the cart and pay for it when you can, and I'll pay you the same I pay Stephen? You've got time to hop on your horse, ride out and see Joseph, and see if he's interested. I think he uses Stephen, but doesn't like him that much."

"How much for the cart?"

"For a man that doesn't understand numbers, you like to have everything settled, don't you, Tom?" said Bill, laughing. He looked at William for a few moments. "How about twelve pounds? Two hands plus two fingers?"

"When do I pay you?"

"When you can. But if you haven't paid in say, six months, I'll take it back."

"What's six months?"

"A half a year—pay me by Christmas."

"All right. Where will I find Joseph?"

"He's at the Cornish Settlement. I'm sure you know where that is?"

"How will I find him when I get there?"

"Ask anyone—there'll be people about."

"I'm in your debt for all your help," said William, shaking Bill's hand. "I'd best be going."

"Good luck, Tom."

William went out, got on Kelly, and rode back along the road to Bathurst for about a half mile before turning off on the road to The Cornish Settlement. He'd not been there before but knew where it was. The mist still hung about and it was cool, only a very light breeze blowing. He'd need to push Kelly along if he was to see Joseph and get back by mid-afternoon. It was pleasant enough riding through the hills, and he cantered where it was flat.

He thought it an hour or so before midday when he rode into the Settlement and asked a young boy throwing stones at birds where he'd find Joseph.

"Why do you want to see 'im?" asked the lad.

William was taken aback. Why would the lad ask such a question?

"I want to see him about some horses."

"He's the right man to see—best in the valley, they say."

"Where will I find him?"

"Back the way you came about a mile and turn left."

William was good with right and left. He thanked the lad and set off, regretting the time wasted to ride a useless mile. It wasn't long before he rode up to a beautiful two-storey stone house. There were several outbuildings and an orchard. William decided he'd like to own such a place one day and was confident that being a carrier was the way to go.

He dismounted and, still holding the reins, asked a man working in the garden where he'd find Joseph.

"He'll be in the house," said the man, nodding towards the house with his head.

William hadn't thought about how he'd approach Joseph and wished he'd spent part of his time rehearsing the discussion. Leaving Kelly, he stepped onto the veranda and called out, "Joseph?"

It was only a few moments before Joseph appeared in the doorway. William got a better look at him in the daylight and wasn't disappointed by what he saw. Joseph had a big smile and a friendly face. He looked middle aged, with a shock of white hair and a long white beard, dressed like a farmer with a checked shirt, vest, cord pants and blucher boots.

"Tom? Is that you, Tom? Goodness me, what brings you out this way?"

"I've come to see you."

"I presumed that!" said Joseph, laughing. "My question is more, why? But, come in, come in. We're soon to have lunch and you can join us if you want."

"I don't have a lot of time. My wife is coming home today, and I want to be there to meet her."

"I won't ask where she's been. But riding out to see me on such a day must be important, so tell me how I can help."

"I want to be a carrier. Bill at the Commercial said you raise cart horses."

"I do, but I have to warn you—they're not cheap."

"I didn't think they would be but I don't have much money, so I've come to see if there's a way that I can still get two horses."

Joseph laughed out loud, and William blushed.

"I admire your courage, Tom. Not many men would get straight to the point. Come, sit with me on the veranda and we'll talk about it. No, better still, let's walk around to where the horses are, and see what we can see."

They walked around the side of the house and William admired how everything was laid out. It reminded him of Robert's place in Victoria.

"Are you any good with horses, Tom?"

"I've worked with them."

"Why do you want two?"

"So I can carry bigger loads."

"You could start small and get another horse later."

"I'm going to do work for Bill at the Commercial."

"I see," said Joseph, thoughtfully. "Come over here."

He led William across to a yard with six horses.

"I've just started training two of those in cart harness. If you take them untrained, they'll be cheaper."

The horses appeared very interested in William. They all walked towards the rail, as though checking out a possible owner. After a few moments, four lost interest and walked away, but two stood still, watching.

"Are they fillies?" asked William.

"Yes, they are."

"Missy and Polly," said William, quietly.

The horses nodded their approval.

"They don't usually do that," said Joseph, cocking his head to one side and sounding puzzled.

"Do what?"

"Why, take any interest in anyone that comes to see them."

"I can train them—not as well as you, but well enough," said William. "Also, the cart's at Bill's, and I'll need the horses to move it."

"Perhaps you could borrow another horse to move it."

*I could. I could borrow James's, although he's bound to not like this idea.*

"How much for each horse?"

"Well, untrained they're twenty-five pounds each."

William's heart sank.

"Bill said you might make them cheaper if I did carrying for you."

Joseph laughed and shook his head.

"He did, did he? You fellers have had a long talk already. Shame I wasn't there."

"I didn't mean offence, Joseph."

"None taken."

Joseph looked from the horses to William several times, as though coming to a decision.

"This is important to you, isn't it, Tom?"

"Yes, it is."

Joseph thought for a little longer, then said, "Tom, you can't tell anyone else about our arrangement. If you do, I'll have everybody west of the Blue Mountains knocking on my door. Do I have your word?"

"You do."

"Take the two that like you—horses are good judges of people. They're twenty-five pounds each, and you can pay me when you can."

"What if I can't?"

"I'll take them back."

"When would you do that?"

"That would be my choice. So, if I think you can't pay, won't pay or you're not working as a carrier, I'll take them back."

"That's all right with me."

"That's not all. I've a set of training harness that's nearly worn out. There's some work left in it, and you may have to do some repairs, but it'll save you spending money right at the moment. I was thinking of replacing it soon, anyway."

William must have looked confused.

"With the horses, the harness, and the cart, you're ready to go," said Joseph.

"I don't know what to say."

"Then don't say anything."

"Can I take them now?"

"If you wish, but I'd like to shake hands on it."

They shook hands and, as they did, Joseph said, "You owe me fifty pound for two horses, and you'll pay me when you can."

"That's right," said William. He had no idea how Joseph got to fifty, but agreed because Joseph said it, and he trusted him.

Joseph went and fetched one of his men from the barn, who carried the harness over and hitched it to the two horses. They decided it would be easier to make the horses wear it for the journey back to Guyong where William could collect the cart. The horses didn't object to the harness, for which William was grateful. He knew he'd look foolish driving a harnessed pair without a cart, with just himself and Kelly behind, but he didn't care. It was so exciting that he'd come up with a plan to make money, and it was all working out perfectly.

William and Joseph shook hands again, and William set out for Guyong. It was early afternoon when he arrived at the Commercial and told Bill the good news. He left out the details, as Joseph had asked, and Bill didn't push him. They harnessed the horses to the cart, which was in poor condition, but William was confident he could fix it. He didn't bother tethering Kelly to the cart. Just removed his saddle and bridle and threw it in the cart. They set off for home and Kelly trotted along happily behind, as though he, too, was pleased with the results of their morning.

As William pulled into his farm, he could see cart wheel marks in the wet ground and knew Caroline was home already. He was disappointed, as he had wanted to be there when she arrived, but he knew she'd be so pleased and proud with what he'd done that his disappointment was fleeting. Caroline appeared in the doorway when he pulled up. Kelly went straight to the barn.

"Oh, Tom! Where've you been?" asked Caroline. "I was hoping you'd be here. I was so excited to come home. I've missed you so much!"

"Look what I've got!" he exclaimed, getting down from the cart.

"Whose is it?"

"It's ours."

"Did you use all our money? I looked and it's all gone. I was afraid we'd been robbed."

"No, I've still got it," he said, pulling the money from his pocket.

"Then how did you pay for it?"

"I'll pay when I can."

"What are you going to do with it? We can borrow Pa's cart whenever we need one."

"I'm going to be a carrier."

"A carrier?"

"Yes."

He thought Caroline would be excited, but she looked both bewildered and disappointed. It shocked and then hurt him.

"I thought you'd be pleased," he said.

"It's just that I thought we'd work the farm, like Ma and Pa, and we'd be happy here."

"I can't see us making enough money, just working the farm."

"What do we want money for? We've got ourselves and now we've got Elizabeth."

"That's why I want money—I want to be able to take care of you both, properly."

They stood, looking at each other crossly, as though they had found out something new about each other and didn't like it.

"Let me see to the horses and then I'll come inside and we'll talk about it. It's cold and damp out here. I'm sure you'll like the idea better with a warm fire in front of you and a pannikin of tea in your hands."

Caroline turned without a word and went back into the house. William went to see to the horses and introduce them to their new yard. Kelly looked happy to have new friends, but the two horses looked disoriented. William got them some oats and topped up the water trough. He'd have to make a bigger one now—three horses could drink a lot of water on a hot day. The thought occurred to him that he'd need to keep the horses in good condition if they were to pay their way, so he'd have to get extra oats too.

Fetching some more wood from the stack outside, he went into the house to join Caroline and see his daughter. He knew Caroline would see his point of view when the money came in. In the meantime, he knew he'd better keep his excitement to himself and concentrate on getting carrier work. He'd need to see Bill and find out what he wanted, and see storeowners in Guyong to work out their needs, too. There'd be a lot more work when the harvest came in, but he'd need to find work until then to cover the cost of the horses, fixing the harness, and repairing the cart. Perhaps he'd bitten off too much, but he could never say that to Caroline. In his heart, he knew he'd always have to be sure of himself and positive about his new job.

CHAPTER 23

# LIFE AS A CARRIER

William worked harder than ten men. He continued with the farming work, doing it as best he could. The new horses were very useful for ploughing, as he didn't have to borrow James's horses anymore. He did manage to buy an old plough, that he also fixed. While it was clumsy, it worked—and he was just that bit more independent of his in-laws.

One day, when he told Caroline he had a job in Orange, she asked if he could register Elizabeth's birth. Charlotte, who William learned was Mrs Sykes, had told her it had to be done or they'd be fined by the Government, and that William should do it at the Orange Court House.

"What do I have to do?" asked William, nervously.

"Charlotte said you just answer some questions."

"What kind of questions?"

"Oh, who we are, where we were born, things like that."

William was fearful of the government. What if they found out who he was and what he had done in Victoria? He had no idea if the police were still looking for him, but certainly didn't want to fall into their hands by his own stupidity.

"Wouldn't it be better if you did it?" he asked Caroline, tentatively.

"But you're in Orange. It'll be easy for you, you'll see."

William presented himself at the Registry Office at the Court House in Orange. It was a bitter cold day, with a strong westerly wind blowing. He hoped that all the clothes he wore, the handlebar moustache, and the fact that he could hardly speak due to the cold, would mask any description of a wanted man.

The man at the courthouse dealt with a number of people registering births and deaths while William watched on. When his turn came, William answered as best he could the same questions that he'd heard asked of others.

There was no problem with their names, but there was a problem with where they lived, with Caroline's age, and with the witness. William tried to describe where they lived, even told the man the name of their road, but the man hadn't heard of it, so he just wrote, 'near Orange'. William described Caroline, and said it was their first child. The man asked, "Is she eighteen?"

William had no idea, but said, "Yes".

When the man asked for the name of the witness, William had to ask what a witness was.

"Why, a person who was present at the birth," said the man.

"My wife was there," said William.

"It can't be your wife. Was someone else there?"

"Yes—Charlotte."

"Who's Charlotte?"

"Mrs Sykes."

It was that easy. His daughter was now a person, but William was glad to get out of there and hoped Caroline would do it the next time.

It took a while to find carrier work around Guyong. Some people wanted to stay with Stephen, the existing carrier. William reassured people that he wasn't trying to take work away from Stephen, he just thought there might be enough work for two carriers. It wasn't exactly true, but he didn't want to make enemies in the town.

Bill from the Commercial found more work for him, in addition to his own. That worked out better than William initially realised, as Bill had to tell him what he already paid for carrier services, so it gave William an idea of what to charge.

When he wasn't working on the farm, he was out and about carrying. Kelly would look wistful sometimes when he'd harness the other horses and set out early of a morning to find work. Caroline, on the other hand, became very supportive and did many of the jobs around the farm that William used to do, like cutting wood, fetching water and tending to the crops and vegetables. She did so without complaint or instruction. It was as though they'd always been her jobs.

William found he could sometimes arrange to do work beforehand, like bringing supplies from Bathurst for the storekeepers, and sometimes for the farmers. But most of his work came from him being in the right place at the right time. He'd drive around the town and the countryside, asking people if they wanted any carrying done. Sometimes he'd find work because people were angry with Stephen, or because they had a job to do and William was ready and available.

He paid Bill and Joseph the money he owed them whenever he could—a pound here, a pound there. He'd mostly see them in Guyong, and would ride in on a Saturday night for a few hands of cards and a whisky. It was about a year before Bill said he was fully paid and congratulated William on how well he'd done. William wasn't so sure. He didn't seem to get ahead. There was never any money left after he bought oats for the horses and repaid Bill and Joseph, and he was working long days. He could only ever work the farm on a Sunday, which James and Philis disliked intensely.

Harvest time was the worst. He had to cut and thresh his own crops, as well as carry wheat and supplies for his customers. Still, that's when he made his best money, even though most of it went to Joseph. He wished he understood numbers better, so that he could work out if all his hard work was for a purpose.

"Look at it this way," said Caroline, one night after supper, "when you pay the money back to Joseph, all the money will come to us, and you'll own the horses and the cart."

He wasn't sure the cart was worth it. It broke down often and he spent long hours and precious money fixing it. Sometimes it broke when it was fully loaded, and he'd have to unload it before he could fix it. More than anything, the cart tried his patience, but he couldn't afford another one while he still owed money to Joseph.

Elizabeth was always asleep in the morning when he left and at night when he came home. It was the same if he worked on his own farm. He'd start early and finish late. Caroline told him he was missing out on something special, but there wasn't much he could do about it. He had to make as much money as he could to pay back his debt to Joseph.

Sometimes, in the spring and summer months, he didn't get home at all. He'd be able to take longer jobs, and he'd sleep under the cart. It always reminded him of his earlier life, and he found there were parts of that he missed, too.

Then, almost at the same time, Caroline told him another baby was on the way and Joseph said his debt was paid. He was excited about the baby, but he was much more excited that his debts were now cleared. Well, he thought they were.

He'd got a job to take a load of wheat from a farm near Guyong to Blayney. There was a little-used road he could take that involved crossing the Belubula River. It was autumn and the rains had been good, just what was needed for the crops, but it meant the rivers flowed fast and the crossing would be difficult. He'd only been offered a few shillings for the job but took it anyway. It was money and if he took the back way, it would be a quick job and he'd get it done easily in the day.

The farmer's men loaded what they said was forty bushels onto the cart. One of the men remarked that it was a heavy load, and would the horses manage it?

William remarked that they would, they'd pulled more before.

"Good horses, then," said the man.

"Aye, that they are," said William.

He set off. It was mostly downhill at first and William took it easy—he didn't want the cart to get any momentum and be out of control. Missy and Polly did their job well, as though they understood their role was not to pull but to steady the cart.

It was a beautiful autumn day. Blue sky, no wind and a nip in the air. The road was rough, he saw no one else, and it wasn't long before William wished he'd gone the long way. But it was too late to turn back. He'd just have to make the best of it.

He could hear the river before he saw it. It was swollen from the rain and flowing quickly. He'd used the crossing before. It was wide, but that meant there was more time in the water and more time for things to go wrong. The weight that he was carrying also meant that the cart would be difficult to pull over an uneven surface. He sat for a while before entering the water. The option to turn back was still there, but he'd waste half a day if he did. As he pulled into the water, the thought crossed his mind that, since he was alone on the road, there'd be no one to help if anything went wrong.

It was difficult going at first and the horses worked hard to keep the cart moving. The river's flow was fast but because the crossing was wide, it wasn't that deep, so there wasn't too much sideways pressure. William started to relax. It would be all right and he'd made the right decision.

There was sudden, sodden *crump!* and the cart listed to the side.

"Whoa!" called William, pulling on the harness. He jumped from the cart to see what was wrong and was immediately relieved. The water came only to his knees. He'd expected it to be a foot or so deeper. Going around the back, he saw that one of the rear wheels had collapsed.

"Damn the cart," he muttered to himself. He'd thought there was at least another year in it, but what he could see of the wheel told him it might be finished. "Now what?"

If he could support the cart, he might be able to fix the wheel and get it back on, but he'd have to take the wheel to the wheelwright in Guyong. Water lapped at the base of the cart, and it wouldn't be long before his load was spoiled. He cursed himself for all the things he should have done differently and spared himself the problem.

There was no way he could remove the wheel with the cart loaded. First things first. He removed the harness from the cart and walked Missy and Polly back to the side from which they'd entered the river. It wasn't easy, and he slipped and fell several times before they reached the bank. He took the harness off the horses and dumped it in a pile on the ground. The horses watched for a while, as though in sympathy for his plight, then grazed nearby. He knew they wouldn't go far.

Sitting on a rock, he studied the cart. One choice was to go back to the farm where he'd got the wheat, get some men and another cart, come back, transfer the load and go on to Blayney. Going straight to Blayney might work too, but he didn't know anyone there that would help. No, if he decided to get help, he'd have to go to Guyong. The water lapping at the cart would mean the bags on the bottom would be ruined, but those on the other layers would be all right, so he'd still be able to save part of the load.

While he watched, another sudden *crump!* signalled the collapse of the other wheel at the back. All the wheat at the back of the cart was now exposed to water. He tried to think of the value of the load and guessed it at a few pounds, probably the same value as the cart. Yet the cart was necessary if he wanted to continue as a carrier. He'd have to do his best to save it, so the load had to be sacrificed. Perhaps he could get Missy and Polly to drag the cart to dry land where he'd be able to fix it. The water might help lift it up and make it easier to drag.

He went back through the river, again falling a few times, climbed up on the cart and threw the bags into the water. The ones already wet were so heavy, he couldn't lift them and had to push them off the back. He was soaked and exhausted when the job was done. Going back to the shore, he reharnessed Missy and Polly and walked them back to the cart. It was hard to harness them to the cart because the shafts now pointed up at a sharp angle. For a few moments he was glad of the water, because it helped support the weight of the cart as he dragged the shafts down to fit the harness. He'd come to love the two horses, and loved them even more as they stood quietly while he wrestled with the harness.

Finally, it was done. And what a sight it looked! The shafts pulled the harness upwards, as though trying to lift the horses out of the water. At least the back of the cart was off the river bottom, and he realised, with relief, that he'd be able to walk the cart to dry land. Of course, as they left the river, the water no longer supported the weight of the cart, and the horses weren't sure how to pull it with it trying to pull them upwards. Once they were clear of the river and far enough up the bank that even if the river became more swollen, it wouldn't reach the cart, William stacked some wood and rocks under the back before unharnessing the horses. Thankfully, both wheels stayed on as they dragged the cart out, and William was glad he'd taken steps to secure them first. The wheels had been off so often that it was easy to loosen the axle nuts, and he put them back on once he removed the wheels so they wouldn't be lost. Most of the grease was gone and he'd have to remember to bring more.

It was almost dark when he finished. He stacked the harness in some bushes nearby and tied the wheels on either side of Polly. Hopping on Missy bareback, he told Polly to follow, and headed for home. The ride home was miserable as he was cold, wet and hungry, and there was no moon to guide him. He relied on Missy to find the farm and was grateful that she did.

He pulled up in the yard, put the horses away, fed and watered them, and went in to report to Caroline. She was asleep in front of the fire, Elizabeth also sleeping in a cradle nearby.

Caroline woke with a start when William stepped into the room. Her hands came to her face and she almost screamed, "My God! What's happened?"

William was startled. What did she see?

"Why?" he asked.

"Your clothes!" she exclaimed.

William looked down. His clothes were in tatters. It looked like he'd been through a shredder. It must have happened when he wrestled the shafts down so he could attach the harness.

Notwithstanding his fatigue, he laughed.

"I've had a rough day," he said.

"You poor man. Sit down, warm yourself by the fire, and I'll get you some supper."

William fell more than sat into a chair and was asleep in moments. He woke when Caroline shook his arm, then he sat at the table and ate what she had prepared. It was only eggs, bread, cheese, tea and jam, but it tasted like a feast. Caroline was keen to hear what had happened, so he told her while he ate and she had some tea.

"I think you should stop being a carrier," she said, when he finished the story.

"Why?" he asked.

"Well, we don't have much to show for it. I mean, look at us—we're no better off for all your hard work. I'm going to have another baby, so I won't be able to do much on the farm, and your little girl is growing up without a father. Wouldn't you like to see her grow up?"

"I'm hoping to fix the cart and earn enough to cover the cost of the wheat I lost."

"Perhaps when you've done that, then? You could stop?"

"I'll have the horses and the cart. What will I do with them?"

"They'll be useful for many things. Why, instead of being a carrier, you could just carry goods for Bill at the Commercial, and our neighbours. That would only be a few days a week and the rest of the time you could be a farmer, and then you'd be here with us."

William was silent as he thought about it, and Caroline started to cry.

"I'm sorry, Tom. I miss you so! It's hard here, all day, every day, wondering if you're all right, and trying to work the farm. It's not easy, Tom, and I'm sure I'd do a better job if you were here to help. I was hoping we'd have a life together, but you're gone so much, I hardly know you anymore."

William held her.

"Will you think about it?" Caroline asked, her voice trembling.

William promised he would.

CHAPTER 24

# LIVING ON CREDIT

William was up early the following morning and took the wheels to the wheelwright in Guyong. Kelly looked excited that he'd be going out for a change, but was ill-behaved when William fixed the broken wheels to each side of him. He'd thought about borrowing James's cart but didn't want to tell him about the accident yet.

He had to wait for a while before the wheelwright opened his store. He busied himself getting the wheels off Kelly. He saw with disappointment and guilt that the broken rims had rubbed and cut Kelly on both sides. Apologising, he rubbed Kelly's ears.

"We're both having a bad time of it, aren't we? You get to go out and all I do is hurt you."

The wheelwright came out of his shop and William showed him the wheels.

"Can you fix them?" he asked, hoping, against all expectation to the contrary, that they could be fixed.

"I'll do my best. They look bad though."

"I know, but I'd rather they were fixed. I can't afford new ones."

"You might be better with new ones, Tom. None of the spokes look any good," said the wheelwright, shaking his head. "Leave them with me and come back later."

William then rode out to the farm, dreading a confrontation with the farmer.

The farmer was furious when William told him the wheat was lost.

"You'll pay for it, by God!" he thundered.

William wondered at his anger, thinking it was only wheat.

"Yes, I'll pay for it," said William, and the farmer lost some of his anger. He even looked sympathetic when William told him what happened.

"All right, Tom. I'm sorry I was angry. It's five shilling a bushel, so it's an expensive mistake."

"How much do I owe you then?" asked William, hoping the man would give him an honest answer.

"It's ten pounds," said the man.

"That's a lot," said William, although it was the sort of number he expected to hear. "I haven't got it. I'll have to owe it to you."

"I hear you're a man of your word, but I was relying on that money and was promised it as soon as the wheat reached Blayney."

"I'm sorry."

"You'll have to borrow it from someone—I need it."

"All right. Will you give me a week?"

"A week is all I can give you. I'm sorry, Tom, but that's how things are."

William rode back to Guyong with a heavy heart. Things had looked good for such a short time, and now it was all a mess. He decided to see Bill at the Commercial, to see if he could offer any advice. Maybe, he could lend William some money. If he couldn't, then maybe he knew someone who could.

The day was grey and overcast—a perfect match for his spirits. He pulled his coat tighter around his shoulders. There was always the money that Scott owed him, but he'd arranged several letters to Scott, and had not ever heard back from him. He knew Scott wouldn't keep his money and that either something had happened to both Scott and Tom, or he hadn't received the letters. Not that sending the letter to what he remembered as the address in Ballarat, would in any way ensure success. One day, he'd learn how to read and write.

Robert's letter had been lost long ago, and he had no idea how to contact Robert or his family. Anyway, he was afraid to let Robert know where he was, as it was Robert who had given the horse back to its owner. He was the most direct link to the events of that awful day, and he'd feel stupid if a letter to Robert led the police back to him.

William sighed as he rode along. His life had taken some twists and turns and he was in the biggest mess ever, if you didn't count the attempts on his life. Still, someone had tried to kill most of the men he knew at one time or another.

If there was anything he regretted, it was not understanding numbers. He was sure that if he did, he'd be better with money. There was no doubt he was hopeless, but it hadn't really mattered until he was married. Since he was married, the money problems had only become worse.

*What is it about being married and not ever having enough money?*

Bill was pleased to see him, expressed concern about his worried look, and suggested he have a whisky and sit in front of the fire, and try not to think about his problems for a few moments. There was no one else there, so they could talk and it would remain between them.

"I need your help again, Bill," said William.

Bill ushered him to a chair, got him a whisky and sat beside him.

"I'm happy to listen, if you're happy to talk," said Bill.

"I need some money," said William.

"Do you want to buy something else? I thought things were going well, now that you'd paid off your debt."

Bill only knew about William's debt to him. True to his word, William didn't tell anyone about Joseph's arrangement.

William told him the sad story about the wheat.

"I've heard of similar things happening at that crossing," said Bill. "You were unlucky, of course. You nearly got through."

"Nearly wasn't good enough," said William.

"I know, I know. How can I help?"

"I owe ten pounds for the wheat, and I have to pay it within a week. Can you lend it to me?"

"Oh, Tom, I'd like nothing better, but you can see this place. The fire's going and it's still as cold as charity in here—place has more holes than a Swiss cheese. I need all my money to fix it up. I'm losing customers, especially in the winter."

"I don't know what to do, Bill."

"What happens if you don't pay it?"

"I don't know, I didn't ask. The problem is, I said I'd pay it. And if I'm not worth my word, I'm not worth anything."

"I understand—it's how we all feel."

William struggled to stop becoming more depressed by the minute.

"Can your family help?" asked Bill.

"I don't want to ask. You know how it is."

"Sometimes, you don't have a choice."

"This is not one of those times," said William, sharply.

"Sorry, Tom. I wish I could be more help."

"You can be."

"How's that?"

"Get me another whisky."

"Can you afford it?"

"That's all I can afford."

Bill took William's glass, filled it, and returned.

"You could sell your horses," said Bill. "Plenty of people would buy them. They're fine animals."

"I don't want to do that. I'm lucky to have them. If I sell them, I've nothing to pull a cart."

"Your cart's no good anyway."

"I'll fix it. It'll be as good as new—you'll see."

"There is a man who might help. He does lend money, usually only small amounts, and he'll charge you interest."

"What's interest?"

"He usually charges ten percent of the whole loan per year."

"How does he do that?"

"Well, let's say you borrow ten pounds from him. You'll owe him a pound every year until you pay the full amount back to him."

"If I paid him back in the year, what would I owe him?"

"The ten pounds you borrowed, plus the pound of interest."

"Where will I find him?"

"It's John, the feller who lives in the big house just over the way. You know—the blacksmith."

"Is he in the church? Have I seen him?"

"No, he's not in the church. He's Church of England. Never comes in here, either."

"How do you know him?"

"He's done work for me, and I see him around the town. He's a good man, very friendly. Everyone likes him. They say he's hard when it comes to money. You have to pay him whatever you promise, or he puts the bailiff onto you."

"What's a bailiff?"

"He's the man that will sell whatever you own, to pay back your debts."

"Like what happened to Euphemia?"

"Yes. Like what happened to Euphemia."

William finished his whisky quickly.

"I'm going to see John."

"Why don't you think about it? Go home, think about it, and see John tomorrow if you're still of a mind to do so."

"No. I want to see him now. I've made up my mind—it's the best thing to do. I don't ever want to be known as a man who is not as good as his word, whatever it costs me."

He paid for his whiskies and went out into the cold. He got onto Kelly and walked him the few hundred yards to John's home. The house was set well back from the street. It was a nice, two-storey stone home with the new corrugated iron roofing. It looked like whatever John did, he did it well, and well enough to afford a good home. At least it looked like he had enough money to lend William ten pounds.

William got off, dropped the reins and walked to the door. He raised his hand to knock but before he did, the door opened, and a man appeared in the doorway. The man was older than middle aged, with a shock of white hair, and he was very well dressed. He held a pipe in his hand and wore slippers.

"I saw you ride up," he said. "How can I help you?"

"I want to borrow some money."

"How much?"

"Ten pounds."

"And what do you plan to do with it?"

"I owe a man some money and I promised him I would pay in a week but I don't have it. I have to borrow it and I'm told you might help."

"I like your directness. I'm John," he said, thrusting out his hand.

"I'm Tom."

"Come on in, Tom, out of the cold and let's have a talk."

He led William into a room immediately to the side of a long hallway that went back into the house. The room was warm, with a fire crackling in a fireplace opposite the door. There was a desk pushed up against the windows at the front and William could see Kelly outside. No wonder John saw him arrive—the windows occupied most of the wall above the desk and provided an excellent view of the front yard and some of the buildings in the town.

"Sit there," said John, indicating a chair beside the desk. "Where did you hear about me?"

"Bill at the Commercial."

John just nodded.

"How do you know him?"

"I drink there sometimes."

John just nodded again.

"If I lend you the money, what can you give me as collateral?"

"What's collateral?"

John laughed.

"I take it this is the first time you've borrowed money."

William blushed with embarrassment. Why did people laugh when confronted by ignorance?

"I'm sorry, Tom. I didn't mean to embarrass you. It's nice to meet someone who is not wise to the ways of the world. Collateral is something you have that is worth ten pounds, so if you can't pay the money back, I can take something of yours worth ten pounds."

"I have two cart horses and the saddle horse you see out front."

"Yes, they're worth more than ten pounds. Why don't you sell them to raise the money?"

William was irritated and it must have shown.

"All right, all right," said John, raising a hand. "Where do you live?"

"On the Pretty Plains Road."

"Kings Plains."

"I've heard it called that."

"What do you do there?"

"I'm a farmer."

"Why do you owe the money?"

"Does it make any difference? Don't you only want to know if I can pay it back and if I can't, you can sell something of mine for ten pounds?"

John laughed again.

"I like you, Tom. I don't meet many people like you, especially when they ask me to lend them money. They sit there, almost begging. Most don't have whisky on their breath, nor do they tell me how to behave. I expect you'll pay me back if it's the last thing you do."

William didn't know what to say.

"Have you borrowed money before?" asked John.

"Yes."

"And paid it back?"

"Yes."

"Then I'll lend you the money. I'll charge you ten percent interest. Do you know how that works?"

"Bill told me."

"All right. The ten percent is on the whole amount for every year you still owe me any money. Do you understand? If you owe me the money for one year and one day, you owe me two pounds interest."

"I understand."

"I have a document here. It explains everything. I'd like you to read it and sign it, and then I'll give you the money. When you pay the money back, I'll give you the document."

He passed the document to William, who pretended to read it. The trouble was, he didn't know how long it took for someone to read such a document, so he passed it back and said, "I can't read."

"I thought not," said John. "Don't worry—there's nothing in there that I haven't told you. Can you do your mark?"

"Yes, I can make a mark."

"Here then," said John, pointing near the bottom of the paper. William made his mark. "Tom, today is the last day of June. If you pay me the ten pounds by the last day of June next year, then you owe me one pound extra."

"Thank you, John. I will."

"I believe you will. And to help you, it doesn't matter if you pay me tomorrow, or by the end of June next year, it's still one pound."

He reached into a drawer, took out some money and counted out ten pounds before handing them to William.

"Thank you, sir, but I don't like owing money, so I will pay you as soon as I can. Also, do you mind if I have a part of the money and give it to you and you tell me when it's all paid back?"

"No, Tom, I don't mind at all. It would be a pleasure to see you and, provided you don't come too often, we might have a whisky together."

The men stood, and John showed William out of the house.

William went back to thank Bill for his help. The bar was now crowded, so William didn't stay, just whispered to Bill and left. He then went to the wheelwright's to see if the wheels were fixed.

"No, Tom," he said. "Come back tomorrow. I'm still not sure if I can fix them, and I won't know until I try."

"If you can't fix them, do you have two others I can take?"

"I do, but they're a pound each."

"I can't help that, and neither can you."

The day was already well advanced, so William decided to take the money to the farmer the next day, collect the wheels if he could, and take them to the cart. With luck, he'd get it all done in the day. His day looked better at the end than it had at the beginning.

As William rode home, he thought that John reminded him a lot of Robert. He liked men who had wealth but didn't pretend they were better men because of it.

Caroline was pleased to see him and asked how it went with the farmer.

"It was good," said William, reluctant to tell her that the man demanded money and he'd had to borrow it.

"See?" she said. "I told you it would be all right."

"I still have to pay him though, so I'll have to fix the cart and continue as a carrier until I get enough money."

"I know, you said you'd do that. But perhaps when you've paid him back, you can go back to being a farmer."

"We'll see," he said, taking a seat by the fire. He was dozing in a few seconds and had to be woken for supper.

"You missed Elizabeth," said Caroline. "I fed her while you were asleep."

They went to bed and made love. It seemed to William that it had been a long time since they last did so. He fell into the deepest sleep and dreamt that the hut was swept away in a flood and everything they owned was ruined or lost.

He woke long before dawn, worrying about the money he'd borrowed and how long it would take to pay it back. John seemed tough, but fair. Nonetheless, William didn't want to get on his bad side and resolved to work as hard as he could to pay it back as soon as possible.

CHAPTER 25

# LIFE BECOMES HARDER

William woke to a cold, wet, miserable morning. He dragged himself out of bed reluctantly and looked at his sleeping wife and child. He didn't know who had it best—Caroline here all day on her own, or him out and about in miserable weather like this. It had been nice a day or so ago, and that day had brought him nothing but trouble. He couldn't blame the weather, perhaps he should just blame God, like his mother and father did. Briefly, he thought of them and wondered how they were. Perhaps they weren't alive anymore? He had no way of knowing. And what of his sisters and brother, Jimmy? How were they?

He stood in the doorway for a quick piss, knowing the rain would wash it away. The rain dripped off the roof, clouds scudded across the hills, and patchy mist hung low to the ground. An equally quick breakfast of tea and damper, a saddle on Missy, a lead on Polly, and he set out for Guyong. Caroline didn't wake and he was glad of it—he could do things more quickly if he was left to his own devices. Looking briefly at his daughter, he marvelled how quietly she slept, her face serene and not a problem in the world.

Once again, he arrived before the wheelwright and fretted the whole time he waited. The river might rise again with the rain, and he might be wasting his time. The cart might have been swept away.

At last, the wheelwright appeared and gave him the bad news that the wheels couldn't be fixed.

"I can use the hubs, some of the spokes and the rims, so I'll give you two shillings each for them."

"I didn't bring any money, so I'll owe you for the new wheels."

"That's all right—next time you're in town. Don't leave it too long though."

"I won't."

William and the wheelwright tied the wheels to Polly, who liked them no better than Kelly had. They put some old sacking over her first so there'd be no chance the wheels would rub and cause wounds. William still felt badly about Kelly.

The weather was no better as he set out for the river. If anything, the rain was heavier and the mist thicker.

"This is not a day to be out," said the wheelwright by way of farewell.

It took about a half hour to get to the crossing and William was relieved to see the cart still high, if not dry, and well above the water line. He looked down at about the middle of the river and judged it was still only up to his knees.

*Be grateful for small mercies*, he thought, and went to the other side.

The harness was still where he stowed it, so he left it and went back to the cart.

Now came the hard work of fitting the new wheels on his own. He'd have to work out a way of lifting the back of the cart, so he could get them on the axle. Even unloaded, the cart was too heavy for a man to lift. He pulled the wheels off Polly, and that was no easy task either. They both made a big *bang*! When they hit the ground, startling Polly.

"Sorry, Polly. It's all right, you've nothing to fear," he whispered to her.

He measured the wheel alongside the cart. He'd need to lift the cart about a hand.

Looking around, he was grateful that he'd pulled the cart far enough up the bank that there was a tree beside it. There was a solid branch overhead on the other side of the tree so the tree, not the branch, would take the load. A rope tied to the back of the cart, looped over the tree and attached to the horses might be enough for him to raise the cart a little and attach the wheels.

*I'll need to be careful though—don't want to pull the whole lot down on my head.*

Luckily, there was always rope for tying things down. So he took some from the cart, tied it to the back on one side and, after several attempts, threw it over the branch above him. He took the saddle and bridle off Missy and threw it in the cart. Then he retrieved the harness and put it on the horses, drew the rope tight, and tied it as best he could to the harness. It looked awful, but if the branch and rope held and he could get the horses to take small steps, he might be able to raise the cart enough to do the job.

What followed was a very frustrating hour of trial and error. He found the horses' instinct was to throw their weight into pulling something forward, so when he told them to get moving, they'd try to get the cart moving and keep it that way. The first time he called them to move, they nearly upended the cart and he startled them by calling, "Whoa!", so loudly he also startled himself. He eventually solved the problem by being in front of them and getting them to move forward only a little. Then, he'd go and try to attach the wheel. It worked after two tries with the first wheel and on the first with the second.

The job was finally done, and so was William. As far as he could tell, the wheels were attached properly, and the cart was again useable. He checked the front wheels— they looked all right, and he supposed that without the weight of a load, they'd at least get him back home. There was the river to cross, of course, but he didn't expect any problem, again because the cart no longer had a load.

He attached the harness and manoeuvred the cart around, so he was again poised to cross the river. The rain was still misting, the wind had picked up a little, and he was now cool after his hard work. He pulled his oilskin on, more for warmth than anything else, because his clothes were soaked under it.

"All right, Missy and Polly. We're about to do this again. I expect you'll be happier this time, without a load, but let's see."

William flicked the reins and eased the cart into the river. The water lapped the bottom of the cart, so it had risen a little. Of course, he'd forgotten that now being unloaded it was more likely to float.

*If it's not one damn thing, it's another.*

The current was strong, and he could feel the cart drift a little sideways from time to time. His pulse raced and his heart skipped beating a few times when the cart lifted, but each time it caught on something in the river and held its ground.

He couldn't remember a time in his life when he'd been more relieved than when they reached the other side and were free of the river. Stopping briefly, he muttered a silent prayer to whichever God had helped him. Exhaustion threatened to overwhelm him so he shook off his tiredness, flicked the reins, and told Missy and Polly they were headed for home.

It wasn't an easy trip back and the gathering darkness made the road indistinct. Like the previous night, he relied on the horses to find their way home and they didn't let him down.

As he pulled into the yard, Caroline was framed in the doorway.

"Oh, Tom!" she exclaimed. "I've been so worried—I didn't think it would take all day!"

"I'll be there in a moment," he said. "I'll see to the horses first."

The rain hadn't let up all day, so he put Missy, Polly and Kelly in the barn with some oats, hay and water. He stopped for a moment to say some special words of thanks to Missy and Polly, and to rub them down and make them comfortable. There was no doubt he loved the horses now and would keep them for life. Kelly looked a little older, but he was still a good and reliable horse. On the other hand, he could expect fifteen to twenty years from Missy and Polly and realised he should really think about mating them soon, when the spring came. If not this year, then perhaps the next.

When he went inside, Caroline already had some supper ready. He collapsed into the chair and ate like a man who hadn't eaten for a week. Caroline sat and watched, like she was waiting for him to finish, knowing he couldn't hold a conversation until he was done.

William thanked her for the supper, and got up to sit in a chair by the stove, where he sipped hot, sweetened tea from a pannikin. He thought to get his pipe, then thought better of it.

On the rare times he used it at home, it made the room smell and it always took a day or so for the lingering odour to leave.

"Can I sit beside you?" asked Caroline.

She pulled the other chair closer, resting her hand on his knee and her head on his shoulder. It thrilled him as he thought how much he enjoyed her gesture and the moment.

"Was it difficult?" she asked.

"It wasn't easy."

"I was going to come with you, but you were gone when I woke."

"What about Elizabeth?"

"She has to learn about being the daughter of a farmer sooner or later."

"It didn't stop raining all day."

"I thought about that. I would have wrapped her in your coat."

"Why did you want to come?"

"I want us to do things together. I'm sure you could have used another pair of hands."

"Another pair of men's hands, perhaps."

He saw the quick look of hurt but didn't know what to say to fix it. What he said was the truth.

"I could have made some tea, or even cooked something to eat."

"It's done now."

"Yes, it is, isn't it?"

Caroline took her head off his shoulder, her hand off his knee, and sat quietly.

As tired as he was, William wanted to talk.

*It would be good for us*, he thought, but wasn't sure what to say.

"I haven't seen your ma and pa in a while," he said finally. "Are they well?"

"I saw them this morning. When I woke and you were gone, I thought I'd go to see them."

The food and the warmth in the room began to take their toll, and William started dozing and snoring in the chair.

Caroline shook him awake.

"You best go to bed," she said. "You've had a long day."

William got up, took off his clothes, pulled on his night shirt and fell into bed.

When he woke, he could see glimpses of daylight through the walls, so knew that dawn had probably already happened. Caroline slept quietly beside him, so he took a moment to think about their conversation from last night. He had been working too hard, spending too much time out and about, neglecting his farm and family. Perhaps he should do more work for neighbours and friends, and it would be local too, so there'd be less wear and tear on the cart. He owed John eleven pounds but didn't have to pay it until next winter. Still, he wanted to earn the money and pay it back as soon as he could.

There was so much to do, he hardly knew where to start. If he continued to do carrying, then the wheelwright should take a look at the cart and make sure nothing else was wrong with it. William was confident it was all right, but it didn't hurt to make sure. He'd lost ten pounds to the farmer because he hadn't been careful. The farmer wanted his ten pounds within the week, so he'd be better to give that to him sooner rather than later. The ploughing needed doing, the hut needed fixing, and the horses needed a bigger yard.

"Good morning," said Caroline, sleepily.

"Good morning."

"What are you doing today?"

"I thought I'd do some ploughing and take the cart into town to make sure it's all right."

"When are you going to give the farmer his money?"

"What do you mean?" asked William, cautiously.

"I saw some extra money in the jar and wondered about it. My brother said yesterday that he'd heard in town the farmer was angry and demanded his money within a week. He heard you'd had to borrow some and wondered why you didn't ask him?"

William was silent. He hadn't told a lie, but he hadn't told the truth either.

"Are you angry?" he asked.

"No—more disappointed. When I heard, I thought it might have been a problem we could solve together. We could have asked our family. They might have given it to us."

"Given it?"

"All right, loaned it."

"If I couldn't get it somewhere else, then I would have asked your family."

"Where did you get it?"

"John."

"The blacksmith?"

"Yes."

"They say he's a hard man."

"He seemed nice enough."

"They say he is until you can't pay him back, then he's hard and heartless."

"Well, we'll see. It's not a lot of money."

"It's always a lot of money when you don't have it."

After a few moments, Caroline said, "You could give it back, and get the money from Pa."

"That would make no sense. I already owe a pound for borrowing it for a year, and I have to pay that anyway."

William had to pay it back as soon as possible. He didn't care about the year anymore and was afraid he'd made a terrible mistake.

CHAPTER 26

# IN DEBT

William decided not to have the cart checked out that day, but to do so when he next took it to Guyong.

After breakfast, he worked around the farm for the morning. He tried to plough, but the soil was too wet, so it would have to wait for another day. For the next few hours, he did a little of everything—fences, repairs to the hut and barn, checking the cart again and making sure the animals were in good order. Caroline worked with him where she could. They had lunch together in the early afternoon, and he played with Elizabeth. He wasn't sure if she liked him. She seemed nervous at first, and Caroline said it was only that Elizabeth saw more of her uncle and grandfather than she did of William.

Once lunch was done, William said he'd take the farmer's money to him, then call by the Commercial to see if he could find any carrying work. He'd said to Caroline that his best chances came from word of mouth and since people in the town were talking about his accident with the wheat, then he'd need to make sure people heard the right story.

Caroline just nodded and told him she'd see him when he came home. He wanted to tell her how badly he felt about taking out the loan without talking with her, but didn't know how, so thought it was better to leave it. All the money was kept in a big jar on the shelf in the corner, and it was easy to identify the farmer's money. He'd tied a piece of string around it, so he took that and another pound besides, for whisky at the Commercial. He didn't go to the Commercial often enough to run an account there, and Bill had never offered.

It didn't take him long to saddle Kelly and climb into the saddle for the trip. Waving *goodbye* to Caroline, her standing in the doorway with Elizabeth as he rode out of the yard, reminded him for a moment of when he left home in Ireland. He was saddened by the memory.

*It's nothing like that*, he admonished himself. *I'll be home in a few hours.*

The cool of the evening wasn't far off, a stiff wind blew, and the sun cast long shadows from the trees. He'd be lucky to make it to the farmer's and to Guyong before nightfall, so he hurried Kelly along, making him canter for the first time in a long time. Pulling his coat tightly around his shoulders, he wished he'd set out earlier.

The farmer was pleased to get his money, but didn't make a fuss, as though he'd expected William would pay him. William thought it might be a compliment, and that people thought him a man of his word.

He thought about it all the way to the Commercial, and was startled to hear and see so many people there when he arrived.

Stopping out front, he slipped to the ground and let the reins fall. He pushed the door open and stepped inside. There was quite a crowd, a few of whom turned to look and acknowledge him.

"Look who's arrived!" called Nicholas, sitting at a table not far from the door. "Hello, Tom. Do you want to play a few hands?"

It was hard to hear him over the general din.

"Don't mind if I do. Let me see to my horse first—I was only stopping by, but now I'll stay for a few hands. What's happening? Why so many people?"

"It's Saturday."

"Of course—I'd forgotten. I'll be back."

He went out and took Kelly to the stables out back. There was no one there, and he found an empty stall. He took the saddle off and settled Kelly with some oats and water, and then went around the front and back inside.

Shaking hands with Nicholas and Frank, he asked after Joseph.

"He's all right as far as I know. Not here tonight, but meet Mick."

"Mick," said William, shaking hands, "Tom."

"I heard," said Mick, tersely. Nicholas looked at him in bewilderment but didn't say anything.

"I'll get a whisky first," said William.

"Get one for us all. We've not had any yet."

"Why so slow?"

"Just got 'ere."

William went to the bar, got four whiskies and paid five shillings for them.

*Only four for me tonight. Unless I win at cards, for a change.*

They played a few hands and not much changed. Frank went to get more whisky, and Nicholas asked William, "Carrying business all right?"

"Carrying?" asked Mick, looking up quickly. "You're a carrier?"

"Sometimes."

"I need some supplies brought out from Orange. I've been chasin' Stephen for a week and gettin' nowhere. If you want the job, it's yours."

"Where will I find you?"

"Why do you want to find me?"

"So's you can tell me what you want, where to get it, and where to take it."

Mick laughed and William was taken aback. He thought Mick the difficult sort that never laughed.

"I'm on the Orange Road, about two miles out of town. Come by Monday mornin' and we'll go together."

"How much will you pay?" asked William.

"How much do you charge?"

Mick was looking at him intently. William noticed Nicholas was holding up all his fingers, but Mick didn't notice. Luckily, William knew the number.

"Ten shillings," he said.

"Good. Done," said Mick, reaching to shake hands. "I'll see you Monday in the mornin'."

Frank came back with the whisky.

"Let's get to the cards," said Nicholas.

William took it carefully.

*Nothing rash*, he kept telling himself.

They played until they'd all had four whiskies and Mick said he had to go. William was relieved.

"I have to go too," he told them.

Everyone agreed it was time to finish, so they settled up. William was pleased he'd won a few shillings.

*All in all, it was a great night—I've got a carrying job, won some money, and had some whisky. Not all bad.*

Caroline was asleep when he got home and he tried not to wake her as he made some supper, but it was impossible in the one-roomed hut. She got up, sat him in a chair, and cooked some supper for him. He couldn't help being excited about the evening and told Caroline it might be the way for him to secure work and have some fun. She didn't say much, so he took that as agreement.

She was up early the next morning and asked if he was coming to church. He said he had too much to do around the farm and he would likely come the next week. James, Philis and the children came by not long after, loaded Caroline and Elizabeth onto their cart, and headed off to church. James and Philis were a little cool, but Caroline chatted gaily, so William decided he was imagining things and set to work mending fences, gathering more firewood, seeing to the chickens and animals, and doing some more ploughing.

*There's always something to do. I know the Lord would understand that, as a family man, I have responsibilities, things that have to be done, that wouldn't get done if I went to church.*

It was bitterly cold outside, with a strong southerly wind blowing. Grey clouds fled across the sky, pushed along by the wind. A drizzle started, and he thought it might turn to snow before the day was done. His hands felt like blocks of ice most of the time and he was glad he'd decided to do the ploughing last. It meant that when it was too cold and too uncomfortable, he could stop and that would be it for the day. At one point he noticed smoke from the chimney back at the hut and knew Caroline must be home, so he figured to do a little more ploughing and then give it away.

He used both horses with the plough, as it meant he could work faster. The horses always worked well as a team, regardless of what they did, and they seemed not the least tired, so he thought he'd work on regardless of the weather. Caroline didn't come down, but he hadn't expected she would. In addition to the weather being so awful, she was probably miffed that he was working on a Sunday, when there were six other days set aside for working and the seventh for God and family. There was only a little more to do when the lack of daylight beat him, and it was time to put the plough and the horses away.

As he went into the hut, he hoped there wouldn't be a problem. He was tired, cold and hungry after a long day. Notwithstanding his apprehension, Caroline was in a happy mood and chatted about who she had seen and what she had learned at church. She wasn't yet big with their next child and as she laughed and chatted about her day, he thought how much he loved her.

They finished supper, put Elizabeth to bed, and sat by the fire, drinking pannikins of tea. Caroline told him she'd chatted with her pa and he was happy to come and help Tom to build another room on the hut. She thought they'd need it with another child on the way. William confided that one day he'd like to own a stone house like Joseph.

"We need to do things slowly, Tom. I worry that you're trying to do too much, too soon. We'll have a big house one day, even if it's a hut like this one with more rooms."

"I worry that I don't do enough. I came to Australia looking for gold, but I haven't found much. I do see people who came with nothing, like me, and didn't find gold either, but still live in fine houses. If they can do it, why can't I?"

"I don't know, Tom. Maybe they came with brothers and sisters and maybe they had an education. I don't know why, Tom. All I know is I want us to be happy."

"Aren't you happy?"

"Yes, I am. Of course I am."

"What do you want to change then?"

"I think you work too hard. Ma says she thinks the Sabbath isn't a day when the Lord says you can't work, she thinks it's a day when you shouldn't work."

"Why does she say that?"

"She says you work too hard and there's no time left for your family. She thinks you should come to church with us on Sundays. You can meet people there, too. Annie asked after you this morning."

"And how is Annie?" asked William, not interested in the answer, only wasting time while he thought about what his mother-in-law had said.

"She's well. She's excited we're having another baby. You are too, aren't you?"

"Yes, I am, but it's another mouth to feed and as you say, we'll have to do more here to allow for more people."

Heavy rain began to fall, and it was hard to continue the conversation with the noise of it hitting the bark roof. There was a *plunk! plunk!* where water found its way through the roof and onto the wooden floor. Caroline found a cooking pot and put it under the drip. The sound became a *plonk! plonk!*

The rain stopped and William could almost feel the stillness. "It might snow soon," he said.

"I think so too. When will I ask Pa to come over and help build another room?"

"We've a few months yet, and I want to do as much carrying as I can to pay John."

"We might need to hurry—Ma thinks this one might come early," said Caroline, patting her stomach.

"How would she know that?"

"She didn't say, just said she thought it might."

CHAPTER 27

# MORE TALK OF GOLD

Philis was right—his second daughter came early. William was proud to name her Margaret, after his mother.

The growing season had been good, and William had a lot of wheat to harvest. Carrying had been good, too, and he was able to pay John back before Christmas. He was very excited when he made a payment and John said, "If you can give me another shilling, you will have paid off your debt."

William was glad to do it and couldn't wait to get home and tell Caroline that the debt was paid, and they could both stop worrying. He told Caroline that they might run accounts in the stores, like everyone did, but he'd never borrow again. It wasn't the interest that he paid, it was owing the money and that whoever he borrowed from, could come and take things to cover the debt if they thought William couldn't pay.

It was a hot summer, and William stayed around the hut as much as he could to help Caroline. She was big with her child, and couldn't do a lot, so William looked after Elizabeth and cooked the meals, as well as working around the farm. There was little time for carrying, and little need for it now the debt was repaid.

Philis suggested Caroline come and stay with her and James when the baby was due. William was relieved and glad that Caroline accepted. He was more than happy for Euphemia and Philis to manage the delivery and for him to stay at home and look after Elizabeth. Elizabeth proved to be a great companion. She went everywhere with William, no matter the task. Caroline was gone for only a week when young James came down to tell him he had another daughter. It was close on supper time, so he didn't go over and see Caroline until the next morning. She astonished him by being ready to come home straight away, and he thought he was quite the family man as he drove home in the cart, his oldest daughter sitting on the bench beside him, and his newest in his wife's arms.

Elizabeth was taken with the newest addition to the household and mastered '*baby*' quickly, although there were noticeable twinges of jealousy when she realised she was no longer the sole centre of attention. There was also the occasional tantrum when William tried to return to normal and no longer took Elizabeth everywhere with him.

A few months after Margaret arrived, William went into Bathurst to see Daniel to talk about adding an extra room and whether he was still willing to pay for the materials they'd need. William took Elizabeth with him for the trip, and she snuggled against him the whole way. He wished she could talk, but she was still only able to mutter a few words. Daniel and his wife fussed over Elizabeth, who welcomed the attention as though she had never received any. When William raised the matter of the extra room, Daniel went one better and also arranged for some corrugated iron for the roof. The building materials were delivered within a week, William picked them up from

Bathurst, and William and his father-in-law added the extra room and changed the roof in two days of hard work.

Harvest came soon enough, and William got nearly two hundred pounds for his wheat. It was the most he'd earned in a year, and more than he'd ever received from carrying and farming. He decided that he'd stick to the farming and use the horses for ploughing, and only do the odd job of carrying—if the money was good and he had the time.

William was too busy with the harvest to register the birth, so Caroline took the little ones and, helped by Euphemia, went into Orange to tell the Court about Margaret. She told William later that the man wanted to know about any previous children, and it was hard to tell him that their first child, a boy, was stillborn. However, she brightened up and smiled when she told William that when the man asked what William did for a living, she told him her husband was a farmer.

The next year, he was able to sow more wheat and the harvest was even better. He only ever did the odd job as a carrier, mostly for a change from the drudgery of farming. It was a hard life, not without its problems and uncertainties—too hot in summer, too cold in winter, and he was much too dependent on the weather. Hardly a day went by where he didn't regret that he'd failed to find gold like so many others had—it wasn't as though he hadn't tried.

Elizabeth was five now, and talking up a storm. Caroline wanted to send her to school. She'd found some other neighbours with children and had arranged they would take turns in dropping them off and picking them up in Guyong.

Caroline was pregnant again and William realised that with the growing family, he might need to get more carrier work to make ends meet.

When the harvest was done, and he had some time on his hands, he thought he'd go to the Commercial to see if he could find some carrier work. He saddled Kelly and set off late in the afternoon, promising he'd be back early and would go to church with Caroline the next day.

It was dusk when he arrived, the days were still warm and the flies still bothersome. There were a number of other horses standing outside—tied to carts, veranda posts, or with the reins simply lying on the ground. Nevertheless, William took Kelly around the back to the stables, found an empty stall, removed his saddle, made sure he had food and water, left him and went inside.

There was the usual crowd, and several other men besides.

"What's happening?" William asked when Bill brought him his whisky.

"Haven't you heard?" said Bill over the din of others talking loudly.

"Heard what?"

"There's a lot of excitement at Hill End."

"What's happened at Hill End?"

"People are getting rich."

"Gold?"

"What else?"

Bill needed to serve some customers, so he left William scanning the familiar faces for someone who would know what was happening at Hill End. He saw Frank and Nicholas sitting at a table with two other men, all in animated conversation. Not knowing what it was about, he went over anyway. He could always move if the conversation was of no interest. It also appeared as if the place was too noisy for cards, so he wouldn't need to stay at the table.

"Hello, Tom," said Nicholas, making some room and pulling a vacant chair from a table nearby. "This is John and Anthony."

They shook hands. John was a man about William's own age, good-looking and alert. Anthony looked older and had a constant smile. The smile caused William to wonder what was coming next.

"What's happening at Hill End?" he asked.

"We were just talking about it," said Nicholas. "They're mining for reef gold. There's been some rich finds. Some people are buying and selling shares in companies that have already been set up, and some fellers are banding together and staking new claims."

"Where?" asked William.

"Hill End, of course," said Nicholas.

"No," said William, "where in Hill End?"

"There's action all about the place, but mostly on Hawkins Hill, south of Hill End," said Frank. William was startled when Frank spoke, as he didn't ever say much. In any event, he wasn't interested in the answer because he knew nothing about Hill End. He just wanted to be sure his companions did.

"John was with Edward Hargreaves when he found the gold around here," said Nicholas. "He's been trying to find his fortune ever since."

They all laughed, John not as much as the rest.

"Did you know Thomas?" asked John. "Feller that ran the Wellington Inn here? Left in 1860 to go to Hill End?"

"No," said William, "I didn't get here until 1864."

He couldn't help smiling with pride, and the fact no one noticed he could say a year.

"Ma owned the Inn before him. Anyway, he's got the Metropolitan Hotel in Hill End," said John. "His brother's got the Reefers' Hotel there too. He found the first gold on Hawkins Hill when he was tryin' to find a lost horse about twenty years ago."

"I thought you said they'd just found gold?" said William.

"They've just found a lot more by mining for it."

"All right, but why are you telling me this?"

"You asked about Hill End," said John, looking offended.

"I know I did. What's this got to do with Thomas and his brother and them owning hotels?"

"I've just come back from Hill End," said Anthony. "I was tellin' Frank and Nicholas about the excitement in the town. John was there, too. Thomas is formin' a company called the *Star of Peace*. Lots of people buyin' shares."

"It's not only John and Anthony talking about it," said Nicholas. "Everyone's talking about it."

"What are shares?" asked William.

"You tell him, John—you've been there and you seem to know what you're talkin' about," said Anthony.

"Well, I think I do. I think it goes like this. To find the gold, they're having to mine for it, sometimes at hundreds of feet through hard rock, and that costs a lot. So, a group of people get together, and decide to form a company. There are so many shares in the company that can be bought for say, a pound each. People can buy as many as they want, but not more in total than is available. Then, if the company is successful, the people can sell their shares for more than a pound."

"What's successful?" asked William.

"In this case, they sell the gold for more than it costs to find it."

"Why do you form a company? Why don't the group just go and dig for gold?"

"Why, some do, but it means they have to put up all the money and do all the digging. This way, the company uses the money from the shares to employ men to mine and if they find gold, the people that bought the shares and put up the money get to share in the profits."

"What about people that don't have much money?" asked William.

"Like us," said Frank.

"Yes, like us," said Nicholas.

"Like all of us," said Anthony, still smiling.

"They do like you suggested, Tom—they put up as much money as they can, pick a likely spot for a claim, spend their money digging, and hope it's not a shicer."

"Then what's different? Isn't that what diggers have always done?"

"It is. But here rich people buy shares, that money goes to the cost of the digging, and the shareholders don't do the digging. Now, even people living in the city can put up money to find the gold."

"They were doing that in Victoria years ago," said William.

"What do you know about Victoria?" asked Nicholas.

"Oh, not much," said William, "I heard something about it."

"What about it, fellers?" asked Anthony. "Are you interested?"

"Interested in what?" asked William.

"Anthony staked a claim when he was there. He's after people to come in with him," said John

"Oh, work the claim," said William, thoughtfully.

"Yes," said John, hopefully.

"I thought you said we had to go hundreds of feet through hard rock."

"That's what the big companies are doing. I'm hopin' that my claim is in a good spot and we won't have to go that deep," said Anthony.

"What happens if we have to?"

"It won't work. If we don't find shallow gold, we'll have to sell the claim to someone else."

"I think that's what people always did."

"The difference now is that the people who buy it are people with money who don't care where the mine is—they just want to share in the profits. There'll be someone that wants to buy the mine if it does well."

"How many of us would there be?" asked William.

"Five," said Anthony.

"We five," said Nicholas, signalling the table with his hand.

Bill arrived. "More whisky?" he asked.

"Yes," said everyone at once, and the others counted out some money.

"Are we in a shout?" asked William.

"No, we're not in a shout," said Nicholas, "I have to go soon."

"Why we five?" asked William.

"We're sitting here. There were four until you came," said Frank. "We decided we'd ask whoever came to join us and you've joined us."

"So, it's just luck you've asked me?" said William.

"Gold is only ever about luck," said John.

"Can I think about it?" asked William.

"No," said Anthony quickly, "I have to get back to the claim and I want to know where I stand before I go."

"I've got a family," said William.

"We've all got families," said Nicholas.

"So, you're all going?" said William.

"Yes," said the four at once.

"How much are you each putting in?"

"Twenty-five pounds," said Anthony.

William noticed the smile was gone now, and needed some time to think. It was a better arrangement than when he'd gone with Reginald, when he put up all the money. At least everyone shared in this adventure. Nonetheless, he knew Caroline wouldn't like it. She was pregnant and with two small children. He doubted she'd like that her husband was again off to seek his fortune on the gold fields.

The others sipped their whisky, staring at him. He wanted to tell them to stare at something else. It was irritating, trying to make a decision with everyone watching.

"How long will it take?" asked William of Anthony.

"How long will what take?"

"Finding gold, of course."

"I don't know," said Anthony, shrugging his shoulders. "Some find it straight away, some never find it."

"I've dug for gold before," said William. "This doesn't sound any different."

"It's different," said Anthony. "We don't make our money from diggin' the gold out of the ground and sellin' it. We make our money by findin' gold, then sellin' the mine. I know people used to do that too, but now there's a hunger for people with money to own a mine."

"How much do we make when we sell the mine?" asked William.

"Do you want in or not?" asked Anthony. "All I'm gettin' is a thousand questions, a headache, and a ragin' thirst."

"It's not like playing poker, is it Anthony? When I play poker, I know what I'm gambling because I see what I might get. Here, I'm gambling my time and twenty-five pounds, and I might get rich or I might get nothing."

"Then stick to poker," said Anthony, irritably.

"Take it easy, Anthony," said Nicholas. "You already know what you're doin'. Tom here has come by for a whisky, now he's got to make a hard decision that involves his family, and you want an answer straight away? What does it matter to you if it's four or five men?"

"From what I've seen, it's got to be five. Two for a twelve-hour shift and one to help."

"We work at night?" asked William, baffled. His couldn't do numbers, but he knew from the ship about a twelve-hour shift.

"If we can," said Anthony. "We won't waste any time if we can avoid it. If it's not Tom, it has to be someone else."

"I don't think there is anyone else," said Nicholas.

"Then it has to be Tom," said Anthony. The smile was back.

Bill arrived with more whisky.

*I suppose, if I'm to do it, now's a good time,* thought William. *Harvest is in, so I have some money. Ploughing and the baby aren't due for a few months, so while it's bad for Caroline, if I do make some good money, we're a step closer to the stone house.*

"Tom, I haven't seen such excitement about gold in years," said John. "If you went to Hill End, you'd feel it too."

William remembered the excitement when he first found gold with Tom in a creek outside Ballarat.

*Gold! Gold!* He said to himself, remembering the excitement all over again. And this might be the last and best chance to be rich.

"I'm in," he said.

"You won't regret it!" shouted Anthony. "I'll tell you what, I'll buy a last drink and we'll meet at the Metropolitan Hotel in Hill End next Saturday night."

"What do we all bring?" asked William.

"Yourself and your money," said Anthony.

"What about mining equipment?" pressed William.

"Don't worry—we'll buy it from someone who's failed," said Anthony. "There's plenty of those."

The drinks arrived and William kept his concerns to himself. It not only worried him that there were plenty of failures, but he was also apprehensive that he'd already made the decision without talking to Caroline, and nervous that his experiences in Ballarat and Tuena had in no way prepared him for Hill End. He finished his drink, agreed to meet the next Saturday night, and before leaving, he put sixpence on the bar for stabling Kelly and waved *goodnight* to Bill.

He rode home in the dark, slowly, dreading telling Caroline about what he'd just done. There was no doubt the gold fever still smouldered, and it took nothing but faint hope and a tiny spark to rekindle the fire.

CHAPTER 28

# THE ROAD TO HILL END

There was no doubt the silliest decision they made that night was to meet in Hill End the following Saturday night. It was already dark when William arrived. The noise and the drunkenness were nothing like anything William had seen, and he thought he'd seen it all. There were more pubs and hotels than he remembered in Sydney, all were crowded and noisy. His heart sank as he walked Kelly slowly up the main street, asking every now and again for the Metropolitan Hotel.

Caroline had taken the news better than he'd expected. There were no tears and anger. It was as though she was expecting it, but he knew she couldn't have been. She said she'd be fine with the little ones, and she'd ask young James to come over and help if she needed it. He busied himself for the rest of the week, trying to make sure she wouldn't need to do any hard work while he was away. She couldn't anyway. The next baby was only a few months from arriving. All the fences were done, the hay stored, and he went and bought some more oats and made sure there was plenty of wood cut. His tarpaulins, blankets, and gold panning equipment looked tired, but he decided to take it all anyway—there might be a chance to look for alluvial gold, if there was any spare time.

He and Caroline worked out what was twenty-five pounds. It took a while and made a noticeable reduction in the pile of notes they had in the jar. Caroline pushed him to take another five pounds. She said she could get more from her da if she needed it, and Tom had no one to ask if he ran out of money. He tried to reassure her that there was plenty of money where he was going. Why, all he had to do was dig it from the ground! She laughed, pushed the money in his pocket, hugged him fiercely and told him he would be missed.

As he was leaving, Elizabeth woke and made a fuss. She wanted to go too, and wasn't about to take *no* for an answer. William finally solved the problem by telling her he was going a long way away, and that he'd take her the next time. There was sadness in his heart as he rode away, unsure of what he was doing and already regretting what looked like a rash and hasty decision.

The ride to Hill End took him to Bathurst first, then over the mountains on the bridle track. Autumn wasn't far off, and William enjoyed the crisp morning air, the blue sky, and the stillness without the wind that would surely come later. The country had changed with more people moving into the valley, so there was more traffic on the road. No one took any notice of each other apart from the odd nod, wave of the hand, or dip of the hat.

He stopped in Bathurst to see Daniel at the hotel, but he was away in Sydney. Daniel's wife readily accepted he was on the hunt for gold again and wished him well over some tea and scones. She made him promise to bring his family to Bathurst when the baby arrived. As he left, he asked her about the bridle track.

"I've heard people talk about it. They say it's the best way to go if you're riding a horse. Cross the Macquarie and take the road north out of Bathurst. Follow the road until it forks. Take the left fork. There's a few more forks, but always take the left one until you cross the Turon and then you're at the bottom of Hawkins Hill. Hill End is at the top."

"How will I know when I get to Hawkins Hill?"

"Kelly will turn and look at you like you've taken leave of your senses to want to go up it."

"How long will it take to get there?"

"About two days. It'll be a good test for you and Kelly—they say the track goes up and down a lot."

"Is there water?"

"Plenty, but not always easy to get to. They say you follow the river for a lot of the way, but you're often high up on a ridge, with the water too far below. Then at the end, after you cross the Turon, you'll both want water going up to Hill End. I'd take a water skin, if I was you."

William stopped at a store and bought a skin. He'd seen them before, but he'd not used one.

"What's it made of?" he asked the storekeeper.

"Skin," said the man.

"I know that," said William. "The skin of what animal?"

"I think it's a water," said the man with a straight face. Some of the customers in the store smiled. William blushed, hated himself for it, paid, and left the store without another word.

He stopped and filled it as he crossed the Macquarie to make sure it worked. Once he left the river, for the first hour or so, he rode through farming and grazing land. The wind had picked up, but the day was still warm and the ride pleasant. He found the first fork without difficulty and not long after, the country changed—the hills became steeper and more timbered. The road lost all its shape, and it was clear that once he took the first fork, it was only riders that used the road.

For the rest of the day, he rode up and down endless hills, and sometimes the side of the track fell away dangerously when the track followed gullies. He took it easy so Kelly wouldn't tire and lose his footing. It was hot and dusty, and he was glad when the track followed close beside a river.

It was nearly dark when he pulled up beside the river and set up camp for the night. He had no idea what river it was, nor did he try to find anyone else to share his camp. After he'd set up, he thought he could hear distant voices, then decided it was birds or the river—or both—and regardless of the possible presence of others, stripped off all his clothes and took a dip. Like always, the bottom of the river was more rocks than sand, so he hurt his feet as he tried to move around, but felt so refreshed when he emerged, he thought to do it again. The darkness made such a decision unwise, so he cooked his supper, and drank several pannikins of sweetened tea while enjoying his pipe for the first time in a long time.

He liked the way the wind soughed in the she-oaks and the water bubbled through the rocks. An occasional night bird or animal made a noise nearby, but since most of the bush rangers were gone, the noise didn't ever startle him as there was nothing to fear in the bush.

When he rolled into his blankets, he was asleep in seconds and slept soundly and without dreams.

Once he was awake, there was no point in wasting time, so he was up with the birds and back on the road again first thing in the morning.

It was about mid-morning when he saw two riders coming the other way. He'd been climbing and descending all morning, mostly following the river beside which he'd camped the night before. There was often a good view back the way he had come, but never in front. When he reached the top of a hill, there was always another to climb, even if he had to go down first.

The riders pulled up and told him without him asking that he had about six hours to go, and that the road would only get more difficult. One man told him about the journey, the other passed the time of day by noting that it was a nice day to ride, and then they rode on.

"What river is it?" called William, to their backs.

"Macquarie," one of them said. "It's the river you crossed when you left Bathurst."

Around lunch time, William decided to pull up, being beside the river, and have some tea and damper. Everything was still open, the vegetation sparse, the ground dry and rocky, and the sun easy to see. Nonetheless, he found a lovely spot with a big pool, got a fire going, and made some tea and damper. When he finished eating, he stayed for a while to enjoy the peace and quiet of the moment.

Not long after he started again, the track climbed away from the river, rising steadily, the drop precipitous and the ground rocky and uneven.

It was still hot with plenty of the day left when he came upon a junction between the river he'd been following and another one. He was high above the junction at that point and had a wonderful view of the two rivers. The track was only about the height of a man wide, and the drop to his left made him nervous. He kept Kelly close to the rock wall, well away from the edge. Thinking that his time on the masts would have made him accustomed to heights, he puzzled over his nervousness. However, the drop was much more than the height of a mast, so he reassured himself that he was just being careful.

The track now followed the new river and his height above it gradually reduced, so he was finally able to take himself and Kelly for a drink. It was a typical Australian mountain river, about knee deep, with large rocks and boulders scattered everywhere. He found a spot where he could lie face-down on the bank to drink. The water was clear and cold. He'd already had a drink when he realised the diggin's may be just up ahead and all manner of things could be in the water. The skin was about half-full, so he didn't bother to refill it with what might be polluted water.

Back on the track, he and Kelly continued to climb, the river sometimes close and sometimes inaccessible. About mid-afternoon, he heard sounds from higher up and it wasn't long before he found men digging. He doubted he'd done the big climb he was told would come at the end, so he bypassed the diggings, following the track when it crossed the river. There were more diggings and then the track began to rise more steeply. None of the diggers took any notice of him, so he guessed a lone man on a horse on the track wasn't unusual.

As he climbed further up the hill, sometimes it was too steep to ride, so he got off Kelly and walked. It was tiring work and perspiration flowed freely. He sipped the water frequently, sometimes giving Kelly a little in his hat. The noise from the valley floor was long behind him and he worried that he might have taken a wrong turn. The road twisted and turned like a snake, always climbing, but not always on the same hill. He crossed through gullies and creeks, which sometimes had water that he allowed Kelly to drink, but took none himself in case it was polluted.

It was almost dark when he finally reached the top and he could see the lights of what he presumed to be Hill End in front of him.

When he reached the Metropolitan, several men stood around drinking outside, occasionally slapping at mosquitoes. The men all looked and talked like diggers. William rode up and got down tiredly from Kelly. He dropped the reins and stood looking at the building. It was a low building with an iron roof and posts holding up the roof of a shallow veranda. A few men nodded at William, but most ignored him. He nodded back and went through the door nearest to him. More noise came from the doorway, so he thought it would be where he'd meet the others.

The noise inside hit him like a wall. The bar was like every other one, except for the number of people. It was as though they'd all come for free drink, or they'd been told drink was about to run out. There were a few tables and chairs, and most of the men stood in groups. From time to time they would put their drinks on some tables of about waist-height that were all along the walls, jutting out in some parts to accommodate more men. It took a few moments to spot Nicholas and Anthony. They were lucky enough to be sitting at a table with two vacant chairs, and William slipped into one of them.

"That's good," he said, smiling when the others laughed.

"Good to see you," said Anthony, shaking William's hand firmly. "Let me get you a drink. Whisky, I suspect?"

William nodded.

"Where are John and Frank?" he asked Nicholas.

"We were just wondering about all of you. Did you just arrive?"

"Pretty much. Had to ask a few people to find the Metropolitan. Town's busy."

"Saturday night," said Anthony, coming back with three whiskies. "Have you seen John and Frank? We thought they might be comin' with you."

"I came on my own. What about you, Nicholas?"

"I came with Anthony. We got here a couple of days ago."

"What have you been doing?"

"Not a moment wasted," said Anthony. "We bought some minin' gear, had a look over the claim, and made some plans. We'll be ready to start diggin' on Monday."

"What will we do tomorrow?"

"Go to church," said Anthony, laughing.

"Apart from going to church."

"We'll show you over the claim, set up somewhere to live, and have a look around the town."

"Where will we stay tonight?"

"Here."

"Then I'd better see to my horse."

"Take him around back to the stables—ours are there, too. They'll look after him tonight and we can put him somewhere else tomorrow."

"Where else is there?"

"Feller's got a paddock up the road. He looks after everybody's horse—used to be four pence a week, might be six pence now. He does a good job—none of the horses ever complain."

William stood up, finished his whisky, and went to look after Kelly. When he got back, John and Frank were there. He was nonplussed at how pleased he was to see them. Everyone shook hands again, and Anthony went to find another chair. He came back with a chair and two whiskies. Nicholas remarked how clever he was to hold two glasses in one hand.

"Worked in a bar for a while," said Anthony.

"When did you fellers leave?" William asked Frank and John.

"Yesterday. We left a little late though and camped for the night not long after we reached the bridle track. We pushed it pretty hard today."

"Well, we're all here now and that's the main thing," said Anthony, and he again explained his plans for the next day.

"Where will we set up to live?" asked Frank.

"Why, we've got five acres, so we can set up a lean-to on our claim. That'll do for the moment, and we can build somethin' better if we find gold, or when winter comes."

"Five acres?" asked William. "How big is that?"

"I thought you had a farm?" asked Nicholas.

"Doesn't matter," said William, blushing. "Forget I asked."

"So, let's have supper," said Nicholas, draining his glass.

"I haven't had a shout yet," said William.

"We're not shoutin'. I'm taking the money out of what we all contribute," said Anthony. "Which reminds me, I've only received money from Nicholas so far, so you others can give me your money now too." The smile was back.

William felt uncomfortable about what he saw as a change of arrangements. He hadn't expected to contribute the money all at once, but held his tongue as Frank and John took money from their pockets and passed it to Anthony.

*Perhaps this is the way it works*, thought William. *The others don't seem the least bit troubled about handing over their money.*

William reached into his pocket and pulled out the wad of money he and Caroline had counted out.

"Thanks," said Anthony, taking the whole wad.

"There's too much," said William reaching to take it back.

"Oh," said Anthony, handing the wad back, "count out the twenty five and keep the rest."

"No, you do it," said William. "I want to be sure you can count."

"And why is that?" asked Anthony, stiffly.

"If you're handling the money, I want to know that you can count."

"Fair enough," said Anthony, keeping the wad and counting an amount quickly on the table. His lips moved as he counted, but he made no sound. He passed the rest back to William.

William put it in his pocket.

"Shouldn't you check it?" asked Anthony, "to be sure I took only twenty-five?"

William made a pretence of checking it.

"That's right," he said, putting the money in his pocket.

Anthony looked at William for a few moments, saying nothing, and just staring.

"What's wrong?" asked William.

"What's wrong? A minute ago, you didn't trust me. And now you do. I'd like to think that we're partners who trust each other without question."

"I trust you," said William. "Now that I know you can count, I trust you."

"It takes one to know one," said Anthony.

"One what?"

"A person that can count."

"Oh," said William, blushing.

"I know you can't count," said Anthony, peeling off a pound from the money William had given him. "This is yours—I counted out twenty-six, just to show you that you can trust me."

"Sorry," said William. He didn't know if he was more ashamed that he couldn't count or that he had made a stupid mistake in testing Anthony.

"It's all right," said Anthony, putting out his hand to shake William's, "you'll all have to trust me to manage your money. If anyone doesn't, I'll give him his money back right now and he can leave."

Everyone sat still, the others looking at the ground, possibly avoiding eye contact with both Anthony and William.

"Have we finished here? Are you all ready to get on with it now?"

Everyone nodded.

"Then let's have supper," said Anthony, rising from the table.

The next morning, they rose to the sound of roosters and church bells. It was a beautiful day, the sun not yet warm and a chill lingering in the air. Anthony said they'd look at their claim first thing and then plan the rest of the day. They walked down the main street, going back the way William had come into the town the previous night. William spent more time looking about and saw buildings of all types lining both sides of the road. Several with two or three storeys, some of brick or stone and most of timber. Not many people were out and about, and dogs made them unwelcome at almost every house they passed. Many of the houses were well presented, some with flowers and most with gardens.

"We're just across the creek from the Star of Peace mine in Nuggetty Gully," said Anthony. "I think it's a good claim."

The diggin's were mostly quiet. The inevitable dogs made a racket, but no one took any notice. Most of the claims had huts or tents, so it was very different to what William had known at Ballarat and Tuena, where people rarely lived on their claim. Some of the diggers were out getting breakfast and William could smell the distinct odour of a gold field, mixed with wood smoke and cooking. There were no trees about, and Anthony explained that they were used for fires and to stop the shafts and tunnels collapsing. He said that some men were making good money bringing timber and trees, often from camps several miles away. Most of the gold hunting in Hill End involved tunnels and shafts, so wood was in great demand.

William could see a creek, not far ahead, with good water. The sides to get into it were steep, the gully was over the height of a man deep, and he and his companions slipped where it was wet and stumbled where it was uneven. They climbed to the other side and Anthony said, "This is our claim."

Looking around, William thought it just like any other place he had seen—scrubby bush, steep sided hills, and nothing to show there might be gold.

"Like I said, we've got five acres, so we can pick a spot to build a place to live in while we're here. We can't drink the water, although some of the fellers say they make tea from it. I don't know that I want to do that."

"Does our claim include the creek?" asked John.

"Here it does," said Anthony. "We go to about that big rock there on the Hawkins Hill side and quite a way on the other side. You can't see it from here, but it's marked, so we can't make a mistake."

It didn't take long to explore all their claim and, after checking out several places, they agreed on a spot to erect a tent using poles and their tarpaulins. They could see some trees some distance away and they agreed that two of them would get their horses and axes, and ride off to get some for the structure. The others would go with Anthony and fetch their digging equipment, tarpaulins, and anything else they had brought.

"Sorry—no time for church," laughed Anthony, acknowledging the sounds of church bells in the distance.

It took most of the morning to complete the tent and when they stood back to admire it, William thought it looked like it might fall over at any time. The corner posts were sunk in the ground, but not a single one stood straight. The other posts were lashed to them with rope and the tarpaulins were stretched across, leaving gaping holes everywhere. He kept his thoughts to himself, deciding that after his experience with the money he'd be better to go along with whatever was decided.

Working out where each man would be in the tent wasn't an easy task. Eventually, they decided three would be at the back and two at the front. Anthony said he'd take the middle spot at the back because he was in charge. Nicholas and William would be either side of him and John and Frank would be at the front.

William was the target of a few jokes when they realised he'd brought some panning equipment.

"Leave him alone," said Anthony, finally. "There's still gold to be found in the creeks around here."

They set up a spot to do cooking and agreed that, until they had better accommodation, they'd need to do all their cooking outside. Anthony, who appointed himself cook, had brought some mutton and vegetables, so they had mutton stew and damper for lunch.

"You're a good cook," said John.

"You might get sick of it. It's all I know how to cook."

After lunch, Anthony volunteered to take the horses to the feller that would look after them. William wanted to see more of the town and volunteered to go with him.

"What'll we do while you're gone?" asked Nicholas.

"Find somewhere good to dig. Diggin' starts tomorrow," said Anthony.

Taking the two horses that had been used to get wood, they headed back to town. They had to walk the horses quite a way up the creek before they found a place where the horses could climb the side of the creek to get out.

"Been a lot of diggin' done up here a few years back," said Anthony, as they climbed out of the creek. "Fellers diggin' here were very lucky. I'm hopin' some of what was here also found its way down to our claim."

They passed a few people working their claims, but most claims were empty, showing that many of the diggers respected the Sabbath, or at least, took the day off.

The man to look after the horses was busy taking horses in and letting them out. It seemed many people wanted to make use of their horses on a Sunday. Anthony negotiated the price for five horses. William thought he could easily become accustomed to someone else worrying about the money.

They took their time going back, walking on some of the side streets, and checking out the stores. Nothing was open, but they could look in the windows and see what was available. William liked Hill End. It had a sense of order about it. Many of the buildings looked permanent, and there were many signs that people with money lived there.

"We'd better be gettin' back," said Anthony. "The boys might be fightin' over where to dig."

When they got back, the others were sitting around, waiting for them.

"We thought you'd got lost," said Nicholas.

"Did you find a spot to dig?" asked Anthony.

"No," said Nicholas, "we talked about it for a while, then decided to leave it up to you."

It was nearly dark, so Anthony cooked supper. It was mutton stew. William understood what Anthony meant by them getting sick of it after a while. He decided a while might be only a few days.

"Where do you think we should dig?" asked Nicholas when supper was finished and they were sitting around on rocks they had found for the purpose.

"I think we'll put down a few holes first—we don't have to go very deep. Maybe twenty or thirty feet to bed rock. We can do that near to the creek, so we don't have to carry the wash far."

"Isn't the creek on bed rock?" asked John.

"It is, so if we put down a hole near the creek, then it's probably only as deep as the bank of the creek. I think we should do them away from the creek."

"Why?"

"Ground water for one—too much too close to the creek. Then I'm hopin' we find a spot where the creek used to go when all the gold was still here."

"Will we work at night?"

"Not at first."

"Five's too many to work a shaft," said John.

"You're right," said Anthony. "We'll dig two holes—one man diggin', and another pullin' the dirt out and taking it to the creek. The fifth man will do the washin'."

"How long will it take to dig twenty or thirty feet?"

"Two or three days."

"And if we don't find gold?"

"We start on a shaft and go lookin' for a vein."

"What's a vein?" asked Nicholas.

"Gold bearin' quartz. If we find some, we'll take it to the crusher further down the creek."

"How do we do that?"

"Use bags and horses."

"Why'd you choose here?" asked Frank.

Even Anthony looked stunned. They'd already become accustomed to Frank not saying much.

"A few reasons. First was that a feller wanted to sell it and didn't want much for it."

"Isn't it any good?" asked Frank, suspiciously.

Anthony laughed.

"He hasn't worked it, so he didn't know. No, he'd made the claim thinkin' he'd be able to work it. He's a city feller—knew nothin' about workin' a claim."

"How'd you meet him?" asked William.

"Why, in the Metropolitan. He was tryin' to sell it to Thomas, but he didn't want it."

"He didn't want it?" Nicholas almost shouted. "I thought he knows what he's doing?"

"He does," said Anthony, patiently. "It's too far from his claim. Maybe if he buys the ones between he'll be interested, but he's not interested now. Anyway, feller was miserable and said he'd take next to nothin' for it. I told him that's what I was prepared to pay."

"How much did you pay?" asked Nicholas.

"Ten pounds."

No one said anything for a few moments and William supposed each man was trying to work out if Anthony had paid a good price, or if they were all wasting their time and money.

"Well, it doesn't matter," said Nicholas. "It's ours now, so let's make the best of it. If there's gold, let's find it. If there's not, it won't be anybody's fault. We'll just be like thousands of other fellers that tried and failed."

"Won't be unusual for me to fail," said John, laughing.

"Nor me," said Nicholas.

"Time for bed," said Anthony. "Let's make an early start."

CHAPTER 29

# HILL END

The next few months had all the usual highs and lows of the gold field. They sank four holes in the first two weeks. It took longer than Anthony had thought it would, because they'd run into big boulders and had to either break them up or work around them. Anthony was excited when they found them.

"They'll only be here because the creek water pushed them here," he admonished the others when they complained.

He was right. They found good gold in two of the holes, water worn nuggets gathered in pockets. Once more, William relived the excitement he'd first had when looking for gold with Tom outside Ballarat. Anthony tried to work out how the creek might have flowed, so they could follow it and find more pockets. It was fruitless but didn't dampen their spirits. They'd established there was gold to be found and the team was ready to find more of it.

It took another two weeks to find more.

"I don't understand it," said Anthony. "If we dig where we expect to find gold, we find nothin'. I never expected to find gold in the three holes where we found it."

"Then, you pick a spot where you expect to find gold and we'll dig somewhere else," said Nicholas.

"We could go further away from the creek," said William.

"I've been thinkin' that," said Anthony.

"Then let's not do it," said Nicholas. William looked at him. He was serious.

"I'll tell you what we'll do. Let's keep our two teams goin', one will dig holes and the other will dig a shaft."

"A shaft?" said John, doubt in his voice.

"Yes. The Star of Peace gets all their gold from a vein in the side of Hawkins Hill."

"But I heard they went down one hundred and twenty feet before they found it, and they've followed it down for hundreds more!" exclaimed John. "We can't do that with two men."

"We're further down the hill. We won't have to go so deep before we find it."

"Can't we just keep digging the holes?" said Frank.

"We can, but we're not makin' much and it's all hard work."

"We can't go under the other claims, can we?" asked William.

"No, we can't. We have to find a vein under our claim."

"How far up Hawkins Hill does our claim go?" asked Nicholas.

"Like I said," said Anthony, "to those boulders. Maybe a hundred feet or so."

"And we'll have to shore it up with timber," said Frank.

"Yes, we will."

"How much money do we have left?" asked Nicholas.

"I don't know—maybe one hundred and fifty pounds."

"Is that enough?"

"I don't know."

"How much did we get for the gold we found?"

"One hundred and twenty-three pounds."

"Shall we take a vote?" said John.

"Look," said Anthony, "this is Saturday. I, for one, am sick of mutton stew. Let's go into Hill End tonight, have some supper and a few whiskies at the Metropolitan, and talk about it."

They gathered their tools, putting everything away as best they could, and headed up the hill to the town in the increasing darkness. A strong, cold wind had come up, and black clouds fled across the sky.

"Storm comin'," said Anthony.

The weather did nothing to improve their mood as they hurried to the sanctuary of the Metropolitan.

They had some whiskies in the bar, standing around one of the tables. Once again, the noise was deafening—the conversation to do with digging, tunnelling, and the impending storm.

"It's too noisy to talk here," said Anthony. "Let's wait until we have supper."

William overheard a group behind talking about some card games that would be held nearby that night. He thought he'd like to join in, if there was time. When he asked about it, the men said the Hill End police didn't like cards in the hotels, so the players gathered at different places. He was glad he'd put a few pounds in his pocket as they left the tent earlier, and hoped he'd get a chance to join. It was hard being part of a team, doing everything together every day. He told Nicholas and Frank about it, and they were excited too, but regretted they'd brought no money, thinking Anthony would pay for everything. They didn't want to ask Anthony for any money for cards. William assured them they'd be able to use the money he'd brought, as he was happy to share it and they could pay him back.

They discussed what to do about the gold over supper. In the end, Anthony's idea of pursuing both holes and a shaft prevailed. They agreed he had the most experience, knew the area best, and they should all be guided by him. Anthony ordered a bottle of claret to have with their supper, and appeared miffed when John took a sip and told him he'd tasted better from a billabong that hadn't had rain in six months.

"Doesn't matter," said Anthony. "More for the rest of us."

As it transpired, no one else liked it either and Anthony stubbornly drank the bottle on his own while the others settled for another whisky.

When they finished supper, William went back to the bar to see if they could join the card players.

"We were waiting for you," they declared. "We're ready to go when you are."

Anthony and John wanted to go back to the tent, but they'd brought only one lamp, so they had to stay together.

"We won't stay long," said William. "Just a few hands."

"All right, all right," mumbled Anthony, clearly the worse for the claret.

They joined the men, and everyone ran through the pouring rain just a few doors down the street and into a store. A lamp was burning to guide them, and they went out the back to where the owner lived. They went into an unexpectedly big room with three tables, with card players sitting at two of them. Some other men were standing around watching.

"We're only here for a few hands," mumbled Anthony.

"That's all right," said one of the men standing, "so are we."

The man that had spoken joined William, Frank and Nicholas at a table. John stood back and watched, while Anthony slumped into a chair and was snoring loudly in seconds.

"I'm glad he's only staying for a few hands," said one of the players at the nearby table. "I don't think I could stand too much of that."

They agreed the stakes and William got out his money and shared it with Nicholas and Frank. The fourth man introduced himself as Les.

"What'd you do? Bring paupers?" said Les, watching the men share the money.

"What's a pauper?" asked Frank.

"Doesn't matter," said Les. "Let's play."

They played ten hands and William was very lucky, gathering a tidy pile of winnings in front of him, largely funded by Les. Both Nicholas and Frank lost only a small amount. Les was put out when William said it was time to go.

"You'll have to come back next week," said Les. "You have to give me a chance to win my money back."

"That's all right with me," said William. "But like we said when we came in, we're only here for a few hands."

"Good. I'll see you next week," said Les, and stomped out the door.

William scooped up his winnings and pushed them as far down into his pocket as he could. When they came out the front, the rain was torrential.

"Lamp won't work in this," said Nicholas. He and John carried a still-snoring Anthony between them.

"It's worse than that, I think," said Frank. "The creek'll be up and we won't get through it—be madness to try."

"He's right," said William. "What'll we do?"

"Let's go to the stables at the Metropolitan. We can each find a piece of dry ground there and spend the night. Hopefully the storm'll be gone by morning, Anthony'll be able to walk, the creek'll be down, and we can get back to the tent and sleep the day away."

They struggled back to the stables, and all were soaking before they'd even gone a few steps. Finding some empty chaff bags in the darkness, they made themselves as comfortable as they could. William took a little more time and found a spot that was on some bales of hay, so he could be sure that even if the rain came in, he wouldn't get wetter than he was already.

He woke in the dim light of early morning to a rough voice saying, "'Ere! What're you lot doin' 'ere? These aren't rooms for the likes of you."

William struggled to his feet, feeling stiff and sore in every joint and hardly able to move.

"Jesus!" said the voice. "That you, Tom? Who've you got with you? My sainted mother, it's Anthony and your other mates. Why didn't you come inside? The boss would've found a room for you all."

"It was too late, Cyril," said William. "We played cards and couldn't cross the creek."

"You don't have to worry about that. Come inside the next time—you can do better than this."

"No matter now, Cyril, but we'll remember that. It wasn't such a bad night."

"You speak for yourself," said Anthony. "My head's splittin' and I feel like I slept on a bed of rocks."

"Be careful of the creek," said Cyril. "You're right that it'll be hard to cross, but you might get across higher up."

They left the hotel and decided to try to cross the creek at the usual spot. The noise of the creek was evident long before they got to it. Water roared, foamed and tore at the banks of the creek, flowing fast in the narrow gully. They realised they'd made a mistake putting their camp on the other side. It might be days before they could get to it. What was worse, the holes they'd been working on would be full of water and would take days to empty without a pump.

William looked at his companions. What a bedraggled, sorry looking lot they were. None of them shaved, so they all had beards. Their clothes were torn, wet and dirty. None of them looked like they had a home to go to and that was the truth. Their home was on the other side of the creek, and it might be days before they could get to it.

"Let's try higher up," said Frank, "like Cyril said."

"Even if we get across, it'll take hours to climb down past Prince Alfred Hill."

"We've got hours," said Anthony.

"We could go to church," said Nicholas.

"What? And pray for a miracle?" said Anthony, a sharp edge to his voice.

"No. At least it'll be warm and dry."

"I don't think we're dressed for it," said William.

"I'm for trying higher up," said Frank again. "Even if it does take hours, at least we can get dry and sleep in our beds."

"I don't think it's going to be dry," said William, pointing at the tent. The tarpaulin at the top was split down the middle.

"It must have filled with water," said John. "I've seen them do that in heavy rain."

"It's no wonder some of the diggers've built proper huts."

"Why don't we do that?" said John. "We sure won't be able to dig for the next few days."

"Where'll we stay for the next few nights?" said Nicholas. "The pub?"

"I don't want to spend the money," said Anthony, "but I'm not sure we have many other choices."

"Are there any abandoned huts?" asked William. "We could use one of those while we fix our tent."

"I think there are," said Anthony. "Good idea. There's some up near Golden Gully."

"Do we want to try and get our blankets and supplies?" said John. "It'll be cold without the blankets and there's no point in wasting the supplies."

"All right," said Anthony, taking control again. "Tom, you and John try to get across the creek and get our stuff. The rest of us will try to find an abandoned hut, and one of us will meet you outside the Metropolitan when we find one."

"What'll we do if there's no one at the Metropolitan?"

"Wait, but I think it'll take you longer to get our stuff than it will us to find a hut."

William and John set out and tried several places before they crossed the creek. It was still dangerous, and William was relieved that they crossed without incident. He remembered the tale of the pastor in the Wollondilly and knew the high price for a mistake.

When they got to their tent, they found most of the food ruined and all their clothes and blankets soaked. They threw the supplies away. It hardly hit the ground before the birds fought over it. Using two of the tarpaulins, they put the clothes and blankets in one and cooking pots and things in the other, rolled them up and carried them over their shoulders. It was a dreadful struggle back up the hill, through the torn up and uneven ground. They slipped and fell countless times, cursing the job they'd been given. It was mid-afternoon before William and John finally got to the Metropolitan and met a bored and irritated Nicholas.

"What kept you?" he said when they arrived.

"The girls," said John.

"What girls?" asked Nicholas, suspicion and envy in his voice.

"No matter," said John. "Did you find a hut?"

"We did. I reckon we should use it all the time. It's got a wooden floor, a fireplace inside, and two bunks."

"Two bunks? That'll be nice and comfortable," said John.

"We can build some more. There's not a lot of room, but there's enough for us to put three more beds in there. Anyway, it's a lot better than what we had down by the creek. There's a well out the back, and a privy too."

"All right," said John.

"What about our stuff?" asked Nicholas.

"Supplies were ruined, and our clothes and blankets are soaked."

"We'll need some food. There's nothing at the hut."

"None of the stores are open," said William.

"I'll see what I can do here," said Nicholas, going into the Metropolitan. He came out a few minutes later with a flour bag.

"They said we can have this—not sure if it's any good. She said they were about to throw it out, so we're lucky."

"What is it?"

"Some mutton and vegetables."

"Good—at least Anthony will know what to do with that."

It took about twenty minutes to get to the hut, and William was grateful to find it was bigger than he had expected, and well built. It would take them a while to get to their claim each day, but maybe it would be best to use it, for a while at least. They all set out and spent another hour looking for wood for a fire, bringing it back by the arm load. It was hard work as wood could only be found in inaccessible places, like the sides of steep gullies, or the tops of hills.

As darkness fell, they had a good fire going and their clothes and blankets strung out and hanging around the room, trying to dry them by the heat of the fire. After a while, it was so hot and steamy in the room that they had to open the door.

"This'll never dry," said Anthony. "What a bloody mess."

"It'll dry tomorrow," said John.

"What'll we do tonight? Two beds and wet blankets," said Anthony. "Anyway, let's see what they gave you, Nicholas. We can have some supper, at least."

He looked in the bag and wrinkled his nose.

"Doesn't smell too good."

"The cook said she was going to throw it out."

"Good idea—I think she should have."

"Do you think we could catch a possum?"

"Maybe if we'd thought about it earlier. Too late and too dark now."

"What else is in there?"

"Some vegetables."

"Why don't we throw the meat away and cook the vegetables?" asked Frank.

"There won't be enough."

"I've never heard of rank mutton hurting anyone," said Nicholas.

"Neither have I," said John.

"All right," said Anthony. "I'll cook it all together and let's hope it doesn't kill us. Did you bring the sugar and tea?"

"Threw it all out," said William. "It was all ruined."

"We can't eat this without tea," said Anthony. "They'll have some at the Metropolitan."

He looked at Nicholas.

"Why didn't you get some?"

Nicholas shrugged and said, "Didn't know I had to."

"Go back and get it," said Anthony.

"It's too dark."

"Since when've you been afraid of the dark?"

"I'm not afraid of the dark. It's just that it's too dark to see where I'm going, and I might fall down a mine—it's happened before. Somebody else can go."

"Jesus, we've a well out the back with fresh water to make tea, and no tea or sugar!"

"I'll go," said William, getting up stiffly from where he'd been squatting on the floor, his back against the wall.

*I'll be glad to get away from this for a while—the bickering and the nonsense.*

He wasn't bothered by the dark and knew that if he stuck to the road, he couldn't fall down anything. The night air was chilly and still damp from the rain. He was still wet from perspiration from climbing the hill, and the condensation in the hut. Shivering, he walked quickly in the hope that he'd warm up a little. There was enough moon to see the way.

When he arrived at the Metropolitan, there were a few travellers in the bar. Thomas worked behind it, chatting with his guests.

"Hello, Tom," he said when William stepped through the door. "My lord, you're soaked! Come stand by the fire. I'll get you a whisky to warm you up."

William, not being a traveller, could accept the whisky for free and Thomas would not be breaking the law. He resolved to pay Thomas on a later day. The fire was wonderfully warm, and he stood as close as he could.

"Here you are," said Thomas. "I know you're not here for the whisky. How can I help you?"

"All our supplies were ruined in the storm. I'm hoping you can give me some tea and sugar."

"Of course I can. Stay a few moments and dry off though. Your mates'll last a while longer without tea."

"Where're you from?" asked one of the guests.

"Local—working a claim in one of the gullies here. You?"

"Bathurst. We tried to get back this morning but couldn't get across the Turon. You look worn out."

"We've had a hard day. Tent was ruined and we had to move everything."

"Are you ready for another whisky?"

"I'm not a traveller. Like I said, I'm local."

"I think I can buy one for you. He serves me, I give it to you."

"That'll be all right," said Thomas. "I'll get it for you shortly."

William had another drink, collected his tea and sugar, thanked the guest for his hospitality, and headed back out into the cold. The time by the fire had warmed him but hadn't dried his clothes. He was chilled within moments, clutched the flour bags with their precious cargo, and walked as fast as he could back to their hut. As he walked, he thought of Caroline and the girls. He hoped they were all right, warm and safe. When he reached the hut, he opened the door and went quickly inside.

"Here he is!" said Anthony. "We thought you'd fallen down a hole."

The room stank of wet clothes, dirty men, and rank stew. William would have preferred to be back at the hotel in the company of the man from Bathurst.

"I've got the tea and sugar. What are we going to do tonight? I'm not dry, and none of this stuff is either," said William, indicating the blankets and clothes hanging all about the room.

"We were just talkin' about that," said Anthony, taking the tea and throwing some in a billy, already boiling over the fire. "We think that if we keep the fire goin', it'll be warm even if it is wet. Lie wherever we can and get whatever sleep we can."

They had the stew and some tea. Everyone agreed the stew was better with the tea and thanked William for getting it.

William nodded wearily, pulled one of the wet blankets off the wall, lay down in a corner, and made himself as comfortable as possible. He was asleep in seconds. As he drifted off, he heard someone say, "Luck of the Irish."

The next day, Anthony organised that he and Nicholas would stay at the hut and hang all the clothing and blankets outside to dry, then busy themselves building some more beds, and doing whatever other jobs were necessary. The rest would go to the claim, make sure all the tools were still there, rescue whatever was left in the tent, and see what damage was done to the claim by the water.

William, Frank and John went to the claim, crossing the creek up high and following the route Frank and William had used the previous day. They passed by other claims, many of them suffering water damage. When they reached the claim, the holes were only half-filled with water, and John predicted confidently that all the water would be gone in a day or so.

"We're high up on the hill," he said. "Water drains quickly."

All the tools were still there, and they managed to rescue the rest of the tarpaulins and some clothes they hadn't seen on their last visit. Water still flowed quickly in the creek, but it was nothing like the day before.

Again, John predicted confidently that they'd be able to cross the creek at the claim site the next day. Once they had done all they could, they gathered their belongings, hid the tools, and headed back to the hut.

When they arrived back, the others had just got back with some wood and bark to make the extra beds. They'd retrieved their horses to make the job easier. Anthony went to buy supplies, the rest busied themselves building the beds. It wasn't hard to do, and the job was completed by the time Anthony returned.

All their clothes and blankets were stretched on rope between the hut and some poles they'd rigged as a clothesline. There was enough warmth in the sun and dryness in the wind that it looked like everything would be dry by nightfall.

Anthony busied himself getting some lunch while the rest went in search of more wood for the fire. They took Anthony's and Nicholas's horses and had to go a mile before they found anything suitable. There were other groups in search of firewood too, and they decided it was a job someone would have to do every day, or they'd need to buy it.

"We'd better find good gold at some point," muttered Nicholas to no one in particular. "This is all hard work, just like being at home with none of the benefits."

Over the next few days, they finished work on the hut and went back to digging holes and started a shaft on the eastern side of Nuggetty Gully. Anthony picked the spot where they'd start. John was keen to know why he'd chosen where he did.

"It's on a line with the Star of Peace. With luck, we'll find the same vein."

"How did they find theirs?" John asked.

"Joseph, Thomas's brother, did. He found it on the surface. The whole side of this hill is meant to have veins of different widths at different depths. No reason we won't find some. We're further down the hill, so it might be closer to the surface here."

John and William were to work on the shaft and Frank and Nicholas were to dig more holes. Anthony would help out where needed. Frank and Nicholas decided to stop trying to work out where the gold might be and to just dig holes in a pattern all along the western side of their claim, but close enough to the creek to reduce the effort required to move the dirt for washing. They had mixed success, sometimes finding enough to maintain interest, but never enough to make them rich. The real hope lay with William and John digging the shaft.

William went back for cards each Saturday night. Frank and Nicholas sometimes came with him. William did well when Les was there. He decided that the best men to play against were the ones who had found gold and were more willing to bet on their luck. They seemed to think that if they were lucky with gold, they'd be lucky with cards too.

The next Sunday, William decided to try his hand at panning. He realised late in the week that the recent storm may have dislodged more gold. Anthony told him he would need a licence if he panned anywhere but their claim, and if he panned on their claim then he'd have to share it with the team. There were no claims on some of the other creeks, which were as good as anywhere, so William decided to go it alone. Anthony had told him a lot of gold had been found further up their own creek, so it stood to reason the storm would have dislodged some from other creeks too.

William bought a three-month panning licence on the Friday and couldn't believe his luck once he went out. There was coarse gold in many of the crevices, and he had a pannikin-full by the end of the day. He tried to share it with the others, but Anthony wouldn't hear of it.

"You found it, it's yours," he said.

"But I'm still part of the team!"

"No matter. We can search, too, if we want."

The others agreed, and thereafter William spent each Saturday evening playing cards and Sundays panning the creeks and gullies wherever he could. It got him away from the others for a while and gave him some gambling money, and he'd forgotten how much he enjoyed panning for gold and playing cards. He gave the gold to Anthony when he went to sell what they had found in the holes, and Anthony always brought his money back to him—sometimes as much as ten pounds.

"It's the best way," said Anthony. "They'll think it's all from our claim, and they never ask why we weigh it separately."

Around the middle of the year, the shaft was down to about thirty feet, and they had to shore it with wood as they went. Every now and again, they'd dig out on the sides to see if they could find a vein, but it was always only dirt and rocks. The weather had turned chilly, and Frank and Nicholas complained every night about how cold it was digging the holes. One night, John offered to swap the shaft for the holes. They didn't complain any more after that.

John and William took turns about, one being at the top and the other at the bottom of the shaft. It was cold at the top, waiting to pull a bucket of dirt up, then hot work doing it. It was always hot digging at the bottom, and more dangerous.

One day, William was at the bottom of the shaft when he thought he heard John calling to him from above. He stopped digging, looked up and could see John framed against the sky at the top. William thought he heard "woman" and wondered what the devil John was saying. The wind blew hard across the top and William eventually decided that John wasn't coming down to give him the message, so he'd have to go up. It took a while to climb the ladders, and he had to be careful as he went not to slip and fall. He was sure his experience from the ship was very useful in the shaft.

He was about halfway up when John stuck his head over again.

"There's a woman here!" he called.

"What woman?"

"She says she's your wife."

"My wife?"

"That's what she says."

*Jesus. What's happened?*

He scrambled to the top faster than he should have, mindless of the danger.

As he emerged into the grey light of a Hill End winter, he looked and saw Caroline wrapped in shawls and warm clothing standing beside John, a huge smile on her face, and the baby bump clearly visible.

"Tom," she said, and if anything, the smile became broader. "Hello."

*Well, at least nothing's wrong*, he thought, with relief.

"What on earth are you doing here?" he asked, unable to keep the displeasure out of his voice.

"I came to see you."

"Why?"

"Aren't you pleased to see me?"

John discretely made himself scarce.

"Of course I am, but you shouldn't have come here."

William finished climbing out of the shaft and stood beside her.

"You don't sound like you are."

"It's just that this is no place for a woman."

"I saw women in the town when I arrived."

"How did you get here?"

"Aren't you going to give me a hug?"

"Of course."

They tried to hug, but each went to the wrong side, and their bodies failed to join properly. After disengaging, they sorted it out and hugged briefly.

"You can't stay here."

"Then let's go back to the town."

"No, I mean in Hill End."

Anthony, Frank and Nicholas stood staring from the other side of the creek. John was also staring, from a discrete distance.

"I'll be back later!" William called to them all, and took Caroline by the arm. "C'mon, let's go back to town."

"I can wait until you finish for the day, then go back with all of you."

William looked at her. The wind tore at her clothing, pushing back against the baby bump, showing her advanced pregnancy. Her nose and face were blue. He took her hand—it was freezing.

"No, c'mon—if you're going to wait, you're better to wait in front of a fire."

He held her hand and they struggled up the path from the gully. It was still muddy and slippery from frequent mists and morning dews, and several times she nearly fell.

As they walked, he fretted about where to take her.

"Where will we go?" she asked.

"You can wait at our hut, but you can't stay there. It's only got one room and we all sleep there. I'm hoping we can find somewhere for you to stay until we can arrange for you to go home."

"Go home? I just got here."

"What about the baby? You can't have the baby here."

"Yes, I can. There's no problem with having the baby here. In the meantime, I can look after you and the others."

"We don't need looking after," he said, tersely.

"Have you found anything?"

"Not much yet."

"Then, why are you here? Why don't you come home?"

They'd reached the main street where the mix of animal dung and mud made for even harder walking. William tried to pick paths where it would be easier for Caroline, but he decided after a few moments that he was only making things worse. He stopped and turned to her.

"I'm trying to make a lot of money the only way I know how."

"I don't care about money. I want my husband and the children want their father."

"Where are the children?"

"Ma's got them."

"I'm surprised you didn't bring them."

Caroline started to cry.

"I thought you'd at least be pleased to see me."

"This is no place for you. It's a mining town. We're living in a one-roomed hut. The hut stinks, and the men stink. We work hard and we work all day. We're doing all we can to make as much as we can, and it's not easy."

Caroline stood in front of him—her head and shoulders bent—shaking and sobbing. A few people took notice, but most ignored them. William decided it might be a familiar sight in the gold town. He hugged Caroline and she clung to him fiercely.

"C'mon," he said finally, "we have to get you out of this wind."

"Where can we go if we can't go to where you live?"

"There's a coffee shop up here. I've never been in it, but I've seen women there, so I'm sure it'll be all right. At least we'll be out of the wind and we can work out how to get you home."

"I'd rather tea," she said.

"Have you ever had coffee?"

"No."

"Then I'll get us both tea."

"Will they have something to eat?"

"We'll ask them. If they say *no*, we'll go somewhere else."

They went into the coffee shop and found a table, and William went to find help. He already liked the shop a lot. There were several pretty, young and well-dressed girls serving behind a counter, on which stood racks of cakes and pies. The scent of baking filled the air, and he could smell pastry, bread, cakes, and fruit like apples, peaches, apricots and pears. This was a secret place that had been hidden from him the whole time he'd been in Hill End.

He asked for tea and an apple pie.

"Would you like cream with that?" asked the girl behind the counter.

"Yes, please."

She put the pie on a plate, some cream on the side and gave him two knives and forks and winked at him.

"I think you should share it," she said. "That's what I'd do. That'll be a shilling."

He gave her the money.

She put some tea into two china cups that looked so delicate he thought they might break under the weight of the tea. He blushed when he went to pick them up with his dirty hands, still covered in mud and dirt from digging in the shaft.

"I'm sorry," he said, pulling his hands away.

"You sit down, sir, and I'll bring them to you. I'll bring the pie, too, and if you want more tea, just wave. There's milk and sugar on the table."

"Milk?" said William.

"Some people like it with their tea."

She brought the pie and cups at the same time, balanced on her hands and wrists.

"Here you are, missus," she said to Caroline. "You look like you might enjoy this. It's cold outside. Wave if you want more."

There was enough noise from the customers and staff in the shop that William and Caroline could talk and not be overheard.

"How did you get here?" he asked, taking the delicate cup in his hardened, dirty hands like it was a flower.

"I came on the mail coach from Bathurst."

"But that often doesn't get in until late."

"I stayed in Sofala last night. The coach driver asked a man from there to bring me today. He said I'd have to climb more hills on foot if I came with him. The man was very nice. There was just the two of us in his gig and we left very early this morning. He said we had to use a cutting called Cockatoo before the teams from Hill End started using it. There's only one-way traffic, and it's almost impossible to even turn a horse around, the road is so narrow in places."

"I've heard of it."

"Didn't you come that way?"

"No, I came on the bridle track."

"No one told me about that."

"It's only for riders. Anyway, it must have been an awful trip."

"It wasn't easy, and the coach was the worst," she said, and smiled. "Some of the heights are very scary and the road is very rough. We were thrown all about the place in the coach."

"I'm surprised they brought you, being pregnant."

"Me too. I think the driver was glad to get rid of me in Sofala."

William couldn't help it—he put his head back and laughed. The other customers looked at him quickly, probably to see if they had missed something. Caroline laughed too. He'd forgotten how much he loved that laugh, and how beautiful she looked.

"Where did you stay in Sofala?"

"At the man's house."

"The man's house?" stammered William.

"Yes," said Caroline with a smile. "He and his wife were lovely and made me very welcome. They wouldn't take any money. Said I was better at their place, anyway. They said the hotels were all crowded and noisy."

"What does the man do here?"

"Said he's a partner in a mine."

"What'll we do?" he asked, after a small lull in their conversation.

"About what?"

"About you being in Hill End."

"If I can't stay at the hut, perhaps I can stay somewhere else?"

"Wouldn't it be better if you went home?"

"No. It wouldn't. I didn't come here to go home—I came here to be with you."

"What about the girls?"

"Ma said she'll look after them for us. I told her it wouldn't be for long."

"I don't understand. What do you mean? It wouldn't be for long?"

"I told her we'd send for them."

"And live here?"

"It's where you're living, isn't it? I want to live where you live. The girls want to live where we live."

William sat back, then signalled for more tea. It gave him a moment while he thought about what to do. While they waited, Caroline helped herself to the pie.

"This is delicious," she said, as though the pie was all that mattered.

The girl arrived with more tea and poured it from a large pot. William wasn't used to drinking tea from such a small cup and was tempted to ask for something larger but decided against it—it would only show him up as a digger. Then, he laughed.

*Show me up as a digger? What else do I think I look like?*

"I'm sorry, sir," said the girl, "is everythin' all right?"

"Yes, it is," he said. "I was just thinking how silly I must look, drinking tea from a delicate cup and dressed like a digger."

"You don't have to worry, sir—we get a lot of diggers in here. The pies are very popular. You should bring your lovely wife more often."

"I just arrived today," said Caroline.

"Not much of a day to arrive, is it?" she said. "It's better in the summertime."

"Too many flies in the summer," said William.

"Oh?" said the girl. "You live here?"

"I do."

"Well, you'll be ever so pleased for your wife to join you."

"I'm not too sure about that," said Caroline, and laughed. "He lives in a hut with some other men and there's no room for me."

William blushed. He wasn't sure about this instant friendship between the women, nor how Caroline was sharing their family issues.

"Are you lookin' for somewhere to stay?" asked the girl.

William was about to say she wasn't, when Caroline said, "Yes."

"I know someone. She's lookin' for someone to stay with her. Her husband died. She's not that old but hates livin' on her own. She doesn't have any children."

"How do you know her?" asked Caroline, as though it mattered.

"She's my auntie—my ma's sister. Ma wants her to stay with us, but she won't hear of it."

She looked nervously at the counter.

"Look, I have to get back to the counter. If I pour you some more tea, will you stay for a few more minutes? Then I can show you the house and you can go to see her."

"What's her name?" asked William.

"Lizzie. Her name is Lizzie."

She poured some more tea and went back to the counter.

"It won't hurt us to look," said Caroline. "Does she mean us both?"

"I don't know," said William. "Why did you come now? Why didn't you wait until the baby is born?"

"I want to be with you when our child is born."

"When is it due?"

"Not long now. That's why I had to come."

They drank their tea, and the girl came back to their table.

"Are you finished?" she asked.

They both nodded.

"Then come with me—I can show you from the door."

They went to the door and the girl pointed across the road.

"See that street there? Go down it and you'll see a place with a lovely garden out front. She'll be home now. She doesn't like the cold."

They thanked her and left. There was nowhere to cross that wasn't muddy, so eventually William scooped Caroline up and carried her across the street, avoiding the traffic that paid them no mind. Caroline put her arms around his neck, her head on his shoulder, and hugged him fiercely.

"Oh, Tom. I know you don't like that I've come here, but I do love you so."

He put her down on the other side and they walked hand in hand up the side street, seeing the house as described. It was painted white, and everything was so neat—there was no doubt someone loved it. They walked up the path to the house and William knocked on the door.

The door opened almost straight away, and a soft voice said, "May I help you?"

"Are you Lizzie?" asked Caroline.

"Yes, I am," the voice replied.

They still couldn't see her clearly.

"May I help you?" she asked again.

"We were told you might have a room for rent?"

"I do. Would you like to come in?"

The door opened wider and revealed a middle-aged lady with a soft, smiling face and bright, intelligent eyes, wearing a colourful apron. A rush of warm air came as soon as she opened the door wider.

William did his best to clean his boots, still muddy from the road. She waited patiently, still holding the door open.

"Sorry," he said, "it's the best I can do."

She reached to her side, behind the door, and passed William a brush.

"Use this," she said. "It'll do a better job."

"That'll do," she said, after a few moments of vigorous effort on William's part.

She ushered them both into a very comfortable sitting room, with a fire glowing from the hearth.

"Sit yourselves down. Here, dear, you sit by the fire. You'll catch your death. Would you like tea?"

"No, thank you," said Caroline. "We just had tea at the café. I'm Caroline and this is my husband Tom. Your niece told us about the room."

"Ah, Libby—sweet girl. She's named for me, of course. Would you both be wanting the room? If so, you'll be disappointed. It's only a room for one."

William and Caroline looked at each other. Caroline shrugged.

"One's all right."

"Come this way then."

She showed them the room. It was very small—with a narrow bed, suitable for only one person—but very neat. The bed covering looked like knitted wool. There was a bedside table with a jug and dish, and floral curtains covering a window that looked out on mist-shrouded hills.

"It's five shillings a week. You can use the kitchen, of course. Water closet is out the back. I use coal for the fire, so it's better heat and not as messy as wood. Easier for you too, dear, I think, in your condition. There's a bath in the wash shed out back, and you can use that too."

She watched them both of a few moments.

"Perhaps if I leave you here to talk? I'll go back by the fire. Once you've had a talk, come and tell me what you think."

She left the room, pulling the door closed behind her.

"She seems nice and it's only for a while," said Caroline. "Maybe only a few days until we find somewhere that we can all live."

William's heart sank. Decisions were being made and they hadn't talked about it. Now certainly wasn't the time for discussion, and Caroline needed somewhere to stay. None of the hotels would be suitable, and he needed time to think.

"All right," he said.

They opened the door and went into the sitting room.

Lizzie was back by the fire, knitting.

"That's good," she said, and laughed. "There's no privacy. I could hear you through the door. It's no matter, of course—most people only want it for a few days, so a few days is fine."

Caroline laughed too.

"I think we'll get along, dear," said Lizzie. "Now you, young man, you fetch your wife's bag, and we'll get her settled."

William looked at Caroline, conscience-stricken. He hadn't even thought of her bag.

"Of course. Where is it?" he said.

"I left it at the All Nations Hotel."

"I know where that is," said William. "I'll be back shortly."

He went out into the cold and blustery day. Darkness was coming, and the earlier mist had already turned to light rain. It wasn't far to the All Nations and, even in that short distance, he tried to think about Caroline being in Hill End. He couldn't see it working, but he was already glad they'd found Lizzie. It was cheaper than a hotel, and certainly safer and better for Caroline.

When he got back, he found Lizzie and Caroline chatting amiably over a cup of tea. He'd left the brush outside the front door, and did his best to clean his boots. It was hard to see the mud in the fading light and, without Lizzie to approve of the result, he spent more time over the job.

He knocked, pushing the door open when Lizzie called, "Come in!"

"Cold out there," he said, putting the bag on the floor. There was now the smell of something cooking. "Whatever that is, it smells good."

"Will you stay for supper, dear?" asked Lizzie.

"No, thank you. There are some men who'll be wondering what's become of me. I should let them know."

"It won't be long before it's ready, Tom," said Caroline.

"I know. Perhaps tomorrow night."

"All right, tomorrow night," said Lizzie, and disappeared into the kitchen.

William gave Caroline a hug.

"I hope you'll be all right here."

"I'll be all right—Lizzie's really nice. She's a midwife, too, and that might be useful. Will you come back tomorrow night?"

"I will," he said, and kissed her on the forehead. "I have to bring the money for Lizzie anyway."

He reached the door to leave, turned and waved his hand. The light in the room was poor, coming from only one kerosene lamp and the fire. Caroline was framed against the light from the fire, her bump clearly visible.

*Any day now*, he thought. *Life has changed quickly in less than a day—I'd better find a doctor.*

"Tomorrow night," he said, opening the door and stepping out into the darkness, closing the door behind him. He headed straight for the Metropolitan for a whisky, and for some time to think before he went to his hut.

*What a mess.*

After a whisky at the Metropolitan, he headed back to his hut in the dark and steady rain. He'd decided that he couldn't stay in Hill End.

When he reached the hut, he was very wet and a little nervous. Some laughter from inside the hut made him relax slightly, although he had no idea what to say to the others about his decision to leave, nor what they would do about his share.

Pushing the door open, he stepped into the room. It smelled of damper and stew.

"Ah, Tom," said Anthony, "how are you? We've been worried. I was thinkin' I might come lookin' for you after supper."

All the men were seated around the table on the chairs they had built. He was glad he'd not considered bringing Caroline to this hut. How stupid that would have been. There was a steaming pot of stew in the middle of the table, from which the men were ladling into their own bowls. William took his customary seat, picked up the only unused bowl on the table, and ladled himself some dinner. He wasn't really hungry, but it gave him something to do.

"How's your wife?" asked Anthony. "More importantly, when's the baby due?"

"Good, and soon," said William. "I want to talk to you all."

"I expect you do," said Anthony, his face no longer friendly. "How did you let your wife follow you here? And in her condition?"

"I didn't—she made up her own mind."

"You shouldn't let her. No wife of mine would do that."

"Well, it's done now," said Nicholas, his face showing concern, and still friendly. "What are you going to do? Is she staying?"

"She is until the baby comes, then we'll both go home."

"What about us?" asked Anthony.

"That's what I want to talk to you about," said William.

"You can't be a partner and not be here," said Anthony, "but I expect you know that."

"I do and I understand."

"Will we be able to find someone else?" asked Frank.

"We'll concentrate on the shaft," said Anthony. "We won't need someone else."

"Why don't you take your wife home and come back?" asked Nicholas. "It would only take a few days."

"That's an idea," said Anthony. "A good idea. I hadn't thought of that."

"It's not what she wants," said William.

"I know what I'd do," said Anthony.

"I don't care what you'd do," said William, tersely. "What my wife and I do is nothing to do with you. I'm sorry that things have changed, but there's nothing that can be done about it, and I need you to think what we do next."

"All right," said Anthony, stiffly, "I'll work out how much money there is and give you your share. Once you've gone, you'll no longer be part of it, no matter what we find."

"I'll work until the baby comes and share in whatever we find until then," William said.

"How long will that be?" asked Anthony. "I don't like the sound of that—I'd rather you left now."

"I'd rather he stayed," said John. "We can work both the holes and the shaft until then, so there's still some money coming in."

"I agree," said Nicholas. "The holes've been good. We wouldn't have anything without them."

"All right," said Anthony. "I don't like it, but it's not up to me. I'd like you to leave as soon as your wife and baby can travel."

The meal was finished in stony silence. William wondered why Anthony had behaved the way he did. Surely he'd expected one of them might want or need to leave early?

They went back to digging the next day, and William went to visit with Caroline that evening to have supper with her and Lizzie, and to give Lizzie some money. Lizzie said she knew a doctor who would tend to Caroline, if necessary. She'd worked with him before and he was very good.

William skipped his cards and whisky on the following Saturday night, spending it talking with Caroline and Lizzie over endless cups of tea instead. Lizzie turned out to be fun and she and Caroline got on well, as promised.

The baby was born the following Tuesday. William was working down the shaft when a boy arrived to tell him the baby was here. Lizzie had given him a penny to tell William that mother and son were well. The others clapped him on the back, shouted congratulations, and made him promise to come for a whisky that night. Even Anthony appeared pleased, although William wondered if the pleasure came from the sure knowledge that William would soon leave.

As dirty and dishevelled as he was, he couldn't wait to see his son.

*A boy! A boy!*

Knocking on the door of Lizzie's house, he could hardly contain his excitement.

Lizzie opened the door, and told him to come in.

"The brush," said William. "I need to clean my boots."

"You need to clean more than your boots," laughed Lizzie. "Come on in. This is such a happy occasion, I don't care about the dirt. I'll fix all that later. Come and see your son."

William defied Lizzie's protest, taking a few moments to brush himself down and clean some of the mud off his boots. He went through the door and headed for Caroline's room.

"No, no," said Lizzie, "she's in my room. It's a bigger bed. Birthing's better with a little extra space."

William followed Lizzie into another room. It was the same as Caroline's, only bigger. Caroline sat in bed, holding a bundle to her breast and looking like she'd not even given birth.

"Oh, Tom. You have a son," said Caroline, smiling. "He's got all his fingers and toes, and he looks just like you."

She passed the baby to William, who stood looking down proudly at his son and trying not to get dirt on the blanket. William started to cry. Lizzie left the room.

*A son. A son. What would Ma and Da think? Now, more than ever, I want to go back to Guyong and be a family. Caroline was right to come, right to want us to be together.*

He bought some whisky for his mates at the Metropolitan that night. After a while, it was like the old days—a crowd gathered and everyone was happy, telling stories, and reminiscing the humorous side of their troubles. Even Anthony had thawed and told William how he'd done a good job and had worked well with everyone. The crowd was more sombre when he told them he was leaving soon.

The next week, William and Caroline decided she was well enough to travel. Caroline didn't argue when he told her they'd go back to Guyong and wouldn't stay in Hill End. It was like she'd expected it. She didn't like it, though, when he told her that she and the baby would go back on the coach, and he'd ride Kelly. After a while, she agreed he had to get Kelly home and the only way to do that was to ride.

They both left the following morning, William taking the bridle track and Caroline going in the coach. The plan was they would meet up at Daniel's in Bathurst. Caroline would get there first, of course, as speed was important to the mail coach. William would push as fast as he could, but they both expected Caroline to be in Bathurst that day, and William the next.

In the end, Anthony looked sad to see him go. When he went to say *goodbye* that morning, Anthony told him he had fifty-three pounds, thirteen shilling and four pence for him. It was his share of the money they had accumulated. William took it and was grateful. Anthony told him he'd doubled his money, and that sounded like it hadn't been a complete waste of time even though it felt like it had. He'd already collected Kelly and settled with the feller. There were as many horses there as ever and the feller said he was pleased to see one go. He saddled Kelly, then collected his things and left his mates with a wave. They all looked forlorn, standing outside the hut and waving.

"I hope you do well!" shouted William.

"Yes, so do we!" shouted John in reply, the others just waving.

The morning was cold and it looked like there might be snow on the way. William decided he shouldn't waste time getting on the bridle track and crossing the Turon. He went to buy supplies for the two days and set out in heavy fog, taking his time with the slippery, dangerous descent down Hawkins Hill to the river and walking more than riding.

When he put Caroline and the baby in the coach earlier, she'd made him promise to be careful. He told her he was more worried about his wife and child and wished they could travel together.

"We'll be together soon enough," she whispered and gave him a hug. He supposed he looked forlorn, waving as the coach sped away.

She was right. The coach made Bathurst in good time, and Caroline was at Daniel's Inn a day before William. They stayed overnight, and the next day, William borrowed a gig, hooked a hapless Kelly up to it and drove his wife and child back to Guyong. He decided later that the people back in Hill End probably heard Elizabeth's shout of delight when she saw her mother and father were back at home. Caroline explained that she now had a brother. She wasn't too sure about that and took to pouting if the new baby had any undue attention from either Caroline or William.

They put the money that Anthony had given him into the jar and agreed while it wasn't much, it was something to show for his time in Hill End.

It didn't take William long to ride into Orange and register his son's birth. He didn't know Lizzie's name, so he decided it would do no harm to say his son was born locally. He described the location in general terms and the man suggested it would be Chain of Ponds. William had told him that Euphemia was the midwife and the man said that Euphemia was the midwife for a lot of children born in Chain of Ponds.

"Yes," the man confirmed, "that's definitely it."

Caroline didn't object when he rode into Guyong each Saturday night for whisky and cards. It was months before Nicholas and Frank came back. Nicholas told him they should all have left when he did. The shaft was never any good, and when Anthony was badly hurt in a fall in the shaft, they decided they'd all had enough and sold the claim for a few pounds.

"You did the best," said Nicholas. "Although Anthony thought at the time that we'd still find a vein and hoped we would prove to you that you should have stayed."

"It was worse than that," said Frank. "Many of the claims turned out to be useless and there was a lot of money lost looking for gold that didn't exist."

"The Star of Peace was always good, but they went a long way down. It was so deep, if Anthony'd fallen in that mine, he'd be dead now."

They all settled back into Saturday night whisky and cards and William went back to being a farmer.

CHAPTER 30

# BACK TO THE FARM

In the years that followed, two more sons were born—James and William Henry. William and his father-in-law added another room to the hut. William kept talking about moving to somewhere bigger but had to agree that it was useful to live close to his in-laws, and that the farm had so far been good to them, as had Daniel from Bathurst.

William found that it was easy to ride into Guyong and spend Saturday evenings drinking whisky and playing cards and, in the manner of farmers, he eventually bought his whisky on credit. Everyone else did it, so he did it too. It was a matter of settling the bill when the harvest came in.

There was a new innkeeper called Matthew who didn't approve of them playing cards in the pub, so they'd have a few whiskies, buy a bottle or two, and go to someone's home in the town to play cards. It was like being back in the gold fields and William loved it.

Caroline's father died unexpectedly only a few months after the birth of William Henry. The extended family was devastated and felt his loss greatly. He had been the foundation on which the family was built. William did his best to support

Caroline, who in turn did her best to support Philis. The family all expressed concern that the light had now gone from Philis's life, and with it perhaps her will to live.

Elizabeth and Margaret were older now and could help Caroline with the little ones. William would sometimes play cards all night, getting caught up in the game, going to sleep on the floor and then home the next morning. Caroline and the children would mostly already be gone to church, so he could get his own breakfast and see to the animals. The children would all be excited to see him when they got home, so Caroline's displeasure would be lost in the fun, laughter and chasing games that took place.

He and Caroline didn't talk much, but as far as he could tell, that was normal in marriage. The children were always around and there was little opportunity for intimacy. Mostly, bed was for sleeping after long days of hard work. They'd find a moment in the middle of the night sometimes, and it would be like a dream the next morning. People with money seemed to have the better of it, because they could pay other people to do the boring jobs. They had bigger houses, too, and their children weren't always underfoot.

William began to fret about money. He didn't always win at cards, and he was always caught off guard by how much of the harvest income would be consumed on paying the outstanding bills to the stores, the school, and the pub. He thought he should get more work—perhaps do some carrying—to add to his income.

Missy and Polly were still young and very useful at harvest time, so it wouldn't pay to sell them for a short-term gain. Kelly was very old now, and William worried about him, too. He'd have to get another horse if Kelly died, but he didn't have the money for it.

The idea of making more money was never far from his mind.

One Saturday night, he and his drinking mates had gone to the home of a feller called Alfred, who lived not far from the pub. They'd go to different houses, so as not to upset the families too much. Alfred owned a few farms in the area, and often talked about the difficulty of finding workers.

During a break in the cards, Alfred said, "I bought a steam thresher a couple of years back in the hope that I'd save time at harvest."

William thought it an odd topic, but decided they'd have to talk about something while they filled their pipes and glasses.

No one but William was listening, and he was not interested. Alfred went on as though unaware he was mostly talking to himself.

"It worked out well, but it sits idle for most of the year. I heard there's a feller who has brought one into the area and takes it from farm to farm and charges for threshin'."

Alfred looked up and asked, "Is anyone listenin'?"

"What's this to do with us?" asked one of the players.

"Well, I was thinkin', I might do the same thing," said Alfred.

"Why don't you?" asked William.

"I've too much to do lookin' after the farms. I was hopin' I might find a feller who could do it for me."

"Like a feller who worked for you?" asked William.

"No, I've thought about it—if I pay a feller wages, he doesn't have to do anythin'."

"What do you mean, he doesn't have to do anything?"

"Well, I have to pay him even if there's no threshin' to do. That's why I was thinkin' different."

"Let's play cards," said someone now, and the game started again.

William rode home after the game, thinking all the way. It had been one of those nights where no one won a lot—where there wasn't a lot of excitement—so the game finished early, and Caroline was still awake when William arrived.

Talk was of the children and the farm. He delighted Caroline by telling her that he'd be at church the next day.

After the services, he found Alfred. He stood on his own, looking bored.

"Tell me about the thresher, Alfred. What are you thinking?"

"Why?"

"I might be interested."

"Well, I'm thinkin' that I can take someone in as a partner."

"How would that work?"

"Like a mine, I think—we'd have shares."

"Would the feller buy half your machine?"

"That's what I was thinkin'."

"What would you do?"

"When?"

"While the feller took the machine to people's farms."

"Nothin'."

"How is that fair?"

"What do you mean?"

"Well, the feller buys half your machine, does all the work, and you get half the money?"

"All right. What do you think?"

"What if the feller bought your machine?"

"What about my threshin'?"

"What if the feller did your threshing for half price?"

"It doesn't cost me anythin' at the moment."

"Yes, it does. You paid for the machine, so if the machine only does one harvest each year, then that's what you pay for the harvest."

"I thought you weren't any good with numbers?"

"I'm getting better."

"I suppose it's better than the machine sittin' around, doin' nothin'."

"What did it cost you?"

"Three hundred pounds."

William knew he got around two hundred pounds for his annual harvest.

"How much would you charge the feller?"

"Two hundred and fifty pounds?"

"That's too much."

"How do you know what too much is? I think it's worth it."

"I don't."

"Thanks for talkin' then," said Alfred, tersely. "I'll find someone else."

"As you wish."

William turned and walked off, looking to find Caroline and the children. He didn't know if he was disappointed or not. It was a lot of money, and wouldn't easily be repaid, even if he could find someone to lend it to him. He'd heard about the machines and knew they could do in a day what it took a horse a week to do, so it seemed like a good idea and would be popular. It would make short work of his own crops, so he'd be able to put more of his land under crops and make more money come harvest. Still, if it wasn't to be, he could live with that and maybe he'd find another way to make some money.

"Just a minute!" Alfred called behind him.

William stopped and turned. Alfred joined him.

"All right," said Alfred, "I need the money, so I'll do it for two hundred."

"Can I pay you as I earn the money?"

"No, I need all the money now."

"I'll try to find the money. If I can't find it, I can't do it."

"You just made a deal. We agreed you'd pay me two hundred."

"You didn't say anything about needing the money now."

"All right, Tom, I'll give you a day to come up with it. If you don't, I'll find someone else."

Alfred turned and walked off, back ram rod straight, shoulders held back, head held high, and obviously angry.

William's enthusiasm was deflated.

*Why does Alfred need the money now? Is there something wrong with the machine? Am I being tricked?*

"I want to see the machine before we agree!" he called after Alfred.

Alfred stopped, turned, and said, "All right. Now?"

"Now's as good a time as any."

He talked to Caroline on the way to Alfred's. It wasn't far.

"Oh, Tom," she said, "a steam thresher? You don't know anything about them!"

"I can learn," he said, more defensively than he had intended.

*She's right. What do I know about a steam thresher?*

"How much does he want for it?"

"Two hundred pounds."

"Tom! That's about what we get for a harvest!"

"I know."

"Where would you get it?"

"I don't know. Maybe John who loaned me the money for Missy and Polly?"

"He may not have that much!"

"Alfred said he'd give me a day to find it. I might find it in Bathurst, if I don't find it here."

"Tom, why don't you put these foolish notions out of your head?"

"I have to make some money, Caroline. I don't make enough from the farm."

"The boys will be old enough to help soon."

"Old enough? John is only six. Willie can't even walk yet."

"Why is Daddy foolish, Ma?" asked Elizabeth.

"He's not foolish, little one. I didn't mean that."

"That's good. I think he's the best daddy in the whole world."

Caroline was quiet for a while.

"All right, Tom. If you want it, ride back and see John this afternoon. I suppose if you don't ask him, you won't know. But I'm very scared. Remember how it was when we owed him for Missy and Polly."

"It didn't take long to pay back. It'll be like that again—you'll see."

They arrived at Alfred's, and he took William to see the machine.

It was huge and in three parts. William didn't know what any of it was, and Alfred had to explain. William was glad he'd left Caroline and the children in the cart—it wouldn't do for them to see him so ignorant.

There was a steam engine. He knew what they looked like from working in the gold fields, but this one had wheels. It looked like a much smaller version of the engine from the ship. There was another machine that had a large drum, was driven by the engine and separated the grain from the chaff. The third part was a tall stacker, which Alfred said took the chaff after separation and stacked it.

"How many men does it take to use it?" asked William, not knowing what he'd got himself into.

"Three, but the men would be supplied by the farmer."

"What if he doesn't have three men?"

"His neighbours'll help."

"What if they won't?"

Alfred laughed. "Neighbours always help—that's what they're for."

William inspected all the parts, climbing on the stacker to see how it worked.

"It looks a bit old and rusty," he said finally.

"Of course it does—that's why you're not paying three hundred pounds for it!"

William continued to look at it, checking for wear and tear.

"Well?" said Alfred, clearly sick of waiting. "Do you want to buy it?"

"Yes," said William, "you said I have a day to find the money."

"Less than a day now."

"All right," said William, "If I can find it, I'll be back with your money tomorrow morning."

"Until then," said Alfred, shaking William's hand.

"You look serious," Caroline said, when William got back to the cart. "What's it look like?"

"Big," said William.

"How big?" said Caroline, alarm on her face.

"I'm glad we've got Missy and Polly," said William, "but they might not be enough."

"We don't have to do this, Tom," said Caroline.

"I know," he said, "but I know it's a good idea, and I know I can make it work."

William didn't bother going home and drove straight to see John.

"Why aren't we going home?" asked Elizabeth. "I'm hungry."

"Me too," clamoured all those who could speak.

"I won't be long," said William, "then we'll go home."

John was pleased to see him, took him into the same room as last time, and asked if his family wanted to come inside.

"No," replied William, "they're all right."

William couldn't help himself and went straight to the point.

"I need to borrow two hundred pounds."

"Christ!" said John, dropping his usual delicate speech in his amazement. "What on earth for?"

William explained.

"That's a lot of money, Tom. What if your idea doesn't work? How will you pay it back?"

"It'll work."

"I admire your confidence, lad. But sometimes, confidence is not enough. It needs to be a good idea, as well."

"Will you lend me the money?"

John looked at William, and at his family outside.

"It's a lot, Tom. Are you sure? What if this doesn't work? What about your family?"

"I'm doing it for them."

"All right, Tom, I'll lend you the money at ten percent a year on the full amount. Do you know what that means?"

"The same as the last time?"

"Yes."

"Then I know what you mean."

"You don't have anything else worth two hundred pounds, do you?"

William couldn't help laughing. John joined him for a few moments, then looked serious.

"I'll get you to sign a bill of sale, Tom."

"What's that mean?"

"If I think you can't repay me, then I can sell the machine and take my money."

"What if I've already paid some of it back?"

"Then I take only what you owe me and you'll get to keep the rest."

"Without the machine, I won't be able to do any more threshing."

"That's right. It's the price of a mistake."

William was doubtful. He could still back out. Yet, it might be his only chance to make some good money. Gold had failed, farming was hand to mouth, and maybe this was the best chance.

"This may sound harsh, Tom, but it's what businesspeople do. I have to protect my interests, too."

"I understand. It's what I want to do, so if that's the only way, then so be it."

"Do you want your money now?"

"In the morning."

"I'll prepare the bill of sale, put your money together, and see you in the morning. You have up to the time you sign the bill of sale to change your mind."

"I won't."

"I thought not—I'll see you in the morning."

They shook hands and William left.

William lay awake that night, until early in the morning. How was he to solve the problem of three pieces of machinery and two horses to pull them? Missy and Polly could probably pull only one at a time, so he'd need three trips to take the machine to anyone who wanted threshing. He'd have to find farmers all together, and maybe if he gave them a good price he wouldn't have to move the equipment much and they'd all help each other.

What was a 'good price'? How much would he charge them to do the threshing? Would he have to get some help? What if he had to pay people to help him? What did Alfred say? Three? How much would he pay them, and how would he find the money to do it?

Perhaps this wasn't such a good idea after all, though Alfred had said others were doing it and doing well. If he didn't take a chance, he'd never be able to look after his family. He'd certainly never own a stone house, and no one would ever call him *Mister*.

He got up to sit by the fire. He looked at Caroline, still sleeping. She'd been horrified at the idea, then said his family would support him if that's what he thought best. James and Willie were in a bed in the same room, and he stood for a few moments and watched them too. Their faces were just visible in the dull red glow of the firelight, sleeping peacefully and without a care in the world. Elizabeth, Margaret and John were in the room he and James had built. He didn't go to see them. It was hard enough to look at his family in this room and wonder about his decision. What would it do to them if it all went wrong?

So much money. It was a gamble, there was no doubt about that—mostly because he didn't know what he was doing. Still, most men who went gold hunting didn't know what they were doing, and some walked away with a fortune. He'd made little money from gold, so perhaps this was his future. Like gold, he'd found it by accident, and all he had to do was to take advantage of it.

Perhaps he should talk to Caroline's brother, Warren. He always seemed to make the right decision. Instinct told him Warren would advise against it, so if what he really wanted was to go ahead, then there was probably no point in talking to him.

Then, what if it did go wrong? What did he have to lose? He only owned the furniture, the cart, Missy, Polly and Kelly. The thought of losing the horses was unbearable, so he shied away from that immediately. He'd never looked for gold thinking he wouldn't find any, nor did he play cards to lose. No, if he did this, he'd go into it thinking, even *knowing*, it would work.

He left the hut before dawn and went to John's to get the money. If wheat threshing failed, it wouldn't be because he didn't try as hard as he could.

CHAPTER 31

# OWNING A STEAM THRESHER

The next two years were the most harrowing, difficult, and stressful years of his life so far. If anything could go wrong with the venture, it did.

He took the machine home in three sections. It took him all morning, and the children were so excited that it lifted his spirits, too. The part that took the hay and stacked it was the most ungainly. Alfred didn't help him at all, just took the money and said, "It's yours—take it when you want," so he decided to take it all home and work it out from there.

Cleaning, greasing and oiling all the parts taught him a lot about it, and he learned how to raise and lower the stacker. It would certainly be easier to move with the arm lowered. He worked out how the huge belt from the engine drove the thresher, which in turn drove the stacker with another belt. After he cleaned it and was feeling very confident, he set it all up and got a fire going in the engine. He'd use wood at first, and coal later if it was better. Wood was certainly cheaper and easier to get. The children wanted to stay, but he wouldn't let them. He wouldn't even let himself think about what would happen if the children became caught up in the belts, wheels or grinding drums.

It made so much noise the children lost all interest in watching, and all peered fearfully from the safety of the hut. He'd got it all working but had no wheat to thresh. So, disappointed, he turned it all off and cleaned it. It would be several months before harvest, so he thought he'd make good use of the time by getting his own crop ready and going around the district to find customers, so they would be ready at harvest time.

Most of his success in finding customers so far came from the pub, so he'd go to the pub in Guyong as often as he could, and if he was in Blayney, Orange, Bathurst or Millthorpe, he'd spend time at the pubs there too. Of course, he still had the problem of how to move three large pieces of machinery with only two horses, but if he didn't find customers, then it wouldn't be a problem at all.

Of everyone he spoke to, Matthew was the most interested in his project. He told William that he admired people who took a chance and said he'd support William as best he could, and he would certainly extend him credit at the bar, the money to be repaid when William was successful, which he had no doubt would be soon. It meant that William favoured the Commercial and went there more often.

Matthew also told William he'd heard that others with the machines were charging thirty shillings for a hundred bushels threshed, and that people were doing six or seven hundred in a day. William had to admit that the numbers meant nothing to him, but Matthew smiled and asked if he had borrowed money to buy the machine. The look on his face said he knew the answer was *yes*.

"How much interest are you being charged for the loan?"

"John said twenty pounds."

"Then, based on what I understand about how much you can process with the machine, you need to use the machine for between two and three full day's work to pay John his interest, and apart from upkeep to the machine and paying off the loan, after say, six days, all your money is profit."

William was overjoyed. He'd already arranged work in Guyong and Blayney, and without thinking, asked Matthew to help with the numbers.

"I can help," said Mathew. "How big is your farm?"

"I think forty acres," said William.

"How much do you have under wheat?"

"I'm told about a quarter."

"And how much do you get for your wheat each year?"

"About two hundred pounds. Does that sound right?"

"It does. I expect you're right and your farm is around forty acres. That's the smallest block you can get, so that's probably right. How big are the farms where you've found work?"

"I don't know," said William, miserably and feeling very foolish.

"Don't worry, Tom," said Matthew, patting him on the shoulder, "let's say they're about the same size as yours. You'll get about ten pounds from each of them for threshing their wheat."

"Ten pounds?" said William, horror on his face. He didn't understand the numbers all that well, but well enough to know that threshing wheat for two people was nowhere near enough to pay John, keep the machine, and feed his family. He could thresh his own wheat, and would save money doing that, but he'd expected that to be a benefit, not why he bought the machine.

"I'll need a lot more than two, won't I?" he asked Matthew, fear gripping his stomach.

"Well, the farms might be bigger than yours, so it might be too soon to worry."

"Too soon? Matthew, I think it might be too late."

"Tom, the harvesting season is about a month, maybe six weeks long, so that's twenty to thirty farms you can thresh, if they're all close together and you can move your thresher overnight. If you get ten pounds from each of them, that's two hundred to three hundred pounds you can make."

"Overnight? I can't move the thresher overnight between Guyong and Blayney!"

"Then you want all your customers in Guyong, or in Blayney. Get on your horse and ride to the neighbours of your two customers. See if you can convince them to use your thresher. Then, thresh only where you find the most customers."

William left the Commercial almost in a state of despair. The season was nearly on him, and he hadn't even used the thresher yet—didn't even know how it worked! What was he thinking? He should have gone to Matthew in the beginning, asked him about the numbers. Hell, he should have done that even before he bought the machine!

He got up early the next morning, saddled Kelly, and rode around Guyong, visiting as many wheat farmers as he could and trying to convince them to use his thresher. Some were prepared to talk, others had no interest. The few that considered it, asked questions about how the machine worked, or about the condition of the wheat once it was threshed. William was furious with himself because he had no answers. The farmers who had already agreed to use his thresher had used one before, so they had no questions. Now the farmers that he met had nothing but questions, and he couldn't answer any of them.

Late in the day, he went back to the Commercial. It was a weekday, so there weren't many customers. Sad, dispirited, and fretful, he accepted a whisky from Matthew and joined a group at a nearby table.

"Here he is," said one of the men, "the thresher man!"

"What's it to you?" asked William, angrily.

"Nothin'," said the man. "What's got you all riled up?"

"Will you use my thresher?" asked William.

"No, I won't."

"Why not?" barked William.

"I hear they bruise the grain."

"So what? It'll be bruised when you make flour, won't it?"

"I hear bruised grain won't grow."

"Then, flail some, thresh the rest. What's wrong with you people?" demanded William. "Won't you even try it once?"

"We only get one harvest. If the thresher makes a mess of it, then we have to wait a year—it's not worth the risk."

"Other people have done it."

William couldn't help himself now. He knew he wasn't winning friends or customers, but he didn't care. He was angry. Angry at himself mostly, but he couldn't control his anger.

"More fool them," said the man.

"Then to hell with you lot!" yelled William, and downed his whisky. He walked over to the bar to get another.

"Calm down," said Matthew. "You won't get customers by yelling at people."

"I know, I know. Christ, Matthew! I've made such a mess of it. I don't even know how the machine works."

"Tom, think about it—you've got your own harvest. You can thresh that with your machine and learn how it works. Then, you've two customers—that'll get you a few pounds. You can do some harvests for free and show people that the thresher works well. You'll lose money this year, but put that down to experience. You'll do better next year."

"Matthew, thanks—I'll think on it. Can I take a bottle of whisky with me? I don't think I should drink here anymore tonight, but I'd like another whisky."

"Of course. I'll put it on credit. I know you'll be good for it."

Matthew fetched a bottle and gave it to William, and put another entry in William's ledger.

"You're building a debt, Tom. It's nearly ten pounds, but I know you'll pay me when the money comes in."

"I will, Matthew. I will," said William, taking the bottle and heading towards the door. He went out and wearily got onto Kelly, the reins in his left hand, the bottle in his right. He would normally have put it in the saddle bags, but he thought he might drink as he rode.

*Damn it all*, he thought. *How did I get to here? Living on credit, and nothing but debt. Just like Euphemia.*

He uncorked the bottle, putting the cork absently in his pocket and took a deep drink. Lord, it tasted good. Whatever else, whisky always tasted good. He tried to remember some songs from his youth, from the ship or from the gold fields. Nothing came to mind.

"C'mon, Kelly. Can't you help?"

Kelly plodded on, heading for home. William kept drinking, no longer concerned that he couldn't remember any songs, and only that people wouldn't use his thresher. He wished he'd made more of it in the pub. Perhaps if he'd pushed harder, the men might have agreed to use his thresher. He needed a piss and told Kelly to stop. Kelly did and William tried to get down from the saddle.

"Christ, Kelly! Stand still, damn you!" he barked.

Holding the bottle carefully, so as not to spill any, he struggled with the task. The movement was nothing like the quick descent he usually made, where he'd throw a leg over the pommel and slide to the ground. He had to think very carefully—left foot in the stirrup, right leg over Kelly's arse, stomach on the saddle, bottle held firmly in the right hand, pommel in the left, and slide down. Once on the ground, he had to be careful taking a piss that he didn't get any in the whisky bottle. Life was more complicated now, although Kelly was older so he had to be more considerate.

Getting back on Kelly was almost beyond him, and he had to tell Kelly often to stand still. Once he was back on, he tried to take a drink but found there was no more whisky in the bottle. Had it spilled? He threw the bottle away absently. Kelly started walking and William dozed, swaying in the saddle, not waking up until they arrived back at his farm. He fell off Kelly, more than climbed off, and lay on the ground, dazed and trying to get his bearings.

Somebody was talking to him. He wasn't sure, but he thought it was Caroline, although he couldn't understand a word she said. Perhaps she talked Chinese? Yes, that was it—she was talking Chinese, like he had heard when he was at Lambing Flat. He tried to tell her not to talk Chinese, but of course he couldn't, because he didn't know how to talk Chinese. How did she learn it and why was she using it? Hang on, it wasn't Caroline at all, but Kelly that was talking. How did Kelly learn to talk, and learn to talk Chinese? Why didn't Kelly talk English, like William? If he didn't speak English, William would have to sell him. In the end, it didn't matter what language Kelly spoke. William still had to get the saddle and bridle off and turn him loose in the yard. He'd never had such trouble before, and it took him longer than it should have, but eventually he turned Kelly loose and put the saddle and bridle in the barn. He was very tired and lay down where he was for a brief rest before going inside.

He woke in the morning with Elizabeth peering at him.

"Daddy?" said Elizabeth. "What are you doing out here?"

"Out where?" he asked, confused at why Elizabeth would want to know such a thing.

"With Kelly."

"Oh, I was just checking on him."

"Mummy said you're drunk."

"Drunk?"

"Yes. She said when you have too much whisky."

"She might be right. Where's mummy?"

"Inside. She told me to get you for breakfast."

"Breakfast?"

"Yes, breakfast."

"All right, I think I can go in now. I think Kelly is all right."

"He looks all right to me."

"Then I should have asked you in the first place. What are we having for breakfast?"

"I don't know. I expect we'll find out when we go in."

"Yes, I expect we will."

Elizabeth took his hand and led him inside. The children and the baby were all at the table, silent, watching William as though they had never seen him before.

"Good morning, Daddy!" they all chimed, as though they'd all received a signal to speak at the same moment.

Caroline had her back to him, fussing at the fire.

"Porridge," was all she said, not looking at him.

William sat down, painfully aware of mosquito bites and his rumpled clothing.

"Sleep well?" asked Caroline, looking at him for the first time. "You might need a bath—you smell like you slept in a vat of whisky and covered yourself in a blanket made from horse dung."

"If you say so," said William.

He got up from the table, heading outside and down to the creek. The pool where he'd sat and thought all those years ago was still there. He waded in until he was up to his knees and fell forward into the water. It might have been summer but the water was cold, and the effect was instant.

"Christ!" he yelled, stumbling out of the water. He couldn't believe how cold it was and was now more awake than he wanted to be. Still, he knew what he had to do. He went back to the barn, sloshing in his wet clothes and boots and shivering in the cool breeze. Still wet and not caring, he saddled Kelly and set out for Blayney.

Tired, cold and hungry, he rode into Blayney about two hours later. He found a baker and bought a half loaf of bread for a penny. It wasn't much but it filled a hole, and there was a little left for Kelly. The baker saw him feed Kelly and called out, "Hang on a minute, mate! I've still some bread from yesterday—I'll give you some of that!"

"Sorry," said William, "I can't afford it."

"Don't worry about that, mate!" the baker yelled. "I won't charge you. It's only going to the horses anyway—yours might as well have some."

He came back with a loaf and something else wrapped in a piece of paper.

"This is for the horse, and this is for you. It's only a piece of cake, but you look like you need it. You look like things aren't going too well."

William protested.

"It's all right, mate," said the baker, "if you don't want the cake, give it to your horse. You both look like you need a good feed and a good night's sleep."

"Thanks," said William, moved by the man's thoughtfulness.

William went to see his customer, who was confused to see him.

"It'll be a few weeks before I'm ready," he said.

"Do you think any of your neighbours might want me to thresh their wheat too?"

"Ah, I see why you're here." The man considered William's question briefly. "No, I don't think so," he said. "I've used a machine before, and you gave me a good price. The other fellers prefer to do it by hand. I'll tell you what I'll do. I'll tell 'em to come and watch—might be some change their minds this year or next. That might get you a few more customers."

The man stopped talking and looked at William.

"Things not going too well, I suppose? Not enough fellers want to use your machine?"

"I could do with more."

"People don't like new ideas. Might take a while to catch on. I'll see what I can do. I'd like you to be around for a while. The machine makes the job easier, but not everyone will like it."

"Thanks," said William, and climbed into the saddle.

"See you," said the man, waving. He walked away, shaking his head.

William didn't know what to do. He could ride around Blayney, asking farmers if they'd like to machine thresh, but he knew in his heart it would be another difficult day. Watching the man walk away, William wished for happier times and bitterly regretted buying the thresher and taking out the loan. Selling a new idea was not what he did. Working hard with his hands and following orders was much more his line of work. With a heavy heart, he knew he had no choice. He set out to call on as many farmers as he could in the day.

The sun was a dull glow in the west when he climbed onto Kelly for the last time that day and set off on the road to Guyong. A few farmers had expressed interest, but none would make a commitment. Others said they'd come and see the machine at work, if he would tell them when they could see it in Blayney. The way back took him along the main street. He liked Blayney—it reminded him of Bathurst. Wide streets, and some imposing buildings. He shivered a little. Summer was on them, but the evening was cool. There was laughter and music coming from a two-storey pub a little way ahead. A few horses were tethered outside. Perhaps that's what he needed—some company, a drink, something to laugh at for a change.

Drawing up to the pub, he stepped off Kelly and dropped the reins.

"I won't be long," he said to Kelly. "If the publican doesn't give me credit, then I'll be right back."

He pushed the door open and stepped inside. No one took any notice of him. He supposed he looked like any farmer, since most of the people in the room were dressed the same. As he approached the bar, the man behind it said, "What'll you have?"

"Can you give me a little credit?"

"Where are you from?"

"Guyong."

"What're you doing here?"

"I've a steam thresher—I'm trying to find business."

"Looks like you haven't found much."

"How is that?"

"Not exactly dressed like you don't know what to do with your money."

"If you can't give me credit, then I'll not waste your time."

"You from Ireland?"

"A while back."

"Name's James. You?"

"Tom."

They shook hands.

"I'll give you credit, Tom—only a few pounds though. Pay me when you do some threshing."

"I will."

"What'll you have?"

"Whisky."

James poured him a whisky. The first sip burned all the way down on an empty stomach.

"Do you have anything to eat?"

"Dining room's out back. I suppose you want that on credit too?"

William nodded and said, "I don't want much—bread and jam will be all I need."

"I think we can do better than that—let me see. But before I do, are you drinking on your own, or do you want to join some fellers?"

"Anyone playing cards?"

"Not here—police station is too close. I can introduce you to some fellers if you want to talk though."

William looked around. There were a few people in the bar, mostly seated at tables. One group in particular caught his eye. The four men were dressed like him, probably farmers, but one man was telling stories and the others laughing from time to time.

"What about them?" he asked James.

James shook his head.

"They work on a farm not far from here. They've just brought some produce to send on the train for Sydney. Stopped in for a quick drink on the way back. They won't stay long—said they wanted to be home before dark."

"I suppose that's what I should do."

"You might get home before dark tomorrow."

William laughed. He liked James. It was good to laugh. He hadn't felt like it for a while. James went away to serve some other customers. It was some time before he returned, and William's glass was empty by then.

"Another?" said James.

"No," said William, "I might see if I can get home before dark."

James laughed.

"Go out to the dining room and have something to eat before you go."

William shook his head.

"No, thanks all the same, James. I'm living off credit and it's not what I want to do."

"I could understand if you were the only one doing that, but you're one of many. Don't worry—I'll chase you when I need to. Besides, we Tipperary boys need to stick up for each other. Wait here—I'll be back in a few minutes."

William waited, tired and miserable.

"Here—take this," James said upon his return. "If you don't, it'll be thrown out, so you might as well have it. It's just some vegetables and a piece of steak. Cook had it ready for you—no point in wasting it."

Taking the flour bag, William was overwhelmed by thoughtfulness for the second time in the day.

"Thanks, James. I'm grateful. I'm hoping thanks is enough, but if not, I'll owe you for this too."

"It is. Call by next time you are here. I'll see if I can find some more customers for you."

James shook hands and turned away to deal with some other customers.

William went out into the night, mounted Kelly and rode off, over the railway lines and out of Blayney. He followed the Belubula River for a while and just after he crossed it, he got down, unsaddled Kelly and turned him loose to graze. Even though there was enough moonlight to see, he couldn't really tell what was in the flour bag but didn't care and settled down to eat his supper.

Once he was done, he stretched out on the sand and, using the saddle as a pillow, he thought about his day. The stars filled the sky, animals rustled in the grass nearby, and the river rattled and murmured through the rocks. No one could get him here, so at least he could ignore his problems for a few moments. Lying beside a river, thousands of miles from Ireland, he prayed to a God he thought little about, that he and his family would be all right.

Then he realised Matthew was right—he could use this year to find more customers, convince farmers that machine threshing was the best way to go, and to learn how to thresh quickly and efficiently. Everything wasn't lost, and thinking it was would only distract him from getting on with the job at hand. He had to make a success of steam threshing.

When he woke, the day was well advanced. The sun was already hot in a cloudless, brilliant blue sky. A gentle breeze blew, and he sat up to find Kelly. He wasn't far away and came when William whistled. William got up, and thought he might keep the flour bag, but decided not to when he noticed it was swarming with ants. He saddled Kelly and set off for home. The meal and the sleep had refreshed him, and he rode with renewed purpose.

There was no one at the hut when he got there, and he wondered where Caroline and the babies might be. He had no idea what day it was so decided it might be Sunday and they would be at church, but the cart was in place and Missy and Polly in the paddock.

He unsaddled Kelly and set him loose. The wheat looked good and only a week or two from harvest.

*Good, good,* he thought, *I can try the thresher now and have a better idea of how it works.*

It was late afternoon before his family arrived home. Caroline's brother, Warren, drove the cart, Caroline beside him and all the children in the back.

Elizabeth stood and pointed at William.

"You're in trouble," she called.

"Be quiet, Lizzie," said Caroline, sternly. "Warren, you stay with the children."

She got down from the cart and walked to where William stood outside the hut.

"Come inside," she said. "We have things to talk about."

When they stood inside, facing each other, William could see that she was very angry.

"Where have you been?" she demanded.

"Blayney."

"Why? What's in Blayney?"

"I've a customer there for the thresher. I was hoping to find more."

"Why did you go without saying anything?"

"There was nothing to say."

"You slept in the yard and left without eating. Elizabeth saw you fall in the creek. She was worried you might have drowned."

"I'm all right."

"Of course you're all right, but how were we expected to know that? Anyhow, were you drunk?"

"I suppose I was, but so what?"

"So what? So what? What do you mean, *so what*? Tom, I'm so angry I could hit you."

"Go ahead, if it'll make you feel better."

"What are you doing, Tom? What's happening to you?"

She reached forward, buried her face in his chest, and held him fiercely. She sobbed, and William could feel her tears through his shirt.

"You stink, Tom. When did you last have a bath?"

"The other morning, when I fell in the creek."

"That's not a bath!"

"It was cold and wet enough."

She pushed him away.

"So, what's happening? Where's my husband? Where's my children's father?"

"I'm still here."

"No, you're not. We were worried sick about you. I got Warren to drive me into Guyong, looking for you. Matthew said you had a fight with some of his customers."

"It wasn't a fight."

"He said it was. What's happening to you?"

"I'm worried I can't find enough work for the thresher."

"That wretched thresher—I wish we'd never seen it."

"So do I."

"Sell it, Tom. Get rid of it."

"I can't. Matthew went through the numbers for me. The only way forward is to find more customers. James said he'd help."

"Who's James?"

"He runs the Exchange Hotel in Blayney."

"Is that what you did in Blayney? Did you go there drinking?"

"No. Like I said, I went looking for customers. I found the one here in Guyong through the Commercial, and he put me onto the one in Blayney. I thought if I had a drink in the pub in Blayney, I might find some more."

"You can't afford whisky. We haven't got much money. The jar is nearly empty. The children need to go to school, and we've got to feed and clothe them. You can't be drinking whisky when we can't afford it."

Her voice rose, her face was red from crying, and she was visibly shaking with anger.

"All right, all right—I understand. I'm going to cut and thresh our wheat next week, then I'm going to take the thresher to Guyong, and then to Blayney. I'll get some money for that, and I'm sure that will help."

"How much are you going to get?"

William was thrown by the question. *What did Caroline know about money?*

"Why?"

"Why? Why? What do you mean *why*?"

"Why do you want to know *why*?"

"Because it's my family too, that's why! I'm going to manage our money from now on."

"What? How are you going to do that?"

"I've learnt about money and numbers and now I'm going to put it to good use."

"Where did you learn about it?" asked William, astonished.

"Elizabeth."

"Our Lizzie?"

"Yes. She learnt about it at school, and she taught me. So, how much will you get from the farmers for threshing?"

"Matthew said I might get ten pounds each."

"I went to see John. He told me you borrowed two hundred pounds at ten percent interest."

William was aghast. *Caroline understands the numbers? She's been to see John?* Here he was, making a terrible mess of everything, and here she was, using her head to make things better. Yet, his pride stood in the way. Common sense told him he should discuss every aspect of the thresher with Caroline, but he couldn't bring himself to do it.

Caroline studied him carefully, not saying anything for a few moments.

"That's it? Two customers? Twenty pounds?" she said. "Do you know you owe him twenty pounds in interest every year until you pay all the money back? And if you don't pay the interest, you owe interest on the interest."

Just then, Elizabeth stood in the doorway.

"Can we come in? Uncle Warren says he wants to go home."

"Tell Warren that's all right. Look after Willie for me, will you? There's a good girl. Play in the yard for a while. We won't be long."

Elizabeth looked at them both for a few moments, then turned and walked away.

"She's right, Caroline," said William, "I don't think there's anything left to talk about."

"Nothing left to talk about? There's a lot left to talk about! If you're not going to sell the thresher, we have to talk about how we're going to pay all that money back to John."

"If you understood the numbers, why didn't you stop me doing it?"

"A wife's job is to support her husband, not get in his way."

William looked at Caroline and, for the first time in his life, he was afraid of her. Afraid of what she knew. She understood things now that had only ever confused him. What did a man do when his wife was smarter than him? She would run the family now. It was like being a boy again. Whatever money he earned, he'd give to Caroline to manage for them, like he did when he was young and gave the money to his mother.

"What do you think we should do?" he asked, miserably.

Shame and guilt ran through his mind in equal measure. Guilt because of the mess he'd made, and shame because he had to ask his wife what to do.

"You can only do one of two things," she said, "either sell the thresher, or find more farmers to use it. You're probably right that it makes no sense to sell it. I think you paid too much for it and I doubt you'll find a buyer. Of course, we could sell it for whatever we get, pay John as much as we can, and you can become a carrier again to make the rest."

William wished the ground would open and swallow him. *Paid too much for it?*

"No," said Caroline, "you have to find more farmers—that's all there is to it. I tried to get John to take less, but he wouldn't.

He said a deal is a deal. So, we just have to make the best of this. I'll bring the little ones in now. We'll talk again later."

She went out and brought the children in, all of whom exclaimed they were hungry. Caroline set about preparing supper. William went out into the yard. He needed time to think. The feeling that he'd been demoted as head of the family didn't sit easily with him. What would John think of him now, with Caroline trying to renegotiate the deal? She had decided that he had to find more customers. Well, he'd decided that too—so perhaps he wasn't all that stupid after all. He decided not to tell her he bought whisky on credit. That wouldn't do any good. No, he'd give her the money that he earned, no matter how he earned it. That might at least get her to respect him again. It bothered him a lot to think he'd lost her respect.

He went out, called Kelly over, put his arms around his neck, and leant on him, close to tears. After a while, he went and looked at his wheat again. The colour was right, and he tested some to see if the grains were hard. He was sure he could cut it and stack it next week, using the thresher. Perhaps he could thresh some of it early, just to make sure he could work the thresher. It wouldn't matter if he ruined it, at least he'd know how to work the thresher when he was called to use it. The farmers could come any day now, asking him to thresh their wheat, and he'd better be ready.

Elizabeth called from the hut that supper was ready. She waited for him, out of hearing from those in the hut.

"Daddy," she whispered when he came close, "bend down."

He did, and she whispered in his ear, "I can teach you about the numbers too, if you like."

"Oh, darling," he said, pulled her close and hugging her. Once again, he was close to tears. "You'll always be Daddy's wonderful little girl, but I think it might be too late for me to learn about numbers."

They went inside for supper.

Over the next few days, he visited the two farmers who had agreed to use his machine. Neither was ready yet, and they both said it would be a few weeks before they were.

Things settled down at home, and nothing more was said about the thresher, although William was constantly afraid that Caroline would want to talk about how he might find more customers. He was sure Caroline would find fault with his plan, as he wasn't too keen on it himself. It hadn't worked this year, why would it work next? But try hard as he might, he had no idea how to improve it. The plan was to show farmers how well the thresher worked whenever he could, and drink whisky and make friends with as many farmers as he could. The drinking whisky part, he would keep to himself.

The next week, he cut his wheat. It took all week, and he worked from dawn until dusk, cutting and stacking. He convinced himself that he was better to cut all the wheat before he used the thresher, but he knew he was only postponing the job. What would Caroline say if he couldn't work out how to use it?

Eventually, he could postpone the moment no longer. He got the boiler going and, when he thought the time was right, he started the threshing machine. The noise it made was deafening, and the belt that ran from the engine to the machine whacked and jumped, and he prayed he'd never get so used to it that he'd forget about it and walk into it. He wasn't ready to use the stacker yet, he only wanted to understand how to thresh the wheat.

It took him a full day of trial and error. The boiler went through the wood at an alarming rate, and he found he had to give the fire constant attention. It took some time before he worked out how to change the settings on the drum so the grains would be released and not crushed. Then he positioned the elevator and managed to stack the straw. He worked out how to change its elevation so the straw could be stacked directly onto a cart. At the end of the day, he was satisfied he knew how to work the thresher. But of his wheat, precious little had been threshed. The real test would come the next day, when he could see how fast he could work, but he already knew he couldn't do it alone. He would need help, and whoever helped him would also have to know how to use the machine.

Exhausted, he had his supper and went to bed. He said nothing to Caroline about needing help. Once again, money was the problem.

That night, it rained. He awoke to the sound of thunder and heavy rain on the roof. Carefully, so as not to wake Caroline, he got out of bed and stood in the doorway, watching drops fall from the roof. Each drop was a message that he was no match for the elements. He hadn't bothered to stack the wheat in the barn. Thinking he'd get it threshed in the day, he'd left it in the open. Now he'd have to restack it to dry.

*If it's not one thing, it's another.*

The next day, the farmer from Guyong rode up and asked him to be there on the following Monday to thresh his wheat. William just nodded and agreed—of course he'd be there. He asked the farmer if he'd be able to help.

"Doubt it," said the man. "Don't know a thing about the machines other than they're way too noisy for me. I'll be as far away from it as I can get."

"What about your men? Can one of them help?"

"I don't have any men."

William watched the man ride away. He'd have to solve the problem sooner than he thought. Maybe one of his neighbours would help, or at least know someone who might. He sighed and went to talk to Caroline.

Caroline took it well when he told her she and the children would have to restack the wheat. Now the machine would be at Guyong, then at Blayney, and it might be weeks before he could bring it back to thresh his own wheat. His harvest money would be delayed this year.

She didn't take it anywhere near as well when he told her he'd need to hire help to work the thresher.

"How many men will you need?"

"I think I can do it with one."

"How many days?"

"I'm hoping to thresh all the harvest for each farmer in one or two days."

"That's four or five shillings a day. Can you find someone that won't want their money until you get paid?"

William was again intimidated. He should have talked to Caroline before he bought the thresher. It impressed him how much she knew about the numbers.

"I'll see if I can find someone in Guyong. It's going to take me three trips to get the thresher there, so I'll ask around."

"What if you can't find someone?"

"Then I'll do it on my own. It will just take longer."

He hitched Missy and Polly to the engine and started his journey. It took him much longer than he thought it would. The road was rutted and pot-holed, and the wheels on the engine would often get jammed in a rut or caught behind a rock.

The farmer was pleased to see him. He said he thought William would be able to thresh all the wheat on the Monday, so he hadn't bothered putting any of it in the barn.

"Rained over my way last night," said William. "I can't thresh it if it's wet."

"I know," said the farmer, wearily. "We were late getting started. We've still got some to do to be ready for Monday. I'll tell you what—I won't get you to thresh until Wednesday. That way, we'll take time to put it in the barn and then we can thresh whatever happens."

William struggled to control his anger. He now had the engine in Guyong, and the thresher and stacker at home. Even if his wheat dried out in the next few days, he couldn't thresh it with the machine. He then realised that the farmer was only being sensible, and there was no point in anger.

"All right," he said. "Wednesday."

He put a lead on Missy, mounted Polly, and rode back to his farm.

It was dark before he arrived home, and he knew it would take three full days to get all the parts of the thresher to Guyong. He dreaded now the journey from Guyong to Blayney, and prayed that the farmer there wouldn't be ready for at least another week.

Waking up early, he went outside to decide which piece of the machine to take next. He decided the stacker would be the most difficult, so that would be best. Remarkably, it moved more easily. Perhaps because the wheels were further apart and smaller than on the engine. It took about half the time to move it to Guyong, so he had time to stop in town to see if he could hire some help. There was no one. It turned out all the workers were committed to reaping, stacking and threshing on the many small farms in the area. He was annoyed that he had a machine that could do the job faster and no one wanted to use it, but glad there was time for a whisky with Matthew before heading home.

When he got home, Caroline told him that the farmer from Blayney had ridden over that day and wanted him to come and thresh his wheat Friday or Saturday.

"What did you tell him?" said William.

"He didn't give me a chance to tell him anything—he just told me and left."

"Maybe I can do it, if I can do the job in Guyong in one day, then move the thresher in two days. Oh Caroline, all this work for so little money!"

"Don't worry, Tom—we'll be better at it next year."

"I'll stay here tomorrow and help with the stacking."

"Don't you have to move the rest of the thresher to Guyong?"

"He doesn't want to thresh until next Wednesday, so I'll take it over Monday, set it up on Tuesday, and be ready for Wednesday."

"Did you manage to get some help?"

"No, there's no one."

"Take John. He can help with the boiler."

"He's so young."

"He can put wood on a fire, so at least the boiler won't go out while you run the machine. We're a family and we're all in this together."

William stayed and helped to stack the wheat. Elizabeth, Margaret and John all helped. It was a hard job, not made easier by the heat and the flies. The job was mostly done and the day nearly over when he asked Caroline if he could have a pound to go into Guyong to have a whisky and see if he could get more customers.

"Farmers in Guyong won't do you any good—you're taking the thresher to Blayney on Thursday."

William cursed himself for his stupidity. All he'd really wanted was a few hands of poker and a couple of whiskies.

"Perhaps I should go to Blayney?"

"It'll take you three or four hours to get there."

"You're right. It's been a long day."

They all had supper and went to bed. As he drifted off to sleep, William resolved that he'd get a bottle of whisky at the next opportunity and hide it somewhere on the farm. At least then he'd be able to have a whisky when he wanted.

He and John hitched the horses to the threshing drum on Monday and took it to Guyong. It took all day to get there. The drum was the heaviest of the three pieces and, again, the wheels were caught in every rut and pothole, and behind every rock. He wished he hadn't brought John as it was a long walk, and he was exhausted by the time they arrived. John sat in front of him on Polly for the return journey and slept all the way.

They rode out again on Kelly the next morning to set up the thresher. It was working by lunch time. John was a quick learner, and William stressed he must only ever approach the engine from the front and must never go near the belts that ran the drum and the stacker. The smoke, noise and heat all terrified John, and whenever William watched to be sure he was all right, John stood with his hands over his ears. Still, he kept the fire going. The farmer promised he would have plenty of wood the next morning.

John slept all the way home and was the devil to wake before dawn the next morning. Caroline had packed some pieces of chicken, bread and jam for the day. They had to be gone before the sun was up so they would have most of the day to thresh.

William decided they would take Missy and Polly and stay overnight at the farm after the threshing, and then William would take the thresher over to Blayney on the Thursday and Friday. Caroline would ride over on Kelly on the Thursday morning and bring John back. John was disappointed when he heard the plan—he had thought he might stay with his father.

When they arrived at Guyong, it took about an hour to get the steam up and the thresher going. The farmer put a cart nearby to stack the hay and, contrary to what he had said, had some men to help put the wheat through the thresher. To William's relief, everything worked, and they filled bushel bags with wheat steadily and quickly. John was good with the fire, and the men helped load the sheaves and took the filled bags and put them in the barn. The job was complete by mid-afternoon. The farmer's men said he was working away from the noise, and one of them went and fetched him. The farmer was delighted with the result. He counted the bags and said he had five hundred and thirty bushel bags. Moreover, he was thrilled that all the wheat had been threshed in the day.

"You've done very well, Tom. I'll take this and sell it tomorrow. You can have your money next Monday. I make that seven pounds and nineteen shillings, so come as early as you like on Monday."

William asked if he and John could stay in the barn that night as he had to take the thresher to Blayney the next day.

"Of course—you and your lad can join us for supper. I'll send the missus for you."

William and John joined the farmer's men, who had made some tea on a fireplace probably used for branding and shoeing. They had their chicken, bread and jam, and shared some around. William had thought they would have what was left for supper, but now they would eat with the farmer and his family, there was plenty to go around. John had hardly finished eating when he was sound asleep. The last few days had taken their toll.

Putting John on some hay in a corner of the barn, William busied himself dismantling the thresher for the journey to Blayney. He was happier than he'd been for a long time. The thresher had worked well, and he was confident it could do the job and would work when needed. Moving it around was a problem but unless he had more men and horses, it was a problem that couldn't be solved. He would have liked to take John to Blayney to help with the threshing on the Saturday, but perhaps the farmer would help.

John was still asleep when the farmer's wife came over to tell them supper was ready.

"Och! The pur wee lad," she said when William went to wake him. "Leave 'im be. I'll fetch your supper to ye. Ye can 'ave yers, and 'im if 'e wakes."

She went away and came back with some damper, pannikins and a billy with stew. It smelt wonderful, and William's stomach growled in anticipation.

"Ye sound like ye are ready, even if yer lad isn't!" said the farmer's wife. "Do ye 'ave some tea and sugar?"

"Aye," said William, reverting to his old speech.

John didn't wake at all, but William kept some of the damper and stew, knowing his boy would be very hungry in the morning.

It wasn't yet dawn when they set off for Blayney, hoping to meet Caroline on the road. They would wait at the Pretty Plains Road turnoff, if they didn't meet her before they got there. Not long after they set out, they saw her in the distance. She looked so tiny on Kelly.

"Do I have to go with Ma?" John asked.

"I'm afraid so."

"All done?" asked Caroline, pulling up beside them.

William lifted John up and sat him in front of Caroline.

"Did the thresher work all right?" asked Caroline.

"Better than I expected."

"How much did he pay you?"

"He'll pay next week."

"How much?"

"John?" asked William.

"He said seven pounds and nineteen shillings."

"When will you be home?" asked Caroline, passing William a flour bag. "There's some lamb, cheese, damper and peaches in there, so be careful with it."

"Sunday or Monday. Depends on how I go with the threshing on Saturday."

He looked in the bag.

"I will. Thank you. I hadn't thought much about eating."

Caroline rode with him until they reached the turnoff, then she headed home, and William headed for Blayney. Not long after Caroline left, the rain started—big summer drops, falling quickly and making the road difficult. The country was rolling hills, so there was little to climb or descend. William tried to guide the horses to avoid the worst of it, but there was more traffic now, and often he'd have to wait for carts or wagons to pass him, before he could take advantage of all of the road.

It rained all the way to Blayney, and he was glad he didn't have to cross the river. Unfortunately, the farmer lived on the other side of Blayney, so he had to go through the town, clashing with the traffic and short tempers due to the rain. It was late afternoon when he dropped the drum off at the farmer's and told him he'd deliver the other two parts and be ready to thresh on Saturday.

"Might not be able to," said the farmer. "Be hard if the rain keeps up."

"I know, but I'll be ready if God is," said William, casting a doleful eye at the sky.

"Do you want to stay tonight? You can use the barn if you want."

"No—I have to bring the rest tomorrow and I have to start early."

"As you wish."

William didn't even stop at the Exchange. It would already be well into the night before he got to Guyong.

The sun was a pink and blue hue on the horizon when he rose the next morning, exhausted before he had even started. He decided to take the engine next, as the stacker might be easier if he had to finish in the night.

Once again, he set off for Blayney, encouraging Missy and Polly to hurry. His feet were sore from all the walking, but there was no way to ride and help the horses at the same time. It was just after lunch when he arrived back at Guyong to take the stacker. The food was exhausted and so was he. As he set off, the farmer's wife hurried some damper and cheese to him. He was very grateful, but she dismissed his gratitude with a wave of her hand.

It was too dark to assemble the thresher when he got to Blayney. That job would have to wait for morning. The sky was a dull red as the sun set, a portent for a fine day on the morrow. He settled down to sleep in the barn, but the farmer woke him just as he dozed off.

"We've supper on if you've a mind to join us," he said.

William nearly hugged him and joined his family for supper. It was hot and humid in the house after the rain but that didn't stop William, who fell upon the meat and potatoes as though he hadn't eaten for days.

"Will you need some help tomorrow?" asked the farmer. "My boys can help if you need it. They know how—they've done it before."

"It's dangerous," said William.

"They know that, and they know how to be careful."

"If I have some help, we can do it in the day."

"Good. We'll see you bright and early. The wood is stacked by the boiler and there should be plenty—but tell me in the morning if you want more. You look exhausted, Tom. I've prayed to the Lord that it goes well on the morrow."

"Thanks for supper. I'll see you in the morning."

William was up early but he still spent the best part of an hour assembling the thresher, and it took another hour to get the boiler going. The wood was wet from the rain and the fire refused to cooperate. Nothing went right and William fretted that a bad start would be a bad finish.

The farmer brought him some tea and damper.

"Take it easy, Tom—the weather looks all right, and we still have time to finish in the day."

Once the threshing started, things went well. The hay and the bags piled up, and his helpers were kept busy stacking. To everyone's delight, it was late afternoon when they finished. As the farmer had said, his boys knew what to do and they did it well.

"I've been countin' 'em, Tom. That's six hundred and eighty bushels, give or take. That's about a hundred more than I got last time, and all in the day. The machine's a ripper!"

William smiled. Ripper was the latest expression, but it was mostly used by young people. It sounded odd coming from the farmer.

"Tell everyone if you can—I could do with some more customers."

"I've already told everyone I know. Can't tell more than that. Don't know what's wrong with 'em!"

William and the farmer stood looking at the bags of wheat, both contented with a job well done.

"Do you want to stay tonight?" asked the farmer.

"No, I have to get back home and thresh my own wheat. I've still a few hours of daylight and I want to take advantage of them."

"I'll get you your money. It's ten pounds, four shillings."

William was thrilled. Ten pounds! Caroline would be pleased.

The farmer came back with the money and William put it carefully in his pocket. His clothes were dirty, smelly and dishevelled from the many days of hard work. A bath would be good, but it wouldn't happen until he got home sometime tomorrow.

He put Missy and Polly in the traces to pull the drum. It didn't seem to matter which part he chose first, all three parts tested endurance and patience. Heading back through Blayney, he pulled up outside the Exchange. It was late on Saturday afternoon, and the pub was already lively. There was some grumbling as he drew up out the front, some patrons complaining about the size of the drum and how much room it took up, and others admiring the mechanics. William was pleased at the attention—it meant no one would steal his machine. *Might be better if they did!*

Missy and Polly looked pleased to stop for a while, and William went into the bar. There was a fearful racket from the patrons, and William had to push his way through. It was obvious that Saturday was in full swing. James looked hassled, but pleased to see William.

"Tom, just a minute, wait there—I want to talk to you."

He came back a few minutes later, a whisky in hand that he gave to William.

"I might have another customer for you. I didn't know how to get you, so he said that if he didn't talk to you by tomorrow, he'd have to do it by hand."

"Is he here tonight?"

"He is. Come and meet him. It's grand you've stopped by."

"I wanted to see you, too—I have some money for you."

He pulled the money from his pocket and tried to give James the four shillings. Caroline would be happy with the ten pounds and wouldn't ask about the shillings.

"Don't be silly. Your account is only a few shillings, so use that for something else. Some new clothes or a bath might be a good start."

William flushed red.

"Sorry, Tom—I didn't mean to offend you. Come and meet Patrick."

They pushed their way through the crowd.

Patrick was sitting at a table with two other men, all were dressed like farmers.

"Patrick," said James. "This is Tom who I told you about—he's got the steam threshing machine."

Patrick leapt to his feet and gripped William's hand warmly.

"James has told me about you! I'm very pleased to meet you."

William heard a strong Irish accent.

"I've part of the machine outside. We can do your wheat on Monday, if you like. Have you used a steam thresher before?"

"No, but James says it's real fast, and as far as I'm concerned, fast is good. If James says it, then that's good enough for me. Here, Tom—sit down, have a drink. James, will you fetch another round and one for Tom?"

William sat wearily into a spare chair. If he could do more threshing in Blayney before going home, so much the better.

"Where's your farm, Patrick?" asked William.

"About five miles out on the Newbridge Road," said Patrick. "It's not far. Where's the thresher?"

"Part of it is outside the pub. The rest not far from here."

"Tom, I'm Ned," said one of the men sitting at the table. They shook hands.

"Mine's Michael," said the other man, also shaking hands.

"Do you fellers want your wheat threshed too?"

They all laughed.

"We might," said Ned. "Depends on how you go with Patrick."

"When do you want it done, Patrick?" asked William.

"Monday. Can you get there Monday?"

"I can. How much do you have to thresh?"

"I've got about five hundred bushels. Can you do that on Monday?"

"I can. I can't leave the drum outside the pub though—I'll have to move it tonight. Can we take it to your farm tonight?"

"Is it big?"

"Yes."

"We have to cross the Belubula."

"I haven't tried to cross a river. It might be too heavy."

"It's up to you. The work is there if you can get the thresher to my place by Monday. I have to go now. Remember, I'm about five miles out on the Newbridge Road."

"We have to go too," said Ned, finishing his drink and standing.

"I'll be there," said William, not at all sure he would be. He didn't want to cross the river at night but if he could, then he'd easily be able to get all three parts there by Monday. He went to the bar.

"Can I get something to eat?" he asked James.

"Of course. Does he still want you to do his wheat?"

"If I can do it on Monday."

"Can you?"

"I can try."

"Go out to the dining room. We'll get you fixed up."

William had dinner and two more whiskies. James was happy to provide it all on credit. After dinner, William went outside and walked the horses down to the Newbridge Road and walked as far as the river. It wasn't far, but it was dark and hard to see. When he could hear the river ahead, he went carefully and stopped when he got near to it. He took the harness off Missy and Polly and turned them loose to forage. Some oats would be good, but he had none—and no nose bags, even if he had.

At least the night was warm, and the rain was gone. He curled up near the drum and went to sleep.

When he woke, he could hear the sound of voices. Two men rode from town towards him.

"Mornin'", one of them said. "Where are you off to?"

"Patrick's farm."

"He's not far. Only a few miles down the road. Left side. House on a hill. You can't miss it. You going to take that?" he said, pointing at the drum.

William nodded.

"Good luck," said the man, and he and his companion rode on.

William took off his boots and walked out into the river. His heart sank. The bottom was sandy. He was hoping it would be rocky, in which case the drum wouldn't bog. The lure of the money was strong, so he put Missy and Polly in the harness and started towards the river. When they reached the edge, the horses didn't want to go any further. He pulled at the lead, but neither would budge.

*Is their intuition better than mine? Do they think we might get bogged?*

It wasn't very wide—only twenty or so yards—but wide enough to get bogged. He didn't know what to do and was about to turn back when he heard horses coming from the other side of the river. It was Patrick, with four more horses.

He laughed and waved when he saw William.

"I thought you might be in trouble here. I've brought some help."

"The harness only takes two horses."

"I thought of that. I brought a harness too, and we can rig it to take six."

Once hitched, the six horses had no trouble pulling the drum across. On the way to Patrick's, they crossed the railway line twice. William wondered if the railway made people in the area more accepting of new ideas.

They dropped it at Patrick's farm, then took all the horses back to Blayney and collected the rest of the thresher, using all six to pull each piece across the Belubula.

William stayed overnight at Patrick's and got up early the next morning to rig the thresher, and they easily threshed all the wheat in the day. Patrick gave William eight pounds, three shillings and sixpence.

"Where's Ned's farm?" asked William.

"He's at Newbridge."

"Do you think he'll want me to do his wheat?"

"He said he would if I was happy. He's this side of Newbridge, so he's only a few miles away—said he'd come by this afternoon and see how we went. Why don't you pack up your gear? And if he doesn't come, I'll take you there tomorrow. You can stay again tonight, whatever happens."

Sure enough, Ned arrived, and Patrick advised all had gone well.

"Good," said Ned. "Can we do mine tomorrow?"

"It'll take me all morning to get the thresher there."

"I'll help," said Ned.

"So will I," said Patrick, proudly. "I know how to do it—Tom and I brought it all over from Blayney yesterday. Stay here tonight, Ned. That way, we can all get an early start."

William liked these men—they made decisions and didn't question what he did and didn't know.

They drank too much whisky that night but were still up early to hitch the horses and, taking a part each, set out for Ned's farm. It was only a few miles through pleasant, undulating country, but the summer heat and the flies destroyed any pleasure the journey might afford.

Again, William assembled the thresher, and with help from Patrick, Ned and some of Ned's men, the job was done in no time.

William was feeling more confident about the thresher now. He knew how to work it, though the transport was still a serious shortcoming—too much time was wasted moving it around.

Ned suggested they all go to Michael's pub. He'd leave his men to take the wheat to the station for transport to Sydney, and he, Patrick and William could enjoy a whisky or two. Then they could all stay at Ned's overnight, and Ned volunteered Patrick to help to move the thresher back to Blayney on its way to Guyong.

Newbridge was a small town, unlike Blayney. However, like Blayney, the railway line ran past it—so it was a busy town with produce coming from all around the area for freight to Sydney by rail. There were gold fields near to the town as well, so an itinerant population made good use of the town's pubs and stores. Patrick and Ned agreed William would do better selling the use of his thresher in towns like Blayney and Newbridge, where farmers wanted the wheat threshed early for the Sydney market and which was accessible by rail.

William liked Michael immediately, not the least because Ned said he permitted an occasional game of poker on the premises. It was quiet that night though and, there being no more customers for his thresher, William thought it wise to start the journey back to Guyong at first light. Patrick agreed but said he couldn't afford William to take his horses, however, he would help William back into Blayney with the thresher. But after that, it was up to William to get it to Guyong.

When William arrived home with the first part of the thresher, his family were overjoyed to see he was all right and hadn't had an accident. Caroline was even happier with the money he gave her, and they agreed they could yet make a success of the venture.

The news wasn't all good though. Caroline and the children had managed to hand-thresh some of his wheat, but the rain had caused it to sprout and none of it would go to market. It was devastating news. While they had saved enough for seed for the next season, they would receive no income for his crop. Caroline said that while he was away, earning about thirty pounds, they'd sacrificed about two hundred pounds through the loss of his own harvest.

They wouldn't be able to pay John anything, and the debt would mount. William was devastated. He'd been so confident, so proud, that his plan might work, but it involved him having his own harvest.

"It will have to be done first each year," he said to Caroline. "The machine doesn't leave here until we do our own harvest."

"We'll have to plant sooner than anyone else. That'll be risky if there's a frost."

"Unfortunately, if that's what we need to do, then we have to do it."

Caroline was interested that William had learnt it might be more successful for him to look for customers in Blayney and Newbridge. They resolved that the next year—long before harvest—he'd go and meet as many farmers as he could and, with help from his existing customers, it would be a better year.

CHAPTER 32

# A HARD LIFE

William went to see John and told him that he couldn't make any payments on the loan. He explained what had gone wrong and said they had better plans for the next harvest. Thinking it was better not to tell him that they would look for more work in Newbridge and Blayney, he said only that the thresher had worked well and the customers had been pleased with the result.

"What's the problem then, Tom? Why don't you have more customers?"

"It's a new idea, John—people have to get used to it. It'll be all right next harvest. You'll see."

"I know I don't have to tell you about our arrangement, Tom. You owe me interest on two hundred and twenty pounds each year until all the money is repaid."

"I know, John."

"Your wife came to see me."

"I know that too, John. I'm sorry."

"Don't be. I hadn't expected it, but I was impressed at the same time. You've got a good one there, Tom."

The family lived as frugally as they could, but Caroline wouldn't hear of them not sending the children to school. She also wouldn't let the credit get out of hand at the stores in Guyong, so she and the children spent long hours in the vegetable garden.

"I'm not going to end up like Euphemia, scared to go to a store and buy anything because we owe too much money."

While he waited to do the next season's ploughing, William got some work as a carrier, and sometimes as a labourer. He gave most of what he earned to Caroline, and only had the occasional game of poker or whisky in Guyong. Whisky was on credit but the cards required cash, so he kept a few shillings for himself. He found the risk of losing sharpened his game such that he rarely lost money, and he was able to pay off a little of what he owed Matthew. Every now and again, he would bring a bottle of whisky home and hide it in the paddocks.

*A little sip every now and then will do no harm*, he told himself. He had to have it early so Caroline wouldn't smell the whisky when he came home from his work. A thought that it wasn't right did nag him, but he pushed it away.

*Life's not all about hard work and self-denial. It can't be—not worth living if you can't enjoy some of it.*

They expanded the area of the vegetable garden and raised more chickens and pigs. Autumn came and he finished ploughing and planted the next season's wheat. He reassured Caroline that he wouldn't move the machine until they harvested and threshed their own crop.

He kept the machine in top order, greasing and oiling it, getting it ready for the next harvest. Sometimes he showed his son John how to use it if he wasn't at school, hoping that he'd become more familiar, less afraid, and able to help with more of the jobs.

When spring came, he pulled out all his old tarpaulins and camping gear. He saddled Kelly and set off for Blayney and Newbridge, expecting to reach Blayney later in the day—which by coincidence, was a Saturday. He reassured Caroline he would only be gone a few weeks. She worried about him sleeping out, but he told her he might get to stay a few nights with Patrick or Ned. He didn't mention that if he did, he might get caught up in the pub.

Blayney was first, only because it was closer. He didn't go to Guyong, thinking that if his mission failed in Blayney and Newbridge, then he'd visit Guyong on the way back.

James was very pleased to see him and didn't mention the money he was owed. It was Saturday night, and it was hard to have a conversation. The pub was noisy as usual, so William drifted away from the bar, whisky in hand, looking for Patrick and Ned. Neither was there, and although he tried to talk with people dressed as farmers, no one gave him the time of day. When his whisky was finished, he went back for another. He was hoping to talk further with James, but he was nowhere to be seen.

It was too late to get to Newbridge now, so he'd squandered a Saturday.

*I should have come Friday.* He'd expected more interest, especially since the thresher had gone so well at the previous harvest. Even worse, the next day was a Sunday—so most people would be at church and not the least interested in talking business.

*I haven't just squandered a Saturday—I've squandered a whole week!*

He sensed a presence. Looking up from his whisky, James stood there with another man.

"Tom, this is Andrew," said James, talking loudly above the noise. "He's interested in using your thresher."

William could have kissed him.

"Andrew," said William, shaking hands, "can I buy you a whisky?"

William spent the evening chatting with Andrew and drinking whisky. Andrew told him where to find his farm and William said he'd be back closer to harvest time to decide a day. After camping by the river that night, he rode out around midday to see Fred, his other customer in Blayney. Fred wasn't home, so William decided to sleep by the river again and ride to Patrick's the next morning.

Patrick, like James, was pleased to see him. He said he'd been in Newbridge on Saturday night and insisted William stay overnight before going on to Newbridge.

"There's a couple of fellers interested in your thresher," said Patrick, "and it won't be hard to find a few more—Ned's got a few, too."

William's spirits rose.

*Doesn't take much to cheer me up.*

The next morning, after a night of drinking whisky, he set out for Ned's. Ned wasn't home and his wife said he'd gone to Bathurst for a few days. She asked where he might find William when he got back and, without thinking, William replied, "Michael's in Newbridge."

"I know he'll know how to find you there," she said, sarcasm in her voice.

William left quickly and went to the pub. Michael was there and made him welcome. He asked if he could have credit, and Michael didn't hesitate.

"A friend of Patrick and Ned is always welcome here."

"Ned is going to meet me here when he gets back from Bathurst, but I don't know when."

"That's all right—you can play some poker while you wait," said Michael, laughing.

*This could be good.*

"Will there be a game tonight?"

"If there's enough people, and there usually is, but you'll need money to play."

"I've got some," said William, instantly regretting the statement, as it would be obvious to Michael that if William had money he wouldn't need credit.

"Good," said Michael, seemingly oblivious to William's regret. "Come back later for the cards, stay now for whisky or something to eat. Whatever you'd like to do is all right with me."

"When should I come back for the cards?"

"End of the day, around dusk."

William left and went across to the store. The supplies Caroline had given him were nearly exhausted, and it would be cheaper to buy more at the store than to eat at the pub. There was only one main street, two pubs and three stores. William wondered why a town on the railway line would be so small.

In the first store, the storekeeper took little interest in him. He guessed that many strangers patronised the stores and pubs in Newbridge. Selecting bacon, flour and some vegetables, he was told he'd have to buy oats at another store.

"This is a people store," said the man, without interest or conviction. "Horses down the road."

After buying some oats, he rode out of town to find somewhere to camp. He hadn't seen much on the way, and there were only two other roads to choose. Not knowing what to do, he went back to ask Michael.

"What are you doing?" said Michael, astonished. "You're sleeping out? What do you think this is? A prison?"

"I can't afford to stay here, Michael."

"Of course you can! Stay here on credit and pay me when you can. Everyone does it, Tom—no reason you should be different."

"I've bought some bacon and vegetables for me and oats for my horse."

"Give it all to me. We'll give you some money for it. You'll need money for cards. I'll fix you up with the cheapest room we have, and we can put your horse out in the stables. If we're not prepared to help each other, why did the good Lord put so many of us here?"

William tried to thank him, but he wouldn't hear of it.

"You look half starved, Tom. I don't know what you eat, but I'll warrant it's not much. Be off to the kitchen and get the cook to feed you. Tell her I sent you. No, better still, I'll tell her myself."

Michael organised some food for William, then showed him a room.

"It's usually a storeroom, but you can sleep here. I don't know what it's like in winter, but I'll warrant it's better than sleeping in the open. You can have it for threepence a night. And put that poor horse of yours in the stables—he looks worse than you. Give him some oats. It's all part of the service."

Once again, William tried to thank him.

"Ned and Patrick tell me you've got a thresher. They said you'll be by from time to time, either trying to get people to use it, or using it. If you need a room, this room's yours. That's the end of it, Tom. You look like you might have fun when you're not half starved, so if you're half good at cards, people will want to play with you, you'll bring business, and I'll win in the long run."

"I can help, if you need help. I've worked in an Inn."

"Have you now? I might just do that. See you at cards."

William put Kelly in the stables and wandered around for a few hours. He didn't see any trains, and there was little else to take his interest. Despite that, it was a pretty and sleepy little town with huts and cottages scattered about. He found a creek crossing what he later heard was called the Caloola Road and going under the railway line that ran parallel with the road. There was more water in the creek than he expected, so he went and sat in the shade under the railway culvert and watched the water. It was very peaceful. Listening to the birds calling, the crickets and insects flicking and chattering, the haze of the heat, and the breeze moving the trees, he thought of home and wondered about his family in Ireland. What were they all doing now? Did they think of him at all? He supposed, if anything, they thought he might be dead.

The venture with the thresher worried him all the time. There had been some hope in the last few days, but he was scared that he'd bitten off way more than he could chew. His confidence in the machine and his ability with it had grown, but he worried that he'd never find enough farmers to use it. He felt better about his prospects in Blayney and Newbridge and was glad he'd taken the time to find more farmers. Michael was a godsend, but he wondered about his resolve not to live off charity. Already he was running up bills in Guyong, Blayney and Newbridge—not to mention the money he owed John for the thresher.

He drifted off to sleep and dreamed terrible dreams of being shipwrecked and chased by cannibals. Fighting them off with rocks and sticks, he saw them stuffing Caroline and the children into big pots. They were calling to him, but he couldn't move to help, and any blow he landed with a stick or a stone on the cannibals had no effect.

"Are you all right?"

He woke with a start. There was a man standing on the road, looking at him in the culvert.

"Are you all right?" the man called again.

"Yes, yes. I'm all right. I must have fallen asleep."

"It's a good spot. I sometimes fish here."

William went back to the road. It wasn't easy, as the side of the creek was rough and overgrown with bush. He joined the man, who looked old and was wretchedly dressed, had several days' growth of stubble, and white hair that pointed everywhere.

"I didn't see any fish," said William. "How do you catch them?"

"I bait a hook with a small frog. That way, if I don't get a fish, I might get an eel."

"A frog? I've not heard of them being used for bait."

"You don't know much, do you?"

"I suppose not."

"I always 'ave a bottle of whisky when I fish. That way, if I don't catch anythin', at least I've 'ad a good time. "

The man studied William for a few moments before talking again.

"One time, I fell asleep and woke to see a big snake crawling across my legs. It 'ad a frog in its mouth. I snatched the frog and the snake turned to me, mouth open and ready to bite."

"Christ! I can't imagine a snake crawling across my legs. I hate snakes."

"So do I. Anyway, before 'e could bite me, I pushed the neck of the whisky bottle into its mouth and forced it to take a drink."

"What did the snake do?"

"It swallowed the whisky, looked at me for a moment and slithered away."

"I would have been too scared to do anything!"

"I suppose I should 'ave just 'it 'im with the bottle. Waste of good whisky. I fished on for a while, and next thing I felt a tap on my shoulder. I looked around and 'ere was the snake with another frog."

William looked at the man in astonishment.

"You're not from 'round 'ere? I 'aven't seen you before," said the man, without smiling, and looking at William as though he might be a fugitive.

"No, I'm not. I'm from Guyong."

"What are you doin' 'ere then?"

"I've a steam thresher. I'm looking for farmers to use it."

"I'm goin' up to the town. You 'eadin' that way?"

"I am. I'll walk with you, if that's all right."

"It is. What's a... what did you call it?"

"A steam thresher—separates the wheat from the stalk, runs on steam."

"Like a steam engine on a train?"

"Just like that."

"Where is it?" asked the man, looking around.

"In Guyong. I'll bring it here at harvest."

"I'm goin' to Michael's for a drink," said the man, proudly, as though it was an accomplishment.

"I'm staying there."

"Then you might buy me a drink."

"I haven't got much money."

"You must 'ave if you're stayin' at the pub."

"No, I'm afraid I don't—but I will buy you one."

"That's all right. Somebody else might buy me another."

They walked up the hill from the creek, passing buildings to the left and the train station and other buildings to the right.

"Do you live in Newbridge?" asked William.

"Wouldn't live anywhere else. Just there behind us, over to the right lookin' back. Wasn't always like this, though—more people here now the train has come."

"How often do the trains run? I haven't seen any."

"Comes from the west early in the mornin', and the east late in the afternoon."

"Every day?"

"'Cept weekends."

"Where's the gold around here?"

"Why so many questions? What do you want to know for?"

"Interested."

"I do a bit of diggin' myself. Gets me some drinkin' money."

"Then why do you need me to buy you a drink?"

The man stopped, turned, looked at William, and laughed. He doubled over he laughed so hard.

"Aren't you the one!" exclaimed the man. "I 'aven't heard that before!"

They continued their walk and, reaching the top of the hill, saw the pub in front of them.

"This the best pub?" asked William, turning and looking at the other.

"You're stayin' 'ere, aren't you?"

"I'll buy you that drink but, before I do, I like to know the name," said William, stretching out his hand. "Tom."

The old man took it in a surprisingly firm grip.

"George."

"The story about the snake isn't true, is it George?"

"As true as I'm standin' 'ere."

They got the drinks and sat at a table in the corner.

William looked around. Every pub he'd been in had been the same—cool enough inside to escape the heat of outside, a few annoying flies that wandered around the lips of glasses and never got drunk, a bar to serve drink, and doors out to the privy, the dining room and the accommodation.

Michael saw them and waved, calling out, "Usual?"

The men nodded and he brought the drinks over to them.

"My shout," said William.

"I thought so," said Michael.

Once Michael had gone, William asked again about the gold.

"It's everywhere. They're diggin' at Caloola Road, Sugarloaf Mount, Dry Diggin's—just to name a few. Even around here, the creeks produce gold. That's where I go—always find some, but never enough."

They chatted for a while. Other people were coming into the bar, and George introduced William. All expressed interest when George told them William ''ad a steam machine that did somethin' with wheat'.

After a while, George wasn't part of the discussion, and he left without buying William a whisky. William didn't care—he'd met new people who expressed interest in the thresher. He was careful not to get caught in a shout, protesting that he would have to go soon. People he met seemed to understand, and no one pushed him.

William worried the drink was getting the better of him when Ned finally arrived. He was delighted to see William, made a big fuss, and insisted on buying him a drink. Someone suggested cards and William nearly whooped for joy. This is what he'd come for. Well, he wanted to meet some farmers, but he wanted to play cards, too. A pipe, whisky and cards—life was again how he loved it.

There were five of them, including Ned and William, and they only played for an hour or so—most were due home for supper. It was a good game with friendly players, and William won a modest amount. He loved the battle of wits, the bluffing, and the tension, knowing he couldn't afford to lose. Ned said he could come and stay at his farm, but William said he'd found a room at the pub so he'd be all right. William thought Ned looked relieved, and wondered if Ned took a risk bringing a guest home from the pub.

William spent a week in Newbridge and decided to head back to Blayney for the Saturday night. As well as Ned, four other farmers committed to using his thresher. It wasn't much, but it was a better start than he'd had the previous year, and he was confident he'd find more before the harvest. He played cards most nights, won a little money, and drank some whisky. When he insisted Michael take some money to reduce his debt, Michael would take only a few shillings.

"Pay me later," he said. "I know you'll be good for it."

He stopped to see Ned as he went back to Blayney. Ned was pleased to see him and pleased to hear he had some more customers.

"That's good, Tom," he said. "It'll work—you'll see."

William stopped in to see Patrick, too, and check if the fellers that Patrick had said wanted to use the thresher weren't the same as the ones he met in Newbridge. They weren't, so William now had six farmers. Patrick insisted he stay for lunch, so it was evening before he rode into Blayney.

James asked how he had gone in Newbridge, and William couldn't contain his excitement when telling him that things had gone 'very well'. Once again, the pub was noisy, but William was determined to get more customers in Blayney, so he stayed longer and drank more whisky than he should have. James insisted he have something to eat and put him at a table with some farmers. He told the farmers all about his thresher but he could sense they were only pretending to be interested. Try hard as he might, they didn't answer any question that might have given him a clue as to their lack of interest. Wary that he might get angry, he finished his meal and made a fruitless search for James, who was busy elsewhere.

William went down to the river and spread out his tarpaulins, turned Kelly loose, and went to sleep. He couldn't go back to Guyong before he found out why the farmers didn't want to use the thresher.

It was a beautiful Sunday morning and, while William was a bit sore and tired from sleeping outdoors, he didn't miss a chance to have a swim in the river. There hadn't been much rain and there wasn't a lot of water, but he found a reasonable pool, took off all his clothes, and lazed around in the water for a while. He was startled by the sound of a horse and gig and only managed to get his clothes back on a few moments before it crossed the river.

They didn't see him but stopped when they saw Kelly, and he heard the man on the gig say to the woman William presumed was his wife, "Must be a stray."

"It's not!" called William. "He's mine!"

"Sorry," said the man, then looked startled as William approached.

"Sorry," said William, "I didn't mean to startle you—I was just looking at the river."

"There's no saddle on your horse," said the man, suspiciously.

"Come on, darling," William heard the man's wife whisper, "it's none of our business."

"All right," he said and, flicking the reins, drove off.

*They'd be more concerned if they'd seen me naked in the river.*

He saddled Kelly, packed up his gear, and rode into Blayney. He was a traveller, so he could have a drink, but only wanted to ask James what was happening and why the farmers had no interest. James was pleased to see him but said he only had a few moments, as he and his family would soon go to church.

"I wanted to talk to you anyway," said James. "There's another feller trying to convince the farmers to use his machine. He's offering low prices—lower than you—and no one wants to tell you. He was here last night, by the way. People thought if they told you about him with him being here, there might be trouble."

William thought at least he knew what was going on, though he had no idea what to do about it. He remembered the competition between the storeowners in Tuena, and how upset they'd be if they thought one of the others had made a better show.

"Why don't you stay around for the week, Tom? Ride around a little, talk with the farmers, have a whisky here? Farmers'll be more open if the other feller is not here, and they say he's gone back to Orange."

"I'll think on it. I'm planning on going home today, so I might come back tomorrow."

"No point in staying today anyway—come back tomorrow."

Caroline and the children were not long back from church when he stopped outside.

"Daddy! Daddy's home!" cried Margaret when she saw him.

He stepped off Kelly, saddle sore and tired, and pleased to be home.

"I was hoping you'd be back before the baby was born," said Caroline. She was only a few months pregnant, but already showing. William didn't know if she was being sarcastic, but decided not to find out. "How was your trip? Did you find some more people to use the machine?"

They walked inside, out of the sun. The children gathered around, anxious for news.

"It was good. Hold up your hands, Elizabeth."

He said the names of the farmers he had engaged and touched one of her fingers for each them from Newbridge, Blayney and Guyong. He ran out of fingers.

"Put up your hands, Margaret," said Caroline. She did as bidden.

William went on, stopping after two.

"That's twelve!" exclaimed John.

"I'm hoping for ten pounds from each one," said William.

He looked at Caroline and was startled to see she looked anxious. He thought she'd be excited by the news.

"What's wrong?" asked William.

"I was hoping you'd have more customers. I don't like the look of our wheat—I think there's something wrong with it. I was thinking to get Warren to come and look at it."

They all went outside. William picked Willie up and carried him. He was too little to keep up.

The wheat looked to be ripening, but the plants appeared neither vibrant nor strong—and were sparse.

"I should have seen this before," said William. "Not enough seed, not enough rain."

"We did the best we could," said Caroline, her voice breaking.

"I know, I know. But I should have bought some more seed."

"What with?"

William was near to tears.

*Can't I do anything right?*

Once again, he wouldn't get a harvest. He'd been away, trying to earn more money, and failing at home. The thresher was a disaster. He wished he'd never even heard of it.

"Come inside, children. We'll get supper," said Caroline.

Supper was a sombre affair, everyone's mood affected by the impending failure of the crop. For the older children and the adults, the prospect of even less money was frightening.

"We'll get *some* wheat," said Caroline at one point, but there was no answer.

Later that night, lying in bed, Caroline said, "What'll we do, Tom?"

"Do? I'm afraid to do anything—nothing works for me."

William couldn't shake a sense of failure, and a sense of impending trouble. Things were bad and only getting worse.

"I said I'd go back to Blayney tomorrow. There's another feller selling the use of his machine. They said he wants less money."

"Less money? You can't do threshing for less money! The man's a fool!" said Caroline.

"I suppose if he can stop me, then he'll have everyone for himself."

"I know I didn't agree with you getting the thresher, but I didn't think it would be this hard, Tom."

"I didn't either. Other people find gold, grow wheat, make money, and build fine houses. Not me—I doubt I could start a fire and boil a billy of water."

They held each other by the dying light of the fire, overwhelmed by the problems they faced and the absence of a solution for any of them.

At first light, William saddled Kelly, Caroline gave him a bag of meagre supplies, and he set off for Blayney. He wanted to spend as much time as he could meeting with farmers in the area. If he could get as many farmers again as he had in Newbridge, then there would be a fighting chance. Taking the shortcut that had caused trouble a few years before, he bypassed Guyong. Guyong didn't matter. If he could find all his customers in Blayney and Newbridge, it would be easier to work them as he would have to move the machine less.

The week was a bitter disappointment. By the end, he only had two more farmers. He suspected people had accepted the other man's offer, but no one would say. Camping by the river each night, he stretched the supplies that Caroline had given him to last the whole week. He didn't stay the Saturday night. James had hinted that he might want to settle at least part of his account.

He rode back home on the Saturday morning. He thought Caroline knew by the look on his face that he'd had little success, so she didn't ask how he went.

CHAPTER 33

# A MOVE TO NEWBRIDGE

A few days before harvest, William cleaned, oiled and greased the thresher, ready for use. He and John cut and threshed his own wheat. It took so little time, and John said they had only forty-five bags. Caroline said they'd be lucky to get twenty pounds for it. William put it on the cart and took it down the road for Warren to sell with his harvest. They didn't talk about why Warren wouldn't use his thresher. Caroline asked him not to—she said it would only make him angry.

William rode over to Blayney and Newbridge to work out where to take his machine first. He met with all the farmers and found that he'd have to take it backwards and forwards between Blayney and Newbridge.

*If it wasn't so sad, it'd be funny.*

The first job was in Newbridge the following Monday. He'd need to bring the thresher over on the Friday and Saturday. Still being nervous about crossing the Belubula, he decided to stop in and see if Patrick would help him across the river. It was late in the afternoon as he rode through Newbridge, and he thought Patrick might be at the pub. If he wasn't then he'd be at home, but he'd be a fool to go to Patrick's and find he was at the pub.

Dismounting from Kelly, he walked into the bar. It was surprisingly busy and some of his customers were there too. Next year, he'd arrange to meet them all at the pub and work out their threshing times.

Michael gave him a wave.

"Why so busy?" William asked.

"Just one of those nights. You staying?"

"Depends. I came to see Patrick—I'll ride by his place if he's not here."

"No, he's not here. I expect he's at home and he'll still be there tomorrow. There's a card game on later. You might want to join—some people you should meet."

William laughed.

*If all else fails, there's always cards and whisky.*

"I'm in, of course."

"Wait a minute," said Michael, pouring a whisky for William. "Take this and join your mates."

"Mates?"

"They think you're a mate."

William took his whisky and joined the others. There was animated chatter and stories, and he was made very welcome. His new customers exclaimed how much they looked forward to using the machine and that they'd heard such great reports. One of the men was unknown to William, although his face was familiar, and it was a few moments before the group realised William didn't know him and they were introduced.

"Tom, this is Bernard. He's from over at Guyong."

"I hear you're from there too," said Bernard. "I've heard about you."

"Would you like to use my thresher?" asked William, and the group laughed.

"No," said Bernard, "not this year, but maybe next. I hear you play cards."

William flushed red. It wouldn't do for someone from Guyong to tell Caroline that William played cards in Newbridge.

"Sorry, Tom," said Bernard, looking alarmed, "I didn't mean to offend you."

"No offence, Bernard—I hadn't realised I was known as a card player."

"They say you're quite good, so that's probably why. I'd like to play a game with you. There aren't many places to play anymore."

"I suppose Newbridge has the advantage of no police station," said one of the group.

"Yet," said Michael, arriving with a round of drinks. "On me."

"Can we set up the game soon?" asked Bernard. "I'm looking forward to matching wits with young Tom here."

"Whenever you like," said Michael. "Just go on out back—you know where."

They all headed out to play cards. William couldn't remember a game he had enjoyed more. No one drank too much and the stakes weren't high, of course, but his constant fear of losing heightened his skill, and he finished up the winner on the night.

"You're good!" exclaimed Bernard at the end of the evening. "I want to do this again. I won't rest easy until I've beaten you."

He clapped his hand on William's shoulder.

"Are you staying here tonight?"

"I am."

"Then let's have breakfast together. I have something I want to discuss with you."

Over breakfast, Bernard explained that he wanted to buy a Conditional Purchase block of land in Newbridge.

William knew about Conditional Purchase. He'd harboured a notion of buying such a block himself, but he'd not ever had enough money. Such blocks of Crown Land had become available about twenty years before. It was the government's way of opening up land to more than just the wealthy, and before it was surveyed. Once it was surveyed, the land could be reclaimed by the government, which did happen sometimes. Nonetheless, for a pound an acre and a deposit of a quarter of the price, with the rest paid off over time at five percent interest, many people took advantage of it. William hadn't understood the interest part until he took out the loan with John for the wheat.

*Experience is the best teacher*, his father used to say.

Bernard continued to explain Conditional Purchase, possibly thinking William didn't know about it.

*There's not a farmer in New South Wales that hasn't thought about Conditional Purchase*, thought William, but allowed Bernard to explain it anyway.

"My problem is that it has to be occupied for three years, and requires improvement to the value of a pound an acre."

"Why is that a problem?"

"I live over at Guyong. Some of my children are on other properties, but I like Newbridge. If anywhere is going ahead, it's here."

"Looks like a sleepy little place to me."

"Not with the railway line going through. Farmers from all around will bring their produce here. It'll be big one day—mark my words. Anyway, the point is, I need someone to occupy the block for me."

"Are you thinking of me?"

"I am."

"I live in Guyong."

"I know, but I'll bet you rent."

"I do."

"You can live here for free."

"Where's here?"

"I found a place on the Caloola Road. It's only a few miles out of town, not far from the Caloola Creek gold field."

"What's on it?"

"Nothing."

"I'd have to build something to live in."

"Of course, but I can do that. It needs to be improved, so buildings are improvements. Your job would be to live there. That's all. I wouldn't expect you to do anything else."

"Can we have a look at it?"

"After breakfast, if you like."

"How long could I stay there?" asked William.

"How long would you like?"

"Five years, at least."

"That's all right—could even be longer, too. I hope to sell it one day, but if no one buys it then you can stay there. I might charge you rent after five years."

They rode out after breakfast. The day was already hot, insects and cicadas buzzed and flicked, flies made their endless personal intrusions, and dust rose as the horses walked, stirred along by a hot breeze from the west. Most of the land was covered by endless gum trees, and after about thirty minutes, Bernard said, "This is it."

Sitting astride his horse, looking at the block, William thought the only redeeming feature was that it was rent free. Bernard wasn't right that there was nothing on it—there were plenty of trees—but after the initial shock, he thought that might be a good thing. He'd need wood for buildings, fences and fires, and he wouldn't need to pay rent, at least for a while.

"Is that a creek down there?" he asked Bernard.

"I believe so, but you might need to sink a well for permanent water."

"Is there gold in it?"

"If there is, you can have it."

"Then I suppose there isn't any."

The men laughed.

"Are you interested?" asked Bernard. "If you are, I'll finalise the purchase and have my men put some buildings up for you."

"I'll have to tell Daniel I'm moving on."

"Your present landlord?"

"Yes."

"As you wish, but he can't make you stay."

"I wasn't thinking that. I've been there since I was married. He thought I might buy it one day."

"Can you do that?"

"No, I can't."

"I've heard that."

"What do you mean?" asked William, looking at him sharply.

"I hear you're trying to get your business going. I think this might help us both."

"I start threshing next week. I don't have time to put up buildings and move my family."

"I'll do the buildings. I want this block, Tom—so I'll do all that. You just say the word. That's all you need to do, and I'll do the rest. Besides, you're better off here. From what I hear, the farmers here like your machine, and most of your work will come from this area."

"What about the children? They go to school in Guyong."

"There's a school here. It's summer holidays soon, so they can start here in the new year—best time for it. Think on it, Tom."

"You sound like you've been thinking about it for some time."

"I have. I'm a man who does his homework."

"All right," said William. He reached out and shook Bernard's hand. He knew Caroline would be thrilled when he rode home and told her. With her new-found money awareness, she'd welcome the notion of no rent to pay.

"Good," said Bernard.

They turned and headed back, separating at the road to Bathurst.

"I'll go and finalise the purchase in Bathurst," said Bernard.

"Thanks, Bernard."

As he rode off, Bernard called back, "See you at the next card game!"

William rode and saw Patrick, who said he'd help him cross the river, and all he had to do was ask.

"Can you help me Saturday? I'll bring the three parts to the Belubula on Friday and Saturday morning, if you can help me Saturday afternoon?"

"Of course. Just ride and tell me when you're ready."

William rode home, beside himself with excitement to tell Caroline the good news.

"You've done what!" she exclaimed. "We've a baby on the way! Who'll help with the delivery? And, what about all this? You say there's nothing on the block? No wonder it's free! Did you even think about the children? What about their schooling? What about their friends? What about our church? What about my ma? And Warren? When will I see them? While you're wandering all over country, at least they're there to help! Oh, Tom, what next?"

"I've thought about it, Caroline—I know it's the right thing to do."

"Like buying the threshing machine? At least you asked about that."

The children had all gone to bed before William raised the matter with Caroline, but William didn't doubt the older ones would now be awake. He didn't want them to find out like this—overhearing a heated conversation—but he knew it was too late.

*Can't I get anything right?*

"I'm taking the thresher to Newbridge on Friday. Can we talk about this in the morning, when the children have gone to school?"

"I don't think sleeping on it will help. Anyway, it's their last week at school for the year, so if you want to talk while they're at school, then you raised it just in time."

It was clear in the morning that Elizabeth, Margaret, John and James knew what was happening, but no one said anything as they waited for their neighbour to pick them up for school. William dreaded the children leaving. As soon as they were gone, the argument would start. Caroline was right—he should have asked her first, or at least involved her in the decision. It seemed right at the time, but nothing was right about it now. Newbridge wasn't far away, but it was a big change that affected the whole family. He'd seen other men make changes and their families just went along with it. His family was different. Caroline was smart, willing to learn and understood the numbers—he would have already made better decisions if he'd talked to her first. Perhaps he wasn't cut out to be the head of a family. Maybe all he'd ever be good at was playing cards and drinking whisky. He liked digging for gold, but he wasn't all that good at it.

When the neighbour left, there was only Willie, Caroline and William.

Willie happily played on the floor, moving pieces of stick around as though he was building something.

Caroline and William sat at the table, with pannikins of tea in front of them. The day was already hot but William didn't dare say he didn't want the tea.

"Christmas is soon," said Caroline.

"Oh," said William. He'd forgotten—there were no presents in his family.

"Do you want to move by Christmas?"

"I don't think we can—there are no buildings there yet. I thought I told you that last night."

"You did. I just wondered. Tell me again, why are we doing this?"

"To save money."

"How much money?"

"I don't remember," said William, miserably.

"I do. Three pounds, ten shillings a year. Daniel hasn't changed the rent since we moved here."

"How do you know that?"

"How long since you paid it?"

William shook his head.

"Have you told whoever it is that we'll move?"

William nodded.

"Then we have no other choice. Do you like it?"

William shrugged. It would be better when the discussion was over. It would be the last time he would ever act without talking with his wife first.

"When do we move?"

"When he finishes the buildings."

"When might that be?"

"He didn't say."

"Who is he?"

"Bernard."

"I think I've seen him at church."

"He says he knows of us."

"Everybody knows of us—we're the people with the threshing machine."

Caroline said nothing further. William hoped the ordeal was over. Once again, he wished he'd never heard of the threshing machine.

"I'll talk to Euphemia—she might come to Newbridge this time. After that, we'll have to find another midwife."

"I didn't think there'd be another child after this one."

"We're not getting divorced, Tom—just working out how to manage changes in our life. Besides, as much as I wished you'd talked it over with me first, we would probably have come to the same decision."

"Do you want to come and look at it?"

"No, I'll see it when we move there. It might be less frightening with some buildings."

"I'm sorry."

"I know you are. Pa used to say big plans don't always produce big results."

"I've met some people there, and they're all right. It's on the rail line, too, so you can go to Bathurst on the train."

"In the one day?"

"That's what they say."

"The children might enjoy that. I won't put them back in school here. We'll start them in Newbridge, whenever we get there."

"Will you tell them what's happening?"

"We can both tell them."

"I might take the thresher to Newbridge today."

"You said tomorrow."

"Tomorrow is the latest I can go. It's better if I start today."

"Are you going to take John?"

"No. I'll be gone a few weeks once I take all the parts there."

"He'll be disappointed."

William shrugged.

"I suppose you won't be away as much when we live in Newbridge," said Caroline.

"Why is that?"

"Well, most of your customers will be from there."

"Sounds right. Anyway, I'll go and organise the drum. I'll do a trip each day, so I'll be back tonight."

William took his time and moved the thresher to the Blayney side of the Belubula River. Then he rode to Patrick's and got his help to move the thresher to the first customer's farm. The job was done by late in the day, so they went and spent the evening at Michael's. William hoped that Bernard would be there, so he could confirm that he'd purchased the property. It would be terrible if the deal fell through and he'd upset Caroline for nothing. William ate, drank and slept at the pub, and Michael didn't mention money. He wondered how much he owed Michael but was afraid to ask.

The next few weeks were busy, and William enjoyed the distraction of working hard, even if the work was mind-numbingly boring. Feeding the wheat into the thresher then stacking bagged grain and hay was demanding and exhausting, but speed was imperative because he had to do as much as he could in the shortest possible time. The farmers all knew he needed help with the machine, and they did the work themselves if they had enough men, or their neighbours helped if not. On some farms, a festive atmosphere prevailed, and the farmer's wives and children helped a little and provided food and drinks. William always warned them about the belts and moving parts, and he worried that the adults would become complacent, or the children would forget.

Each farmer paid him when the job was done, and he carefully put all the notes together in a bundle in one pocket, and all the coins in another. The coins became a problem, rattling in his pocket, and he continually worried that the pocket would break, and he'd lose them all. He finally solved the problem by giving the coins to Michael each night, to take off what he owed. Michael wouldn't take any of the notes and insisted that William finish all his threshing before he worried about paying off his debts.

One day, one of the farmers from Blayney rode over and asked when he'd be there. He said there were three customers who wanted to see William as soon as possible. William said he still had three more to do in Newbridge, but he'd be able to be in Blayney the next Monday.

"How did you find me?" he asked the farmer, shouting over the noise of the thresher.

The man laughed.

"James said he thought you might be in Newbridge. I rode by the pub and Michael said I'd find you here."

"I have to take all three parts across the Belubula. I'll do it Saturday. Can you meet me late in the day with four horses and harness to pull it all across?"

"I can do that if you buy me a whisky when the job's done."

"And I can do that. See you on Saturday."

The man tipped his hat and rode off. William went back to work.

On the Friday before he left Newbridge, Bernard met him at the pub and said that he'd bought the land and asked if William would ride out with him so they could work out where the buildings should be erected. There was enough time left in the day, so they rode out together, chatting amiably on the way. Once they reached the land, it took some time to work out where the house and barn should go—far enough up the hill so that they wouldn't be flooded, but close enough to sink a well and find water. They put some markers down so that neither Bernard nor William would need to come back and show the men what to do.

Bernard promised his men would start the buildings soon, and William and his family could move in around March. William was excited, and hoped Caroline would be too. It was almost dark as they rode up the hill, and William thought he saw a cemetery.

"What's that? Is that a cemetery?" he asked Bernard.

"Yes, it is. I think they plan to move it—odd place to put one, if you ask me. Too far out of town."

William thought Caroline might not like it being there. She was superstitious about those things. He'd have to tell her though, as she liked surprises even less.

Bernard suggested they have a few whiskies and try to find others for cards. They couldn't find anyone, so they had an early supper and William went to bed. He was exhausted after all the threshing. Nevertheless, he was up early the next morning and moved the thresher to the Newbridge side of the Belubula.

The farmer came early in the afternoon and woke William dozing under a tree. They moved the thresher to his farm. The farmer hadn't expected that William would need help to run the thresher and said that neither he nor any of the other farmers would be available. He suggested that he and William go to James's pub, have the whisky they talked about, and see if William could hire someone to help. The farmer also said he had a spare bed and William could stay with him, so he could be ready early on the Monday morning. The farmer's wife said William could come to church with them the next day, and William said he'd think on it.

The pub was heaving, with people scattered out onto the road. It was a hot night and many of the patrons drank beer.

After several hours of drinking and trying to both find more farmers to use his thresher, and someone to work, he found a man called Joseph who said he'd work for five shillings a day. William tried to negotiate, but Joseph wouldn't hear of it—it was five shillings or William would have to find someone else.

They finished all three jobs over three days, and William put some more pounds and shillings in his pocket. The farmer said he was welcome to leave the machine on his property until it came time to take it to Newbridge. There was no point in taking it to Guyong, then back to Newbridge. William and Joseph rode into Blayney and went to James's pub to celebrate the end of the harvest, and for William to settle his debt with James and Joseph.

It was quiet at the pub, and William proudly put his pounds on the bar and told James to take what he was owed and then Joseph would do the same.

James smiled and said, "It's gone well then, Tom?"

"We've been busy, and Joseph here has been a great help. I think it's gone well, but the proof is on the bar there."

James counted the money.

"You're wise not to carry all you've earned around with you, Tom," he said.

"What do you mean, James? That's all there is. That's all I've earned."

James pushed it back.

"You keep it for the moment then, Tom."

"I thought there was a lot."

"Perhaps if you add it to your harvest, then you might have enough."

"I owe Joseph here money, too."

"How much?"

"Five shillings a day for three days," said Joseph, "but if there's not enough, then pay me later too."

William's mind was in a turmoil—he thought he'd made a lot of money, and now he found out he didn't have much at all. Putting the money back in his pocket, he didn't feel in the least like celebrating. Life was in every way too hard. Now he'd have to go to Caroline and tell her that the money in his pocket was all he had earned. The thresher was a failure. He put all his coins on the bar and said he'd like to buy whatever whisky he could for himself and Joseph to drink, then he'd ride on home.

James said that would buy them four whiskies each. William shrugged and pushed the money over. They drank the four whiskies, he shook Joseph's hand, went out and got Missy and Polly, and went home. It was dark and everyone was already in bed when he arrived. He gave Missy and Polly some oats, turned them loose in the yard, and went in to bed, dreading the morning.

When he woke in the morning, he waited until the children went outside to see to their chores before giving the money to Caroline.

"Is this all?" she said, shock on her face. "I expected nearly two hundred pounds!"

"That's all," said William miserably.

"Did you drink it?" asked Caroline.

"Drink what?"

"The money."

"You can't drink money."

"No, but you can buy whisky with it and drink that."

"No, I didn't buy whisky with it."

"You'll have to tell John we can't pay him anything this year either."

"I thought we *had* to pay him this year—we didn't pay him anything last year."

"If we can't pay, we can't pay, and that's an end of it."

"I wish I understood the numbers."

"So do I, Tom, so do I."

William was crushed by the words. He'd never thought he could be or feel as big a failure as he was at that moment.

CHAPTER 34

# INSOLVENT

William busied himself with the farm and did his best to try to make amends. He worked long hours in the gardens, on the fences, and with the animals.

"Don't waste your time, Tom," said Caroline. "I thought we'd leave all this behind soon."

"We will, we will. But I thought I'd make it as good as it could be for Daniel. He's always been good to us."

"I agree. We'd like to go and have a look at the new place."

"Who's we?"

"The children and me."

"We could go tomorrow."

"Tomorrow's Saturday."

"Saturday might be better."

They woke the next morning, had breakfast, loaded the cart with some provisions and the children, and set off for Newbridge. William stayed on the better roads, even if it took him a little longer. Everyone was in a festive mood, and even though William had dreaded showing them where they would soon live, he was glad it was finally happening.

Nothing had prepared him for his family's disappointment.

Fortunately, Bernard's men had already started work on the buildings, and while William thought of it as progress, his family thought otherwise.

"Oh, Tom," said Caroline, disappointment in her voice.

The children stood in the cart and no one else said a thing.

"Let's have a closer look," said William, hoping to find something positive.

He drove over the track from Caloola Road and pulled up alongside the first building.

"This will be the house," he said. "It's bigger than the one we have now, so you children will have more rooms."

"Oh, good," said Elizabeth. "Can I have my own room?"

Caroline got down from the cart and encouraged all the children to come with her. William thought she looked like the baby could come at any time and encouraged her to be careful. The children ran from room to room as best they could using the half-finished floors, claiming things for themselves. William felt relief—perhaps it would work out well after all.

"How long do you think they'll take to finish it?" asked Caroline. "Do you think our baby could be born here?"

"I'd like that," said William. "I'll ride and find Bernard tomorrow and ask him."

"Tomorrow is Sunday."

"Then I'll come with you to church, and we'll see him there."

"He's not often at church—I think he goes somewhere else."

"Then I'll ride to his home and ask him."

Caroline just nodded.

It was late and dark by the time they arrived back home.

"I'm glad we went, Tom," said Caroline as they sat sipping tea later that night. "The children are more excited than I have seen them in a long while."

"I'll come with you to church, and if Bernard is not there, I'll ride over to his house."

"Have you seen John about the loan yet?"

"I'll do that tomorrow, too."

William saddled Kelly the next morning and rode with his family to church. Bernard wasn't there, so he rode on alone to his home. Thankfully, Bernard was there and made him very welcome.

"Good, good," said Bernard when William told him they'd been to see the block in Newbridge. "I'll bet your family is excited."

"They want to know when we can move in."

"Two weeks, Tom. Do you want some help to move?"

"No, we'll be all right."

They shook hands and William left. He didn't see John on the way back. He wasn't sure how to tell him that again he couldn't pay him. A sense of failure wouldn't leave William, and he wasn't sure he could put on a brave front and tell John that he was still confident of success.

The next day he rode into Bathurst and told Daniel he would no longer rent the farm and that he would pay the outstanding rent as soon as he could. Daniel didn't look well, and William was worried for him.

"Don't worry about me," said Daniel. "You should only ever worry about yourself and your family. Pay me when you can and not a day sooner."

Two weeks later, the whole family took a week to move what they could to Newbridge. The furniture was easy—there wasn't much of it. The animals were more challenging, so they only moved a few. It took William and his son, John, all their patience and perseverance to move them. The rest they left with Warren, Caroline's brother.

The house was bigger with a wooden floor and an iron roof. There was plenty of wood for fires and to build fences, and the next few weeks were busy for everyone. Euphemia was happy to come to Newbridge to help deliver Richard. Willie was miffed that his place as the baby had been taken, but soon got over it. Caroline took the older children to school at Newbridge. It was closer than the school had been at Guyong, and the children were more than happy with their new teacher.

William said he'd go and get the thresher and bring it to their new home. It was time to get it ready for the new harvest. He'd decided not to plant any wheat himself so the full harvest season could be used for threshing for others, and planting his own had not been successful.

Everything looked much better, and the days—though cold, as autumn would soon turn to winter—held more promise.

Then, John struck.

The farmer from Blayney appeared at the farm one day. William thought he might have come over to tell him to move the thresher.

"No," said the farmer, "John seized it—told me he'd sold it."

"Sold it? How could he sell it?" asked Caroline, who had joined them standing outside in the cold wind, with the new baby in her arms.

The farmer shrugged.

"He had a piece of paper. He showed it to me. It meant nothing to me. He said it was a Bill of Sale. Said it meant he could do what he wanted with the machine. He said he had sold it to the man that came with him, and other men would soon take it all away."

"Tom, what does it mean?" asked Caroline.

"I'll ride over and see him," said William. "He got me to sign what he called a Bill of Sale—I suppose that's what he used."

"Didn't you go to see him? Didn't you tell him that we thought we'd do better next year?"

William reddened, as was his habit.

"Oh, Tom," said Caroline, "if only you'd seen him!"

William and the farmer rode back to Blayney together, and William continued on to Guyong. It was late in the evening when he arrived. The sun was about to set, and the chill of the evening was already upon him.

John was delighted to see him and ushered him into the parlour. William was grateful for the fire, but unsure how to ask John what had happened and why he sold the thresher. He needn't have worried—John was more than ready to talk.

"I got a good price for it," he said proudly. "More than your loan, so I have some money for you."

"I don't know why you sold it," said William, bitterly. "We did better this year than we did last. Can we get it back?"

"Now, Tom, don't make too much of this. You signed the Bill of Sale so I could sell the machine if you failed to pay off your debt."

"I was going to pay it back—it was only a matter of time!"

"Tom, you hadn't come to see me. I didn't know what was happening. Like I said at the time, I'm entitled to protect my money. That's why you signed the Bill of Sale. I asked around Guyong. Farmers here said they hadn't heard from you this year."

"The opportunities came from Blayney and Newbridge."

"How was I to know that? Anyway, no point in talking about it further. Here's your fifty pounds. It's what's left after what I got for the thresher and deducted the costs. The man that bought it said you'd looked after it very well and he was prepared to pay a good price."

William just nodded and took his money.

"Thank you, Tom," said John as he closed the door behind William, who stood in the yard and looked at the moon. The moon was such a cold and lonely thing, providing only light and sometimes not even that. As he mounted Kelly, he knew that life had suddenly become much more difficult. He had no source of income because he had neither a thresher nor a farm—no machine and no harvest.

What was to become of him and his family? He had debts in Guyong, Blayney and Newbridge and, including the fifty pounds from John, he had only the money he'd given Caroline that he'd earned from the thresher. The path forward was in no way clear. Did he give the fifty pounds to Caroline, and she would use it to pay off the debts? He'd already made the mistake of not involving her more than once. At least she now understood the money.

It wasn't far to Matthew's pub so he thought he'd stop in on the way home.

Matthew was pleased to see him and was already aware the thresher had been sold.

"Everyone in Guyong knows," he said. "We were all disappointed we haven't seen much of you lately."

"I've been busy in Blayney and Newbridge."

"What will you do now?" asked Matthew.

"I don't know," said William.

The men stood quietly at the bar. There were only a few other customers, none of whom took any interest in William.

"I know I owe you money," said William. "I'll pay you as soon as I can."

"How?" asked Matthew.

"My wife understands the money," said William, unable to keep a hint of pride from his voice. "I'll ask her."

"You'll ask your wife?" asked Matthew, unable to keep the astonishment from his voice.

William reddened. "What's wrong with that?"

"Does she know how much you owe me?"

"No," said William, embarrassed all over again. "I haven't told her."

"That's what I thought. Tell her to see me the next time she's in Guyong. I'll tell her how much and tell her that I'd like it to be repaid."

William thought for a few moments, then pulled out the fifty pounds.

"I got this from John. You should take some of it."

"Can't I take all of it?"

"All of it? Do I owe you that much?"

"You do."

"I want to give some to other people too."

"I'll take ten pounds and you can have a whisky and tell your wife to see me."

William thought Matthew had changed and said so.

"What's changed, Matthew? You've been very helpful, but now you're different."

"Everybody will want their money now, Tom—now that your source of income has been sold. I've seen this happen before. You owe me money and I suspect you owe others, too. The murmuring will become shouting, and you'll be under a lot of pressure."

William thanked Matthew, downed his whisky, and went out into the night. The moon was still out, and he could see well enough to ride. It didn't matter—the faithful Kelly walked along as though he knew the road. It wasn't long before William was frozen. He stopped Kelly and rummaged in the saddle bags for whatever he could find to fend off the cold. A smile followed when he found his old possum fur coat in there and, while dilapidated and worn, it was still serviceable. He wrapped it carefully around his shoulders. They'd travelled a long way together.

He took a detour and stopped for Kelly to drink when they reached the Belubula. Sitting on the bank, he looked at the silent pools and wondered what things lurked in there that might wish him harm. It seemed that the world was full of things that wished him harm, and he longed for happier times. He'd made such a mess of things and, try hard as he might, could see no way out. He thought it might be easier if he put some rocks in his pockets and fell into a deep pool.

Then, a feeling of calm came over him. The she-oaks soughing in the wind on the riverbank, the chuckle of the water among the rocks, and the odd croak from a frog, were all familiar sounds—and he knew that they had been for a very long time. They'd be here long after he was gone, and little would change due to his passing. It was time to stop feeling sorry for himself, and time to do something about it. In a moment, he was glad that it was over. The machine was gone. John had done him a favour. If he no longer spent money he didn't have, and found some way to pay back the money he owed, everything would be all right.

Matthew had said that all his creditors would now start pressing for payment. The night was too cold to sleep out so unprepared, so he'd go on home first and then see Michael the next morning—he would know what to do.

Caroline was in a state when he came home.

"I've been worried sick about you!" she said. "What did John say? It must be close to dawn. Where have you been?"

"As the farmer said, John has sold the thresher. Here's the money left after he took what was owed to him."

"Forty pounds?" exclaimed Caroline. The children awoke and appeared in their doorways.

"Off to bed," said Caroline, sternly. "This is nothing to do with you."

They left the adults to it.

"I gave some to Matthew at Guyong—I owed him some money."

"Matthew? You owed him some money?"

"You might as well know," said William, "I also owe money to Michael in Newbridge, and James and Joseph in Blayney."

"I know Michael. Who are those other people?"

"An innkeeper and a man I hired to help me," muttered William.

"How much?"

"I don't know."

"What for?"

"Mostly lodging, and Joseph helped me with the thresher."

William hoped he didn't have to mention the whisky.

"And whisky, I suppose?" said Caroline.

"Some," said William, crestfallen.

Caroline sat heavily.

"What will we do, Tom?" she asked. "We have no thresher, no wheat, and no farm."

"Do we owe anything at the stores?" asked William.

"No—I paid them all."

"I'm going to see Michael in the morning—he'll know what to do."

"But you owe him money! He'll only ask you to pay."

"I don't know what else to do," said William, miserably.

The weak rays of the sun appeared in the doorway, and the birds and fowls began their cheerful welcome of the day.

"I have to have a few hours' rest," said William, "then I'll go to see Michael."

Caroline nodded, numbly—the blood drained from her face, and tears in her eyes.

"Oh, Tom," she said, "what's to become of us?"

She stood suddenly and held him fiercely.

"It's not your fault," she said.

"Yes, it is," he said, all the emotion gone from his voice. "If only I'd understood the numbers."

"Will you come back and tell me what Michael says we should do?"

He nodded wearily and lay on the bed. Caroline went to take off his boots, but he was asleep even before she'd undone the laces.

When he woke, Caroline had already taken the older children to school. She was pottering at the fire and Willie was playing with Richard on the floor. William watched for a while, amazed how the little ones never seemed to feel the cold. He supposed that now they'd lose everything, as had happened to Euphemia. She'd told him how bad it was, and he was sure Caroline already knew. His heart was heavy, but he knew that he had to see Michael and do what he said—no matter the shame. He couldn't bring himself to eat, so he saddled Kelly and set off not long after waking.

"Oh, Tom, that's dreadful," said Michael, when William told him what John had done. "It happens sometimes though, and it's not the end of the world."

"Yes, it is," said William, his voice breaking.

"It isn't, Tom—it just feels like it is. Do you know how much you owe?"

"No."

"Go around to all the people to whom you owe money. Tell them what has happened. Get them to write the amount down for you. Wait here a moment."

He came back with a note.

"Here—once you find out what you owe, take this and give it to TH in Bathurst. Do everything as soon as you can. It'll go better for you if you do it voluntarily."

"Who or what's TH?"

"A lawyer in Bathurst."

"A lawyer?"

"Yes—you need legal help. Don't worry. Everyone knows him as TH. You'll have no trouble finding him."

"Legal help? I can't afford legal help. Anyway, do what voluntarily?"

"Become insolvent."

"Like Euphemia?"

"Who's Euphemia?"

"She's a midwife from Guyong."

"I don't know her."

"She was insolvent a while ago."

"How is she now?"

"All right—she delivered our last child."

"You see, Tom—she survived and so will you. Now, before you go any further, we need to talk about your animals."

"Animals? What animals?"

"Chickens, cows, sheep, goats, pigs and the like."

"Most of them are at Caroline's brother's place."

"Leave them there."

"Why?"

"If someone comes looking for your animals, they won't find them at your place. Horses? Carts?"

"Yes. I've got three horses and a cart."

"You are about to lose everything you own, so you sell them to me, now, and I'll sell them back to you later. You can't mention them to anyone. If anyone asks about them, tell them you sold them to me months ago to cover your debts. People may wonder how you get around—say you borrow a horse and saddle from me. Wait here a moment."

He came back a few minutes later with a ten pound note.

"Here you are—this is for your horses and cart."

William went to take it.

"Hold on, Tom. That's mine."

"I don't understand."

"Well, when you want your horses and cart back, I'll give you the ten pounds and you can give it to me. In the meantime, it'll be safer with me."

"Thank you, Michael. I don't understand and I don't know how to thank you."

"Seeing you get on with your life will be thanks enough. You'll get some work and get back on your feet, and all this will become a distant memory. By the way, I wrote how much you owe me on that piece of paper. Bring your horses and cart to me soon. I'll take good care of them for you."

William nodded, went out to Kelly, and leant against the saddle before getting on. It would be a hard day, and he wasn't looking forward to it. He spent the rest of the day going to Guyong and Blayney, talking to the men to whom he owed money and, as instructed, getting them to write the number on a piece of paper.

The next day, before dawn, he rode into Bathurst and visited Daniel to get details of his debt. Then, after asking for directions in several places, he found the offices of TH. William was awed by the offices—clean and neat with glass, polished wood, and leather seats. He realised how dirty he was and was self-conscious asking for TH. He knew Michael wouldn't be playing a trick on him, but who on earth was called TH?

"He's not here at the moment," said the pretty, young girl at the front desk. "If you'll take a seat, I'm sure he won't be long."

As William sat and waited, he was conscious that it had been some time since he'd eaten—or taken a bath, for that matter.

When William's tension and nervousness were about at breaking point, a man with a leather bag in hand walked through the door. He was well dressed, balding, bearded, and a little overweight.

"TH," said the girl behind the desk, "this is Tom Stewart. He's here to see you. He has a note from Michael."

TH took the note, read it, nodded, and said, "Come on in, Tom. This way—follow me."

William got up, relieved that whatever was going to happen was now underway. They walked into another room, not unlike the one they had just left—chairs, wood, leather and glass.

"Sit down, Tom."

TH indicated a chair near to a desk, hung his coat on a stand near the door, closed the door, and went and sat in the chair behind the desk. It looked like he did those things every day that he walked into his office.

"Tom, tell me about it," said TH, smiling.

"What do you want to know?" asked William, struggling to speak.

"Tell me why you can't pay your debts. Take your time."

William told him how he'd bought the thresher with a loan from John, couldn't repay the loan, the thresher had been seized using a Bill of Sale and sold. And now, without a source of income, he couldn't pay his debts. TH sat and listened, saying nothing, and nodding from time to time.

"Who do you owe the money to?" asked TH.

William handed him the pieces of paper.

"Michael said he wrote the amount on the note I've given you."

"Indeed he has."

TH did some scribbling on a piece of paper.

"You owe a lot of money."

William flushed.

"Sorry, Tom, but you can't be embarrassed anymore. Do you know how this works?"

William shook his head. He had an idea from what Euphemia had told him, but it couldn't hurt to hear again.

"It's quite simple—you are about to lose everything you own. It's sold to pay your debts. But once it's done, you won't owe anything anymore and you'll be able to start again."

William felt hollow, weak, and helpless. Anguish and hurt rose in him like a wave, threatening to engulf him, and he was close to tears. He struggled to hold his emotions and stammered, "I can't start again, TH—I have a wife and children!"

"Tom, this isn't *can't*. This is *must*. You have no choice—you can't possibly repay this money."

"I can get a job. I can pay it back over time."

"There's no point, Tom. You'll carry this burden for years."

"Most of the people I owe money to are my friends."

He hesitated, thinking of his friends. For a few moments, he was too emotional to continue.

"I'm a failure to my family, and now I'm a failure to my friends. I don't want to let them down. There must be a way to repay the money."

"Do you think Michael sent you to me so I could talk you into repaying the money? He sent you here knowing I would talk you out of it."

TH held up the pieces of paper.

"I know most of these men, and I've had dealings with them. They're all good men, and they will only want what's best for you."

"How will I pay you?"

TH laughed.

"You'll find a way, one day. The best thing now is to get this started. You tell me again what happened, I write it down, then you agree to it, and sign it in front of an authorised witness. We'll list all the people you owe money to, and all those who owe money to you. Then we'll list all the things you own and have them valued. A person to handle the process will be appointed, and he'll take over from there. He'll call a meeting, at which the people to whom you owe money can argue the amount, and whether they want you to sell everything."

"Everything?" asked William.

"Yes. They're entitled to sell everything but the clothes off your back if they wish. What do you own? Clothes? Furniture? Horse? Cart? Farm? Animals?"

"I rent a farm. I have clothes and furniture. I borrow a horse when I need it. There's a few chickens and pigs."

"Good. Good."

"When does it all happen? I'd like it to be over soon."

"We'll do all the documents first, then I'll take you to the court and turn the matter over to them. After that, the court's in charge."

TH went out and came back with a man who he called an authorised witness. They wrote out what William described as to why he was in the mess, listed all the people to whom he owed money and the one farmer that owed him money. William guessed that amount—he couldn't remember. TH said it didn't matter a lot. The farmer would tell them the actual amount when the time came.

TH laughed and William was shocked by the sound.

"They usually say they owe nothing and it's not worth chasing them. As I have said, the amount doesn't matter."

TH then read the document to William, who agreed with it all and made his mark.

William and TH then went to the courthouse to register his insolvency. It wasn't far, and the morning was damp, overcast and cold. William shivered in his threadbare clothing and, as much as he had been dreading it, was glad to step into the courthouse. It didn't take long for the clerk to write out the details. TH did most of the talking and answered all the questions. Whenever the clerk looked at William for confirmation, he just nodded.

When it was done, the clerk said, "A court date for the creditors' meeting will be assigned. It will be advertised in the Government Gazette. You have to be here for that."

"C'mon, Tom," said TH, putting a hand on his shoulder, "let's go. That's the hard part. I'll let you know when it's on, so you can be sure to be here."

William nodded and stepped out wearily into the cold.

"Go home, Tom. Tell your family it's done and get some rest. I'll get a message to Michael when you're to be here for the creditors' meeting. See him every week."

"I suppose they'll all go to that. I'll have to face them all together?" said William fearfully.

"They don't always, so I don't know. We'll see on the day."

"What about my clothes and furniture?"

"They decide what to do at the creditors' meeting. Don't worry about it, Tom. It's out of your hands now."

William rode home, pulled down by the weight of failure and what he'd done to his family. It was long past dark when he got there. He was so cold his teeth chattered, and he struggled to take the saddle off Kelly.

*Oh, Kelly. Thanks to Michael, at least I've still got you.*

The children were all asleep, and Caroline sat dozing by the fire.

"Oh, Tom!" she said when he came through the door. "You look like death. Come warm yourself by the fire—I'll make some tea."

They sat by the fire, nursing their tea, and William told her about the day and what would happen next. It was far into the night before he had finished, and he was so tired he could hardly put a sentence together.

"Tom, we'll not get anywhere talking any more tonight. Let's go to bed and talk again in the morning. The children want to know what's happened too, and how they'll be affected. I'll keep them home from school tomorrow."

"It might be tomorrow already," said Tom.

"All the more reason for us to go to bed."

In the morning, they all sat around the table and William told them as best he could. There was no doubt that Elizabeth, Margaret and John understood what he talked about, although he often used words he'd not known before. He hoped he used them correctly.

"Everything? We lose everything?" asked Elizabeth when he finished. "Where will we sleep? What will we eat? What will we wear? What about school?"

William looked at the children, who depended on him for everything, and the woman he'd promised to look after. His sense of failure and humiliation was now complete.

"I don't know. TH said it's now out of my hands," was all he could think to say.

"Don't worry, Daddy. I'll look after Richard," said Willie.

"We'll all look after each other," said Caroline. "This is not all your father's fault. Sometimes, things happen. Some say it's God's way."

"Why would God want to hurt us?" asked Margaret. "I thought He loved us— that's what they say in Church."

"I think none of us understand anything right now," said Caroline. "Tom, how will they decide what to take?"

William just shook his head.

"I don't know. I suppose someone will just turn up and take it."

"Can we still go to school?" asked John.

"I'll go and talk to the teacher today," said Caroline. "They might let us pay them later."

"I'll get some work," said William. "I'll earn some money to help us go on."

"If you earn money, won't they take that too?" asked Caroline.

"I don't know," said William miserably. "But I suppose if someone pays me, and we spend it, then it's not there for them to take."

For the next month, William worked where he could and was reminded of what it was like as a young man—earning sixpences and shillings for doing small jobs. It was always humiliating and often back-breaking work, but he was always grateful for it. The money went straight to Caroline, who had taken to hiding the jar. William visited Michael every other day, asking if he had heard from TH. One day, Michael said he had, and William's day in court was the next Friday at 11am in Bathurst.

"I'll ride there the day before," he told Caroline that night.

"Where will you stay?" asked Caroline.

"I'll camp by the river."

"It's winter! It'll be miserable."

"It doesn't matter. I don't want to be late or to miss it. I want it to be over. More than anything, I just want it to be over."

He arrived at the court, and it was some hours before he met TH there.

"Christ, Tom!" TH said when he saw him. "Where did you sleep last night?"

"By the river."

"It looks like it. Well, the court will believe you when you tell them you have nothing—you look the part. C'mon inside where it's warmer." TH consulted a watch. "It's not long now. They don't always start on time, but let's be ready in case they do."

They went inside. William was awed. In appearance, it was a far cry from the court in Ballarat—but the formality was all the same. He was only one of a number of cases being heard that morning, and he nervously watched other people enduring complete financial ruin.

Eventually, William's case was called. William was acknowledged and asked to tell the court whether he wanted to amend his schedule. He looked at TH, who shook his head. The clerk then made some notes and the Commissioner asked William to tell the court in his own words to account for his insolvency. William repeated what he had told TH.

"Are you prepared to come to any arrangements with your creditors?" asked the Commissioner.

"No, Your Honour," said TH.

"Have you sold anything in your estate?" asked the Court.

"My client awaits the direction of the court," said TH.

The Commissioner then asked if there were any creditors in the court, and made no comment when told there were none. He also asked if there were any proofs of debt, and only nodded briefly when told there were none.

"I know it's not your fault that none of your creditors have elected to come, nor to produce any proof of debt," said the Commissioner to William.

"May I address the court, Your Honour?" asked TH.

The Commissioner nodded.

"The Insolvent makes application to be allowed his furniture and his wearing apparel."

"In the absence of any directions from the creditors, and the Insolvent's estate being valued at less than one hundred pounds, the court has no choice other than to direct that your client's assets be sold, and such monies, less expenses incurred, be distributed among his creditors."

"Thank you, Your Honour," said TH.

"Short, sharp and sweet, TH," said the Commissioner. "Meeting terminated."

"What happens now?" William asked TH outside the court.

"They'll sell your belongings at auction," said TH. "They'll turn up and do it whether you're there or not, so I suggest you and your family go for a walk when it happens. It's most unpleasant. Leave everything there for them, and I can guarantee that everything won't be sold. You get to keep what they think is worthless and are unable to sell. But they take a dim view of you hiding anything, so just leave it all."

"When will that happen?"

"A month, maybe two—it'll be over by the end of the year."

"Can I earn some money while we wait?"

"A little. Don't strike gold anywhere."

William stretched out his hand.

"TH, I don't know how to thank you."

"You'll find a way, Tom. I know it's not easy, but apart from the auction, and the time it takes to get back on your feet, the worst is over. You'll be unlikely to make the same mistake again, so you need to put this part of your life behind you. Get on with it, my boy. You've done the best thing. There's nothing to worry about now."

The auction was held in October.

After the court, William saw Michael from time to time to borrow Missy or Polly if he needed them to do some work. One day, Michael told him he had seen a notice in the paper that the auction was scheduled for the following Saturday.

"Don't have Missy, Polly or Kelly anywhere near the place," said Michael. "Get your family away, too. I've seen it before and it's too distressing watching people pick over your personal items."

On the day, Caroline took all the children for a picnic, walking down the road towards the Caloola Goldfields.

"It'll be over soon, Tom," she whispered as they left.

"I hope so," he whispered back.

About mid-morning, some men arrived and moved everything that the auctioneer said had value outside into the yard. It was a beautiful spring morning—cloudless sky, a chill in the air, and no wind. William stood to one side, helping if asked, but otherwise doing nothing.

When the men finished, there wasn't much outside. They had left the beds and the large table in the big room where they cooked and ate. The little tables, the side boards, and the cupboards where they kept their clothes were outside. Most of these had been given to them when they were married. The clothes were checked, but most were left on the beds as 'useless rags'. People began to arrive late in the morning. There were friendly farmers from the area, although some had come from Blayney and Caloola. Most people either shook his hand or patted him on the shoulder. Some of the women looked like they'd been crying.

After a few minutes, William couldn't stay any longer. He went and sat by the creek below the house and buried his head in his hands. Tears flowed and he promised himself, and God, that this would never happen again.

The man came down after a while and said softly, "You can come back now—it's all over."

William walked back and couldn't believe his eyes. Everyone was gone, but most of the furniture was still in the yard.

"Couldn't you sell it?" exclaimed William. "What's it still doing here? Are they coming back to get it later?"

"A few people took the items they bought, but most people left them—said they bought them for you."

William sat on the steps at the front of the house. His chest heaved and his throat ached with emotion.

"I'll leave you," said the man. "You have some good friends."

When the man left, William sobbed uncontrollably. It was a long time before he could stop. He prayed no one would come and find him like this—it didn't do for a grown man to cry, no matter the circumstances. Finally, he went to find his family to tell them there might be a God after all, and to reassure Margaret that God might even love them. Perhaps God's only way of showing His love was through the neighbours.

CHAPTER 35

# LIFE GOES ON

As TH had said, the worst was over, but the daily chores and life went on. He went to see Michael early in December to see if there was any news from TH. Michael smiled and said there was. The matter was completed before the end of November, the papers filed, and Tom was now officially insolvent.

"I wonder what happens now?" William mused.

"Well, you won't get credit—at least for a while."

"That's no bad thing."

"I expect not."

Michael reached into his pocket, pulled out a ten pound note, and gave it to William.

"Here—I've been keeping this for you."

"Thank you," said William, handing it straight back.

Both men laughed, and William thought how good it was to have friends. He wasn't sure how he would have survived without the help he had from friends old and new in Newbridge.

"I'll take Missy, Polly and the cart home with me."

"Please do—they've been fretting. They know this is not their home."

"There must be some way I can pay you for all you've done."

"You'd do the same for me."

"I hope I get the chance."

"I hope you don't."

Once again, the men laughed, and William took Michael's hand and shook it warmly.

"I'll go away, earn some money, and come and buy you a whisky."

"I'd like that. Now, be off—I've work to do."

William collected Missy, Polly and the cart. He took the saddle off Kelly, threw it in the cart, and drove home. Kelly followed obediently behind.

Summer came and went. William was busy working wherever he could, mostly helping with harvests. The irony was not lost on him when farmers using steam threshers asked him to help.

Not caring how hard he worked, he took everything he could, and would sometimes be gone for weeks at a time. However, he brought all the money home to Caroline. She managed it carefully and set the priorities. The children and their needs came first. She made sure they were well-dressed, well-fed, and well-schooled. Once, she told William the school needed extra money for repairs, and he agreed to donate some.

"They were good to us when we needed it," he said.

It was a year before things went back to normal. The storekeepers allowed Caroline credit, although she never let the amounts grow larger than a few pounds, and the children reported that they were no longer teased at school. William always found work, and their income was constant.

One morning, William came out to the paddock to find Kelly lying on the ground. After all the years of his faithful service, Kelly had died. William was inconsolable. He dug a hole on a hill by the creek, in the type of spot that he hoped Kelly would like to spend eternity. Using Missy, he dragged Kelly to the hole, buried him, and sat beside the grave for hours, remembering all the good times with Kelly. Thereafter, he always referred to his home in Newbridge as Kelly's Station.

Later in the day, he decided it was time for a whisky. He asked Caroline for some money, hitched Missy to the cart, and drove into Michael's.

"I'm ready for a whisky," he said to Michael.

"It's about time! There's a card game later, and Bernard will be there. He has waited for you to play again, as he still wants to beat you."

"Good. I have some money, so I'll have a few whiskies and get myself in the right frame of mind."

He enjoyed the cards, the fun and the banter. He drank too much whisky, but still managed to win. Bernard assured him that he would win one day, and said he wanted William to come more often. Caroline said nothing when he came home, and he was glad of that. He went and sat with Kelly the next morning, nursing his first hangover in over a year.

William went back to playing cards and drinking whisky. He found he mostly won, so there was no change to the money he gave to Caroline. If she noticed he was drinking again, she said nothing about it.

There was no change to their physical relationship, although opportunities were fewer now the children were old enough to notice. However, their emotional contact became non-existent. William and Caroline both found work. His was mostly away, but she found work in the village, sometimes at Michael's doing cleaning. Once again, they lived separate lives under the same roof.

In the winter of the next year, both Philis and Daniel died. Caroline had always said that Philis would follow soon after James, and she was proved right. So perhaps being aware made Caroline more prepared for the loss of her mother than her father. It was the first time William had seen many of her family since James's funeral. They had all heard about his insolvency and wondered if they could help. It no longer mattered, William was able to reassure them. As TH had said, life only got better each day.

The death of Daniel hit William hard. He heard about it from Michael, who said he'd read about it in the paper. William told Caroline that he'd go to the funeral. She offered to go with him but he said he'd go alone. The funeral was a sombre affair, and everyone agreed that Daniel was much too young. His wife and children were distraught, and William found he couldn't be close for too long, as the grief was catching, so he left and went home as soon as was reasonable.

As he rode home, he thought about life—what twists and turns it had, and how sad that Daniel would be taken so soon. Still, with one loss, there's a gain. Caroline told him she was pregnant again, so there'd be another mouth to feed. She'd also told him there was a young man showing interest in Elizabeth, so there might soon be one less mouth to feed. William smiled. The ledger of life. It evens up all the time.

He still thought of Elizabeth as a little girl, although the thought he knew to be foolish. She was now fully grown and filled out in all the right places. He supposed that while the children kept coming, Caroline would be happy, and their fun and laughter would bring comfort to their home.

William never grew wheat at Newbridge. He never again wanted to be subject to the whims of nature. There was plenty of work elsewhere—the money was all right and they were comfortable enough to just grow the vegetables they needed.

George was born just before Christmas—a fine lad with a ready smile.

The next few years saw both Elizabeth and Margaret married with children of their own, and Isabella born to William and Caroline.

Not long after Isabella was born, William came home to the sound of Caroline screaming and the children crying. Hurrying into the house, he saw Willie lying on the floor gasping.

"Help him, Tom!" screamed Caroline. "Oh, dear God, help him! He can't breathe!"

William tried everything he could, pounding Willie's chest, trying to force air into his mouth, but Willie just writhed and turned blue in the face. Finally, William scooped him up and tried to run to his horse. Caroline stopped him.

"He's gone, Tom. Willie's gone," she said.

"What happened to him?" muttered William. "I didn't think he was sick."

"I don't know. It started a few minutes before you arrived. One minute he was chatting and laughing, and the next he was on the floor, gasping."

"I never liked the cemetery being over the road, but at least we won't have to go far to visit," said William. "Oh, Caroline, I believe my heart is breaking. I loved him so. Our Willie—gone? It's too hard to believe."

"I know, Tom. It won't happen in our lifetime, but one day there'll be doctors enough to help, and folk will be spared the pain of such pointless deaths."

William put Willie on his bed, and the family sat around on chairs and the floor. Isabella cried softly as though she knew something was amiss. George held her and rocked her to sleep. He'd always loved his little sister. The family all stayed there until darkness fell.

They buried Willie a day later in the cemetery over the road, and Margaret and Elizabeth came back with their families. It was a dull, cold, grey day—the wind chilling them all to the bone. William had dug the grave and insisted on doing it on his own. He held Caroline close, and then he and the boys lowered Willie into the earth. Such a cold and lonely place for a boy so recently full of life. William wanted to scream, to give vent to his barely controlled emotions, but it didn't do for a man to be emotional. He went to Michael's that night and tried to drink away the pain.

"C'mon, Tom," said Michael at one point, "the drink won't bring him back."

"It might help me to forget."

"I doubt it'll do that, either."

"At least let me try. I'm hurting, Michael—I've never known such pain. I'd rather have a tooth pulled."

"How's Caroline?"

"Hurting too."

"Why don't you go to be with her?"

"She's got the children."

"I suppose. Here—take this," he said, handing William a bottle of whisky. "It's on me. Go home. You're not doing anyone any good staying here, drinking away your sorrows."

William left and decided to walk home. He clutched the bottle in one hand and the reins in the other, his horse plodding along behind. Every now and again, he took a swallow from the bottle. The sky had cleared to a cold and cloudless night, and the moonlight was more than enough for him to find his way.

At some point, he sat for a rest and fell asleep. He woke in the morning, the sun already hot, and the whisky bottle lying on the ground beside him—its contents spilled uselessly into the earth.

He went back a few days later to apologise to Michael.

"No need to apologise," said Michael. "I understood. Will you stay for cards?"

William nodded.

The game assembled. Bernard was there and, once again, determined to beat William. Many hands finished with just Bernard and William holding cards. It didn't matter what Bernard did, William always won.

"Let's raise the stakes," said Bernard eventually.

"I'm out," said the other players at the same time.

"What are you thinking?" asked William.

"I'm thinking you always win because the stakes aren't high enough."

"Maybe," said William. "What do you propose?"

"You've been on my land for a few years. You probably think of it as yours."

"I don't."

"Would you like to?"

"Depends."

"All right. Let's put the block on the next hand. If you win, you win the block. If I win, you move off."

"And move my family again?"

"Like I said, I think it has to matter. It's not just money—it's where you live."

William thought for a moment. He was confident he could beat Bernard, but he certainly didn't like the idea of telling his family they had nowhere to live. There was a look of triumph on Bernard's face, so William knew he had no choice.

"All right," he said, "just you and me."

The cards were dealt, and William won. To his consternation, Bernard laughed.

"You're just too good!" he said. "I thought I could force you into a mistake. Well done, and well played, and congratulations! I'll have the papers drawn up. C'mon gentlemen, drinks are on me."

A little later, Michael drew William to one side.

"Well done on the win, but you may not have done yourself any favours."

"Why?" asked William, his voice trembling a little. "What's wrong?"

"You may not remember, but if Bernard hasn't completed the purchase, you will now be responsible."

"Do you mean I'm in debt again?"

"If Bernard doesn't yet own it, it would appear so."

William went and asked Bernard about it.

"Michael's right. I don't yet own it completely, so you'll take over. Don't worry—it's not a lot of money."

"Any amount of money is a lot of money," said William, his heart sinking. He wondered how he would tell Caroline he was once again in debt.

"What's wrong?" asked Bernard.

"If I can't pay it off, then I'll lose it."

"So what? You were renting it from me, and I could have asked you to leave at any time. What's different? At least now you have a chance to own your own place. I've paid some money and done some improvements, so you're part of the way there. Think of it like you're renting it from the government."

"Bernard, I don't understand numbers, so please write on a piece of paper what I owe."

"Tom, I'm writing one hundred and sixteen pounds, five shillings. Interest on that is around six pounds a year, and you need to do improvements totalling one hundred and fifty-five pounds. It's all written here now."

William felt sick to his stomach. *What have I done?*

"Tom, what's wrong? Like I said, you don't have to do anything. Do nothing and wait until they kick you off," said Bernard. "Anyway, I'll register you as owner next time I'm in Bathurst."

"How long before they kick me off?"

"Years. They've got an inspector who goes around, checking that you live on the land and that you're making improvements. I'm told he's very busy, and it takes a while to see all the blocks. Anyway, think on it—you might decide to buy it. I would, if I were you."

On the way home, William decided not to tell Caroline about the block until he better understood what he owed, and how he was meant to pay it.

The next years were busy years. William and Caroline had two more children, Thomas and Ethel. Margaret's husband died, and she remarried. William thought no more about the conditional purchase, nor did he tell Caroline about it. He stayed away from home a lot, travelling the country to find work. It suited him to be away from home, as he could play cards, drink whisky and smoke his pipe as often and as much as he wanted. When he was home, he found the older children were busy with their own pursuits, Caroline relied on them completely to do the tasks that would normally be expected of William, and he was a stranger in his own home. At some point, he stopped sharing the bed with Caroline, and even if Caroline had been able to produce more children, it was never going to happen.

It was the conditional purchase that finally destroyed his relationship with Caroline.

He came home one day, having been away for several weeks. It was already late afternoon as he rode up to the house. As soon as he walked in, he knew there was trouble.

"The sheriff was here today," said Caroline.

"Hello, Caroline. Nice to see you, too," he said, a poor attempt to lighten the mood.

"He gave us this," she said, handing him a piece of paper.

George was the oldest child at home.

"What's it say, George?" asked William, passing the paper to George.

"It's a summons," said George. "It says you are to appear in court about the land."

"What land?" asked William, a hollow feeling in his stomach.

"This land," said George, waving an arm.

"Yes," said Caroline, "Bernard's land. Why do they think we own it?"

After a few moments, William sighed.

"I won it from Bernard in a poker game."

"And you didn't tell us? Any of us? Didn't we have a right to know?"

William shrugged.

"Why do they want me in court?" he asked George.

"It says the land has been inspected, and you have failed to do the appropriate improvements, nor have you paid any monies at the Land Office."

"George, I wonder if you would take your brother and sisters for a walk? I think your mother and I need a few moments alone."

George nodded, gathered up his little sister and, taking the others by the hand, went out into the impending dusk.

William looked at Caroline and remembered the tension in the home back in Ireland—how his parents had little to say to each other and mostly communicated through the children. This person with whom he shared a bed for most of their life was now a stranger to him. He knew he was wrong not to tell her about the conditional purchase, and that he should have done so at the beginning—but it was too late now. They had no money to make amends with the Lands Office and the problem that he created could no longer be fixed.

"Well?" she said.

"Well, what?"

"What do you have to say for yourself?"

"Say for myself? Well, I suppose nothing."

"Nothing? You don't tell me about something as important as our home and you have nothing to say for yourself?"

"Bernard could have asked us to leave at any time."

"I always wondered about that. Wondered why he didn't. Why someone would let us stay for so long without asking for rent. I feel like you have deceived me."

"I didn't deceive you. I just didn't tell you."

"What else haven't you told me?"

"I haven't told you about the cards, the drinking and the smoking."

"I know about the cards, the drinking and the smoking—I can smell it on you when you come home."

They were silent for a few moments, staring at each other across a gulf that would soon be too wide to bridge.

"I'm moving into town," said Caroline. "I'm taking the children and we'll move into Newbridge."

"Why?"

"I want to move on my own terms. I won't have the sheriff turn up and throw us out of our home."

"What do you want me to do?"

There it was, in a single sentence. The response could close the gap, or make it so wide, they would never reach each other again.

Caroline stood silent, as though considering the enormity of the response. She hesitated, as though she hadn't considered that he might ask such a question, or that if he did, she hadn't worked out what to say.

William wondered what he saw in her face. With alarm, he thought he saw pity.

"You should do what you think best," said Caroline.

"Best for who?"

"Just best. That's all—just best."

William nodded and went out to find George. He was playing with the little ones by the creek. George hurried up to him. The others stayed playing at the creek.

"Is everything all right, Pa?" asked George, anxiously. "How's Ma?"

"Can you look after your mother for a while?"

"If John and Richard help, I can."

"They'll help."

"Where are you going?"

"I've some work to do. It might take a while. They didn't say how long."

"What sort of work?"

"They didn't say. Your mother wants to move into town. Ask John to find somewhere for you all, will you? He'll give you money if you need it."

George started to cry.

"There, there, Georgie—you're too old for that now."

William put a hand on his shoulder. He couldn't really be critical. Even though he'd said the words, he'd done more than enough crying himself.

"When will you be back?"

"I don't know."

"What if something happens?"

"Nothing will happen."

"How will we see you again?"

"You don't see much of me now."

"I know, I know, but you're still my da."

"I don't know that I'm anyone's da anymore, Georgie. I've not done much of a job of looking after you—any of you. Most of you are grown up now anyway, and there's older brothers enough to look after the little ones."

"It's not goodbye, is it?"

"It's too hard to say. I've made a mess, Georgie, and I need some time to work out how to make it right."

"We can do that. John and Richard can help. We can all help."

"No, Georgie. Sometimes a man has to stand on his own two feet."

Nothing was said for a few moments.

"So, take the little ones in now—it'll be cold soon," said William.

George did as he was told, and William went and sat by Kelly's grave.

"What a mess!" he said to the night air. "What's a man to do? What's best?"

He looked up at the night sky and marvelled, as he always did, at the stars. There were so many, and he wondered what purpose they served. He knew you could navigate by them, so he wondered if they could help him navigate out of the mess he'd created. George was a sweet and sensitive boy who could be relied upon to help and support his mother. John, James and Richard were older and sensible and would see that the family was properly cared for. He'd told George he was going away, so that might be the best thing. The little ones might miss him, but they had older brothers that could fill the role of a father, and Caroline had done most of the raising of the children anyway.

*It'll be hard to come back*, he thought. *It'll be easy to ride away, but it'll be very hard to work out when and why to come back. Besides, once all the children are grown up and gone, there'll be no life for Caroline and me. She doesn't trust me anymore, and I've brought that on myself. I've let her down—badly—and I'll see that in her eyes every day, for the rest of my life.*

"Best," he said to the night sky. "Do what you think best."

He went and saddled his horse and rode away into the night. He never saw Caroline or his family again.

CHAPTER 36

# A LIFE ALONE

He didn't ride back into Newbridge. There was no plan to what he did, and the direction he chose was as spontaneous as his decision to leave. He was glad of the moonlight, but after an hour, he was emotionally and physically exhausted and decided to sleep by a creek. It wasn't hard to find a place to camp, and he deliberately chose one away from the road where he wouldn't be disturbed by any travellers. He didn't want to have to explain himself if he met someone he knew.

It was spring, and the winter rains meant there was plenty of water in the creek. So in the morning, he boiled a billy and ate some of the supplies he had left from his recent trip away. There wasn't much left of the supplies, but he had money, so it would be easy to buy more.

His mind returned often to the night before, and he had to exercise discipline not to simply get on his horse and ride back home.

He knew the road he was on would lead him to Goulburn, so he decided to stay on it. It was a big town, and it would be easy to lose himself there. He wasn't sure why he wanted to lose himself, but he dreaded someone following him and trying to convince him to come back. The more he thought about the decision, the more stupid it seemed—but his pride had a price.

It was a long time since he'd been in Trunkey or Tuena, so he thought he could buy some supplies in both places if need be and not be recognised. He rode slowly, burying his loss and hurt deep, and refusing to acknowledge it.

When he finally rode into Goulburn on the road he'd used so many times all those years ago, he hardly recognised it. It was coming on dark, and the bustling town had traffic, streetlights, and a railway. He thought of how he'd left there, filled with hurt and humiliation, and his emotional return was not all that different.

Stopping outside Joe's pub, he wondered if Ruth was still there. It was so long ago and so much had happened since then. She'd surely be married now anyway—with grown children.

There were a few horses out front, so he dropped the reins and walked in. There she was, at the front, as though nothing had changed. Even the years had been kind to her, and he couldn't suppress a smile. He hesitated for a moment, thinking he might just pass on. Then impulsively, he took off his hat, and said softly, "Ruthie?"

She looked up in confusion and bewilderment.

"I'm sorry," she said. "Do I know you?"

He knew that his teeth and his youth were long gone, and the Tom standing in front of her bore no resemblance to the one that had left all those years ago.

"It's Tom," he said awkwardly.

"Tom? Oh, Tom!" she shouted, and came out from behind the desk to hug him.

"Where have you been? We always wondered about you and why you didn't call by! We heard you were at Tuena, but that was a long time ago."

She stepped back, eyeing him carefully.

"You look old, and you don't look rich, Tom. Still, some people are rich and don't look it. Are you rich?"

"Why?"

"I always wished the best for you. My ma and pa always said you were the son they missed."

William flushed, as he always did.

"Well, now I know it's you for certain," she said laughing. "Are you staying? Why are you here all of a sudden? And where have you been all these years?"

William laughed. He'd forgotten how much he liked her—no, it was more than that.

"Where's your husband?" he asked.

"Husband?"

"Yes—Ned. I suppose he and your children are hereabouts."

"Oh, Tom—I never married. And Ned was such a fool! Do you remember my sister Eve?"

"Remember? How could I forget?"

Ruth laughed, and with the sound came memories of Beth.

"Her husband, Brian, was killed in an accident. Ned couldn't take his place with Eve fast enough. We used to see them before Pa died, but they don't come by anymore. I think they only saw Pa so he'd leave them some money. More fool them—he didn't leave them anything."

"And your ma?"

"Have dinner with me, Tom. I'll be finished here soon, and I'll meet you in the dining room. We have a lot to catch up on, and it'll be nicer over dinner. Please?"

"How could I refuse?"

"Wonderful! Go on out back and wash up, if you like. Everything's still there. I'm sure you remember. Then go into the bar and get yourself a whisky. I'll find you there, and we'll have dinner. Oh, I'm so looking forward to it, and it's so good to see you!"

As William sipped his whisky, the sadness of recent events swept over him. It wasn't right that he should sit there and later have dinner with Ruth. Yet his family and his children seemed years away, and he was a young William again—sitting in Goulburn, full of hope and promise. A tear gathered in his eye, and he brushed it irritably away.

"Are you ready, Tom?" he heard Ruth say.

"Yes, I'm ready. Shall I bring this whisky?"

"Please do."

They went into the dining room and William realised that, apart from some different furnishings and possibly some paint, little had changed over the years.

The meal was already on the table, and William saw no one else as they ate, so he presumed Ruth was still the cook.

"It's delicious," he said. And it was—fish, peas, and mashed potato.

"I remember you laughed at my cooking once."

"Not anymore," he said with a smile.

"You look like it's been a while since you've eaten, Tom. Where are your family?"

William told her in a rush all that had happened. He lost track of time, he almost forgot Ruth was the listener, and he was glad to get it all off his chest—glad to tell someone, glad to talk of his poor behaviour, and glad to tell how he had failed his family more than once.

When he stopped, Ruth reached across and took his hand.

"Oh, Tom—what a dreadful story! My heart breaks for you all. How sad Mother would be to know what has happened."

She stopped talking and looked at William.

"It doesn't matter. Your wife is a lucky woman."

William shook his head sadly.

"No, she's not."

The ticking of a clock was the only sound to break the quiet that followed.

"You're going home, of course," said Ruth, finally.

"One day," said William.

"Why? Why not go now? They must all be missing you—certainly wondering where you are. You sound like you're missing them."

"I don't know, Ruth. I've been such a disappointment. I have to deal with all that before I can face my family."

Ruth put her head to one side, looking at William with sympathy. He looked away, unable to meet her gaze.

"Is your mother still alive?" asked William, wanting to move the conversation to less emotional matters.

"Oh, no—she died not long after you left. It was very sad for us. I know she wasn't well, but she wasn't a trouble and we loved her so."

"She was wonderful to me."

"She was wonderful to everyone."

She paused and smiled.

"Except Ned," she said. "She didn't like Ned at all."

William laughed. It was good to release the tension.

"What do you do here, Ruth? Do you own the pub?"

"Oh, Lord no! I work for the owner. I tried to run it after Pa died, but it was a waste of time. Evie talked about coming to help, but she was always only talk. So, I sold it. I've always been glad I did."

"Why didn't you marry someone else? After Ned, I mean."

"I didn't ever meet anyone. It's never mattered. I like working here. I help some of the old people in the town. I have a good life."

They had some tea and chatted some more, but William could hardly keep his eyes open.

"There's a room at the back, Tom. You can have that. If you help in the yard, you won't have to pay anything, and you can put your horse in the stables. Stay a few days. Once you feel better, you might make up your mind to go home, and that would be easy to do from here. There's isn't much in the way of hard work, we can fatten you a little, and you and I can catch up on old times."

"I'd like that, Ruth. Now, if you'll forgive me, I'll see to my horse and be off to bed."

"Of course, Tom. I'll wait for you at breakfast. Come in any time—there's no rush."

William stayed four days, helping in the yard and catching up with Ruth. The owner's name was Albert, and William found him to be an all-round good bloke who clearly had a crush on Ruth. As ever, Ruth had no idea—so not much had changed there either. He'd forgotten how lovely she was, but it was on the fourth day he realised she wasn't Caroline, and it was Caroline he loved. But he wasn't ready to go home yet.

He was vague about where he was going, not wanting to leave a trail if anyone came looking for him. If he went home, then he would go home in his own good time. Ruth gave him a big hug goodbye and didn't press him for more information. Riding out of the town as though heading for Tuena, he circled around and headed for Braidwood. He might be able to pan for some gold, or perhaps find some work. He didn't really care. As much as he missed Caroline and his family, he enjoyed the notion of being on his own, if only for a while.

William always planned to go home, but always decided he'd do it tomorrow. It was easy to change his name to Bill. He became an old man, pottering around old diggin's—doing odd jobs and finding gold where people said there was none. There was never a lot, but it was enough to keep him alive. He spent all his time in the gold fields scratching around, finding a little gold, playing cards, drinking whisky, and reliving the carefree days of his youth. A few times, he went to the Snowy Mountains. The cold didn't bother him so much and nor did the snow, which he found mostly to be only inconvenient. He heard stories of home from strangers—things about Newbridge and sometimes about his family—but as much as he assured himself he would go home soon, he never did.

In the spring and summer, he would sometimes camp by a creek or a river for days at a time—living on birds, rabbits, and sometimes a fish. He would pick a place where he wouldn't be disturbed, where he could stay while it suited him.

His needs were simple, his health good, and he was never a nuisance, so the law didn't trouble him. He sometimes had a roof over his head after he'd find an abandoned hut, or a farmer would engage him to help out—mostly with horses or simple tasks around the farm. No one ever bothered to find out who he was or cared where he came from. He was always just Bill, or the old man.

He'd pitched his tent by a river one afternoon and when he woke the next morning, it was a beautiful spring day. It was his favourite time of year. The sun was warm with the promise of summer, and he loved how the birds sang, the sun glistened off the water as it bubbled over the rocks, insects and dragonflies flitted about, and the wind soughed in the trees. Perhaps this was heaven, he decided. Certainly as close as he would ever get to it.

William never thought much about death. It always seemed only to happen to other people. He was sure you didn't go anywhere and that when he died, that would be that. He thought often of Willie and wished he could have done more to save him. It was such a waste. Then he'd feel sad because, to him, it was just one more failure as a husband and a father. Like his own father before him, perhaps he wasn't cut out for the job.

There was only one thing of which he was proud. He came into the world with nothing, and that's how he would go out of it. It was odd to him that it was a source of pride. Once, he wanted to be someone, to own something, to be rich. All his hopes of wealth and a stone house were only the stuff of dreams. Perhaps his children, or even their children, would go on to become wealthy. But it would never happen to him.

The tent flapped a little. Perhaps the breeze was picking up. He lay on a tarpaulin—a blanket over him and his saddle behind his head as a pillow. It was nice to just lie there and enjoy the warmth of the sun on his tent.

*Perhaps it's time to go home,* he thought. *Time to face my wife and children, and deal with my failure as a husband and father. Maybe enough years have passed that they could forgive and forget.*

But like every other time he'd had the same thought, he put it aside. The burden of his failure was often more than he could bear, and it was easier not to think about it.

He'd need to get up soon to tend to his horse. The horse was new—well, at least new to William. He'd swapped his last horse for him. The last horse was getting too old to use in the Snowy Mountains, and a farmer had been keen to swap his feisty one for the older, quieter horse that would be better for his children. It didn't matter to William that he was feisty. He'd always been good with horses. The new horse didn't need to be hobbled either—he always stayed close, as though he knew that he and William only had each other.

William drifted off to sleep, but woke when there was a sudden, massive weight on his chest. He thought a tree must have fallen but, when he looked up, the roof of the tent was still above him.

*What could it be? Oh, Lord, it hurts!*

He tried to call out, but couldn't. It was a waste of time anyway—there was no one to hear. William struggled to move.

*Christ! Get the load off my chest!*

He tried to use his hands to push the weight off, but they wouldn't move. When he looked again, there was nothing on his chest. There was nothing to push anyway, so it didn't matter that his hands didn't work.

*What causes such pain?*

If anything, the pain became worse. He couldn't move and couldn't speak.

The tent flapped again, as though someone had come in. He looked and it was Jimmy! His brother! Little Jimmy!

*Jimmy!* He called, but no sound came.

*Willie! Willie! It's me—Jimmy!*

*Oh, Jimmy! Help me! Something is crushing my chest!*

*It'll stop soon, Willie. I've come to get you.*

*Get me? What are you doing here? How did you get here?*

*I've come to take you home. Ma and Da are there, and so is Caroline and your son Willie. We've all been watching over you, but it's time to come home.*

*Caroline? Willie? What are they doing at home? How did they get there?*

William couldn't understand why he couldn't speak, yet Jimmy heard him and answered.

Jimmy took his hand, and the pain subsided. The hand was warm, just as he remembered. Jimmy gave him a hug like he had done all those years ago and he knew he was home. How good it felt, how much he had missed it—missed everyone. All his family—his brother and sisters, mother and father, but most of all, his children and his wife. His beloved Caroline.

*Oh, Caroline. I have missed you so! Why have I wasted so many years?*

Somehow, he knew that nothing mattered anymore, that every memory he would ever have was now from the past. No more future—only past and present.

The horse came over a few hours later and peered through the tent flap. Sensing his owner would be of no value, he wandered off, foraging on the creek banks. He would later join a mob of brumbies.

William had chosen his camp site well. No one found him and no one ever knew what became of him.